WHEN ALL THE GODS DIED.

Sudarshan Chatterjee

Copyright

Copyright © 2025 Sudarshan Chatterjee

Published by

Dedication

Dedicated to my family - my loveliest wife, Kalpana Chatterjee, and my dearest sons, Attorney Shantanu Chatterjee and Animesh Chatterjee.

Acknowledgements

The idea of the book germinated almost 20 years ago. I had two little boys and a very happy life with my dearest wife, Kalpana. We were busy parents as I worked as a cardiologist and she raised the boys, ran the practice, and took care of our many homes and offices.

Years passed by in research and travel. We went to Greece twice, each time learning a little more than before. Eventually the book began to take shape and the most difficult aspect of interaction of past and present, Gods and mortals and the origin and end seemed to blend like pearls in a necklace, reflecting light and shining as if all the barriers have been broken to bring back the truth, the story and the devastation of a very developed civilization not to annihilation but something more than what eyes meet.

This book wouldn't have been written if I hadn't grown up in a family raised by my mother, the late Pari Rani, and father, the late Binoy Kumar Chatterjee. My mother inspired me to think beyond our home, our country, and our customs. Remembering them with respect and love.

My wife, Kalpana, ensured that we all had a place where we could share our noise, while also preserving our silences and personal space. She was a very kind mother to my sons, and she allowed me to participate in and manage the everyday routine of raising children as I wished. So, I could drive them to school and read them stories at bedtime, but she would care for everything else. She would be blessing us from wherever she is with God.

Special thanks to my publisher, Bookfuel, and the team. Robert Greene initiated the process, and Ashwin Anthony carried out most of the complex tasks, including editing, formatting, and marketing. I am grateful to Ashwin. I am also thankful to my editor, Georgina Williams, for maintaining her composure and patience with me, despite my frequent requests not to change anything, as every word was carefully researched to reveal another story. I am grateful to the design team and marketing teams in BookFuel.

I am grateful to my sons, who have been with me whenever I needed them.

Foreword

What is the difference between how human beings conduct and lead their life versus how immortals do in heaven?

Everything in the Western world is so different than the world I grew up in India. The people behave so differently, moving, dressing, eating, and drinking things that we would consider not refined, with food not well-cooked and cold drinks early in the morning, when they should be serving hot tea. The buildings have columns in either the Ionic, Corinthian, or Doric style.

Men who look handsome are Apollonian, and beauty par excellence is akin to Aphrodite. Who are they, and where do I find them? In sculpture, both Venus de Milo and Discobolus exhibit human and divine beauty. Who is Venus, and where did she arise from?

When Westerners engaged in deep conversation, they drew on the works of Socrates, Plato, and Aristotle.

In the Government affairs of a democratic country like the USA, it all began in the world's first demokratia in the state of Athens.

The Roman Empire contributed to the spread of the new Christian religion, and all those gods and goddesses were no longer to be found.

At this point, I thought I needed to know how everything in the Western world originated and prospered.

My search took me to Athens. After a decade of research, I discovered that my book is a story for everyone, from young to old, designed to introduce readers to the beginnings in Greece, featuring its gods and Goddesses.

I read many books to learn about the gods' behavior and decision-making processes regarding mortals, including classics like The Iliad and The Odyssey, as well as The Aeneid, tragedies such as The Eumenides, and numerous works by authors like Madeline Miller, Edith Hamilton, and Stephen Fry.

I felt the need to understand the lifestyle and behavior of these immortals by examining their cognitive processes, which required an understanding of psychology and philosophy. Therefore, another research project had to be undertaken. Once, I was so overwhelmed that I shelved the project for a few years due to a personal reason.

I felt the Gods and Goddesses were displeased with me for trying to understand their thoughts, and they were sending messages. My wife and I built a very beautiful house near Boston and adorned the long brick paved driveway with statues of Gods and Goddesses. My mind was busy thinking of different Greek customs, rituals, festivals, gods, and goddesses, as well as Andrew and Rhea. One day, our statue of a cup-bearing Goddess Hebe, ready to serve nectar, was found fallen flat on the ground with her Right arm severed from her body. I parked my car and sat near her, once trying to raise her from the ground unsuccessfully due to her weight, then giving up as I sat shocked and sad.

There were a few other incidents that I interpreted as messages to warn me against getting too close in my mind to these divine figures.

So, the publication was delayed. I had suffered irreparable losses in my life.

But one day I woke up and broke through my fear and began the editing, and here it is for readers to know the detailed descriptions of Greek festivals, how their gods and goddesses thought, felt, and reacted or ordained with modern psychological understanding that they did not find in such details in any other previous storytelling that I had reviewed.

If the reader gets close to any understanding, tiny or vast, as the story evolves and they feel they now know who and how Hephaestus is going to react, or Apollo would reminisce, and the reader starts contextualizing and systematizing with empathy, do not be surprised if you become an admirer or even a follower, as akin to what happened to the author.

Birthplaces of Gods:

1. Aphrodite – Paphos in Cyprus.

2. Apollo and Artemis- Delos

3. Ares- Thrace

4. Hermes -Mount Cyllene – Arcadia

5. Poseidon-Rhodes

6. Hera- Samos

7. Dionysus- Mount Pramnos in Icaria

8. Zeus- Crete

9. Hephaestus- Mount Olympus

Table of Contents

Prologue 10

Olympians 11

Chapter One – Hephaestus....................................... 13

Chapter Two – Heracles, Dionysus, Demeter, and Persephone. .. 48

Chapter Three – Aphrodite 67

Chapter Four – Apollo and Artemis.............................. 101

Chapter Five-Poseidon.. 144

Chapter Six – Athena 161

Chapter Seven- Dionysus.. 173

Chapter Eight – Ares... 185

Chapter Nine – Hera. 189

Chapter Ten – Zeus... 205

Chapter Eleven – Thesmophoria.................................. 216

Chapter Twelve – Andrew.. 227

Chapter Thirteen – Apollo 248

Chapter Fourteen – Zeus.. 254

Chapter Fifteen – Athena 267

Chapter Sixteen - Artemis...................................... 272

Chapter Seventeen – Zeus....................................... 293

Chapter Eighteen – Olympus 317

Prologue

How could a nation, particularly a leading nation like Greece, which inspired the rest of the world, especially Western civilization, to believe in supernatural beings, the immortals who governed our planet, meddled in our lives, rewarding the just and punishing the unjust to uphold justice and piety, all of a sudden abandon them all? The vast pantheon of gods, the Olympians, was forsaken as the people devoted their minds and souls to a foreign god. Did they not like their gods? It seems unlikely that anyone could hate a figure as charming as Zeus, the god of gods. He was the chief deity in the heavenly abode called Olympus. True, he wasn't the best husband—he courted too many women and often ignored Hera. Still, as a god with unlimited power and resources, his unceasing desires and passions resembled those of mortals. That's why he was so relatable, so amusing, and close to the Greek hoi polloi.

Yes, the Greeks lived alongside their gods. If they accidentally encountered one in their backyard or on the street, they neither jumped with joy nor bowed in exaltation; they went about their way or even conversed, as they would with their friends or relatives.

Nevertheless, if you visit Greece today, you won't hear people invoking Athena before a war, nor seeking blessings from Apollo or Hermes. Like other Westerners, they attend church, partake in Holy Communion, and ask for forgiveness from the Father, the Son, and the Holy Spirit.

So, what happened to all those gods? Was there a war that consumed them? A plague that struck down the Olympians? But none of that could make those people vanish. They were immortals.

Olympians

Aphrodite (Venus) | Goddess of love and beauty; protector of sailors. Daughter of Zeus and Dione. Symbols: the myrtle tree and the dove. Born near Paphos, Cyprus.

Apollo (Apollo) | God of the arts (poetry and music), healing, archery, and divination. Hunts with a silver bow. Son of Zeus and the Titaness Leto; twin of Artemis. Symbols: laurel tree, crow, and dolphin. Born in Delos.

Ares (Mars) | God of war. Son of Zeus and Hera. He carries a spear. Symbols: vulture and dog. Born in Thrace.

Artemis (Diana) | Goddess of the hunt and protector of children and women in childbirth. Hunts with silver arrows. Daughter of Zeus and Leto. Symbols: cypress tree and deer. Born in Delos.

Athena (Minerva) | Goddess of wisdom, war, and crafts; patroness of Athens. Aided Odysseus and Heracles. Symbols: owl and olive tree.

Demeter (Ceres) | Goddess of agriculture, harvest, and fertility. Daughter of Cronus and Rhea, sister of Zeus, mother of Persephone. Symbols: scepter, cornucopia, corn, wheat.

Dionysus (Bacchus) | God of wine, mysteries, and theatre. Son of Zeus and Semele. Symbols: ivy, snake, grapes. Born on Mount Pramnos, Ikaria Island, near the Turkish coast.

Hephaestus (Vulcan) | God of smiths, metalworkers, fire, and forge. Maker of armor and weapons for the gods. Son of Zeus and Hera. Married to Aphrodite. Symbols: anvil and forge.

Hera (Juno) | Goddess of marriage; consort of Zeus. Symbols: peacock and cow. Born on the island of Samos, off the coast of Turkey. Her largest temple, the Heraion, stands in Argos.

Hades (Pluto) | King of the dead. Ruler of the Underworld; husband of Persephone. Brother of Zeus and Poseidon.

Hermes (Mercury) | God of merchants; messenger of Zeus; trickster and friend to thieves; inventor of boxing and gymnastics. Son of Zeus and Maia. Wore winged sandals and a hat; carried a magic wand (caduceus). Born on Mount Cyllene in Arcadia.

Poseidon (Neptune) | God of the sea and earthquakes. Symbols: horse and trident. Born in Rhodes, raised by the Telchines.

Zeus (Jupiter) | God of the sky; ruler of Olympus. Husband of Hera. Symbols: oak and thunderbolt. Born in Crete, in the Idean Andron cave, about 20 kilometers from Anogeia.

Hestia (Vesta) | Virgin goddess of the hearth, domesticity, family, and the state. Sister of Zeus. Symbol: fire. The firstborn child of Cronus and Rhea.

Born of Cronus and Rhea were Hestia, Demeter, Hera, Hades, Poseidon, and Zeus.

Titans-
Born of Uranus (Heaven) and Gaia (Earth), there were twelve Titans. The males were Oceanus, Coeus, Crius, Hyperion, Iapetus, and Cronus; the females were Thea, Rhea, Themis, Mnemosyne, Phoebe, and Tethys.

Chapter One – Hephaestus

They had flown from New York to Athens and planned to continue to Crete, where they would visit Rhea's ancestral home and Andrew would see Knossos.

Andrew sat spellbound in the cockpit of a small plane, overlooking the vast expanse of Greece. He could see mountain peaks, pines, and firs, and if he looked closely, even the undulating green meadows dotted with olive orchards stretching over acres far below. It is a small country compared to the United States, but what diversity of culture! The Peloponnesian peninsula lay to the south, home to Sparta, Corinth, and Laconia; Thessaly, Macedonia, and Illyria to the north; and Athens, Thebes, and Euboea in the center and east— defined by the rugged Balkan Mountains to the north—with the Mediterranean, Aegean, and Ionian seas surrounding it. To the west lay Ithaca, where the wily Odysseus returned to his wife Penelope after nineteen years, unharmed, unlike what Clytemnestra had warned and plotted against her husband, King Agamemnon, when he returned after the Trojan War. Slightly to the south lay Pylos, where Nestor ruled happily with his many sons. To the southeast was Argos, where Diomedes returned stealthily to his palace, only to flee forever after his beautiful queen, Aigialeia, whispered an order for his execution. Andrew turned his gaze toward Mycenae, from where King Agamemnon had traveled to Anatolia to rescue Helen, ransacking the legendary city of Troy.

Then he turned the plane southeast toward Crete—the site of Minoan civilization, grand palaces, and the land of the Linear A script. How could it all vanish—from the original hunters and Indo-European invaders, through ocean trade, the development of metallurgy and democracy, to a world of philosophers, authors, olive trees, wine, gods, and their pantheon?

Andrew looked at Rhea. She had almost fallen asleep, her face partly concealed by silky blonde hair that scattered as far as the tiny mole at the corner of her mouth. Her abundant hair defined her, and she nurtured it like a symbol. She looked like a goddess when she arranged it with her slender, supple white arms—or so Andrew thought. She wore her long tresses unbraided and uncurled, pulled sleekly back, and rarely tied in a ponytail wrapped over her head, exposing the roots on her long, beautiful neck. Her hair would cascade over Andrew when they danced. She loved the thrill of dancing: the wild music, the rattle of cymbals, the beat of castanets, and every rhythmic jingle or resonance—and she was transformed. Andrew usually slipped away after a dance or two and watched her go wild with others on the floor while he gulped more beer. It was as if he was watching her in the choros, where aulos, lyra, and kithara played the hymn with the singers—the molpoi—and she blended so smoothly as if singing the classics of Apni Zoi or Kai doxa te theo. Rhea would say,

'I like dancing, it's a release. It makes me feel like myself, almost as if I am with my family, my grandpa, and my parents are happy around me, dancing like in my childhood. You won't understand…'

Rhea's grandparents had migrated to the United States from Crete, the largest island in Greece. Her ancestors were priests who had spent centuries tending temples, performing prayers and rituals, and offering oracles. They held festivals where friends and relatives would visit, neighbors gathered, and they followed the age-old traditions of prayer, libation, dancing, and feasting after sacrificing a goat to the deity. Rhea's parents visited their ancestral home when she was a small child. But they knew how to keep family secrets and rarely talked to the children about their past or heritage. The temple rituals were meant to remain secret, and Rhea learned that her grandfather had done something extreme in his middle age during one of those occasions, long after her father was born. Her grandfather had been unable to have any children after that day. Rhea's mother accidentally revealed the secret during a bitter argument with her husband, denouncing his family's traditions.

"We don't have to visit that wretched place. Sell it or give it away."

"No. God will punish us. We must keep it," he whispered.

"I will never let you… Come on, it is barbaric…"

"Don't say that. The gods are listening…"

"We are Christians. I don't believe in those gods."

"The gods never die."

"Then go and do the same. What a gruesome rite… sacrifice your …" She paused upon seeing little Rhea frozen in the corner, terror in her eyes. As Rhea grew up, she pieced together a possible explanation for why her grandparents had no more children after what her grandfather had done. Rhea was never told about the dream her father had seen, in which God appeared and expressed a wish regarding their family. After that dream, they left Greece.

She pouted in sleep and then licked her sylph-like lower lip. Rhea appeared younger than her twenty-eight years, with a five-foot-five-inch frame, hazel eyes, and a narrow waist, unlike Andrew, who at thirty-five eloquently betrayed his age with a graying bald forehead, a prominent midriff, ruddy, plump cheeks, and a figure only slightly taller. Whereas Andrew was happy-go-lucky, Rhea was not the typical cheerful blonde; her countenance was tense. She was likely growing more fastidious as she approached her thirties rapidly. Rhea rarely smiled, and she spoke slowly and sparingly. Marriage was one of the issues they grappled with; personality and lifestyle differences were others.

He again enjoyed her serene posture, unlike back home, where, at her best, she was rarely truly delightful. Something or the other always went wrong in their relationship, and she would retreat into prolonged silences, but he remained in denial. She seemed more responsible, more organized, and, in retrospect, the bearer of the correct opinions, while he came across as an uncaring, insensitive intellectual brute. He knew this was merely her perspective, shaped by growing up in a different world. Still, she believed it was his character and indifference to her world that caused him to forget to show up even when he had promised to attend the theater or critical events like birthdays. Invariably, they argued until returning home exhausted and bitter, where she would retaliate by slamming her bedroom door in his face. He would, of course, knock, but she never budged. Left with no choice, he would go out to find a drink, sometimes two, sometimes too many.

Did this seem like a harmonious and loving relationship conducive to marriage? Then, how could he ever propose or agree to a deeper, more meaningful relationship? Why would he choose to live such a wretched life? But still, he tried, and she seemed to accept his attempts as genuine efforts to build their tenuous relationship, even though it always fizzled out as soon as he made the next faux pas. She would become a hellcat, pouncing again with imperceptible outbursts, forceful door slams, and discomfiting silences.

But it wasn't always so gray and miserable. There were days of sunshine and bright hope when she would wake, amicably move to the couch where Andrew lay unconscious, fondly caress his uneven, unshaven cheeks, and comb his hair with slender fingers as Andrew tried hard to keep his eyes closed, like a child earlier reprimanded but later lovingly comforted by his mother. Then, when she turned her face away to gaze out the window, how could he resist his surging emotions and the desire to end the stalemate by drawing her close, asserting all his manly strength, and feigning just waking?

Some evenings, they strolled to a small Italian restaurant in jeans, where they spoke their minds far more quickly than at home.

"I think we should buy a nice condo and move out of here. I'm sick of sleeping on the couch," and she might reply,

"Not in this town, Andrew. Even if we must pay more…"

Then they would calculate their total bank savings.

"I know how I would decorate the interior," Rhea would claim.

"We both should decide."

"No, you have no idea."

"I do."

Suddenly, the neighborhood eatery would seem intolerably silent; only a word or an order for pizza and calzone was spoken. The couple would sit stiffly, staring at every detail of the place except each other. The once lovely place would turn stifling, the smell of food cloying, and the company less enjoyable. They would resume conversation, attempting to cling to the tenuous thread of their relationship by shifting topics to furniture or paintings they liked, or he might even retreat,

"Okay, Rhea, we won't live in this town. Mauve is fine for the hallway since you're in charge of the shades and coverings. No, I won't ask Dad for the down payment."

On those evenings, he was one of the happiest men in town, and she obliged by keeping the door of her tiny room refreshingly ajar

On some weekends, he left home to fly with an instructor or train in a simulator, learning the intricacies of avionics. He had flown many smaller aircraft like Cessnas, Piper Arrows, and Diamonds. Like many others, he had experienced a few untoward events but had always managed to land safely, except once when he faced an engine issue and had to request an emergency landing. His instructor, a German woman in her fifties, taught him everything he needed with tact and never in a humiliating way.

Andrew's other passions were archaeology and Greek civilization, on which he spent a significant portion of his earnings, despite earning only a modest salary as an assistant professor. He also devoted much effort to researching Greek culture, religion, and language, and he learned Greek ways of living from Rhea. He loved Greek mythology and read every article he could find about the Olympians. He knew how each god and goddess was distinct and unique, which sustained his interest in their nature for many years. He could sketch any deity with utmost precision.

Suddenly, the plane tilted to the right. Rhea opened her eyes, gazed at Andrew as if in a dream, then promptly went back to sleep.

He had been less happy since arriving in Greece, mostly because of what he perceived as Rhea's attitude. She had never been this rude before. Since arriving in Athens, they had not made love. He had planned such a nice getaway from the hustle and bustle of their New Jersey lives, so they could come closer, relax, share their dreams and frustrations, and unpluck each other's thorns from their respective backsides. But so far, they had missed any tête-à-tête they had dreamed of, and he was growing increasingly restless at her taciturn behavior.

Eager to visit Greece, he had laid out a plan that could kill two birds with one stone. He managed to get permission from the University of Athens to become one of their international students and participate in the excavation. They would cover Athens, Crete, Mykonos, and, if possible, Santorini.

He wanted to fly from Athens to Crete in a smaller aircraft. When they reached the airport, she seemed somewhat perplexed.

"What? Are you crazy?" she said.

"No. Rhea, these islands are only accessible by boat or air."

"I'd rather take the boat than let you fly this tiny airplane."

"Rhea, please. I have enough flight hours. I took extra training for this trip. Trust me, baby, nothing will happen to you."

"I'm not only worried about myself…"

"Just hop in and close your eyes. We'll be in Crete in no time."

Andrew had rented a Cessna Citation II for island hopping rather than relying on commercial flights and being at their mercy.

He felt relieved after the weather check. No rain, sunshine at eighty degrees beneath a clear sky with light winds, all perfect for his rendezvous. Some thunderstorms were expected later, but he would have landed by then. He finished his preflight checks, inspected the fuel drain for ice crystals, and reviewed the airworthiness card inside the cockpit. Then he listened to the ATIS (Airport Terminal Information Service) and called ground control,

"Ground control, flight 783 Yankee is ready to taxi to Runway Four Left from the civil terminal with information Charlie." Ground control cleared him and instructed him to contact Athens Tower on frequency 118.5. When he called, he was given the green light.

"783 Yankee, taxi to Runway Four Left, position and hold, clear for takeoff from…"

Then, he took off smoothly. He reached out to touch her hand, but Rhea remained implacable. She felt the sky closing in on her, the blue space wrapping tightly around her, as if she could fall freely into the abyss.

"Yeah, baby, we're at twenty-two thousand!" he shouted with glee. She was astonished by how this gentle archaeologist could fly so skillfully, climbing higher and higher, up and up. She wriggled in her seat as he hesitantly touched her. His mind never stopped; he thought even while asleep, and she was sure, even while making love. Did he fantasize? She shrugged the thought off.

Suddenly, the plane jolted mildly.

Ambition, his ambition was exactly her idea of an ideal mate, a ceaseless hunter. Even when it seemed close enough, good looks matched with humor, education gilded by wealth, avarice still raised its ugly head. Love was never the sole platform for these men.

Losers. She knew why he fretted, but she couldn't take any chances. She had heard too many stories of how things went wrong when one wasn't careful from the start.

"Oh, shit," he said.

"What?"

"I don't like these cirrus clouds. Look how they're covering the mountain."

As he spoke, Andrew realized he had strayed off course and began to panic. This was his first flight in Greece, and he had no idea where his little plane was headed. Yet he concealed his fear and weakness from Rhea. Had he taken off toward the south or veered north? Was he approaching Crete or headed for Mount Olympus? He wanted to call the tower, but first decided to confide in her about a part of his problem.

"You know, we may be heading north. Who knows? This might be Mount Olympus…" he said with a hint of zest, though his voice betrayed his unease. Hearing him, Rhea almost jumped, not in horror, but rather amused by his blunder.

"Mount Olympus? Are you sure? Where the gods live…" She perked up.

"I thought you never believed in your past."

She was hurt again. Men! Reasoning! When would he ever truly know her? Was he missing something? Gods… so many of them live there. Grandpa had often mentioned in the past, when she was a little girl, about gods visiting mortals in his country. Grandpa believed Zeus had chosen them. Why, Grandpa? But Grandpa did not know the reason. Time would unfold the fate that awaited them all. The gods never failed to claim anyone. "We will pay one day."

"Pay, Grandpa?" He had only nodded, "Yes, yes, one day."

She felt a surge of excitement. Aroused, she touched Andrew.

"Let us land here. Andrew, can you land here?" she urged.

"No, this is rough terrain, unknown wilderness. Look." But then, as he met her eyes, he saw two tiny islands shimmering there, where his happiness, his life, gleamed within those tiny irises. He lost himself in her again. This was his Rhea: the one who drove him wild, the one he had chosen to stay with no matter what, the mysterious soul, the faraway woman who beckoned him to come closer but withdrew whenever he tried to make some stride. Andrew knew the futility of their relationship, having tasted the shifting tides of their rapport, yet he relished the risk.

Then he began to descend.

"I don't like this," he said again.

The weather report had changed. They were now surrounded by the darkest clouds.

"We are in heaven," she giggled.

The cockpit grew darker. Fear gripped him.

"I need to tell you something," he tried to warn her.

"No. Let me tell you something. This is perfect, the gods are listening."

"Rhea! This is serious," he insisted.

"Andrew, this is perfect. Listen, I am…"

The plane nearly rolled with the raging energy of the clouds. Andrew sat motionless for a second. The roar swallowed her last words.

Then, suddenly, they could no longer see or hear each other. The noise and turbulence drowned out their emotions and battered the little Cessna Citation.

"Rhea, I realize I have been a jerk. Will you ever forgive me?"

"Depends on…"

The gods showed no mercy. Large hailstones pelted the windshield.

Rhea prayed.

"O God of winds, rain, and all Olympians, please help us land safely. The god of gods, Zeus! Please.

Oh, God of rain and clouds, calm down. Do not unleash your thunderbolt on a mother and her man."

Her supplication deeply moved Andrew. Years of indecision, all his frustrations with Rhea, every argument they had shared, and his last resolve to live without her, if she continued to be petulant, vanished. Suddenly, he asked her,

"Rhea, my darling, will you marry me?"

Rhea froze. Bells in the church rang softly in her tender ears, and she felt as if she were riding the crest of a mammoth wave, just like in her childhood on the beach. Papa was watching, and Mom called her back to shore. Then she closed her eyes to see Papa walking her down the aisle as the faces of relatives in the pews blurred and faded together…

Then the plane roared, as if her wings were ripping apart amid the ferocious wind.

"Ground control, can you hear me? Cessna Citation 783 Yankee calling…"

"Athens Tower, hello? Athens Tower, do you read me?"

"Flight service center, this is flight 783 Yankee… hello? Hello?"

He lost radio contact and attempted to reestablish communication with the transponder.

"The engine idled," he cried, voice breaking like a child.

Relatives smiled, the priest beckoned, and Papa pulled her forward.

"I'm trying to make a hundred eighty…" he explained.

Then everyone rose; Rhea couldn't walk anymore, and Papa tugged at her.

"Tell me, Rhea! Will… you… marry… me…?" he implored.

Then the worst happened. The plane lurched violently; something tore loose, and they started descending rapidly in a nosedive. It seemed as if nothing could hold the aircraft, while Mother Earth eagerly awaited below.

"Why are you so silent? Rhea, I've always been good to you. Why? Why don't you ever speak plainly?"

It was unclear if Rhea heard him. She shrugged, as if waking from a dream, then suddenly exclaimed,

"I see trees. We're close to land."

"Rhea! I want you to know something...really."

Andrew knew they were close, maybe just a thousand feet from the ground. Everything hinged on this moment: his dreams, the excavations, the discovery of an ancient civilization, tenure at a prestigious university, love, and a family with Rhea and children. His father, his fortune, the shipping company, and the entire plan have all been ruined.

"I am not a maniac. I want you to know that I love you. It wasn't my fault you didn't speak much in our relationship."

Then came a loud noise, a steep fall, snapping boughs, rain, and a thunderstorm, and finally, the earth scooped beneath the nose of the plane. And then, the end.

It kept raining. An eagle soared toward an unknown destination. The giant oak bled sap. The ocean sent waves, carrying a silent message.

Life itself seemed perplexed. Was this the end, or a grand new
beginning?

24

"Rhea, Rhea, Rhea... Rhea," he screamed over and over. He peered through the shattered windshield, the torn wings, the twisted tail, and a veil of blood streaking across his vision, thin, fragile lines like the threads of his relationships.

Where was she? Oh God! She must have freed herself and walked away. He tried to move, to wiggle, but a sharp pain shot through him; he couldn't pinpoint it. In frustration, he kicked the door.

He felt glad to be alive. But when he thought of her again, that relief seemed fragile and brittle. Limping, he stumbled away from the wreckage.

The indigo ocean lay calm, its waves retreating into ivory foam, as if nothing had changed. He cupped his hands and splashed water on his face. His eyes burned from the salt. He shifted his gaze to the island's edge. Turning his head, he observed a small but lush green patch, tall trees bending gracefully over it. Then he spotted the eyes watching him like a vigilant sentinel. A golden eagle!

To the northeast, the mountain dotted with scattered, red-tiled roofs resembled a valley blooming with red flowers. Where am I? He wondered. Could she have walked to the beach and...? No, she knew how to swim well. Some wild beasts? But there were no tracks, no signs of a struggle. Why had he passed out? He tried to recall the moments leading up to the crash. The plane had been engulfed in dark, ferocious clouds, mercilessly tilting and turning upside down. He couldn't see any switches, knobs, or controls. Rhea was praying. She was a devout Catholic, yet she had implored, almost invited the gods, the ones no one believed in anymore. Why?

"Hey! Hey! Don't touch, the plane is badly damaged. Stay back."

Though the man prodded and pulled at the door, Andrew was relieved to see someone.

A stout villager wrapped in a cloak, not handsome by any means, but his hands were strong.

"Have you seen a lady?"

He said nothing, instead staring back with intensely bright, suspicious eyes.

"Look, this is my plane; we crashed. I'm Andrew."

"Kalimera!" the man replied.

"Kalimera to you," Andrew repeated.

What a grotesque sight, a muscular yet unsightly man in a sleeveless toga and a long beard. He limped away from the wreckage.

"Where are we?"

Once again, the stranger showed no eagerness to answer. He took his time, bending, shuffling, and waddling through the bushes before approaching Andrew. Strange.

"Have you seen a woman? She's about this tall." Andrew demonstrated her height with his hand.

The man said nothing.

"Listen! Can you take me to the town? I need help; I must report a missing person and a plane crash."

A smile spread across the man's coarse face. He nodded, masking an emotion that made Andrew uneasy. Then he started walking toward the dense trees.

"Where are you going? Are you taking me into the woods?"

The deformed body paused and turned his stoic face toward Andrew. His sickly legs struggled with every step; he was handicapped.

They trudged through thick understory, brushing against shrubs, vines, and trees, often pausing to clear tangled webs of vegetation from their feet. The uneven ground, covered in fallen leaves crushed by their footsteps, rustling twigs, splashes of soft mud, and the occasional chirp of insects and birds, muted his mind for now.

Andrew was surprised. His previous experience of this country had been mostly rocky, rugged, and dry, devoid of such abundant flora.

"Excuse me, I shouldn't ask, but your leg…"

The man frowned, his face contorting with concealed pain and anguish. Andrew felt embarrassed and stepped closer, patting the man's muscular shoulder gently, as if to share the burden of his pain. The stranger relaxed at the gesture and asked,

"Apou pou isaste?"

"America,"

They sat down. Andrew shared details about his home, family, and his reason for being there. The man scratched at his sickly legs, unashamed. Andrew felt a pang of sympathy. Then the man began to speak slowly.

Andrew walked beside the stranger as the man unfolded parts of his childhood. It must have been tough growing up without a father figure; he had been thrown out of a window as a baby!

"You guys have some issues," Andrew ventured.

"Some?" he derided.

After walking briskly, they reached the town, where tiny, whitewashed limestone houses sprouted along the narrow, cobblestone-sloping streets like red and white mushrooms after rain. Andrew observed the Agora, which had many shops, a temple-like structure in the corner, all with stucco walls, and a porch with columns and marble stairs, resembling a scene from classical Greek theatre, and he forgot his bodily pain.

They entered the Agora through a massive northern gate. The Propylon featured four Doric marble columns on the north side and four Ionic marble columns on the south.

The courtyard between was lined with various small and large edifices: stoas, temples, public baths, and the Vespasian. The temples of Hephaestus and Athena crowned the hill, their majestic columns and intricate inscriptions commanding reverence. The Stoa of Zeus stood at a corner, where a small group had gathered quietly for a meeting. The Temple of Apollo was Ionian, and inside the statue of the father of the Ionian race stood lonesome.

Larger buildings included the Agoranomion, with three entrances and a modest façade where the king worshiped, the Bouleuterion, where the council convened, and the Metroon, dedicated to the mother goddess Rhea. The central altar of the twelve gods remained cordoned off, sheltering sacred rites through the ages.

The large odeion held Greek tragedies for a few thousand spectators inside the auditorium. Opposite the hall, they preserved the statues of the Heroes on pedestals as a Monument to the Heroes, and public announcements were also posted.

Andrew surveyed the town center with keen curiosity, struggling to mask his overwhelming excitement; he felt as if he had stumbled upon something extraordinary.

"Temple of Hera," the man said, following Andrew's gaze.

Doric columns with robust capitals supported the entablature, its rectangular metopes depicting scenes from Greek mythology: mighty Zeus on Mount Ida being seduced by the radiant Hera, adorned with Aphrodite's girdle, as dense clouds gather around the couple to veil their divine love.

The altar symbolized ancient rituals, with steps leading up to the sacrificial platform. Andrew's gaze lingered on firewood, whose sparks flickered randomly amid black soot and a faint, steady flame dancing with the breeze. Someone had just worshiped here, he thought. He stepped forward hesitantly, dazed, as an uncanny feeling washed over him upon crossing the porch. The man cautioned him not to enter the cella with his shoes on, so Andrew stepped back to the street, his daze broken by a sharp voice:

"Sir, is this your dmoai?"

A tall, muscular man with curly black hair stood defiantly like a sentinel.

"Does he look like a captive? Son of Alcmene! Don't stop me from entering the town," he said with disdain.

"Uxorious master craftsman, if only you hadn't made me the golden quiver, now hand over the young man. Don't forget I destroyed the Minyans for their arrogance.

"O' Heracles, learn some etiquette. But then, I must not forget how you treated your teacher Linus, the son of Apollo. Wasn't his life cut short by you -one of his pupils?"

Andrew looked at them, baffled by their conversation. What on earth were they talking about? Both spoke with grave seriousness, but neither made much sense to him.

Was he being transported to ancient Greece? Andrew thought.

(Agora- common market, Vespasian- Latrine, Dmoai- slave)

"He hit me first, and the judges released me. For me, I've chosen virtue over pleasure. Now go back and keep an eye on your pretty wife, she might be flirting with some warlord," Heracles said with teasing banter.

Andrew thought he must be hearing lines from a Greek tragedy; these men were excellent actors.

His deformed guide played Hephaestus, while the tall man took on the role of the legendary Heracles, who looked visibly perturbed by the harsh words.

Heracles stepped back, with his glassy, distant gaze as if unwittingly lost in reminiscence. When Heracles was ready to pursue his life and had left his home, he met with two beautiful women: one tall and majestic, the other voluptuous, the virtue and the vice. One promised pleasure; the other, only hardship. Their conversation grew louder, tones harsher, and anger spread its wings, revealing their differences, a clash of power and the profound awareness that each held something unique, something sacred to their sphere of influence; a domain that mortals could call upon and trust for blessings that were unalterable and pure.

"Athena's kindness, my friend. It is her armor that you wield to conquer others," Hephaestus derided.

"Sure, but your golden shield didn't save you from the giants. Had I not held Alcyoneus aloft, shot Porphyrion, and gouged out Ephialtes' eye, the Titans would still reign."

"You have been rewarded amply. You stand among the Olympians," Then Hephaestus said, turning toward Andrew.

"I must let him take it from here."

Andrew, impressed by their act, applauded enthusiastically.

"Spectacular enactment of Greek drama. Impressive costumes!"

The man playing Hephaestus was unamused, while his partner remained stoic. Hephaestus then wobbled away, glancing over his muscular shoulder at Andrew as if perceiving his helplessness, said,

"If you want to live, don't ask questions…"

No words were exchanged for some time as the hush of a threat and peril hung in the air.

He hobbled away clumsily, struggling to maintain balance on his lame feet.

When Hephaestus reached his smithy, he slumped on a couch, but his divine status could not erase the pain brought on by the curious and hateful gazes of mortals. He just felt it when that man looked at him.

It disturbed him, haunted him; he hated his own form repeatedly and cursed the world for what he could have been, and what he was: a lame god, bearing the scars of abuse inflicted by his very own parents. He was uncertain who his parents were, whether Zeus had fathered him with Hera, or if Hera, in her vengeance against Zeus, had borne him without a father. Why? Why, even a god not knowing the whole truth of his origin was beyond divine comprehension.

His name is the most non-Greek among the Olympians, derived from Hephaistia, the capital of Lemnos, home to the Tyrsenoi. There, they celebrated a purification festival, kindling new fire and distributing it among artisans. He holds a special place in Athens as the father of the first king, Erichthonios, and is honored with sacrifices during the Apatouria festival of the Athenian phratriai. He is also celebrated in the smiths' festival, Chalkeia. His grand temple stands atop the hill above the Agora, gazing toward Athena's Acropolis.

His name also signifies fire, and he utilized it during the Trojan War. Hera commanded him to control the river god Scamander's wrath and drown Achilles.

Hephaestus gazed at one of the vases on a mantel, depicting Hera casting him down, and another where she sat ensnared and helpless.

Though he labored to entertain the other gods, serving drinks like the handsome Ganymede, his ego did not suffer; this was his choice: peace and harmony within the family, even at his own expense.

His wife, Charis, was unlike Aphrodite. She lived with him on Olympus in a modest abode where he practiced his craft, fashioning weapons and toiling at bellows and anvils, often covered in black soot and sweat, assisted by his golden automatons.

He brooded endlessly over his misfortune among the gods. "I am crippled. I am no different from the beggar afflicted with polio on the streets, even though it was not polio for me." These were his thoughts during his darkest days. Then he would turn swiftly and pace his house, with blue and white color scheme along with welcoming brick and stone walls, and inside hand-crafted rustic furniture like curved Klismos chairs placed along the columns and curves, and his wife, sweet Charis, wandering about overseeing the mundane chores of a divine household: preparing the dinner table with fresh ambrosia, making sure her husband had warm flower-scented water to wash away the grime and soot he collected all day, providing a new set of underclothes that she carefully tailored to fit his unusual form, and a toga with no sleeves; and, last but not least, searching for a sandal that would fit him so he wouldn't complain at night, when the rest of the world had fallen asleep. He groaned from the pain, some from the effort of carrying his less-than-helpful physiognomy, but more from a mind wounded by humiliation at the hands of those dear to him. Often, this devoted wife would wait on her master craftsman husband for dinner, as lunch had been missed. Charis thought their three golden girls were luckier than she was, as they had more of him. When he was happy, his entire attitude changed, and he challenged all of Olympus with his arguments about beauty and the beast.

He would argue, "You all laugh, snicker, and belittle me, but I've given you something to be proud of, something you carry or show. I have crafted most of the beautiful things around Olympus."

(Charis- a Grace.)

He created numerous jewelry pieces, brooches, armbands, and pins almost as soon as he was a little boy. Hera decided to teach Zeus a lesson for his extreme neglect of her by having Athena born from his head, and then she gave birth to Hephaestus. The baby did not even cry, and the mother was already angry. She looked at him with severe disdain, weighed down by guilt and by his inadequacies. His feet were turned backward, and his legs were thin and rickety. How could she show this infant to the world? What would the other gods say? They would laugh and most likely remind her of the impropriety of having a baby without a father. Zeus would most likely break out into incredible laughter and not hesitate to humiliate her in the council of the gods. A god can have a baby without a goddess, and it would come out just fine, probably better than most, like Athena—but for a goddess, it wouldn't work. Hera bit her lower lip in pain, and ichor drops spilled as she made the hard decision; she would never let the world know or see her baby. It was a painful and indeed very dark moment for a mother to discard her creation, a tiny life with an innocent smile and monstrously clubbed feet.

She glanced stealthily around for the maids, the nurse, and the guards at the door. Then she pulled her silken robe tightly to cover herself fully and walked toward the rear window. The slope of the hill, the pine trees, and the gentle breeze did nothing to soothe her as her gaze pierced what lay at the bottom of the cliff, where the ocean returned the newborn white foam in mockery. Then she turned her eyes to the orchard where a gardener was busy planting, watering, and pruning. She waited until he was done. Then she stood silent for a moment, raised her hands, and called for her grandmother, the earth goddess Gaia. She also called on her mother, Rhea, in obeisance and asked for forgiveness.

"What I have done is not so shameful, but what I intend to do is disgraceful. But what choice do I have with this fruit of my labor besides tremendous humility?" Then she came very near the baby— our Vulcan—and kissed his lips, whispering, "I'm helpless for not being able to love you. I know I'm your only parent, and you have

no one, not even a father, but that is the unfortunate end of this story. Let the world not know of my mistake and your presence; let you be silent and not hateful of your mother. I ask you to cease your short stay peacefully and return your little soul wherever it came from. I am sorry, my baby, the one who would never see my breast and never suckle." Then she hurried to the baby's feet and pulled him by the ankles. The baby Vulcan screamed for the first time as he sensed little love in his mother's fiercely tight grip. But she was desperate and hurled the living god out the window in a flash, watching the baby in fear and pain, with hardly any demonstrable remorse.

The cries, the painful shrieks, and the baby's desperate wails were swallowed by the blowing winds, which suddenly rustled fiercely among the peaks of Olympus.

Hephaestus fell straight down, and halfway through, his cries ceased as he landed in the billowing ocean. White foam smothered his face, blocking his nostrils, making it hard to breathe. After drifting aimlessly atop monstrous waves, a pair of gentle hands reached down and pulled him from the water. The crying baby believed his mother awaited him, rescuing him from the ocean's perilous grasp. Hera appeared to be playing with her baby; as he clasped at her breasts, she embraced him in her bosom. Little did he know it was Thetis instead, along with Eurynome. He had two mothers caring for him.

For nine years more, he grew under the vast ocean. Though he cackled and cooed like a child among strange new sea creatures, he never forgot Hera's cruelty. He hated his feet, yet he never stopped walking. He fashioned beautiful sea corals into fine jewelry for his foster mothers. Eventually, he discovered metal beneath the sea and began crafting pins, brooches, and other glittering ornaments— each piece burning with an unspoken question: why? Why had his mother cast away such a helpless child? And she, the wife of the god of gods, how could she live as if nothing had changed?

"I shall never return to her," he vowed as he swam among dolphins in the cold saltwater. Yet even gods remain unaware of their fate, as decreed by the Fate goddess.

He was lonesome and very bitter, his heart gnawed by rejection from his own family. Restless, he constantly sought something to do or create. "Let me craft a new ornament for Eurynome, or perhaps a necklace for Thetis," he would think. Then, inevitably, he would change course and start something entirely different.

One day, Hera came unannounced while Eurynome and Thetis played with the boy they had raised. In turn, the god proudly showed his metal creations to the two beautiful women.

"What a marvelous brooch you wear, dear Thetis," Hera remarked.

Hephaestus rose and limped away, refusing to sit near her. She was cruel and unworthy of his company.

"My son... he is so skilled with metals," Thetis extolled.

Hera turned her face, wrestling with her emotions as fresh tears welled in her eyes. She had condemned herself, blaming her actions day and night, but the past could not be changed. He was truly the son of Thetis or Eurynome. The little deformed boy, wobbling and casting hateful glances, knew his mother's betrayal. But on that day, she felt something change. She stood and walked to the window. From the underground palace of the Nereids, the sea lay visible, its inhabitants floating effortlessly; one giant mother fish leading a school of countless little ones behind her.

"I want him back," she uttered, almost as if issuing a command. The house of the ocean god trembled as a giant wave crashed over the roof, splashing its sides. Eurynome cast her a look of deep disdain, on the verge of uttering harsh words. She had raised three daughters, the Graces alongside Hephaestus, and they had grown up playing together like a family: Charis, the beautiful; Aglaia, the glorious; and Thalia, the plentiful. All adored the little boy equally. Hephaestus had crafted countless toys and adornments. He was like

a cousin who came for summer vacation and never left—though even that relationship was tenuous, since Zeus fathered her daughters, but not Hephaestus. Eurynome had grand plans; she intended to kill two birds with one stone.

"Why don't you talk to him?" she asked Hera.

Hera knew precisely what she meant. She nodded thoughtfully as she made her plans.

"No. I need my husband to speak with him. Besides, he's just a little boy; why should we seek his permission?"

Tension filled the room. Thetis intervened,

"Hera, you may have a strong urge to right the past wrongs, and I understand your feelings. But let it remain just that, an urge to amend your misdeeds. Let us not make another mistake by sending him away against his will. It's late now, and your family may begin to wonder…"

Hera left the palace swiftly.

Our Hephaestus was deeply grateful to his foster mothers. He kissed and hugged them before retreating to the smithy tucked away in a quiet corner of the palace. Alone, he raised his hammer and beat the hot metal mercilessly; the noise spread to distant places to let people and gods know that the smith god, their god of fire, was working and forging tools the world had never seen before. Thetis had sent Cedalion of Naxos to teach him all the crafts he knew, and she had given Hephaestus this small smithy.

Hephaestus felt abandoned and unappreciated—not only by his parents but by the entire world. He saw no reason to believe he was lovable or admirable. As a child, his young soul recoiled from thought, from pausing or reflecting; it was simply too painful. This was a cruel, ruthless world, where the defective was pitied and kept at a safe distance. His deformity was only skin-deep, something he hardly minded and learned to compensate for. But the flaw inside, an unrelenting feeling of incompleteness, could not be shaken, even as others praised his servitude and eagerness to please. He did not believe he had anything of value to offer the world, nor did he feel he possessed anything worth pride. This gnawing sense of worthlessness haunted him throughout his divine life. He tried his best to act the opposite, carefully avoiding conflicts whenever possible. Some, he could not prevent, and during those moments, he sometimes lost his temper. Yet among the Olympians, Hephaestus was considered steadfast, a rock others relied upon in times of need. He did his best to resolve conflicts, heal suffering, or at least bring opponents together. In transcending his own needs and desires, he often forgot himself. Why did he strive to unite everyone at the cost of forgetting who he was? Self-forgetting Hephaestus sought no place among the gods and did all he could to remain invisible as he grew older.

Hera would not rest. Zeus agreed to welcome her son back. When the king of gods desired Hephaestus' return, no one could refuse—not even the foster mothers. They asked if he would consider returning. He said nothing and immediately returned to his work. The burning wood and glowing iron seemed to mirror his deep-seated anger. He lifted his hammer with all his strength and struck the red-hot metal, shaping the curved handles of a chair. He crafted a fine mesh of pressed metal, joining it like a net atop the chair. After finishing the seat and back, he adorned the piece with gold, transforming it into an exquisite throne.

"Some lucky god will sit upon this throne," the Cyclops said.

Hephaestus instructed the servants to haul it to Olympus and place it in the great hall where the council met.

The next day, during the meeting of the gods, Hera noticed her name inscribed on the throne. Adorned with golden cuckoos, willow leaves, and a full moon on its back, the throne captivated her. Hera eagerly leapt to sit upon it, her chest swelling with pride, knowing only her own Hephaestus could have crafted such a masterpiece. Silently, she blessed him.

But when the council adjourned, Hera struggled to rise and was forced back into her seat. Zeus, embarrassed by his wife's childish antics, looked on as the other gods suppressed soft laughter.

"Invisible net," Ares muttered darkly before storming out in anger.

When Ares arrived at the smithy, Hephaestus was struggling with a faulty bellows. Covered in soot, clutching a flaming torch in his right hand, he barely noticed the war god's furious shout:

"Come with me—right now!" Ares screamed.

The fire god met his gaze with cold, indifferent eyes.

"Oh, lord of war, here in my smithy. How fortunate I am to…" he began.

"Only if you come to Olympus and free our mother from your ludicrous throne," Ares retorted sharply.

"Not our mother, your mother, Ares," he said softly.

"You are so unworthy of her, a disgrace…"

Now angry, Hephaestus stepped forward and thrust the fire toward Ares' face.

"I am ugly, deformed, and don't belong among the gods. So why bother? God of War, do not turn this visit into battle. Mortals will shun you, and even gods will take no pride," he paused.

Ares left seething with anger—and more than a hint of fear.

That evening, as the forge's fire dimmed and weariness settled in, Dionysus arrived, accompanied by his entourage of wine-lovers.

Hephaestus had never experienced such merriment before, and Dionysus made him feel alive.

"You did a fine job, brother," Dionysus laughed. "Hera couldn't even get up. Ha! I don't blame you, not one bit, for what she did to you."

Hephaestus took another drink, sweet but bitter, and soon felt numb. He saw two of Dionysus's, then a mule approached and brayed with laughter. He fell asleep.

Laughter erupted when Dionysus presented the drunken fire god to the council of Olympus, strapped atop a mule. The innocent and unsuspecting Hephaestus came to his senses amid the joyful noise and asked why he had been brought there. Father Zeus greeted him in the chamber of the gods and asked if he would release his mother.

"I bow to the god of gods and warmly greet all other gods and honorable elders gathered here. But my mother... have I ever known a loving mother among you?"

A heavy silence followed; no one knew what to say. Hera lowered her striking eyes, while Zeus smiled, in part retribution, part pity for the lame child.

"Let all gods and goddesses hear today," Hera suddenly proclaimed,

"I, the lawful wife of Zeus, was humiliated by him when he bore a child without me." Hera's large, cow eyes welled with unshed tears; she carefully concealed her sorrow and broken heart from the council. After a moment's pause, she resumed, voice heavy with reproach, pointing toward Zeus. "He desecrated my marriage, and I sought only revenge. Tell me, what could a goddess do against such an unfaithful husband?" She lowered her head in shame and deep remorse, whispering, "What I did was neither unfaithful nor sinful. In my despair and gloom, the goddess Flora brought me a bouquet and grass. I merely touched them with my gentle fingers, and lo and behold, I conceived on my own. I carried him for nine months. But when he was born, oh, Mother! He was a bundle of shame, the ugliest baby I had ever seen, with a clubfoot and disfigurements that seemed to expose my own resentment, as if he had wronged me. I knew you all would curse me, and that my life would never be the same again." She stopped.

Then she couldn't hold it anymore as Athena rose and walked toward her, leaning against her with such tenderness that even the perpetrator of her wrongs seemed to nod as if to thank Athena. Hera began heaving and sobbing very gently.

Hephaestus stood dazed by her intense emotion, thinking she had done what any woman might do under such circumstances. But he was not so overcome as to forget to claim a fitting reward for such a sacrifice. Thus, he spoke his demand.

"Tears of a mother can melt stone and turn devils to saints. But what of me, a poor wretch?" He paused, as if pleased by her remorse. "Only I can free you, O mother of all gods. But why should I?"

Zeus understood and asked directly,

"What will please you, my son? Ask, and I shall grant your wish."

"Then compensate me for my injury. Create a beautiful world around me, one that will inspire others to gaze not with disgust, but with awe at its beauty and elegance. Spare me from curious, hateful looks forever. Father, will you grant my wish: let the goddess of beauty be my bride?" He fell silent.

The council was stunned by his arrogance; his demand for Aphrodite was incomprehensible at first, utterly incongruous and flagrantly disrespectful of how glamour and grace should be revered, how beauty stands apart from the hideous. Above all, it resurfaced the stark contrast, the filthy, unlovely Hephaestus compared to the radiant Aphrodite. Aphrodite erupted in disbelief. She could hardly believe her ears.

"Is he insane? Look at him—what a sight! Have you ever looked at yourself in a mirror, my dear brother? If not, do so now and listen carefully. I am the goddess of love, the cause of mortal joy, the embodiment of beauty, delicacy, and allure, fascination, and enchantment. And you would seek to marry me? To disgrace all that is beautiful and belittle my birth? Why would Father Zeus even entertain such a notion?"

After the initial shock and dismay, the gods began to amuse themselves with the awkward demand. They stared openly at Hephaestus, then at Aphrodite, their glances unapologetically candid. But Ares turned away with disgust.

"Will you all act, or am I to remain ensnared for life? What gratitude is this?"

Then they saw Mother Hera sitting helplessly, and silence fell over the council.

"So be it, Hephaestus. I grant you the most desired goddess as your bride. But honor her and love her as a worthy husband should."

The council remained speechless at the unjust pronouncement. Aphrodite looked at her father, her eyes blazing with anger and filling with tears as she spoke,

"Never! Never shall I consider this man my husband, nor shall I be condemned for refusing to love him. Let Hera rejoice and let father feel satisfied in his peacekeeping, but this foam-born goddess, child of neither, shall remain free to love and bear children with whomever she desires." With that, she stormed out.

Hephaestus walked near Hera with a shifty smile, ready to undo his magic. Hera had waited long for this extraordinary moment, and as Hephaestus approached, she rose, almost trembling with emotion, to embrace him. He seemed hesitant, but once in her arms, he was utterly broken, like a baby, and her warm tears of contrition fell on the strong shoulders of a long-discarded, castaway son. She quivered with disgust as she looked down at his feet, sickly turned-back feet, and her penitence bounced back fiercely. She bent down to reach his legs with her slender fingers. Was she touching her guilt, which had burned ceaselessly since leaving the baby to perish, much worse than what any other mother would have experienced for abandoning her child for others to care for, a guilt neither reasonable nor usual? It was monstrously sickening, and it did nothing good to Hera. She was always guilt-ridden, and she would transfer it to her husband, and later even to Hephaestus. She never felt responsible for her omission nor had any love for the deformed infant, and all that responsibility and love recoiled in her when Hephaestus came near her.

Hephaestus was shown his place in Olympus, and Hera said,

"I've requested a forge for you beneath the hill. I know you love working with metals."

"Yes, goddess mother," he replied.

Hera wished he had said "mother," not "goddess mother."

"You will have the Cyclopes to help you. Cedalion will be there as well."

"Certainly. Would you like me to craft something for you?"

"No, no. Just play and have fun," she said, assuring him of his place in the family.

He set to work immediately. The burning wood and red-hot iron seemed to mirror the fury burning inside him. As the years passed and young Hephaestus grew into his place among the Olympians, he crafted many famed artifacts: the mighty Aegis, the breastplate of his father; a winged helmet for his brother Hermes; a golden chariot cup for Helios, the sun god; the helmet of invisibility for Hades; a bow for Eros; and the renowned girdle of love for Aphrodite, called the kestos himas or Cestus. He also forged armor for heroes like Achilles and Heracles.

But one day, Hera grew upset once more in Olympus. She stormed into the palace, nearly in tears, accusing her husband of infidelity and hurling endless insults. At this, the gods of all gods grew furious and stood near her, saying,

"I have heard enough of your unjust accusations. But this time, Mother Goddess, you have crossed the line by tormenting Heracles. Hera, he is a son any father would be proud of. Yet you sent snakes

to his cradle, and if that were not enough, unleashed terrible storms to hinder him."

"You are to blame for all my actions. Why should a wife live burdened by her husband's secrets and peccadillos? What self-respecting woman could endure such insults and blatant violations of marriage?"

"Hera, I govern the entire universe. Don't you understand? I am the creator of all; I cannot pause. You, of all gods, should know this better than anyone and aid me in preserving what we have wrought. You are not a regular housewife of a mere mortal."

"Marriage demands loyalty and equal partnership. It requires honesty."

"That is true for mortals. But how can we create, maintain, and sustain all we offer the living world if we fail to set examples, produce the finest heroes from our seeds, and condemn injustice? Hera, none can argue with you, and you have conspired with my children against me? Today, you will witness my strength," he said, his voice raging with anger.

Then he suspended her by her fair ankle high in the sky of Olympus. Hephaestus could not remain still.

He promptly spoke out against Zeus. The king of the gods was impressed by his argument but felt humiliated at the prospect of bringing Hera down.

"You, master craftsman, understand nothing of women, and you will forever suffer at their hands. As for now, I cannot stand you—your sickly features and your pity for your cunning mother enrage me. Let me teach you a lesson, so that next time you know your place here." With that, he hurled poor Hephaestus down the slopes of Olympus once more.

This time, he fell for nine days and nine nights. His body landed unconscious on the island of Lemnos, where his legs sustained further irreparable damage.

After this second unceremonious fall from heaven, the Sintians took in and cared for the unfortunate god.

His dedication to his craft earned him respect throughout Greece, and he was venerated in all industrial centers and by artisans alike. In Athens, a temple called the Hephaesteum (or Theseum) was built at the foot of the Acropolis, where both Athena, Ergane, and Hephaestus were worshipped on August 23rd during the Chalkeia festival.

Eurynome's daughter, Charis, was his first wife. A lady unmatched in beauty and grace by any goddess. Yet, Hephaestus could not sustain this marriage. Later, he married his third wife, Aglaia, the embodiment of brilliance. He could often be seen hobbling around the palace, fixing a doorknob or deep inside his smithy, covered in black soot. Draped in a sleeveless toga and wearing a pointed woolen cap, his face sweaty and eyes fixed on the glowing metal, his back bent over the anvil as twenty bellows pumped tirelessly. He had crafted three golden automatons to assist him.

Hephaestus had a tough time believing he was lovable. Then, he was madly in love with our goddess of love, who had never shown him an iota of love except when she needed something. Once, she had come to him for Aeneas, and he'd demanded that she stay over. She consented. But she did regret staying with him. What made Hephaestus so negativistic and resentful, yet appearing as if unperturbed? Aphrodite came close to him and chose to be affectionate to this peaceful soul; she smiled at him and touched his dark, dust-covered shoulder as if needing to feel his strength, then waited for some mild response. He watched her with such delight, thinking he must be asleep again, for that was how he always managed to numb his feelings, drown his conflicts, and wake up refreshed—far away from his own needs. And as the beautiful evening cast its spell, no effort was needed, since she had ensured he was loved; he was deeply touched, and his irritability gradually dissipated. He could find nothing in his heart to oppose, defy, or comment upon someone only sensual, shallow, and utterly carnal, as he always had in the past, which had invariably helped him establish a status of his own where no one could point a finger at him. And if some Olympian dared to make him feel his worth, he would quietly suffer without uttering any counterattack but recoil in sharp, covert indignation. He always knew that no one, no one should tell him what to do, how to live his life, what is good and what is evil. If Zeus or Athena did, he stared at them as if it did not matter; it was a trifle, and they were faced against some dead wall.

Hephaestus had a tough time believing he was loved; he could love, and love was all around. He had ceased to look at others to understand, to connect, and to be present since he was a child, long before he understood that he was in pain, the agony that would serve him relentlessly and finally force him to abandon not only all his family of gods but, most importantly, himself. And how could he remain in love, even with such a wonder of nature, such a splendid creation that would typically turn every divine or mortal head as sweet Aphrodite, when he was never there in the present, when he had escaped from all that is time, space, and stillness, the very elements that instill the most profound sense of affection, longing, and desire to be with someone else other than self, so one could blend, unite, and dissolve in love? Hephaestus had walked away, far away from his boundaries.

One day, Athena visited Hephaestus seeking one of her shields, armor, or something she required. He had been brooding for days over Aphrodite's cold and uncaring attitude. When she arrived, he fell deeply for her. He was so overcome with excitement that, as she turned away from his embrace toward the door, he could no longer restrain himself. Athena received his seed upon her thigh and wiped the last drops to the earth.

Mother Earth bore her child, Erichthonios, whom Athena entrusted to the three daughters of Cecrops, the first king of Attica.

She warned the three sisters not to open the small basket where her son lay sleeping and then departed. The sisters—Agraulos, Herse, and Pandrosus—were overcome with curiosity, but ultimately opened the basket to find Erichthonios lying within, his lower half serpentine. Enraged, Athena cursed them, and they all took their own lives. Erichthonios was credited as the first to use four-horse chariots and was honored with the star Auriga.

His other children included Cacus, a fearsome monster slain by Heracles, and Caeculus, who bore a similar nature to his brother.

Among his gravest deeds—ones he never felt truly justified in—was punishing the Titan brothers Epimetheus and Prometheus. Prometheus had stolen fire from Hephaestus's forge to give to humanity, defying Zeus. The cloud-gatherer grew furious and condemned Prometheus to be chained upon a mountain, where an eagle would eternally feast upon his regenerating liver.

Seeking vengeance against Epimetheus, Zeus commanded Hephaestus to craft a beautiful maiden. Thus, he created Pandora— the most enchanting woman the world had ever known—whom he gifted to Epimetheus. Epimetheus warned her never to open the box containing all evils hidden from humanity. But driven by curiosity, Pandora could not resist. When she opened it, all the evils—anger, jealousy, theft, lust, and more escaped, except hope, which was still inside.

Chapter Two – Heracles, Dionysus, Demeter, and Persephone.

"Please, listen to me, sir," Andrew implored. "I need to find my fiancée." He directed his plea toward the tall, giant-looking man dressed in a lion-skin tunic, who appeared to be a sentry on the island. Andrew was quite disturbed that instead of listening to him and offering help to find Rhea, he seemed eager to take him into custody. He was consumed by sadness and guilt, believing himself to be at fault for the calamity; it wouldn't have happened if they had traveled by boat or a commercial flight. But Andrew was determined to do everything possible to explore this island and pursue Rhea.

"After the crash, when I woke up, she was already gone," he said in a mournful tone.

The whole ordeal was a nightmare for poor Andrew, and he hoped it would soon be over. Rhea was not lost; she would show up soon, and he wouldn't have to make all this fuss or explain everything about her to these native Greek people. The man he faced stood almost seven feet tall, like a colossal basketball player, with strong, sinewy arms and broad shoulders, but gave little impression of insight. Andrew felt helpless in the face of such a human being, as if the giant would be more of an obstacle than any help in finding Rhea. Suddenly, another wave of sadness and despair filled his heart, as if he knew Rhea was lost forever. The bleak prospects of finding her, the poor communication, the utterly deplorable help on the island, and the inexplicable events began to erode his confidence. He lowered his head, misty-eyed, as if this time he truly felt the profound sorrow that would be his fate if he were to live without her. He wished he had known before how he would feel if some misfortune struck them; if, by some act of providence, she was snatched away from his life; a fate which, in the past, he might have accepted without much difficulty, or even with slight relief during moments of frustration, conflict, and disagreements with her, when Rhea behaved nothing less than a hellcat.

Heracles asked him about her features.

"What can I say? You know she's of Greek origin; her grandfather was from Crete."

Then he described her countenance as very pretty and her blonde features eloquently. When he paused to observe the effect on the stranger, he was surprised as a mild softness broke through Heracles' rugged and ruddy countenance, altering to a gentleness tinged with deep, simmering hurt. Andrew waited, then couldn't help but ask,

"Sir, who are you, and what is your business here?"

Heracles did not answer immediately. He studied the stranger before him carefully, and once convinced that Andrew posed no real threat and could be subdued easily if needed, he said,

"I am the son of Zeus and Alcmene. I am Heracles."

Even though mighty Heracles pretended to listen to Andrew's story, he was lost in thoughts about his own life, how he had brought Megara, daughter of King Creon, home after defeating the Minyans, receiving a beautiful woman and a devoted wife who later bore him three sons. But the goddess Hera could not tolerate his joy and sent madness upon him. In a ferocious rage, he turned violent and committed the worst crime, killing all his children and Megara in his frenzy. When he awoke from his insanity, with blood-stained hands and scattered remains of his severed wife and sons, he was filled with deep regret and could not bear the guilt and sorrow. He lamented bitterly for days, until his friend took him away to serve his cousin King Eurystheus for a new beginning, later known as the "Labors of Heracles." It was the mother of the gods, Hera, who had conspired to stain his hands with the blood of his children to halt his rising power and renown, since he, a mortal, had made the immortals appear all the more flawed. Hera had never forgiven Zeus for having a son with the mortal Alcmene.

Heracles tried hard not to let his own life judge another mortal's plight and then gazed at Andrew, who stood before him in supplication, seeking help to recover his lady, who was lost or possibly dead in the accident. For a moment, he felt very akin to Andrew, recalling what had happened to him when his wife Megara had died.

"Was there anyone else with you besides her? Any children?"

Andrew's pain welled anew, and he nodded faintly. How else could he explain to this seemingly orthodox figure that his fiancée carried his unborn child? He could not bring himself to speak ill of Rhea.

Heracles recalled the time when he was courting his second wife, Deianeira.

The river god had appeared, hissing like a bullhead, and a fierce fight had ensued.

"Was there any other man involved?" he asked Andrew.

"Are you kidding? On this desolate Mount Olympus?"

"Mount Olympus?" Heracles echoed in confusion.

"Yes. That is what we thought…"

Heracles glanced at him contemptuously before turning away, clearly unwilling to discuss the matter further. Where should he begin? Like many mortals, this man must believe that the immortals still reside on Mount Olympus.

However, Andrew had only realized by accident how close he had flown his small Cessna to the mountains, mistakenly thinking he was near Mount Olympus based on his data. In truth, he was in a land where ancient civilization still endured.

He sensed he had asked a question Heracles found difficult to answer and waited patiently.

"I don't know who you are or where you come from, mortal, but it's a long story, a tale spanning nearly two thousand mortal years..." He paused, then asked again, as if interrogating, "But what exactly are you looking for here?"

"Mortal? Oh, I see... you're not mortal, then." He studied the towering giant and corrected himself. "Tell me, my immortal friend, where are we? Who is this Hephaestus? And who are you, really?" His voice betrayed his bewilderment.

Heracles remained perplexed as well, glancing at his captive to gauge whether he could be trusted. Then, he shifted his gaze toward the town. After a brief, uncomfortable pause that lent solemnity and gravity to the occasion, he began speaking slowly, pausing repeatedly as he reconsidered whether it was wise to share such a profound tale with a stranger he had only recently met. Moreover, who would willingly recount their own retreat, humiliation, and exile? Heracles had never been one for much reasoning in the past, but he had ample emotions, the anger or the love. At that moment, anger surged within him. His fists clenched as if to strangle someone, that someone being the Roman Emperor Constantine. He spoke slowly:

"It's a long story. We all left after Emperor Constantine adopted Christianity and declared it the state religion. Of course, Zeus was devastated, and mortals were dying, being massacred for their faith in us, by those same mortals. There was no respite; we couldn't change those brutal people. They had gone out of their minds, and it seemed the end was near for that race. There was widespread violence, destruction, and savagery against our old faith and religion. They would only cease if their new faith were firmly established. They were mocking us. That is a sad story, sad indeed," he said, sucking in air and sighing.

Andrew grieved alongside him, though curiosity gnawed at him; he still lacked many answers.

"But where exactly are we right now? I mean geographically, not just in time."

Heracles raised his head and replied, "This is a hidden, small island. Crete lies to the south, while Naxos and Ikaria are to the northeast. To the northwest, you'll find Syros, Tinos, and Andros. Two mountains rise in the center like a crown, concealing us from any eyes above."

"How did you come upon such a place?"

"Hermes once used this island as a refuge for wounded warriors during the Trojan War."

"What about the Greek government? Don't they interfere?"

Heracles smiled amusingly.

"They tried. Several ships came to scout us, but in the end, they gave up."

"Why?"

"I don't know," he said with a grim grin. "Perhaps because no one ever returned to tell the tale..." He trailed off, carefully choosing his words.

Andrew shivered. He didn't know whether to believe this mad giant, laugh at his wild claims, or shake him and say, "Let's be honest, my friend, I'm in serious trouble, and I have no patience for this nonsense."

But he said nothing. Instead, he mourned quietly with him. He now had a rough idea where he was, but that knowledge brought little comfort. This man might truly be honest. It was no dream; he had landed somewhere profoundly strange.

After walking for a while, they reached a small building resembling an old grammar school, deserted and eerie. A tall iron gate barred the entrance, imposing and unnecessary. Andrew lingered outside, reluctant.

Heracles unlocked the padlock and pushed the door with a clang. Noticing Andrew's hesitation, he extended his broad hand almost coaxingly, urging him inside.

Inside was dark, dusty, and dank. The musty odor made Andrews sick.

Heracles lit a candle. Cobwebs brushed Andrew's face like a sacrilege.

Ahead, in small cells, lay gruesome remains, wrist and ankle bones still shackled. Andrew shuddered. He could flee to the shore, but then what?

"This is where you'll stay until the council convenes," Heracles declared, tossing a bundle of Greek clothes toward him.

"What? You expect me to wear this toga and sandals?"

Andrew paused as Heracles turned his steely eyes toward him. Then he noticed a rat scurrying by. There were holes in the wall. What else, he thought, could be creeping upon me? Where is Rhea? It was all his own doing. An unknown pain usurped its head, rising instead of the usual emptiness, and he attributed it to Rhea's absence.

"Look, my father is well known in Athens. He is in the shipping industry and has ties to the government," Andrew ventured.

Heracles opened a small cell. The iron grate rattled, sending dust to the floor.

"He will never know," he said quietly.

The darkness, the scent of bones and dust, and the oppressive stillness weighed heavily on Andrew, foreshadowing a grim fate. What was happening? Where had they brought him, and why? The questions hung unanswered. He could not surrender his fate to these men, remnants of a defeated Trojan tribe trapped in a world frozen in time, as if nothing had ever changed. Fear grew in him, deep and unrelenting. He tried to brace himself, but instead a soft sob escaped. The tears of a man humbled beyond words fell in silence.

Heracles returned carrying a loaf of bread, cheese, figs, and a bottle of Greek wine.

He ate quietly, thinking surely, she must be hungry too.

"Brooding?" Heracles broke the silence.

"No, nothing," he said, taking a deep breath.

And this is how poor Andrew ended up in a tiny Greek penitentiary instead of his lifelong dream vacation on Crete. He wondered whether higher spirits did not wish him to reach Rhea's village, where the old temples, Greek traditions, and her family awaited the little granddaughter of the priest who had left the town in search of a new life. Rhea was reared there as a child after her parents had returned due to financial hardship in America. When her father learned that it was no less destitution and suffering, only more entanglement in archaic family traditions and temple rituals, he felt restricted, stifled, and removed from the world. He had to abandon his father's village again, this time for New Jersey.

Andrew pondered whether Rhea was now paying for her father's past abandonment. If that were true, why hadn't they been sent to Crete to face the hidden history that her parents so carefully concealed? Rhea had once told him that the village's age-old traditions were unstoppable, that the only escape was to flee to a far-off land where no one could punish the family. Her grandfather had fulfilled his duties to the gods, but her father had grown distant, neglecting the rituals and sacrifices demanded of each generation. What the gods asked for was never given.

Andrew wanted to ask why Rhea's father didn't warn or forbid their journey, but before he could voice the question, Heracles interrupted his thoughts.

"Women! My Deianeira—oh, she was unlike anyone I'd ever known," Heracles began.

"Your wife?" Andrew asked.

"Daughter of King Ōeneus, the most beautiful woman in Aetolia. Loving and gentle... but she turned vicious in the end."

"What happened?"

"I was in love with Iole. Her father, King Eurytus, would never agree. Finally, we besieged his army, and I claimed Iole as my prize. Then... yes, I made a grave mistake. I sent her to the palace, right where Deianeira awaited me," he paused.

"How did your wife react?" Andrew asked softly.

"She sent me a cloak, a gift for her husband. I prayed at the temple to Zeus while wearing it. But alas! The cloak tore into my flesh, poisoned by the blood of a dying centaur that she had sprinkled upon it, the poison of jealousy."

"Rhea could never even think such a thing…" Andrew faltered.

Heracles said nothing further, lost in memories.

Seizing the moment, Andrew decided to try escaping once more. He reached out, clutching the wine bottle as if to pour, but suddenly thrust it toward Heracles. The giant was caught off guard and ducked instinctively.

Andrew sprang toward the door and sprinted as fast as his legs could carry him.

He ran on for a long while before daring to glance back. Exhaustion weighed heavily on him; his toga had slipped, revealing his bare chest. He struggled to slip his feet back into the loose sandals.

A stray dog glared at him with harsh eyes. Andrew was in trouble once more.

"Hey, doggie, shoo, shoo," he said, tossing a piece of bread he'd been clutching. The dog sneered, jaws parting.

The dog lunged, and Andrew dodged, tumbling onto an unseen path. He found himself in a ditch, hidden beneath the dry autumn leaves and branches of the fallen trees.

Slipping in the darkness, he slithered down as if descending through a dank, winding underworld. The dog paused at the rim, puzzled, its tongue lolling out of its mouth.

At the end of the glide, he landed with a harsh thud. Panic surged, but he forced himself toward a solitary shaft of sunlight ahead. Once outside, relief washed over him in the open space, a small courtyard.

About a hundred feet away stood a house. Hesitant, he approached, noticing the front door ajar. Inside, dim light flickered, voices muffled but audible.

He knocked softly. A woman's head appeared.

"Stranger!" She exclaimed.

"Who is it, Core?" a voice called from within.

"An extraordinary man, Mother," she answered to the insider.

Andrew studied Core, a soft, willowy girl whose age he couldn't guess. Her hair, framing a pale face, flowed past her shoulders beneath a pink tunic. She was attractive but not voluptuous; her serene black eyes and parched lips gave her an otherworldly air. He noticed her slender ankles and delicate feet. He thought of a biting cold blizzard that never seems to end.

"Please, let me in. I beg you; the sheriff is after me unjustly," he implored.

"Heracles? The slayer of the Nemean Lion chases you? Who can save you now?" Core asked, her voice laced with disbelief.

"I will," the mother snapped angrily. "Heracles brings only misery and destruction."

"Mother, this is not the time," Core scolded softly.

"Core, when then? How long will we turn a blind eye to his bloodshed?"

"Mother, has Hera been whispering in your ear again? I thought she had softened."

"Heracles kills without mercy," she spat. "He slaughtered his own family, razed King Laomedon's city, and abducted Hesione."

Core's mother mentioned something that sounded very trivial, but what transpired after Hesione was abducted made history for the Greeks. Many years later, Hesione's brother, King Priam, sent his son Paris to fetch her back. The rest of the story is well known: Paris brought Helen to Troy, which became the cause of the ill-fated war.

"Mother, you don't make sense. These are irrelevant now," Core replied.

Andrew nearly shoved past Core, desperate to enter. Inside, the mother stood dressed in a dark, elegant tunica beneath a shadowed palla. Her fair ankles gleamed, but a simple headdress modestly veiled her head. Though her flowing blonde hair and golden shoulders remained partially hidden, Andrew sensed her presence, the fragrance, the forlorn eyes, and an aura of timeless grief that inspired reverence rather than fear.

"Who are you?" She asked softly.

"I am a traveler. My plane crashed during the storm, and we landed on your shores," he began. Finding sympathy, he added, "My fiancée, Rhea, is missing. No one has seen her since," then hesitated.

Demeter, the mother, exchanged a meaningful glance with her daughter, Core, which gave Andrew a glimmer of hope. Core, the maiden better known as Persephone, wore an inscrutable expression, yet Demeter appeared calm, as if already privy to Andrew's story.

"And you are...?" Andrew ventured, directing the question to Demeter.

To this innocent query, the air hung still, and the goddess of corn and fertility became speechless. She looked at the young mortal, and all her past came crashing down like a massive wave in her mind.

She had favored mortals when spending time away from Olympus— angry, sad, and deceived by her own. Remembering some mortals she had never cared for, like Tantalus, and she felt the old disgust rise again. Yes, he had killed his son Pelops and fed his flesh to the gods. When she found out, she retched for days. Finally, she restored the unfortunate young man to life, but she missed his shoulder, which the gods had eaten, so she gave him an ivory one.

"You seem to know more than you say," Andrew interrupted gently.

Demeter gave no reply. Persephone's face darkened in unmistakable disgust.

"Is she your wife?" Persephone asked bluntly.

He did not know how to respond and chose silence.

Then they asked all about her. He told her name, and the ladies exchanged glances with that name, though Andrew remained oblivious. Rhea! Rhea! The name echoed in the minds of the deathless goddesses like a restless spirit returning to claim her rightful honor.

Rhea or the Flow, the menstrual flow, Rhea, the ease-ease of childbirth, the daughter of Ouranos and Mother Gaia, the Metros Theon to all the gods. Her name commanded reverence, and the immortals bowed their heads in respect presently.

Rhea, the goddess draped in dark robes, rider of lion-driven chariots; wife of Cronos; mother to Zeus, Poseidon, Demeter, Hades, Hestia, and Hera. She rides with her acolytes—the Curetes and Corybantes—alongside swans and the silent moon. A goddess of wild cliffs and rich hair, she dances to the clangor of cymbals, rattles, castanets, and tambourines. After the Titanomachy, she demanded from Zeus half the earth, the ocean, and the heavens. When denied, she withdrew to the mountains of Phrygia, accompanied by her Corybantes worshippers. To this day, in Crete, her wild cave on Mount Ida is guarded by bees, and occasionally a great flame bursts forth, revealing to mortals the place where baby Zeus was nurtured and fed by the goat Amalthea.

Rhea had helplessly given up all her children to be devoured by Cronos, one by one, until Zeus was born, whom she shielded by deceiving Cronos with a great stone wrapped as an infant. Yet, when Zeus returned, it was she who aided in chaining him and banishing him forever.

At this point, Hekate entered, bearing a basket of fruit.

"Dionysus has arrived,"

Daughter of Asteria and a three-faced goddess, Hekate stands as guardian at the threshold of childbirth.

Persephone acknowledged her presence with a nod.

His sideburns extended almost to his beard, and his skin was tanned, reminiscent of an Asian's, as if he had been raised in an open field. The robe with golden borders glinted like the glow of the sunset.

"Mother, I need some more wine, please. You know Hephaestus encountered some   unusual folks,"   Dionysus   began without hesitation.

"Try some barley water," Demeter offered.

"Barley water? I am not your child, Demophoon. I shall send you some fine old wine from my travels to Phrygia. Besides, father is calling a council meeting later…"

"Father?" Demeter scoffed.

Dionysus fixed Demeter with a sharp look, noting her contorted expression before exploding in anger:

"Why do you torment me so? Persephone, can you save me from her torment?"

"Ignore her," Persephone suggested.

 "Did she quarrel with the god of gods again? Or is Hades back to take you?"

"No," Persephone said quietly, "she worries for a mortal woman here."

"What? Anyway, why mock my father? Why do we endlessly dredge up old family shames? When will the Olympians find peace with their past?"

A heavy silence fell. Hekate stopped slicing apples; Persephone stiffened on her couch. Dionysus hesitated, repulsed, then pressed on with rising agitation:

"Who is my father? Why must I live a deathless life amidst such turmoil? Even mortals would demand answers. Mother Persephone, you were wed to Hades, weren't you? Or should I say, of course, against your wish, the word 'raped' when he seized you from Nysean fields?"

And thus, the inebriated god Dionysus unveiled family secrets, mortifying the women and sowing dismay. Demeter fixed him with a severe glare:

"No more, Dionysus. Even under wine's influence, you have no license to hurl such insults at my daughter."

Pale, Persephone trembled with barely restrained fury:

"Oh, keeper of grain, let truth be spoken to my child." She bowed her head into her radiant lap. Silence fell. Andrew shifted uneasily, longing to vanish, yet unsafe beyond their presence. Dionysus noticed the stranger and raised a questioning brow, but chose silence, yielding to Persephone's gravity.

"What Hades did change my life forever; I can never forgive him. Yet what Zeus allowed was worse. When Hades asked, Zeus neither agreed nor refused. He did not even speak to my mother. Why?

As I was busy picking flowers in a meadow blooming with roses, crocuses, violets, hyacinths, and narcissus, suddenly I heard a rumbling noise as if the earth was breaking open onto a vast chasm.

A dark black chariot with golden rim wheels driven by four horses with tongues of fire leaping from nostrils and dark ruby eyes emerged, and Hades, in a dark floor-length cloak, raven hair on a hideous face, appeared to grab me onto his chariot and all my flowers, wet with my tears scattered on the path to the gloomy house in the neither world.

What violence for a maiden! I wept and begged, but no one, not even Zeus, heard my cries." Persephone paused, her chest heaving as if a wrecked terrain in retribution.

"No one spoke of this vile deed, no one," Demeter said, gazing out the window before turning to her daughter. "I traveled all over the earth, rivers and mountains, my tears dried, my hair tangled, my skin as hard as my heart. Until at last, Hekate and Helios revealed the truth to me."

Hekate stood silent.

"I heard her cries for help. I knew it was Persephone... but I could do nothing."

Demeter sighed, seemingly to contrition-deep.

Time suspended, the immortals lost in memory. Andrew listened closely to the tale, not as sung by the muses but from the very lips of the deathless.

"For nine days, I roamed in vain. My garments torn, my head bare, I was clutching only a torch and a sickle. Surely, I must have looked a dreadful sight," Demeter recalled.

"You hadn't tasted any ambrosia for days… One couldn't say it was a goddess."

Eventually, Demeter paused at Eleusis, meeting the daughters of Keleus and Metaneira while disguised as an older woman left ashore by pirates. She was asked to care for the king's son, Demophoon. She used to anoint him with ambrosia and strengthen him by fire to make him immortal. The child grew so beautiful, like a god, until one day, his mother discovered him while she kept the baby on the fire. Metaneira screamed in pain, and Demeter was disappointed.

Then, she revealed her proper form to them and tried to immortalize their son. Her fair ankles, radiant face, and glorious presence overwhelmed the king. Demeter asked them to build a temple for her and to pray in the Eleusinian way.

"Oh, it was too late for my destiny to bloom. When you descended to the Underworld, Mother, I was already taken. Yet you retrieved me. There in his realm, Hades offered pomegranate seeds deceitfully, watching me every day being starved in agony, and I unknowingly ate a few seeds."

Andrew looked at Persephone, wondering whether she was telling the truth. Her husband had asked her to eat the pomegranate seeds. Who was she really? A ghost? A goddess from the underworld?

And Demeter or Da Mater, the Earth Mother, or perhaps the Corn Mother and her daughter, Persephone, the goddess taken deep into the earth, the embodiment of our soul? What a profound link between life and death, between all that is beautiful and all that is dark. Here on earth, we feed the body, nurture it, and adorn it with togas, flower wreaths, and perfumes, and there, stripped of all adornment, we are left with nothing but our souls, roaming unbound.

"The gods of Olympus decreed you would spend two-thirds of the year on earth, one-third in the Underworld," Demeter explained.

"Oh, I knew it all along, Hades was my father?" Dionysus cried.

They didn't pay much heed.

Demeter had not washed her fair ankles and wished for the world to halt, for everything to pause until the intense pain of separation from her daughter had eased. The earth responded. The weather conspired with her grief, the earth bore no more harvests, no flowers blossomed, and no sweet breeze stirred the tall trees to heal the land. Mortals were in dire trouble, and even the gods were taken aback. There was no grain left to offer in prayers to the Olympians. The earth lay barren, the soil split hard, and people began to starve.

Demeter refused to renew the lease of life. She withdrew far from her family, lonely in her temple at Eleusis. There, among mortals, the goddess found a sanctuary to grieve and to ponder the depths of her existence.

And the mortals seek the gods when struck by a calamity.

Who needs whom?

"It was Hades, wasn't it, Mother?" the god of wine pressed again.

Then Iris arrived as a messenger from Zeus, followed by the Olympians, one at a time, in the temple of Eleusis, but she wouldn't listen. "No, I will not return to that home, the place where my brother seized my daughter, where gods stayed silent far too long. No, it is better here, among the simple folks."

"No, no, no — it was not Hades." Persephone's voice was sharp, quieting the room as others held their breath to listen to her pain.

Outside, it was raining, rain droplets paused in suspension on the glass pane, a branch of a nearby tree, which was swaying, stood still, and the immortals could hear the din of their own thoughts in anticipation of some inscrutable divine secret being revealed by one of them, as if she needed to announce it to redeem herself.

"Father Zeus, as if he hadn't done enough, came to me as a serpent. Rhea knows. Zeus had looked at Rhea with lust, and she, as a mother, was mortified and ran out. Her chagrin burned her to a snake, but Zeus transformed himself before reaching her.

To Rhea's dismay, he glanced at me, and I, like her, turned into a snake with venom. When he was done with me, much to my abject shame, you Zagreus were born.

She sneered, "serpent to serpent—the staff of Hermes."

Dionysus sat speechless, eyes blazing with hatred, and growled,

"Rhea knows, she who nursed me for you. Rhea, who gave me this amethyst to keep me sober."

Finally, Hermes arrived. What a surprise, it was so unexpected that Demeter could hardly believe her eyes and rubbed them in disbelief. But no, it was truly her daughter alighting from the golden chariot of Hades. Persephone came running, and the mother sprang forward to embrace her. Their faces bore a striking resemblance, streaked with tears that fell like gentle rivers. The mother was filled with joy and forgot all her grief. The world seemed fair once more— the earth, the streams, and the mountain peaks all rejoiced, allowing flowers to bloom, barley seeds to sprout, and a fragrant zephyr to sweep across the land, restoring unforeseen fertility. However, Persephone was no longer the innocent maiden she once was; she had grown into the goddess of the underworld.

Suddenly, Dionysus rose, seizing a jar of barley and draining it in one gulp.

"That is why he and I are Zagreus—the great hunter! Mother, you and Demeter, I pity you both. Why didn't you pour out all the venom you possessed rather than mate in incest with a brother or a father? Why? Huh?" And with that, he darted through the door like an arrow.

Andrew watched Demeter's face. She remained distant as if meditating while others fretted.

She revealed her secrets to the king and showed Demophoon-Triptolemus the art of planting a seed. He, in turn, traveled all over the earth to teach her art.

Why should she be bothered by accusations from Dionysus? She never thought much of any mate. She had resisted Poseidon so much when she was grieving. People say she had hidden among the horses when Poseidon came to her, and Arion was born.

She felt something real once, and it was not for a god. It was Iasion. Oh yes, it was a grand marriage for Harmonia and Cadmus. Yet, the bride's brother kept glancing at young Demeter. Iasion had brought her beautiful gifts and stood close, his glistening, strong mortal figure evoking desire even among the gods. And then, she could only remember the field, a desolate, hollow expanse, as silent as a grave, while inside the palace, guests cheered, and laughter mingled with the aroma of food wafting in the air. There, he began to unrobe her. The goddess of grain lay on the thrice-plowed field as if she had waited for this moment for ages. He touched her fair ankles, and she quivered. No, don't, she wanted to say. Do not come close to me, please. You don't know the gods' wrath. Stay away, she whispered, as he drew nearer to her pious self. She closed her divine eyes, and he kissed her nectar-fed lips. Her heart raced, and he began to sweat upon the soft, supple, sweatless goddess.

Upon their return, Zeus saw her crumpled, sullied dark raiment, and his face darkened. Iasion did not live to see his sister's marriage or their children from the union—Plutus and Philomelus.

Chapter Three – Aphrodite

Can love be so distorted that the one who is loved feels nothing for the person loving them? Can it be only received and never given? Was Rhea suffering the same pain of separation, or was poor Andrew alone enduring an unfathomable, endless misery of disunion at the height of a rapturous relationship? What is love, a feeling so many mortals have described, and gods have pondered?

Does love inspire the greatest happiness in mortals? Is it a blissful state, or merely an everyday delight? Do feelings of goodwill, the willingness to sacrifice for loved ones, and fulfillment persist when love is one-sided, and can it still be considered love? Is love tied to a specific appearance, skin tone, hair hue, rosy cheeks, thin, sensual lips, or should it be unconditional? Where does one seek it, and how does one know when it has arrived?

Lost in these thoughts, Andrew slipped silently out of Demeter's palace, leaving the divine family immersed in deep despair. No one was bothered.

Above, the sky was veiled with fluffy, sailing clouds that gradually muted the setting sun. Spring had arrived, heralded by crocuses, irises, and white tulips in jubilation. The bullfrog croaked; a woodpecker lifted its head, then resumed its rhythmic click-click on an oak. Pines and chestnuts rustled mildly in the breeze sweeping in from the Aegean Sea. Temperature and humidity would steadily rise until July, peaking in the driest month, which typically has minimal rainfall.

He strode rather lugubriously, aimlessly, and deep in contemplation of what had happened recently. These people seemed so strange, so uncanny. Their appearance, attire, and dwellings were no less dramatic than what he had previously learned about their culture.

While the history read in books was plausible and imaginable, what truly impressed him was the effort to bring the past, almost antediluvian myths, to life in an organized fashion.

It reminded him of some remote communities back home where people desperately strive to keep "old America" alive, living and dressing in vintage clothing that represent the nineteenth or twentieth century, or even staging Civil War reenactments for visitors. Is it a part of a Greek revival of culture, history, and pagan religion? Andrew wished the people involved in such a tremendous scheme would come forward truthfully rather than mystifying the situation, which made his life so perplexing and complex that at times he would lose track of his true goal: finding Rhea.

"Rhea, I won't give up," he uttered an oath to himself, drawing a deep breath.

Feeling somewhat relieved, his determination to survive and continue searching for his companion grew stronger. He resolved in his mind to forget that these were real people, not phantoms of pagan gods, enacting an extensive drama to preserve their beautiful past. All those characters—Hephaestus, Heracles, Persephone, Demeter, and Dionysus must have real Greek names hidden beneath these mythical personas. Still, he would undoubtedly figure it out when he mingled with them further. That was it: to get to know them, show them as if he believed in them, their bogus appearances, and bingo! They might start talking. But who would betray the information first? He thought Dionysus might reveal almost anything under the ill effect of his wine.

Meanwhile, Hephaestus wasn't very complex to read and could help since he seemed so much against his own family. This thought gave Andrew new hope, and a vague strategy formed in his mind. He resolved to work with these vain Greeks rather than flee like a convict.

At that moment, he glanced up to find the clouds drifting buoyantly, a mélange of shades breaking through: red, orange, and yellow that lifted his hopes.

"Heracles let you out?"

A voice asked, breaking Andrew's reverie as he walked through the woods. He hadn't noticed the speaker; it was Hephaestus again.

Andrew remained silent. What could he say to explain the situation? Was he considered a runaway inmate, a convict, or something else? Would he report him again and condemn him to the same eerie place? He glanced around for a possible escape, but did not move.

"I escaped," he finally said.

Hephaestus seemed troubled.

"Look, I'm dejected. Please help me. Please don't call him again."

Hephaestus listened to him, unaffected by his earnest plea, and showed no haste. He sensed the mortal's pain and could empathize, but what bothered him was the mortal's intense desire to find his lost mate—a woman, after all.

"Dejected, my foot! Not for a wife, they're not worth it," he muttered as he walked away.

Andrew found a hint, albeit a subtle one, at this sudden outburst on such intimate matters. Eager to learn more and draw him closer for his own sake, he followed the great craftsman.

"But she's not my wife yet," he said, the words sounding hollow even to himself.

Hephaestus gave no response, as if his distaste for marriage was deeply rooted. He continued to walk with a comical gait, even as his face betrayed seriousness. Andrew began his story, involving this clown and seeking possible help. He told how he had been happy without women, until he began caring for Rhea, when everything changed. Back home, they had not been so happy. It was a miracle that once they were in the sky and found themselves in midair disaster, his outlook and thinking shifted so significantly that he proposed to her, though just a month ago, he had decided to move out when they were arguing bitterly over something trivial.

"Huh. Marriage. I wouldn't say I like the word. I don't know... You know," he continued, as if confessing his lousy taste in matrimony. "You know what I paid to Zeus, the gifts to appease him for Aphrodite?" He paused.

"You mean the golden Aphrodite, the dazzling beauty?"

"Dazzling? Yes, but she's a bundle of dazzling pain and misery, the cause of all my ridicule."

"Well, the sweet pain," Andrew surmised.

"No. You have no idea. But look, I must go."

Andrew wanted to accompany him, and his desire to see Aphrodite soared.

"May I accompany you?" he asked.

Hephaestus paused, then nodded. Why not let this mortal learn life's lessons, he thought. Let him discover whether beautiful Aphrodite is all we need or if there is more in life than mere dazzling. Hephaestus had learned this the hard way. Glancing askance at Andrew, he tried to decide whether he was trustworthy, whether he could cause trouble to the celestial kingdom. A faint smile erupted on his hardy face before vanishing, replaced by a shadow of mild chagrin. 'He would be the mortal,' Hephaestus whispered, 'whether I take him or not, in the family, since his entry was predestined.' Then he roared to Andrew,

"So be it! You can help me." Hephaestus continued, "restrain your mortal passions, and don't be too quick to judge—what your eyes shall witness is not what your mind must resolve; think, waver, ponder, and vacillate before reaching the truth."

He began walking briskly. Suddenly, the sky cleared, and the sun brightened with a flicker before its yellow-orange hues sank deep into the underworld.

"Rhea and I enjoy the sunset so much. Ah, the soft golden rays, as if reflecting from the sun's chariot, and when," Andrew hesitated, sharing such intimate feelings with a stranger, but continued, "when it colors her pale cheeks, she becomes irresistible, and I forget all my anguish. All I want is to be close to her, to hold her and touch her gently… You know, that is bliss!"

"The chariot," Hephaestus cut in, ignoring Andrew's emotions. "I made it golden for him," he said, looking upward, as if to speak again, as if he'd summon the sun god right there.

He walked across the meadow and found a corner on the ledge where one could see the firmament uninterrupted as the setting sun tinted it vigorously in deep burgundy, orange, and gold. Raising his right hand, he turned his face toward the sun, bright yellow rays falling on his cheek, and began,

"Helios, son of Hyperion and Theia, listen to me. If what you said earlier is true, I shall bring an end to it. If not… You know my wrath. What would you do if Neaira ever slept with another?"

Suddenly, the sun leaped again. The bright light almost blinded Andrew, as if it were not meant for him, the divine intercourse and whatever was being uttered or revealed by the gods for the gods, so he shut his eyes, and his mind seemed foggy. When he opened them, the world had settled into a peaceful evening.

"I shouldn't have said that his children, Lampetia and Phaethousa, might be listening," Hephaestus muttered as he strode on.

The road turned busier, and many men bowed at Hephaestus.

"You know them?"

"No, they are all hard-working people, carpenters, blacksmiths, and jewelers."

Hephaestus seemed in some hurry. Finally, they left the crowd behind and entered a pastureland. The road narrowed, ending in a path trodden by the villagers with doglegs interrupted by dead fallen trees. Andrew felt a mild trepidation, but it didn't show. After a while, a rushing sound reached them, revealing a small brook. Hephaestus glanced around cautiously, cupped his rugged hands, and splashed clear water on his face. Then he waded into the creek, sinking deeper and deeper until only his head remained visible. He beckoned to Andrew to follow.

Andrew began to ford the brook cautiously, like a child stepping in water with its parents, and when he got close to Hephaestus, panic surged as he couldn't find Hephaestus anymore, but then someone grabbed his legs.

After the initial panic, Andrew swam underwater until they reached a break over the other bank. Passing through it, they entered another reservoir, less deep but open to a bright blue sky above. He glimpsed an impressive dwelling a little further away through the boughs of tall oaks, chestnuts, and fruit trees—apples, plums, and cherries—with marble fountains and statues of Greek gods and goddesses.

Emerging from the water, Hephaestus pranced stealthily into a courtyard at the rear of the house. Andrew felt as if an apparition was beginning and tried to keep his eyes open, searching for the source of a beautiful, but unfamiliar fragrance. I must be in heaven, he thought, but I know I'm not dead, he murmured.

For a fleeting moment, Hephaestus considered whether it was worth it to replay a glimpse of divine life for a mortal and reasoned it had to be just a few chosen ones to get a peek of reality, and so be it. He took Andrew with him to a chamber deep inside the house, through some superbly decorated foyers, vestibules, and antechambers, whose walls were painted by Greek artists in various colors, depicting many moods of gods and nature. The floors were covered with silky smooth carpets, and the air carried a most respectful message—gods live here. The serenity raised veneration and spoke of the high moral values observed here.

After spotting the laced apparel neatly folded on one of the golden couches, Andrew hesitated when he perceived the nature of the inner chamber: a maiden's bedroom.

"Don't just stare, help me with the net," Hephaestus said, breaking the silence.

A fine bronze mesh covered the divine bed, which they raised nearly to the ceiling with the help of a ladder. Then, they used thin, wispy threads to hold the net to the ceiling, gently gluing it in place. The transparent net was anchored to the curved figures of angels on the vault, and the thin diaphanous yarn connecting the bed to the gossamer net was carefully hidden beneath the rug and along the walls. When finished, the canopy resembled a heavenly mosquito net, and Andrew stood there rather awed by its elegance.

"Wonderful!" Andrew exclaimed. "What a mosquito net!"

"Now, let's get out quickly. I'll see you out. Careful now."

Andrew stood near the back door as Hephaestus paused, then turned his head toward one of the inner chambers, as if he was addressing someone inside.

"Dear foam-born, do you hear me. I'm leaving for Lemnos."

To Andrew's surprise, a sweet voice responded:

"Oh, my master smith, I shall miss you terribly. I've so much to do with the children here. And make sure those volcanoes aren't erupting in Lemnos."

"I know, dear Aphros. Phobos and Deimos are with Hera tonight, while Eros and Anteros are staying with their aunt Athena. So, if you wish, you can go to Paphos." He hobbled out with a sly smile spread across his grotesque face.

Andrew felt a pang of disappointment.

"I never saw her. You call her 'foam-born'?" he asked.

Hephaestus answered nonchalantly,

"Better than, born of sliced manhood, of Uranus," he sneered.

They then walked toward the town center. People strode in and out of the surrounding buildings at various places. Some soldiers on horseback rode as if the street belonged to them, while hawkers lounged sideways with their belongings spread out to attract the gazing customers.

Andrew felt sultry; the pond water and sand felt gritty after swimming in and out of Aphrodite's palace. "I need a bath," he muttered.

Hephaestus, lost in thought, nodded. Some wealthy citizens were borne on wooden ornate dollies on the shoulders of their slaves, observing the hurly-burly with utter indifference. A palanquin passed, lifted by four hefty, enslaved servants; their perspiring trunks rose and fell in rhythm as their master peeked through a small glass window.

Countless shops, herbaria, and horse stables lined the circular square, offering a variety of goods, including cheese, fruits, and vegetables in the grocery stores, alongside clothing: togas, tunics, pellas, hats, long clothes, silk, cotton, and an array of perfumes.

The public baths bustled with people from various walks of life. Grand marble steps soared magnificently to several arched doorways, constantly spewing men and women clad in togas and tunics. The two men entered an alcove where others were stripping their raiment gleefully. Andrew noticed that Hephaestus wore long underwear.

The next hall was filled with people plunging into a cold pool and emerging when they were satisfied.

The chill stirred Andrew. Hephaestus dipped his head.

"Wow, big like our YMCA pool," Andrew whispered.

"What?"

"Young Men's Christian Association," Andrew spoke a bit louder to explain.

Hephaestus looked at him in horror. Suddenly, two men lunged, pulling Andrew from the pool in a scuffle. When Andrew resisted, a further scrimmage broke out. Other bathers watched in amazement as Andrew stood naked, restrained by two Greeks on the bank.

Hephaestus hobbled out and motioned for his release. The Greeks grudgingly loosened their grip, filled with hateful disgust.

They then moved into a warm-water chamber and sat on a marble bench. Andrew, still stunned, watched as Hephaestus dripped residual pool water from his shriveled, tiny genitals and smiled.

"Don't speak of the new religion here," Hephaestus muttered.

Andrew shook his head, utterly bewildered.

Later, Hephaestus bought some clothing for Andrew, who changed quickly. Some people played games with pebbles and marbles; others played a game called micatio.

Andrew paused near a group busy counting knucklebones.

"Does par impar interest you?" Hephaestus asked.

When Andrew nodded, Hephaestus threw a few gold coins at him, and together they joined a game much like heads or tails. A tall, hefty person with rustic features and burning eyes pushed inside in the middle of the game. He carried a bloodstained spear in one hand.

"Ares, please learn to keep the spear out," Hephaestus murmured in a low voice.

"Dear brother, don't be fainthearted. It punished one of the fierce knaves roaming free outside Father's temple."

They whispered so that others couldn't hear, but with an undertone of anger and disgust.

Then the game resumed.

Ares won, and Hephaestus threw more gold coins.

Ares won again, but Hephaestus soon ran out of coins.

"Brother, you must have something precious to me," Ares scoffed.

The crowd jeered.

"Indeed. But Ares, what Father Zeus has assigned each of us is final. What destiny shall unfold is uncertain, and my dear brother, provoking and winning a war without discretion, shall not turn the winds in your favor in the larger game of love and life."

The crowd grew impatient, and someone suggested,

"Play a maiden!"

"Play your golden girls!"

"Stake your island—Lemnos!"

Ares reviled. Hephaestus had had enough; his patience and reasoning gave way to an outburst of anger. Suddenly, he leaped at Ares, choking him with his working, solid hands, looking eye to eye. As Ares struggled to free himself, his spear slipped and fell off, leaving him helpless. His eyes bulged in horror, and his face turned pale.

People taunted and howled in unbridled passion for violence.

At this moment, a lovely woman appeared, raising her sweet yet imperious voice.

"Get away, get away, you unworthy sons of Zeus!" She moved closer as the crowd parted respectfully to let her approach. Looking at Hephaestus, she hissed,

"Oh, master craftsman, in the name of Erichthonios, release your unseemly grip from his neck that has meant no harm to you." She rested her javelin upon Hephaestus.

The master cautiously moved his gaze to her and muttered,

"Why should Pallas be so reckless in succoring this loutish warrior? Has she not suffered enough? Did he not…?"

Pallas Athena paused, her thoughts drifting back only to her past with Hephaestus. She kept her javelin steady on her target as her green eyes seemed to flit back in years, many years earlier, when Hephaestus had won her over and had gently led her to the bridal chamber. He was serene, and his eyes had shimmered in hope, illuminated by the godly passion of creation intertwined with the ungodly emotion of lust. When he finally approached her, she could not resist, for he seemed so strong, so worthy of creation. Yet, she soon pushed him away, realizing with her feminine intuition the shape of the fruit of their union would bear; she knew it wouldn't be as colossal or magnificent as divine creation demanded. And then, it spread all around her from his manhood, like a pure white rain, upon her and the earth, our mother Gaia, mother of all gods. Then, she fled swiftly, clutching her solemn virginity.

Mother Earth bore his son, later gifting Erichthonios back to her.

The crowd grew restless. Excitement was in the air for a brawl, an exchange of harsh words, blows for blows, primarily for blood. They jeered lustily.

She returned to the fierce present and pushed her weapon deep into his skin, as if for her past arrears, and hissed,

"No. Ares can only fight, but you inflict deeper wounds…" she trailed off, leaving her thought unfinished.

Ares drew a deep breath as his brother released his iron grip, then spat in disdain,

"It is but unworthy of me as the son of Zeus; otherwise, I would expose your lawful but abject marriage with…" he stopped short, unwilling to name the one he loved.

Hephaestus suddenly lost all his zest to hurl further insults. Pallas Athena composed herself and attempted to persuade her brothers to disperse. She noticed the arrogant Ares still simmering, eager to air dirty linen publicly, and warned Ares,

"Lord of wars, strength of muscle should neither diminish memory nor deceive one of the certain stark pasts before you belittle your own. Remember when Otos and Ephialtes bottled you in a jar for years; all your magic vanished, brother, and only your own family came to your rescue. Do you recall how Artemis helped?"

Presently, with more disgust than fear, Ares screamed so loud the crowd scattered. Andrew trembled.

The next day, Hephaestus was seen returning to his palace accompanied by Andrew, who was very puzzled by recent events but had become comfortable with him by now. He asked,

"Hephaestus, can anyone help me find Rhea?"

At first, Hephaestus ignored the question, but then he turned his head nonchalantly,

"Hmm, seems unwise, unattainable task for a mere mortal.

Nevertheless, pray to Hermes, the great messenger."

"Where can I find him?"

"Come with me."

The palace was eerily quiet. A maid bowed and retreated,

"Eurycleia! Has your mistress yet enjoyed the golden daylight?"

"The night was long, my lord, and my lady had much to attend to."

"Be truthful, Eurycleia, you remain under my service," Hephaestus warned her.

"What my eyes behold, my heart fails to discern. Eurycleia shall never be unfaithful to this all-merciful family," she hedged.

"Hun, come with me. We shall escort the goddess of the morning, Eos, to the sacred bedroom I share only with my beloved wife," Hephaestus said.

"Master of my destiny, shall I show your guest to his quarters?" Euricleia asked Andrew.

Hephaestus strode purposefully inside, and she followed him hesitantly. Andrew, burning with curiosity, stepped into a dark hallway devoid of morning glow.

They entered a semicircular chamber where the soft scent of jasmine lingered, and a golden glow filled the space. Gentle, whispered breaths echoed within a restless shaft of sunlight — the breathing of two beautiful, divine figures intertwined like clouds in a rainy sky, oblivious to the unloving world.

The intruders looked away from such a huge revelation, feeling their presence was a blasphemy.

However, Eurycleia, feeling uneasy about her impiety, whispered,

"Master, they are caught in your chain."

Hephaestus trembled, rage surging through him, spite streaming from his heart, and he tried to speak in a shaky voice, raising his hands toward the supreme,

"Oh, Father Zeus! O Olympians, witness my misfortune!" With these words, he alerted the couple and all the residents.

Eurycleia fled hastily, while the couple shrieked in shock. They found themselves bound by the heavy chain of the master craftsman, with no clothing to conceal their personages.

Soon, the gods gathered, men with lustful eyes and women in evident shame.

"Look! Behold what your daughter has done to my sacred bed, where I alone am ordained to be with her in our holy union, defiled by this boorish son of yours, Father. Does she not feel any shame? Should he not be punished harshly for ruining my marriage? If none of you gods act against this immoral couple, it wouldn't be imprudent for me to decide their fate, since all of this happened because I am incomplete. But then, who inflicted the injury to my body but my own, and why should she choose another for only bodily imperfections?"

Apollo and Hermes pushed through the crowd for a closer look. Golden Aphrodite tried to cover her face, but the shackles dug into her petite wrists, and a cloud of remorse flushed her cheeks. This vision of ultimate beauty enthralled Andrew; he stood frozen.

He met her eyes, like two serene lakes where most men would drown willingly; her quivering eyelids resembled a gentle breeze caressing water; her defiant breasts and the silky-smooth stomach leading down to a soft patch of delicate hair nestled between her voluptuous thighs stirred passion in him, Apollo, and Hermes alike.

"They need to be held accountable for this. Hephaestus should insist on repentance," someone declared.

"Move, move, the father of heaven and fate arrives…" an announcer called. A tall, older man, bearing a long beard and a flowing robe embroidered with several precious stones, strode forward, anger evident in his gait.

"Father of all, witness what Aphrodite has done to me; look at these well-formed figures in love, and then look at me. Do not turn away — the time has come for truth. Are you repentant for what you and Hera did in my childhood, tossing an infant down from Olympus?"

No one seemed ready for this serious accusation, which came so suddenly, and most remained utterly stunned. Any mention of indiscretion or digression by a god in public was strictly forbidden, and any analysis of the god of gods and his actions, if done indiscreetly, could lead to incalculable and unimaginable retribution that struck terror into even the bravest gods.

The rainmaker spoke as if on a dark, stormy night; dark clouds clashed overhead, thunder booming deep in the sky.

"Hephaestus, you awaken no more pity in me than I suffer endlessly for you. No self-respecting husband would expose his dear wife, again and again, as my old eyes have seen," the deep voice of the supreme paused.

"Father, will I be compensated for the lavish gifts I bestowed upon her?"

Apollo and Hermes teetered, while Poseidon kept scratching his chin.

The father of all sighed in disgust and turned away.

"I have no part in this foolish hypocrisy," he declared, then he strode away.

Poseidon betrayed no emotion, despite his heart swelling with intense desire for Aphrodite. He uttered very seriously,

"Ares should return all the gifts to secure his release because he is the cause of this harm."

Apollo nudged Hermes playfully. "Hermes, wouldn't you like to be with her?"

Unabashed, Hermes glanced around before lowering his voice:

I will do anything for her, even endure heavier chains, even beneath these lustful mortal and immortal eyes.

They burst into hearty laughter.

Hephaestus, earlier so strident, now looked uneasy and asked,

"What if Ares defaults?"

Poseidon, still admiring Aphrodite's beauty, responded,

"In that case, I shall take responsibility and have no choice but to marry dear Aphrodite. As I said before, when you exposed them many years ago."

Hephaestus stepped forward with fury and stood beside his wife, whose eyes silently pleaded. He then grabbed a robe and tossed it at her after releasing both, his face showing apparent disgust. Ares stood tall, with arms at his sides, chest proud, face unrepentant, thighs tense, and eyes filled with contempt.

Hermes moved closer to Aphrodite, while Poseidon shifted uneasily.

The lady who commands love lifted her eyes gently as she passed, lowering them to each ally in turn, stirring in them wanton dreams deemed unattainable.

The gods left one by one, and the maids moved around again as if to cleanse the palace of its air of transgression. Minds wandered, seeking a reason for another peccadillo, yet silence fastened their lips. Andrew felt numb from what he had seen—initially overjoyed with the pleasure of observing what seemed like the most beautiful creation on earth he had ever laid eyes upon: the perfect feminine silhouette with outstanding curves, the most glamorous face, and lustrous, sparkling-gold skin. When he tried to meet those exquisite eyes, he almost ceased to live or breathe as her restless gaze, aware of all around, locked onto his own as if it knew everything he had been, everything he was, and everything he wanted—and that was enough for him. He lowered his eyes ambiguously, with a mix of reverence, love, and fear.

But the goddess of love, amid all the chaos, humiliation, and hostility, did not pass this mortal carelessly; her all-seeing eyes scrutinized the very unfamiliar barbarian who reveled in her disgrace and shame. Did she not consider teaching him a lesson on modesty, both for the fair sex in general and divinity in particular? Time would reveal Andrew's price for witnessing such divine transgression.

When he was alone with Hephaestus again, he asked softly, "Why don't you just divorce her? There is plenty of evidence and witnesses for her adultery."

Hephaestus looked at him like a child hesitant to talk about his mistakes.

"You bloody hell love her so much, don't you?" Andrew said again.

But Hephaestus stood still. Aphrodite strutted past toward Paphos.

People say she later bore Hermaphroditus with Hermes and had two children for Poseidon.

Cyprus is an island in the Mediterranean Sea, located south of Turkey. It is divided between northern Turkish control and southwestern Greek control, with a United Nations buffer zone in the middle. The island features rich copper mines, and this metal—

known in Greek as "Cyprium"—is said to have been named after Cyprus itself. Historians believe the Greeks arrived on the island as invaders shortly after the Trojan War, around the 11th century BC. Notably, the brother of the famous warrior Ajax is credited with having colonized Salamis. The town of Pafos, as the Greeks call it, was taken over by Agapenor after defeating Kinyras. Paphos is located in southwest Cyprus, near where our goddess arrived after her birth at Petra tou Romiou, or Rock of the Greeks, about ten miles from Paphos, which remains an exquisitely beautiful place today. Aphrodite's sanctuaries still exist at Kouklia, and she visits there with a heavy heart, leaving after moments of reflection. At Lempa village, about a couple of miles from Paphos, locals have built houses that resemble the living quarters of her followers from the Bronze Age. Our goddess of Love bears no ill will toward what Saint Paul did—converting the first ruler of Paphos during Roman times—but she keeps a safe distance from the churches and the Tombs of the Kings, built in the fourth century BC for underground burials of officers.

In Paphos, our goddess of love found the solace she desperately needed amid shame. First, she blamed herself for this impulsive, carnal act, thinking, "I should follow the rules of marriage. I should stay away from Ares. He is such a pest." But why is it so difficult for me? Why can't I be happy with what was assigned to me, even though he is so miserable? Hephaestus doesn't stir even a speck of passion in me. And I do try. Oh, what a face—and then his long, uncared-for beard. His chest, oh, that ugly, dust-laden chest.

Our goddess of love tried to understand her feelings for her husband. It couldn't be just about looks, she thought again. Love, she knows love, she preaches love, and love is what she breathes, filling both mortals and immortals. But then, why couldn't she live her family life with her remedy? Suddenly, she felt a bit guilty for ignoring the real issue buried deep in her heart. Had she been so selfish and busy, failing to recognize her feelings and confusing her attraction with love? Love needs no return; love is meant to be transcendental, and love should lead one to sacrifice one's happiness for the person one loves.

She suspected it was more than looks. He is so different. While she strives to stay at the center of everything, living each moment fully, he prefers to remain on the fringes, unseen, not drawn into company, or left alone. His face flushes, and he stammers when she occasionally glances at him in front of other gods, as if hiding some deep-seated desire for self-denial, almost saying, "Do not come near me; I am not worth your time," while she relishes fleeting glory—some exaggerated story of her past victories, some euphemistic twist on unpleasant experiences. She would have been happier if he had shared her zest for life and made an effort to keep going.

Why does he feel so amorphous? He is not lazy but mentally indolent. While people think Aphrodite is all heart and no reason, I believe I am always thinking. My mind never stops—it looks to the future, the next moment, the next place, the next event that will surpass all before. So, I see utopia clearly, and only I can imagine it in our family. I can hope, instill hope, and bless mortals so they may feel the beauty of living, smell the fragrance of intimacy, and hear the beating hearts of each other. But it is not true that I am all love. I am all joy.

She sat on a long couch and dropped her palla to the ground. The maid entered the room and removed it. She looked at her bosom and smiled with delight at its smooth, golden appearance of pleasure, as mortals and immortals of the other sex would pretend. Yet for her, it was a source of the innermost soul, the character, and spirit—the essence of being a lady, the ultimate nurturing source for the early human soul when it is unsoiled, the frontispiece of gentility and the proscenium of tenderness. Then she removed her long tunic and lay down with her head on a pillow, face down. The maid entered again and carefully removed the rest of her soft underclothes. Then the maid applied immortal oil slowly and steadily over the smooth skin of her mistress as the goddess of love spent a few moments lost in deep, pensive thought.

She felt no more remorse. As she straightened her legs, the maid's gentle hands rubbed them softly. She would not live under any shadow of sadness or penitence.

She would continue to bring the same happiness she reserved for mortals into her own life as well. The room was warm and filled with the scent of bright sunshine, and the maid smiled with an unfamiliar joy.

Our fertility goddess closed her eyes and reflected peacefully on her ageless life and past lovers. Is it possible for one person to love many at the same time, amorously?

Here in Cyprus, no mortal can reach her palace. Hephaestus built it with gold and passion when desperate to please his bride. The steep road to the palace is challenging to climb, and the fence makes it nearly impossible. Inside, he decorated it with marble from distant lands and walls adorned with precious stones.

She felt sleepy and thought of her lovers again—this time, a Cypriot named Adonis.

Pygmalion—yes, the foolish Pygmalion who wouldn't cease loving his own crafted statue of the goddess of love. He even took her to bed and wished she would come alive. When his wish was fulfilled, he had a daughter, Paphos, who became the mother of Kinyras. He was the same man who later founded the city of Paphos and built the temple dedicated to the goddess of beauty.

But his daughter, Smyrna, was arrogant and proud of her beauty. She dared to speak loudly, claiming her hair was more beautiful than the goddess's, and her father supported her. It had ceased to be a mere comparison of their pulchritude; it was the tone and disrespect that had spread among the poor mortals that enraged the goddess. Therefore, Smyrna needed to be reminded that the gods bestow beauty—and can just as easily take it away. Poor Smyrna was consumed by desire, like any mortal woman, but her passion was for her own father. She conspired with her maid to make Kinyras drunk, and, for twelve nights, she indulged in her sin.

One night, the king awoke and looked around. This time, he was sober enough to notice the beautiful face lying beside him in the dim lamp light. When the maid revealed the truth, he sprang to his feet in remorse and fury. The father howled like a wounded animal, and she fled helplessly, running away and praying— but who could save a poor maiden from the wrath of a betrayed king? Our Lady of Love could not bear such cruelty and appeared to the daughter. Exhausted, Smyrna looked up to the dazzling beauty, realized where things had gone wrong, and asked,

"Let my life not be wasted, O goddess I once belittled. If I erred by loving myself excessively, and if you had any hand in it, take me away to a land where neither gods nor mortals will shame me. And let the small life beginning in my womb be born unblemished."

People say she was shown a hollow tree trunk, into which she collapsed; the trunk transformed, exuding a fragrant, spicy sap— myrrh. The goddess was seen carrying away the tiny life in her beautiful hands—the child who would later be known as Adonis.

Aphrodite carried Adonis far away, away from the gods on Olympus and mortals on Earth, to the underground realm of Persephone.

"Will you please help me?" she asked Hades's wife. "Will you feed him, care of him, and raise him for me, please?"

Persephone did what was expected of her. Adonis had grown up with her affection, and she felt her strength fade as he changed into a handsome and powerful young man. And she wouldn't give him up when our goddess of desire demanded him.

Adonis was handsome and gentle. He wouldn't upset either of his lovers. So they went to Father Zeus, but he asked the muse Calliope instead to decide who should keep him. Calliope divided the year into three equal parts—one for each lover and one for himself.

But Adonis gave his share to sweet Aphrodite. Together, they would dress as hunters and roam the deep forests in search of prey. Hunting was his passion.

Yet Ares could not bear their happiness.

"Brute!" Aphrodite suddenly interrupted her reminiscence. "Brute! An animal." She almost wiped away the scent of him from her skin, the smell she had acquired just the night before so passionately. "Oh, what a cruel end to my love." Poor Adonis was mauled to death. "Ares, I know it was you," she whispered. Some claimed to have seen him in disguise.

But when Aphrodite found him bleeding in the woods, she wept bitterly, lamenting to the trees and animals. She begged everyone to revive her lover as he lay there with fresh red blood seeping into the earth. She was aggrieved beyond divine control. Our Lady of Desire sat beside him, cradling his mortal body on her thighs. She tried to comfort him with her soft lips pressed to his lifeless mouth, as if she wanted to nourish herself with all he was before the end came.

The temple in Cyprus still honors their unfulfilled love. Women continue to offer their 'gardens' to Adonis, and the priestesses assist men with whatever offerings they can provide.

Ares claimed it was the wrath of angry Apollo, for Aphrodite had cursed his son Erymanthios, who had seen her naked while she was bathing.

She despised those who compared her and Adonis to Ishtar and Tammuz of Asia. Had she roamed the earth before the twelfth century B.C. as Astarte or Ishtar? The Greeks began calling our Lady of Love "Aphrodite" much later. Hesiod and Homer tried to unravel the mystery of her birth, just as Hephaestus called her:

"Dear foam-born of Hesiod and Botticelli, Aphrodite Urania…"

"Stop it, Hephaestus," she would protest.

"Well then, daughter of Dione, Aphrodite Pandemos, I need to know for sure…"

"Never, never will I reveal myself entirely to such a…"

"Unworthy…?"

"You are my husband…" she would utter softly.

She often wondered why he could never fully grasp the meaning behind his words or the names he used to call her, such as when he referred to her as Urania. She longed to be his heavenly love, even though she was still his wife, not because others told her to be, but for his own happiness. She wouldn't test him or set him on a scale where he'd have to struggle and prove himself, trying to show strength or clear up doubts spread by gods or mortals alike.

But then our god of crafts, Hephaestus, felt extreme loneliness after Aphrodite was ridiculed. Guilt drove him mad, and he could no longer stay away from his wife. So, he left Andrew behind and returned to her golden palace. He did not speak for days after the last incident, which caused such chaos and unbearable pain in their relationship—Hephaestus stayed silent. He confined himself to his workshop, working on another beautiful piece of jewelry he could use if a moment of friendly reconciliation arrived. Aphrodite, unusually cautious, mostly stayed inside her palace.

Presently, Hephaestus entered the chamber, interrupting her thoughts. He moved toward the window as if searching for something. Our *Lady of Desire* glanced at him as he tried to reach one of her golden chests near the window, standing on an unsteady leg. He carefully drew the drawer to prevent its contents from spilling and searched for a hammer.

"You made that for me," she reminded him.

He nodded. The small room in the corner of the house brought them closer together. The drapes over the window, red velvet cushions, and soft rugs on the marble floor colored the twilight inside. She sat still as a strange longing grew inside her, rising from nowhere. She wished he would at least look at her. *I am your wife,* she wanted to whisper. *Let others say whatever they want, but we should—why not?* If you can create the most marvelous things from the inanimate, if what you have done defines beauty in all our possessions—for which mortals and kings alike boast, and if I imbue them with the desire that makes delight possible, why can't you admit your weakness to me, especially when I am ready to listen?

Feeling this surge of intense longing, she approached him and grasped his right hand. He held the chest on his left arm and turned toward her, his wife. She smiled softly—the kind of smile that inspires love among gods and humans alike. He reached out with his right hand to draw her close. She responded in kind, and they clasped hands for a moment. Suddenly, the chest tilted and toppled onto her. She cried out in pain; her tender foot was injured. Hephaestus hurried to remove the chest and saw abrasions on her skin, with ichor seeping from the wound. Searching for something to dress it, he tore a corner from his tunic and gently pressed it against her foot.

After a while, when he took off the cloth, the foot looked better. Our lady opened her arms to him again in a rare gesture of tender affection.

"It hurts…" he asked softly.

She turned her face away. Her anger, pain, and shame all surged back with vengeance. What do you know? What hurts and what does not? It is not what happened in our bedchamber with Ares; it is what does not happen between us. What keeps us apart? Why have I carried this pain all my life, since I was born? It is not you, Hephaestus…

"I don't know…" she mumbled.

It is not you, master-smith. I have endured all my girlhood and adolescence. They loved me for my appearance, not for how I felt or what I carried inside, and I've learned to give you only that sunny side: my pretty face, my eternal youth. You asked Zeus for none of my darker parts; you have never seen my actual face. You only wanted my flowing hair and warm breasts.

"Why?"

"I wish I knew why. Whenever you ask me why, I still await an answer.

I don't even try anymore to understand why. It's not easy, Hephaestus; it's so hard... so tough to dig deep and confront the abyss that haunts me.

"Is it different?"

"Stop!" she screamed and continued,

"No more! No more, Hephaestus. Please, have mercy on me." Then her tears began to flow over her golden cheeks, and she gazed at him with pleading eyes. "I am helpless, and you know why. So why do we keep discussing this over and over? It doesn't bring me any closer to you or myself. In fact, where am I? Where do I belong? How do I find my true self? You cannot even imagine."

"And why not the god of fire? Why not?"

Have you ever made me feel that you loved me? Just me—all that I am, not the polished me? Aphrodite, when she wakes early before the dawn's glow brightens her, as she's shaken on the battlefields of the Trojan War, fleeing after a mortal's attack, when she's reproached at the gods' assembly by Zeus, humiliated by everyone else for just being a lovely goddess, nothing more. And when I decide to make others fall in love, where are you? Why can't you be there for me and say, I need not indulge in others' lives anymore; I first must take care of my life, which seems to fall apart daily. I, of course, cannot blame you for my estrangement, but isn't it the duty of a good lord to at least explain why, for ages, I shall run away from my soul?

"Because..." he began, but hesitated. Then she moved closer, held him without hesitation, and gazed into his eyes so sincerely, so lovingly, that he continued, "Because it may be that I, after all, love you."

And our goddess of love could hardly believe her ears, and she averted her gaze from those burning eyes she never suspected held such feelings. She grew intensely panicked, yet she held onto him, unwilling to let go of the moment—the rare moment of bliss between them. She looked at him now with such deep affection that the iron heart of the fire god started to somersault with unknown happiness, and he whispered repeatedly in her ear, "Be it known that your husband loves you."

Gradually, she loosened her grip on him and let him hold her. His strong arms nearly crushed her delicate ones, turning them pale from his pressure, but she allowed him to come so close that she had to close her eyes when he kissed her eyelids. "My sweet butterfly," he murmured, playing gently with words. She let him be the master he had long been denied, the source of life, alive again and again. During this divine lovemaking, Aphrodite felt—for once—that she was drawing closer to her childhood: her mother, Dione, loving her not for her beauty but because she was her baby. Dione would hobble here and there, picking up her daughter as the girl, not yet Aphrodite, giggled and fumbled away, trying the world on her own. The world did not ask for anything in return; it actively helped the child know, grow, touch, feel, and just before she fell, held her up.

"Hephaestus, stop. Stop being my mother." The goddess could endure no more—the pain of understanding herself, the pain of distancing herself from herself—and she gently pushed him away.

Hephaestus looked at her in disbelief. "Why is she doing this to me, when I am so good to her?" He did not realize that even though he was there for her, she sensed he was not there for himself. Our self-forgetting god had underestimated the goddess, as all gods and men do. She is not all love, and he is not just a peacemaker. They were both more than they seemed—more than they knew, more than they had to understand—to uncover and live into, before their divine powers.

Why did the Fates create such a strange pairing among gods: one of unparalleled beauty, the other the ugliest among Olympians? She possessed desire; he lacked it. She was jubilant, vibrant, and full of energy and vision; he was dull, lazy, and soothing. She engaged in every part of life; he withdrew from it.

As they lingered a little longer in the goddess's chamber, reaffirming their supposedly failed marriage, doves busied themselves in the garden's corner, snuggling neck to neck and nudging each other. Narcissus and hyacinths swayed gently in fragrance—a modest celebration.

But in the end, when Hephaestus turned his curious eye to her for an answer to his eternal query, she silenced him with a gentle kiss.

He would probably never cease asking the same question over and over. He would never know the whole truth about her engendering, the offspring, and posterity in her lineage. Did she have Harmonia, Deimos, and Phobos with Ares, Aeneas, and Lyrus with Anchises, or Hermaphroditus with Hermes, and Priapus by Dionysus? She felt he knew it all—that he had sensed all along how his unfaithful wife had created her world without him, save for the origin of Eros and Anteros, and she preferred to keep the mystery. That was what she liked—a sweet, loving sentiment surrounding her, prevailing over this otherwise barren earth and dry heaven.

When she arrived at Cyprus's shore, people were not amazed but pleasantly overwhelmed as she stood on the giant shell, floating, gently nudged by the south wind toward the shore. The Graces had dressed her slender legs and soft belly in soft silk. She was not upright and proud but softly bent, as if she were a precious gift to the island to be handled with care. She took a step on the ground. The earth greeted her with sprouting green grass; rose bushes bristled, filling the air with scent; doves nearby raised their beaks to the sky; and mortals saw each other differently—sometimes with affection, sometimes with love, sometimes with desire. The goddess smiled gently, knowing well what desire could accomplish.

Then she was brought to Olympus. But her meeting with Anchises was entirely beyond her control. She was far away, near Troy, when her eyes met this mortal herdsman. He was tending his livestock in the valley, and she cast a glance full of awe at him. Struck—the goddess who stirred desire in gods to seek mortals—she unwittingly fell for another mortal, as Father Zeus had cleverly planned. Anchises remained oblivious to the handsome maiden and walked toward his tents.

Fire engulfed her—the fire inside her to behold him —she'd returned to Cyprus. She couldn't rest in peace till she was quenched. Her bosom burned, and her heart was restless, eager to acquire, to feel, to test her womanhood against a mortal.

She entered her temple in Paphos. The Graces knew her thoughts and surrounded her, removing her robe and gently guiding her to the bath. There she lay still as they rubbed her with divine oil, poured water on her, exchanged glances, sensing unusual resistance in her supple body, and added more fragrance that heightened her erotic craving. Then they clothed her in the most beautiful chiton, woven with golden threads on sheer silk.

She hurried, and some say she hummed, as she reached Troy's countryside. The animals sensed her urgency as she strode through the thicket, following her gently. None of them—the lion, the tiger, or the deer- made a sound as she searched for her desired man. She found him sitting in a corner of a hut, playing the lyre. Anchises could scarcely believe his eyes: a woman of unsurpassed beauty had come uninvited—surely a goddess. He bowed in obeisance and uttered,

Indeed, I am speechless regarding your purpose or my fate— whatever brings such a visit—but I will sacrifice my cattle and build a fitting altar for you.

She did not move. Her palla slipped away, revealing the tender, gleaming arms, the fearless breasts, and the gentle curve of her lower abdomen—the woman within her.

"I am a Phrygian princess, and I speak your language," she said. "Hermes brought me to Mount Ida."

The awestruck Anchises believed her, and she continued,

"You may wonder why you? I am destined to be the bride of the son of Capys, the prince known for breeding strong stallions with great strength."

"I certainly did..."

"And now you will stop looking at me—why couldn't you take the maiden so pure and unspoiled that fate has passed to you...?"

Anchises hesitated, but his heart longed for her. She waited patiently until he opened his strong arms to embrace her.

When he woke, the darkness of night wrapped around his tent like a ghost. The sounds of insects, the cold, crisp wind at dawn, and the tempting scent of a woman nearby filled him with an unfamiliar fear.

She stood near the door, tall and defiant. Her breasts now covered; her face radiant—he shuddered.

"I am sorry for what I did..."

The goddess nodded softly. Her tall figure cast a shadow as twilight faded behind her. He looked at her sides beneath stretched arms; outside, his cattle grazed in the early morning calm. Then she spoke,

"Me, too."

"I knew... You were no mere mortal, but why? Why did I love you?"

She heard his helpless cry, came closer, bent over, and whispered,

"I wish you would stay my husband forever. But soon, time will creep up on you, and you'll be carried away—unlike me. But our

son shall be loyal to you, and you will have no wrath of any god, if you reveal no secrets."

But he did not keep his word given to her. Many years passed before he lost all strength in his legs and could barely see light. However, his son Aeneas never left him alone.

But for now, let us see how Hephaestus and Aphrodite continue with their divine lives. She, of course, dealt him such reverse guilt that he spent days and nights cooped up in his palace, mostly busying himself with work. He designed many weapons that had long been requested and remained unfinished. No one could ask him to deliver a product—he would see it as coercion and intentionally delay or procrastinate until the other forgot or he changed his mind.

He was often seen with a gold brooch that he had been polishing, cutting, and melting for years. Once, Aphrodite casually asked for a brooch as she left his house, indifferent, as if it were for occasional wear, not out of urgent desire. He took her request not as a sweet demand from his dear wife but as an order from a proud goddess. So, he began this unusual work as a jeweler but lacked the heart to finish it. He kept adding diamonds, rubies, and other precious stones, then scooped them out to replace them with new, glittering gems. When Aphrodite asked if it was finished, he neither responded nor pointed to the incomplete piece of love, covered with layers of dust. Her gaze would turn cold, as if the pain of rejection might burst into tears at any moment. Still, she smiled and encouraged him to continue his impressive work.

But today, as Hephaestus searched his den, he noticed the diamonds in the brooch shining unusually bright through the dust. He knew what he needed to accomplish soon, before she left again, with lips curved in a despairing smile.

He began polishing it.

She was in the gardens, savoring the gentle glow of the sunset and the scent of soft earth, hyacinths, and wild roses. She moved slowly, as if lost in thought, perhaps influenced by her swirling feelings of anger and embarrassment. Her mind was primarily focused on his indifferent attitude toward her loved one.

She couldn't dig deep enough to find out why all these incidents kept happening in her life, other than her painful conclusion that she was unlovable, even though many admired her. When others approached, they saw what she could offer and what she couldn't, leaving her feeling unworthy despite her fame as the goddess of love. So, she couldn't blame poor Hephaestus for keeping his distance, since she pushed him away whenever he got close—and it almost scared her that he dared.

This sense of emptiness—a void she disliked acknowledging but that nagged relentlessly—led her to seek fleeting joy: new islands, exotic demigods, and powerful mortals. She couldn't pause even for a moment to experience the wholesome delight that might reveal a kernel of truth, for fear of facing the abyss too hard to navigate. She couldn't care less about who she was, where she should be, or where her heart truly resided. Though mortals believed her heart's promises drove her, it was the restless monkey mind inside that had dictated her life's course for ages.

But Hephaestus, on the other hand, was less concerned with himself and more focused on what Aphrodite thought—not for her approval or rejection, but for the messages she was trying to convey. He harbored a profound ambivalence toward everything his wife said, did, or asked. He would resist whenever she reproached him, and if she tried to draw him close to her chest, he would respond with cynicism toward her love. He lived in a conundrum—unable to truly love, yet unable to hate such a wonderful wife, one the worlds of heaven and earth would die for.

"Why don't you think it over?" he urged her.

But how could she think it over? Her thoughts were so tangled—a sharp black-and-white split—that her conclusions seemed more like whims of liking and disliking than reason or rationality. All she could focus on now was his cruel joke, his childish prank of arresting her with Ares. She glared at him with boiling rage, feeling as if she could tear him apart. Instead, she asked,

"And you? Will you ever believe anything I say? Will you ever?"

He paused to listen, appearing so sincere that any other god might have believed he was genuinely paying attention, conceding. He almost nodded twice, causing a speck of dust to flutter from his beard. But Aphrodite recognized it as a practiced gesture—one he would never give up beyond this moment of peace.

While she had no time to explore her inner world, he struggled to navigate his soul. Like an elephant, he moved slowly and cautiously around its edges but never ventured into the center.

"I want you to know... You will not be abandoned."

Hephaestus understood what she needed, but he couldn't fully commit to everything required to satisfy the goddess—his soul pulled away at the very thought. He could never stand being forced into things.

She understood how he could be reversed like a baby needing to know that his mother loved him, but she could not take on the role of the mother.

They were both lost—one longing for invisibility and the other craving all the attention.

Yet, for now, Aphrodite felt the pain again. Why should a goddess feel so lonely? Why should her love for a mortal trouble her so deeply? She told Anchises never to reveal her love, but he disobeyed and was crippled and blinded by Zeus's thunderbolt. Her son carried him but did not reach Italy and died in Sicily.

Why wouldn't she do anything for Anchises, and why did he age? Why did he have to endure such a humiliating defeat and retreat so cowardly on Aeneas's strong shoulders? Was she meant to ignite passion in others, guiding them to love, but not to enjoy herself and see the fruits of her creation?

Aphrodite tucked these memories deep into the crevices of her mind, where they nibbled at her in solitude. But she knew this was no time for daydreaming—her focus had to shift toward the mortal threat looming ahead. Andrew's struggle for Rhea could not be ignored, yet she was uncertain whether to intervene. After all, she had aided Paris against all odds—and still could not save him or the city of Troy. This time, she resolved to be cautious, not to side mindlessly with a likely loser. What if Andrew was mistaken? What if he was hurt? She sat quietly, pondering her course of action.

Let me observe this man a bit longer before deciding. Wasn't he supposed to tie up his donkey instead of searching for it now? It's like looking for fleas in a haystack. What if all the other gods oppose him, and she alone stands by his side? That would be pretty embarrassing—especially since Father Zeus recently warned her about getting involved in war, telling her to focus only on love and marriage. The insolent fool Diomedes wounded her on Troy's battlefield, and Zeus wouldn't even listen. He scoffed at her meddling in the domains of Athena and Hera.

"I will see," she thought. "I will see how deeply this couple loves each other." For that was the crucial factor: whether genuine love existed. If she wished it so, she could alter everything, but she did not want to toy with mortals' lives frivolously. If Andrew loved Rhea and she returned that love equally, Aphrodite made a promise to herself that she would help. But if Rhea did not... then she would have to reconsider this unusual couple. They were both free mortals with their own happiness—it had to be a matter of mutual giving and receiving, a delicate affair requiring sacrifice for each other's joy and a willingness to protect the other's best interests; moreover, it must be the tenderest feeling—one that endures, lingers even as they grow, age and change, when wrinkles deepen, hearts grow weary, minds become addled and at sea, and speech falters and becomes less endearing.

But she couldn't forgive Andrew for witnessing her utter humiliation at the hands of her own—and she could sense who might have granted him that opportunity, who else could have orchestrated such a brazen display of her naked self—something gods yearn for through the ages just for a glimpse. She smiled; now that this mortal had seen it all... wait. She smiled again—but this time, not with mockery. It was a smile of retribution. For retribution, is there much variation other than whether the mortal shall prevail or perish? She did not know for now.

"Where is Rhea, anyway?"

Chapter Four – Apollo and Artemis.

Despair is complete hopelessness. For Andrew, it seemed impossible to fight alone on this remote, alien island, so far from home. Soon, he sank into a cycle of despair after Hephaestus abandoned him; his entire body rebelled, and his wounds now screamed for help. The plane crash had left him with numerous cuts and bruises, which he had ignored until now. But the wound on his right knee looked ominous, with yellow discharge occurring intermittently, clearly needing urgent care.

He stepped outside, thinking of Hephaestus. Why had he hurried to Aphrodite with such urgency after what he had done to her? How would he face her, and how might she retaliate after everything? Andrew couldn't go that far in his thoughts; moreover, a fleeting image of Rhea in a similar situation, or even with minor faults, made him feel extremely uneasy and restless.

Except in the hearts of Andrew and Hephaestus, sunlight poured brightly over the island, illuminating shimmering peaks and gentle slopes among tall, defiant oaks mingling with silver birches and winding streams. He wandered in a damp morning breeze, carrying the emptiness that comes with homelessness, deprived of life's usual comforts. Not even a toothbrush. He scratched his stubble.

Nothing cheered him, not even a bunch of monk seals nesting with their little ones. Even Homer, in the *Odyssey*, had noted these endangered species—their grey-black backs sprawled by the hundreds—as Menelaus had recounted a story to Telemachus about how he had overpowered the old Man of the Sea, sleeping among his seals, to learn how to cross the ocean and find Odysseus and the murderer of Agamemnon. Andrew barely paid any attention to the giant loggerhead turtles with their red-brown shells. The thick forest with junipers, black pines, and brutia pine at the bottom seemed to block the last rays of sunshine from his heart. The imperial eagle and Eleonora's falcon would have sparked tremendous excitement in him at any other time, but not now. As he reached the outskirts of the village, with its olive orchards, sheep, and goats, neither the chirping of the birds nor the greeting of an occasional smiling Greek stranger did anything to ease his pain.

Rhea is not alive, he surmised.

Then he changed his mind again: She is lost here, just like me.

After trudging an unknown distance, lost in deep thought, he paused when he heard someone singing. The gentle, melancholic, yet dulcet notes of an ancient Greek lyre wafted from a distance not readily estimable. He wandered a bit further, looking for a dwelling, then strode briskly, as if inspired all over again.

He followed the note, and when it seemed distinct, he saw a cluster of tall trees concealing a shallow brook with clear water. The music still pulsed in his veins; it wasn't just the tinkling sound of the flowing stream. He hesitated before stepping into the creek, searching for the intriguing source of the melody. Eventually, he waded halfway through the shallow water, then began to swim as it deepened, reaching the other end effortlessly, as if drawn in a trance. Hephaestus had revealed the secrets of such places the last time they were together and shown him the way around. All these locations had multiple entrances, either through deeply wooded caves or under flowing brooks.

Andrew emerged on the other side, where the water was shallow again, amidst thick undergrowth, thorny bushes, and wetlands. He entered a gate with some trepidation and paused near a fountain, noticing a gentleman perched on a marble slab, strumming a lyre, utterly oblivious to the world around.

A towering figure, bent over his lyre, with golden curls strewn over his nape and broad shoulders. His eyes were draped somewhat by indolent lids, as if daydreaming. His partly visible face bore a resemblance to one of Michelangelo's statues, exuding an air of divine masculine purity. A sonorous voice complemented his striking looks.

The lilting, sweet sound of the Greek song filled the air, and for a moment, Andrew felt happy, peaceful, and bereft of his misery. When the leaves ceased to rustle, birds froze with tiny grains in their beaks, and Andrew glimpsed the light. His heart leaped out of a deep despair, and he leaned against a cypress to savor the melody. Time passed uneventfully as the handsome man continued to caress his instrument and sang in a profoundly clear yet deep voice, all about the gods, their golden days and nights of Olympus, and the rich, fertile land and its streams. Then he sang words that usurped from his lips as harmoniously as a rainbow of soap bubbles:

'I, son of Zeus and Leto, sing for all the gods. I see men from a distance and make them work for my temple, and shower them with pleasure, rich fertile land, and endless herds of sheep—but only when they are just. I sing only for the Olympians, and men sing for me-Io Paean, hail the healer.'

It was as if the god of music, medicine, prophecy, and truth sang in the sweetest divine voice, one that resonated throughout this magnificent palace and reached the farthest corners of Earth, including Delos, with the thrumming of his lyre. The lyre's seven strings moved under his delicate fingers like seven seas dancing with gales in a pure melody of waves. He seemed so powerful, as if he could have flayed the skin of Marsyas when challenged to a musical contest or been the one to turn King Midas's ears into donkey ears after the king declared Pan the better musician. The trilling and trolling of this man seemed to echo the famous incantation of the past, when Poseidon built a wall around Troy, but Apollo made the wall grow faster by playing his lyre.

Suddenly, Andrew's back slipped off the wet tree trunk. He tried to regain his posture, but as he struggled awkwardly, his feet began to slide, and in the next moment, he was on the ground, face down, groaning in pain.

The musician was quite startled to hear such a commotion and ceased singing. Then, without showing any panic, he walked closer to Andrew.

"Kalimera!" he greeted Andrew.

"I am sorry," Andrew apologized.

"You seem to be in great pain. Very strange, I don't recall seeing you here before."

Andrew hesitated, then rose with some effort and uttered,

"Strange, that's right. I am a stranger, and I am quite hurt. See my wounds."

The musician saw his cuts and bruises and nodded in sympathy.

"Please follow me," he instructed.

Andrew followed him silently. Once inside, he led Andrew to a chamber with an intensely pungent smell. The walls were lined with shelves holding bottles and jars of various shapes and sizes, and a large table in the center supported a stone slab, knives, a mortar and pestle, and other apothecary tools. In one corner near the window, Andrew saw heaps of dried leaves and shoots in different stages of drying. Another corner was filled with old books, and a large vessel on the hearth emitted faint vapor, as if boiling constantly. He no longer found the smell disagreeable as his wounds began to tear at the flesh. He desperately longed for pain relief.

"Please use this robe," he requested.

The golden-haired healer, a man of striking handsome features, stood upright before him, holding out a crisp white robe. Andrew looked at him openly, up close, ignoring his pain.

"Wounds speak of your character, pardon me!" he said, as he examined with some skill. "Unattended, uncared for, the exuding pus and foul stench—like a small sin left unatoned, spreading to consume the whole person," he paused and looked out the window. Swirling, thick gray clouds, like a dark cloak, hovered on the horizon.

A strong gust rushed against the windowpane, lustily forming dusty, moist sketches.

Lightning struck nearby; the palace seemed to shake, its glass windows trembling. The man looked shaken and dropped the salve to the floor. A maid rushed in, glancing at her master, and quickly took over his task.

"Zeus," the maid whispered.

Andrew sat baffled; his wounds exposed. Outside in the courtyard, rain poured heavily. Suddenly, lightning struck the ground, and a tree seemed to catch fire so rapidly that the area lit up with a fierce orange glow. A second later, another bolt of thunder hit the same tree, as if in vengeance, and the already burning trunk burst into tongues of red and yellow flames dancing recklessly.

The maid mumbled with fear. "You angered him. Master! You angered him!"

The healer looked perplexed, indignant as he walked toward the door, opening it partially. The torrential rain and gale leaped up, drenching his divinely alluring face as he stretched his neck toward the sky.

"No. Master, no!" The maid pulled him in with all her strength. "You have lost enough!" she pleaded, pulling.

He had witnessed the tragic event many years ago. Darkness covered the sky, and Apollo's son Asclepius was busy tending to dying mortals. Yes, just like tonight... the sharp edge of a thunderclap had struck down... down to the center of his chest... splitting it open... leaving a dark, charred stench from a hollow chest.

Zeus had killed his grandson!

Apollo mumbled,

"Oh, Father! Why? Why again? What angers you now? Why did you take away my son...? Why can't you see me doing his work?"

Andrew found his voice faltering—his angelic curls rain-straightened—in profound agony and resentment. It only reminded him of his own father's face during a calamity brought on not by destiny, but by the loss of a beloved family member.

Asclepius—the master loved him dearly. The maid whispered and began to scour Andrew's gash vigorously with a medicated cloth.

This is how Apollo, father of the great physician Asclepius, met Andrew.

Apollo adored Coronis. When she emerged from the lake, Mother Earth paused in wonder, and the sweet breeze stilled, as the god of healing relished with unceasing adulation. Then came the terrible message from a white crow—a revelation that inflamed him with anger: Coronis had chosen Ischys for marriage. In jealousy and boiling rage, he punished the messenger first, and the poor white crow's feathers turned black. Artemis became livid with the news and ran wildly to incinerate the beautiful Coronis. Yet Apollo was able to save the baby Asclepius from her burning womb. He had later asked the centaur Chiron of Crete, who had raised Achilles and Jason, to raise his son as well.

It was Chiron, not Apollo, who trained him in the healing arts. Athena also helped with Gorgon's blood, partly as a healer and partly as a poison. Asclepius became a renowned doctor, but when he resurrected Capaneus and Lycurgus, the fallen warriors of the Seven Against Thebes, and Hippolytus, son of Theseus, many gods were shocked by his actions. Hades, angry, complained to Zeus, who killed him with his thunderbolt like a stag. Apollo was sad at first, but soon became furious with revenge—and yes, that was when he killed the Cyclopes in retaliation. After all, what father wouldn't do the same?

He approached Andrew, still muttering rapidly, as if capitulating without fear. Then, he ran to the center of the ground and screamed, throwing his arms skyward:

Here I am! Here I stand! Go ahead, mighty Zeus! Unleash your might! Pour your wrath upon my chest! Yes, I have killed the Cyclopes for making the thunderbolt for you, after you took Asclepius from me—forever—and then punished me. You have punished me by making me serve mortal Admetus. What now? What now… what now? His voice broke. He bent close to the burning tree.

The glow of the flames neither eased the pain on his handsome face nor dried his tears.

When Apollo was finally supported back inside the chamber by his men, he realized he shouldn't have revealed all his past to a stranger. He stayed silent for a moment, rain-soaked clothes dampening the floor beneath him. Then he asked, "Stranger! Who are you? You've stirred my old pains within me. In a short while, have you felt a glimpse of life quite unlike my music, with cruel disruptions and agonizing bereavements? It has bled my soul. Yet still, I lived." As he spoke those painful words, the clouds began to clear, the rain stopped, and his seething anger seemed to fade.

Andrew felt sorry for him.

Apollo looked somewhat puzzled by Andrew's compassion—a mortal's involvement in the life of a god seemed so sudden and reckless. Though not unpleasant, it was untimely. Still, unexpected emotions welled up in him, and the god started again:

"Some lesser gods may call it haste to speak with a mortal," began a soliloquy. "My soul and sentiments have been torn apart most painfully. Where shall I begin?"

Andrew, remaining befuddled, opened a raw spirit but said nothing further. Apollo continued reproachfully:

"I am destined to create beauty from the ruins of my pain. Unattached to both parents, I seek one in every creature that breathes, god or mortal. Sure, I was raised in my world: a world of fantasy, vibrant imagination, and unbridled emotion." He paused.

Then Apollo recounted his childhood:

"Even before my origin, Mother Leto endured great suffering—perhaps more than most—but she eventually found a place, after traveling countless miles, seeking to give birth to her twins away from Hera's vengeful eyes. She wandered extensively until she arrived on the floating island of Delos to bear me, since Hera had cursed her to give birth to children neither on land nor sea.

Artemis was born first, on the sixth day of the month; I was born on the seventh. Hera had failed, despite sending her son Pythos to attack the granddaughter of Gaia and Ouranos. Many goddesses came to help my dear mother—Dione, Rhea, Amphitrite, and Themis, among them, except the vengeful Hera and Eileithyia. She endured unbearable labor pains for nine days and nights. Swans circled Delos seven times; on the eighth, I was born. The world rejoiced: golden shining sky, sparkling water, smiling earth, and the nine muses singing my praise. Birds and animals called for their mates, and my mother smiled as her labor pains eased," he paused.

Andrew asked, "Was Mother Leto happy?"

"Indeed… and I was fed red nectar, not her breast. But while she rejoiced, I, as a baby god, couldn't just do what babies were supposed to do."

Andrew thought, so what? Of course, you weren't a mortal baby. Apollo felt the same doubts—and more. Why did I flee? What compelled me? Did the God of gods not love me? Was Mother Leto hating herself? The baby had to go stray, escape, and discover why he was unwelcome. What was so wrong with him?

The infant Apollo took flight to right the wrongs that the world had inflicted on his mother, traveling to a place two thousand feet above sea level and in the center of the earth, or Omphalos. Zeus had released two eagles from opposite corners of the world—east and west—and they met over Delos, near Mount Parnassus, which rose over eight thousand feet. The people called the peak the Shining Ones. The old Gaia temple, which had existed for years before Apollo, was a serene, unadorned sanctuary where priestesses known as Sybils, sitting on Sybilline Rock, delivered prophecies to believers. Later, a fierce dragon arrived near the Castalian Spring and made a liar nearby to protect the temple.

When the young god reached the temple, a Sybil glanced up briefly, caught in a trance. Spotting a child nearby, she quickly returned to her ecstatic repose only to be jarred out of her stillness again when the baby with golden locks, a radiant face, and a bewitchingly strong little figure dressed in a tunic asked, "Where lies the great Python?"

Baby Apollo searched for some life, some lost soul to answer his longings. The child had been torn from his origin, from his creators. Yet he was hesitant to feel the distraction; the ugly perception of estrangement pushed him forward. He asked again, "Where lies the great Python?" as if by asking, he might identify himself and later be closer to his true self.

The Sybil exhaled her breath toward the spring, and the tiny god smiled. The sky and earth soon quaked as the golden arrows of the far-shooter pierced the Python. The Sybil was seen bowing at the knees of our god of illumination. The temple was cleansed and rebuilt, marking the dawn of a significant era.

The Sybil, now called Pythia, announced to the pilgrims, "To all from the many tribes of mankind, the most important thing is to know what is His will..." She hinted at Apollo. Darkness was pierced, and humankind was enlightened. The rise of patriarchy challenged the matriarchy, and from Gaia to Themis to Apollo, the art of prophecy was passed down and practiced by the seers whom he established at Delphi.

The sizeable hollow cave in the earth with its narrow mouth formed the temple of Pythian Apollo. Before the inner sanctum, the priestess sat within a chamber called the Adytum, where a bronze trident stood upon a fissure that emitted hallucinogenic vapors. She chewed the bay leaves sacred to Apollo and, at auspicious times, mumbled the truest prophecies, for which the kings' riches were regularly gifted.

Only male pilgrims were admitted after purification in the spring and sacrifice of an animal that ideally did not shiver in cold water (lest both the worshipper and the beast be turned away). Then, the male priest received the supplicant's written question and read it aloud to the priestess, who inhaled the vapor, chewed the bay leaves, and uttered the oracle of the god, always in a manner that was neither affirming nor a clear rebuttal.

The young far-shooter declared, "Let mankind celebrate my victory with games of archery and horse racing every eight years!" The tiny god was filled with joy; he had avenged his mother's torment. The boy looked up at the priestess and smiled devilishly, as if to reassure her of her place, and she bowed in deep reverence. Thus began the endless misery of self-search. Each time he approached an image, it would somehow slip out of his reach, leaving his identity undefined. Who am I? Who am I? Who am I? This question continued to resonate for a million years in the hearts of Apollonian souls.

"The first thing I did was hunt the Python as it ran back to the temple, fearful of a child, yes. It fell beneath my arrows, and for that, Hera made Zeus punish me."

"Why?" Andrew mumbled.

Why, to his son, a newborn god, what was the justification? Would any mortal father ever make his son suffer for such an act of spirit and bravery? But it was no simple matter. Did he not resent the end of the mother goddess's era, when Apollo's shrine would replace those of Gaia, Rhea, Hera, and so on? Zeus had done the same by founding his own lineage, ending the matriarchal hegemony of the mother goddess Gaia.

Apollo continued, "I don't know why, but he punished me many times. Which was worse, I can't say. The eight long, dreary years with Admetus were a torment… But speaking of loneliness, I was most forlorn after Hyacinthus left."

Hyacinthus was not only exquisitely beautiful but also a remarkably kind prince. Apollo could not leave him alone for even a moment, whether he was carrying his fishing net, walking his hunting dogs, or performing any task a prince might perform in those days. Yet someone was resentful of this growing relationship—the West Wind, Zephyrus. One afternoon, after a gathering, Apollo wished to play quoits and hurled his discus far. Hyacinthus, fascinated, chased the flying object, unaware of his fate. The heavy discus came rushing down—and Apollo saw him fall to the ground, unconscious, spurting blood.

"And I, the healer god, couldn't revive him, despite all my might," Apollo sighed.

Outside, deep maroon-purple blossoms released a rich fragrance—one that spoke of unrequited friendship. Andrew felt the god's agony as he gazed forlornly into his garden, searching for the lost Hyacinthus as if he would burst forth, alive and well, from the plant.

Apollo had transformed the blood of Hyacinthus into a beautiful bloom, Hyacinth. People say he inscribed 'ah, ah' on the purple and white petals of the flower.

Apollo had another talented offspring, Orpheus, with the muse Calliope. He was the most exceptional musician ever born. Apollo taught Orpheus to play the lyre, and when he sang his poetry, the gods, humans, animals, and trees alike were enchanted. Orpheus was married to Euridice. The god of marriage, Hymenaios, attended their wedding bearing a blazing torch, but the smoke caused guests to tear up as a bad omen.

Soon, a bad omen appeared on the wedding day as Euridice was strolling with her friends when Aristeus saw her and, smitten by her charm, chased after her. Unfortunately, Euridice stepped on a serpent and died instantly. When Orpheus heard the news, he was so grief-stricken that he decided to visit her in the realms of the dead and silence. He could sing for Hades and Persephone and bring tears even to the hideous Cerberus. They let Euridice leave on one condition—Orpheus wouldn't look back while leading her out to the surface, except he did turn around at the brink between Hell and Earth, to ensure she was behind him. And she was taken back to the grip of death a second time, saying "Farewell" to her darling.

Some say Orpheus desired to share the happiness as she was emerging from hell, but others think it was impatience. Some believe Orpheus did it to freeze her, as he would rather live with her frozen memory than in flesh and blood.

Submerged in despair, Orpheus could only cry and sing of his profound grief. He avoided all maidens who came after him. When the Maenads approached and were spurned, they chased him with a spear to his death. His head was severed in a frenzy of intoxication and thrown into the river Hebros. It washed ashore on the beaches of the island of Lesbos, still singing. After his death, he met Euridice in the underworld and never left her.

"My two talented sons met untimely deaths... Why? Why must a father endure such heartbreaking sorrow?"

Unaware of the ways of gods or the sorrow that the deathless endure upon the loss of their loved ones, Andrew sat speechless. Apollo took a deep breath and continued,

"How I end up in my relationships is mysterious, somewhat tragic, and not blessed in spheres of love and longing, as they all say. I probably should stay away from those my heart desires... and he paused.

"But I'm helpless when it sprouts in me like with Daphne, I was ignorant and forceful... even though I knew about Leukippos, her previous lover..." he trailed off.

Andrew thought of his own difficulties, which seemed now like a minor setback compared to what this divinity endured.

"Fender-benders, yeah, a bump in the road," he ended enunciating.

Leukippos fell in love with Daphne, but she wouldn't let any man come close to her. So, he wore a peplos beneath an embroidered himation when he approached her friends. In love with a beautiful maiden, the prince set aside his pride in being the stronger man and transformed into a winsome maiden adorned with clothes and ornaments. Was it hard? Or was the longing so intense, the lust so unyielding, that manhood could be forgotten, masqueraded away to embrace the tender feelings of his heart?

Subsequently, they all became good friends. Daphne was impressed with her new companion, who was kind, gentle, and an excellent hunter and archer. She spent a lot of time with Leukippos, and in playful gestures, she touched, caressed, and embraced him, perceiving him as an innocent maiden. She walked through the gardens with her new companion, woke up to see the golden rays of dawn with her angel, and always drew him close to her sweet bosom, which exuded the fragrance of purity. He could think of nothing better than being with her, playing with her, being loved by her, and witnessing his love perform all those tender acts befitting a dazzling, delicate woman. She carried her pride and strengthened their friendship, but he defiled it by nurturing ceaseless desire and, whenever he could, satisfying the virile, fearless longing that men possess.

When Apollo learned of Leukippos's deception, he called Daphne and her friends to the Ladon River in Arcadia. There, all the maidens undressed and waded into the water, seemingly for a playful distraction meant to please their softer, more carefree sides—except for one maiden who stayed alone on the riverbank, unwilling to undress. In a clever, mischievous way, the naked girls giggled and teased Leukippos, pulling on his tunic as he blushed fiercely, trying to cover himself. Soon, he was completely stripped, revealing what he had carefully hidden. The same bashful, beautiful maidens suddenly turned fierce, realizing the deception. Their princess stood trembling with shock; her innocent eyes filled with disgust as she shifted from a loving friend to a fierce protector of her pride against this virile intrusion. Leukippos was soon pierced by the very daggers and spears of the maidens he had enjoyed so much in disguise. Daphne had started the harsh game of life by prematurely ending a cherished admirer, destroying his vanity to protect her own pride—or was it her vanity, too?

Daphne was no different from Artemis; both were wild virgins. Was Apollo a victim of fate, like Leukippos? Apollo had just ridiculed Eros as he toyed with his far-shooter bow, and Eros couldn't forgive. A gold-tipped arrow for Apollo and a leaden arrow for Daphne flew, each piercing their hearts with conflicting emotions— flaring love in him, inciting in her a desire for perpetual virginity. This dissonance caused her to reject him, and he chased her relentlessly like a stag.

When Daphne was exhausted, she looked back to see Apollo closing in, desperate to win her love. She knew her fate was sealed. She had seen the terror in Leukippos's eyes just before he was about to be harmed. Apollo embraced her, but she recoiled, praying to Zeus to make her invisible so she wouldn't be violated.

Zeus honored her, and she shriveled, her slender fingers turning into leaves, her unblemished torso hardening into a Laurel trunk. Did she deny nature by mocking Leukippos, and did nature seek revenge by taking her back?

"I didn't lose her. Daphne is forever with me; she lives in my wreath, rests with my lyre, and watches over me. Don't you see my hair almost entwined with hers? She is inalienable. I carry her deep within my soul every moment," Apollo declared.

Andrew experienced a confusing mix of emotions, almost feeling ashamed of presuming Apollo, as if he were a superficial, carefree, and vain god.

But how could he be the god of truth? What was the truth, and what was a lie? Were his eyes witnessing truth or deception? Andrew remained perplexed in such fairy-tale surroundings, given the god's unbecoming episodes and inexplicable character.

When the Seven Sages gathered at Delphi—Periander of Corinth, Solon of Athens, Chilon of Sparta, Thales of Miletus, Cleobulus of Lindos, Pittacus of Mitylene—each offered their own version of truth, except one: Bias of Priene. When asked for his truth, he said bluntly, "Most men are evil," echoing the words of Pythagoras.

Andrew pondered the nature of Apollo's truth, what it truly meant to understand it, and the meaning of "truth" itself. Was it something that reflected reality? Or was truth simply pragmatic and coherent?

"What do you mean by 'know thyself'?" he asked.

The god seemed troubled and glanced at Andrew before walking toward the window. Outside, Andrew observed a remarkable sight: the sun intensifying, beams of bright rays joyfully streaming, swirling with lively dust particles that danced like a celestial waltz. Apollo extended his rough yet steady hands to absorb the warmth, then gently touched Andrew's forehead, softly saying,

Visit your altar; let the rays of dawn guide your journey into the deep crevices you have forsaken—for the unknown, and possibly truth.

Andrew stayed transfixed, like a pilgrim at the edge of Delos.

"Thou art..." Andrew murmured unwittingly.

Then he sat speechless. His entire being underwent a tumultuous change—his pride and conception of truth becoming porous, his shortcomings and emotions trickling through as if the oracle had struck him upon a sieve: hard yet allowing his aqua vitae of life to sift and winnow, drip, drip, drip...

He started to sweat heavily. Andrew had just realized what others had struggled to understand for ages: Apollo's power and his deadly silver arrows—the ones he flicked and used to bring plague upon the Achaeans during the Trojan War and for Niobe's unfortunate children.

Andrew felt pierced and pricked by that same brilliant light, which unsettled his consciousness.

He was humbled. *Know Thyself. Know Thyself. Know Thyself.*

The maid entered, announcing a visitor,

"Heracles, son of Alcmene, is here, master."

Andrew snapped out of his trance. The name sent a jolt through him—he had heard it before, associated with capture and dread. He became restive and fearful of being captive again.

"Heracles, oh my god, sir, please save me from him! He is ruthless. He will throw me back in that dungeon!" he pleaded.

Apollo said nothing. Without a word, he walked to the other chamber to meet Heracles. What did Heracles ask of Apollo, and was he going to surrender? The mortal remained behind the closed divine doors.

But as Andrew sat in that room waiting for him, a colorful veil appeared on the slope of the verdant mountain, gradually obscuring the lonely pines and their scattered needles on the ground. As the rainbow-hued veneer descended, one could discern about fifty or so maidens approaching the fortified mansion of Apollo, dressed in a mélange of clothing ranging from the garb of a huntress to the enchanting peplos of a newly nubile maiden. Were these soldiers of Heracles?

Following this majestic scene of the animal world, two large deer appeared slowly. Artemis held the reins. She was dressed in a belted white half-sleeve peplos, a himation draped over her shoulder and back, and a crown on her proud head.

Andrew stayed fidgety, frantically looking for a way out. As the Amazons encircled the palace, their chatter broke the silence and calm of the divine residence.

Andrew left the chambers and wandered through various nooks and corners of the palace. He stayed anxious, turning different knobs on the doors, peeking cautiously through windows now and then, careful not to be seen, slipping and skirting around the gold and silver goblets, jugs, and statues. Then, a heavy silver door creaked open slowly, and the familiar voice of the god spoke from within.

"What brings the Lady of the Wilderness today?"

"I'm so sick lately, Phoebus."

"Blues of a lonely maiden or remorse of a ruthless huntress?"

"Speak for thyself, god of music. Who is lonelier? I seek no one for my happiness. I have learned to live alone," she paused.

The god of all music felt snubbed. He was painfully aware of his apparent failures—how he had failed to maintain meaningful relationships with those he cared for most. Did he lose them forever, or manage to hold onto them for eternity? Despair seeped through his veins.

Where is Erato, the muse that sings hankering lyrics for adulation, intense amour without lust, burning passionately with eternally faithful? Where is despondent Melpomene with all her sad, dejected, and grief-stricken poetry?

He might have needed Clio to sing about his past, or Calliope to narrate an epic. Euterpe might chant her lyrical verses, while Polyhymnia would recite sacred poetry. Let Thalia make him burst out in laughter, and Terpsichore design a dance.

Urania wouldn't be helpful with her Astronomy.

But nothing could comfort Apollo when confronted by his sister's apt denunciation. He pushed his himation back and smoothed his tunic, uttering,

"Loneliness? There is no time for solitude, sister. When I am alone in my heart, beautiful melodies emerge and sweep me away. But what of you? Why escape? Why do you stay distant from companions?"

Artemis stared at her brother but remained silent, seemingly helpless yet tacitly agreeing. Then she burst into divine laughter,

"How can I… brother? How can I? You should know better. Remember what happened to Actaeon? I don't think I could ever grow close to another… or even like …"

Did the goddess of the wilderness seem to crave companionship? Such longing was unheard of, contradicting all faith and imagination, as she had petitioned Father Zeus to grant her eternal virginity—an oath she zealously defended. She showed no hesitation in ending the life of anyone whose fate brought them near her.

"Oh, fertility goddess, don't be so hard on yourself. Stay connected to the animal kingdom and let no wild instinct creep into your soul. Abandon cruel retributions for sympathetic reasons…" Apollo paused as Artemis derided.

"Cruel retributions? Look who's talking."

"I know, you will remind me countless times about Marsyas… fumbling against Athena's flute, playing for the pleasure of the poor…"

"And you, Phoebus, why flay him?"

"It's not about me anymore. Let's talk about you, my dear huntress sister. Let some fresh, tender feeling grow inside you. Embrace love, sister—taste Aphrodite's potion." Apollo laughed and led her toward his palace, though he was not finished.

"Sister, my sin is minor compared to yours now that we discuss it openly. Cursing Actaeon into a stag was one thing—for witnessing the unclothed goddess—but tearing him apart with hounds? Goddess of fertility, is that just for a mortal who loved you?"

"Dear brother, why are we speaking ill of each other? Why are you so gloomy? Are you in love with a mortal again?" she laughed. When Apollo appeared at ease, she added as if explaining, "Actaeon was part of a ritual—for at the end of his reign, the king had to die, whether a goddess willed it or not..."

A silence followed—a stillness that embodies solemn acceptance of reality, duty over personal feelings, religion over society, and sacrifice over pleasure.

"Have some fresh nectar; wash away the grime of the wild," Apollo offered.

They sat down and continued their conversation in a low tone.

"Phoebus, my Arktois have witnessed a tragedy in the mountains."

Her voice dropped further, and Andrew couldn't hear. He leaned closer to the half-shut door, straining to catch the whispered words:

"Did they see him? You know death awaits anyone who even whispers such rumors to you."

"Not one—many of them saw the massive iron bird crash to its death. The mortals inside lost consciousness, and my girls screamed out of terror." Artemis paused.

Andrew started sweating; his heart raced, and his mouth grew dry. He finally found the answer—the mystery that had surrounded the entire accident was now revealed by a goddess, the one who does not lie.

"And then...?" Apollo asked.

"Then he came. They bowed and scattered, letting him approach the creatures."

"What did he do?"

I don't know. He walked toward the bird, then raised his hand to the clouds, beckoning them to come down and cover the earth. The girls could see no more; the land was wrapped in a soft veil, and their eyelashes grew heavy…

"And then?"

"Then came Hephaestus and drove my girls away, but Phoebus…" she whispered. Andrew leaned against the door to listen, but he couldn't catch the words. Suddenly, someone flung the door wide open, and Andrew fell into the adjoining room, landing on the floor, deeply embarrassed.

The Maiden of the Silver Bow moved quickly. She charged forward like a she-bear, her right foot pressing hard against Andrew's chest, pinning him to the ground as she yelled,

"Who are you, secretly listening to us? Don't try to pull my foot—speak the truth!"

Apollo was taken aback. He rushed over, gently tapping Artemis and saying,

"This mortal has lost his mind since the accident. Let him be free."

Andrew felt a sharp pain in his ribs beneath Artemis's feet. He glanced up, noticing how her feet rested against him and how her shapely legs and firm thighs were tanned golden.

"I'm hurting," he squeaked.

The immortals exchanged looks of mixed pity and dismay. Phoebus said,

"Cease your wandering eyes on the goddess, or, mortal, you'll never see your beloved again. The goddess punishes lust, the desire to possess, and you shall not be an exception if I may warn you."

Andrew lowered his eyes swiftly before the assembled immortals, wondering how he could harbor lust at all. He began to mumble,

"Desire to obtain may be lust, but desire to sacrifice, and to give everything, even risk my own life… what is that? I respect all of you as much as I honor my church," he declared earnestly. The gods laughed heartily at these ingratiating words, and Apollo interjected,

"Honor thy church…?" he repeated, incredulously yet with a hint of complaisance.

"I am helpless here…" Andrew continued, "I must find my fiancé. Whom can I trust? To whom shall I turn for Rhea? I'm deeply hurt even to imagine that she is not alive. Can you help?"

Apollo ceased his condescension and spoke softly into Artemis's ear, and she nodded.

They spoke of the messenger god. Artemis suggested Hermes might find Rhea, perhaps even escort Andrew, before the gods if deemed just.

"Just?" Apollo scoffed. "From Maia's son? Do not expect lofty notions of justice. His deceit might come as a shock to this mortal. Since birth, he has played games with me."

Sibling rivalry flared up again as Artemis reminded him of the lyre he had received in exchange for worthless cattle. He spoke of the golden staff, the symbol of wealth and sleep, which he had given in return long ago, thereby fueling the family's discord.

"He has much more than a staff; he rules over both worlds—the journey for mortals and immortals alike, the very path to the underworld…" she added.

"Surely, but I doubt his fairness to mankind. He may even lead this stranger into a dark alley with no escape," Apollo worried.

"Brother, fine, then you take this mortal to the council of gods; let him plead his case. We have a divine council, after all…"

Apollo consented,

"But you should raise it there and ask him gently."

"Not me. As it is, Hera and my mother are at odds again. The dinner shall not be so peaceful. Let us ask Ares or Hephaestus to stir the air."

"Heracles will surely raise this issue. He threatened me if I harbor any mortal against his wishes."

"He is merely doing his duty."

"Will you escort him?"

"No. You, the god closest to Zeus's mind, should do it."

With that, the goddess of wilderness left her twin brother's palace. Andrew felt a spark of unexpected hope. He would meet the most powerful—the decision-makers on this island. Maybe he could find Andrew's love; surely, she couldn't have disappeared without a trace.

Later that day, Apollo strode confidently with Andrew through the countryside, leaving behind the busy bazaars, grand stately homes, and tree-lined avenues. At one point, he paused carefully, scanning the area for mortals. When convinced no one was nearby, he sharply turned into a dense woodland, with Andrew following. They crept through tall pines and ancient oaks, saying nothing but walking steadily. Finally, Apollo descended steeply into a shadowy hollow where the sun's rays couldn't reach through the thick canopy, and the damp, heavy air whispered secrets. He looked around one last time, leapt to the center of the clearing, and vanished. Andrew hesitated, wondering whether he should follow. Is it safe? Is he going to disappear like Rhea? He shivered with an unknown fear, but took a deep breath and stepped in.

Apollo looked at him with a confused expression, as if to say, '*What took you so long?*' Then, they continued walking toward a narrow tunnel, faintly lit at the distant end—just enough to see their steps.

The small rodents ignored the strangers as the air remained thick and damp.

They moved into a second cave and walked through another dark chamber. Then the cave opened onto a lush green meadow. Andrew took a deep breath, feeling relieved by the fresh mountain air as Apollo climbed up a steep slope once more. Now, on top of the peak, the world spread out beneath them. The ocean gently lapped against cliffs nearby. Tall walls surrounded a palace, at least ten feet high, and farther up, a grand palace nearly touched the sky.

"Who lives there?"

"My father," he paused.

"Wow!"

God of reasoning smiled, his thin lips curling not in joy but in a bittersweet hint of regret as he considered his father's ancient Olympus home. Where did all that go? What could have happened to that magnificent palace? Who lives there now? Is anyone still there at all? All those trivial thoughts drifted past the god's mind.

"You know," Andrew began, "there's a certain irony in the whole thing."

Apollo did not respond.

"I can't believe what you've told me so far..." he left the sentence hanging.

Apollo turned his face back and smiled once more, as if it didn't matter whether he was seen as reality or as a specter. The lingering thought that he inspired through his divine silence once again captivated Andrew and clouded his mind. So, instead of pressing his challenge to prove or disprove their existence, he said,

"May I tell you something?"

Apollo glanced at him with faint curiosity.

Andrew continued

"I'm considered an expert on Greek mythology… yes, this Andrew."

The sun god looked somewhat disconcerted and repeated,

"Mythology?" He laughed mockingly, then his expression grew serious, uttering,

"Am I a myth? Or am I the truth? Who knows?"

"You seem concerned?" Andrew asked.

"No, not at all. Perhaps dismayed and pitying. These mortals will suffer without us. Their gods cannot save them."

"Why?"

Apollo laughed rather loudly, questioning why their god couldn't save them from disaster. Why couldn't he protect them from the hands of evil, the oppressors?

 "God died for all our sins," Andrew muttered, as if he had sensed the question.

All your sins? What sin? Why is a baby born sinful? If He is the Creator, why bring sinful life into being only to seek to cleanse it? But Apollo didn't reveal his thoughts.

"I'm not religious," Andrew said.

God is omnipotent, omniscient, and everywhere—even if He never shows Himself, and people try to prove His existence with all kinds of theories: ontological, cosmological, and more—most are false stories, some are just pure delusions. Like 'visions'—He spoke to me. Talk of illusions; continue to gather endless possessions—those very things they strongly forbid the masses from having. Build more temples, churches, and monasteries. And if not, let us convert the unbelievers, a polite term for those who are not believers.

Andrew smiled internally. What if Apollo traveled to my country? He felt like asking,

Do you ever think of traveling to America? People need to hear you and your polytheism.

Being omniscient, Apollo thought: No, not now. It is silly for me. About polytheism? You have no choice: in monotheism, He is the same, whether you like it or not.

"I never thought of it like this… I wish I had a choice," Andrew mumbled.

People, not gods, control people in the name of gods. The larger the following, the better the loot.

"Do you think we were better off before all these religions usurped us?" Andrew asked.

Those were the days when humans prayed to nature across the globe—when they asked the sun, the moon, the ocean, and Mother Earth all their questions, revered them, cared for them, and lived in harmony. Then they labeled such people as heathens—the most dangerous journey humans ever undertook, the most treacherous act against the very gods who had created everything they had. They bit the hands that fed them.

His chain of thought was suddenly broken by a voice piercing through the darkness.

"Who goes there?" someone screamed suddenly.

Andrew startled, and Apollo looked a bit vexed.

"Charon, don't waste your time. Go watch the banks of Styx," Apollo said.

Andrew was surprised. He suspected there might be a secret passage to the underworld nearby, so he made a mental note of it.

"I was, Phoebus, but Cerberus suddenly woke and ran barking," came the reply.

"Charon, looking for a particular mortal woman who might have succumbed to an air accident, an outsider from a faraway land."

Laughter echoed along the tunnel walls, scattering tiny rocks and dust.

"Admit such a mortal, Phoebus? Uhm…Not me. Unless Thanatos, the god of death, did a favor for a mortal, which would be unprecedented."

Charon, son of Nyx (the goddess of night) and Erebus (the god of darkness), said nothing about what his other siblings were doing.

Phoebus, I've recently allowed passage through Phlegethon and Cocytus. We already operate ferries on the Acheron and Lethe rivers. You know Phlegyas, who transported Virgil, now steers the busy routes to Perdition. I'm here to help the Olympians. Any names?

Apollo looked at Andrew, who answered quickly,

"Rhea."

Charon looked baffled and dismayed. Then he asked Apollo,

"Rhea? Meter Theon? What?"

"No, it is the name of a mortal, this man's mate."

Charon paused for a moment, appearing lost in thought, then told them no one was there yet, unless Hermes had her take a different route.

(Charon's siblings: Hypnos, the goddess of sleep; Nemesis, the goddess of retribution; Eris, the goddess of strife; and Keres, the goddess of doom.)

Andrew's heart leaped; she might be alive, and he prayed for her safety. He remained confounded, though, thinking Apollo should know it all—he is the knower of all, the master of all oracles.

Apollo, knowing what Andrew was thinking, said nothing but beckoned him toward the citadel. No longer cautious, he walked briskly. They reached the mammoth golden gate, gleaming brightly and stretching high, almost touching the milky clouds, which dimmed the brightness somewhat, allowing Andrew to keep his eyes half-shut.

The palace, situated just below the mountain peak, was designed to withstand the strong winds from all four directions, with minimal impact on the towers. Sunlight spread evenly, illuminating every corner to showcase the stunning complex and dazzle the eyes. Compared to this grand structure, the White House looked like a simple monastery. Brick pathways, green lawns, and numerous fountains added to its majestic charm. At the same time, oaks and pines rustled as colorful birds sang songs of eternal joy—a reflection of the everlasting happiness that comes with immortality. Filled with happiness, Andrew's heart shifted from a sad lover, overwhelmed by the recent loss of his beloved, to a liberated soul, joyful and weightless.

Apollo didn't fail to watch him. This mortal troubled him. Something far more significant and sinister than what appeared was approaching—and he was likely a symbol rather than just a premonition. I must be cautious and prevent the looming disaster. Why do I have this foreboding... why do I see the darkness so clearly? Why does reason overpower my passion? Why can't I be like the other gods? What drives me isn't my emotions but something more profound. Why did I struggle with Python as an infant? Certainly not for my ego—babies have none. Killing Tityos was fully justified after what he tried against Mother Leto, but at Delphi... my actions there... no, I must stay strong. After all, the way these mortals see me as a symbol of masculinity, even though all my pursuits for love end in failure, let them know there is a cause, an undying legacy, a continuity in my deeds.

Andrew stumbled against a tree; Apollo caught him again. Andrew felt his hands were steady yet gentle, weightless. His shoulders stretched with quiet pride, his smile radiating generosity. Andrew felt uplifted in the god's presence, as if he were with kin, possibly a distant cousin or an uncle who had left the village long ago.

Andrew smiled back as Apollo preened his hair locks.

"You are not what I learned from the books," Andrew began. Apollo raised his eyebrows, feigning curiosity. Andrew continued: "You seem kind, yet here I am... I've heard all kinds of stuff... like you flaying your grandson..."

Apollo's expression grew troubled. He spoke softly,

"We've discussed this before, but listen. I had two sons with Poseidon's daughter, Aethus, named Eleuther and Linus. Orpheus and Marsyas are Linus's grandchildren. By then, it was very distant, and I am not defending myself. Marsyas took up the flute left by Athena and mistook its sweetness for his own talent. So, his boasting had to be stopped. There's a reason—it was a lesson..." And Apollo appeared arrogantly, perhaps realizing his excessive anger was unjustified anyway. He quickened his step, leaving Andrew behind, who was busy thinking of other times when this god had failed.

"What you're thinking is not right..." Apollo broke the silence.

"Actually..."

"I understand, everyone thinks the same. There's a sadness about Apollo. The world celebrates my victory—the slaying of the Python and my taking over at Delphi. Some say I was justified in bringing the plague on the Achaeans' camp during the Trojan War, but when I fall in love, trouble follows, and misery is born, and lives are shattered— as if all I need for my life are just some tombs, memories, or symbols. Like this one," he said, pointing at the Laurel tree. "Daphne lives strongly within me. I know Eros caused me to fall for her, yet years later, I still cannot forget. I chased her like a fox after a dove, and just as I caught her, she transformed right before my eyes into bark, stem, leaves, and boughs. I wept. What was my problem?"

Andrew remained silent. Then the mighty, graceful, and only god who valued reason lifted his lyre and played a melody that echoed through the woods and touched Andrew's heart, just as it had captivated others before, like Hyacinthus.

Andrew thought Apollo looked somewhat exhausted in that fragile moment, unlike the images on the frieze at Delos, where he appeared as an intense male beauty, unaffected by his surroundings. He seemed quite the opposite: shoulders slumped, eyebrows furrowed, and golden locks hanging flat.

He destroys everything he desires to pursue. How then can he be the god of light and reasoning? Is reasoning merely a synonym for ravaging, slaying, or annihilation? Or is it the capacity to think logically and rationally and arrive at a conclusion? What was the logical explanation for singeing the mother of Asclepius, when he surely knew she carried his son in her womb? Was it simply a failure to understand, or a lapse in perceiving the cause behind his actions, decisions, or convictions? Why did he chase Daphne to the point she had to embrace Mother Earth and transform into a tree, emptied of everything human? Is that an intellectual failure, or is the reason inexplicable in mortal terms? Intuition is the perception of facts or truths without rational processes, like when he threw the discus, striking Hyacinthus on the head and killing him instantly. Where was his intuition to anticipate such a disaster?

Apollo remained silent and stood near the slope of the dense peak. He wondered why he had to go on living as expected, bound by the ways of the gods, the realm, and the reign of the deathless forever. It is so tiring, repetitive, and dehumanizing for a god. Reason does not always lead to responsibility, as it comes from an agreement with society, law, or one's conscience. This creates obligation, defines duty, and—for a god like him—becomes a burden in his endless life.

The lyre attracted his winged horses, and as Andrew opened his eyes from the music's spell, a strong chariot waited, drawn by four winged steeds. Apollo patted his beautiful creatures, fondly stroking their manes and eliciting tender neighs and snorts. A crow flew toward the vehicle, landing on the back of the chariot. Apollo smiled and ceremoniously placed a laurel wreath on his head.

But suddenly, they had to stop. A woman appeared out of nowhere and looked at Andrew as if questioning his identity. She was thin, wearing a floral, half-sleeved chiton, with a pink belt at her narrow waist. She wore a crown decorated with flowers. She did not speak a word. Apollo was busy with his horses, and Andrew remained confused. Two other women then arrived, carrying a sense of alarm.

The second lady wore a brightly colored peplos with designs of apples, grapes, and strawberries on her fabric, as if it depicted the autumn harvest.

"What is going on, Carpo? Why is Thallo so indecisive about a mortal entry?" asked the third lady, who appeared to wear a chiton in earthy tones with pictures of a sheaf of grain, as if she reflected summer.

"Andrew is my name."

They introduced themselves as Thallo, Carpo, and Auxo, who attended the entrance to keep mortals out. Apollo tried to explain his reason for bringing this mortal. Apparently, these three were the Horai.

Thallo smiled, pulled a bud from her hair, brought it close to her beautiful lips, and as she exhaled, it blossomed, spreading tender white petals.

Auxo said softly, "Do not cross my path, mortal." I help things grow every summer from the ground, and as she mocked, a small plant near her began stretching as Andrew watched it grow to a tall tree.

Carpo took the sheaf of grain, which had a green stalk and soft, flowery grain, and she laughed at it with her breath. Andrew saw the green grain turn golden and then brown, like a drying kernel ready to be eaten.

Apollo convinced the Horai to let Andrew slip in for a few hours, but they warned him that if he stayed longer, he wouldn't be able to breathe through this gate again.

In the grandeur of the celestial palace, as Apollo stood contemplating his eternal existence, he also rode his chariot up the hill toward the palace. Other gods and goddesses arrived from different parts of the earth to gather for a council and make essential decisions that would affect not only mortals but some of themselves as well.

The path leading to the palace entrance was filled with the sweet smell of fragrant roses, crocuses with orange-red blossoms, and orchids shaped like insects among mating bugs. White daffodils—symbols of death and loved by Hades—lined the way. Goats browsing and brushing against white cliff roses, whose petals the pheasant girl would later gather from their fur. High chaparral bore large red leaves filled with poisonous milk that cats avoided, alongside clusters of blue-violet hyacinths. As the gods arrived on their chariots, servants whispered, recognizing each deity with such subtlety that only divine ears could hear.

Hera returned from a trip to sacred Argos and Samos and settled in the palace garden, feeding her peacocks. She occasionally picked a grain of pomegranate to scatter near her feet before rising to enter the council hall.

Poseidon arrived on his golden chariot drawn by white horses. Alighting, he balanced his trident, scratched his beard, looked around, and pulled his himation up before proceeding straight inside, nearly chafing the door's edge with the tip of his trident in frustration since no help arrived promptly upon his arrival. He was exhausted from a recent journey to Corinth.

Hades arrived on his black, horse-drawn chariot with his wife, Persephone, and helped her dismount like a gentleman. He was dressed in a business-like dark tunic and robe, a tall, dark figure beneath his helmet of invisibility.

Athena entered with an unusual smile for a goddess: her green eyes shone with hope, and her tall chiton outlined a form of feminine strength — not the harsh, husky kind, but tenderly resilient and compelling — draped by a silk cape flowing over her shoulders that barely hid her flawless bosom. She was at peace, as was her city, Athens.

Artemis was at Ephesus before she visited Apollo and hurried toward him. She was helped down from her chariot, drawn by deer, and handed a small puppy to a maid, who took it inside to be cared for. She wore a short, sleeveless chiton draped over her dark, peaked shoulders, belted just below her bronzed bust. Her legs were boldly bare above tawny feet in leather sandals, and a narrow headband rested on her head. The maid brought her silver bow with a quiver, and Artemis signaled for her accompanying nymphs to vanish.

Aphrodite arrived, not veiled in a mist of love but plainly, lacking licentiousness or libidinousness, her exquisitely bewitching face clouded by recent events. She stood cheek to cheek with Ares—her head covered with a Kalyptra, her gold-orange chiton fastened over the right shoulder. At the same time, the left hung gracefully, revealing her lovely pink bosom without a hint of prurience, radiating natural gleam and glitter that was so beautiful and divine. She stood atop her shell-shaped chariot, driven by the ever-arrogant Ares.

Ares, who cared little for his appearance, wore a simple monochiton with his right shoulder exposed. His sinewy build fully displayed the heat and hunger personified in pomp and show. He helped the goddess step down, slapped the dogs, and loped to the master as Aphrodite rubbed and dabbed her swan before looking up at the sparkle. Then, she lifted the august girdle as if to confirm its existence.

Demeter arrived alone. She wore an orange peplos with dark borders. Her tresses spilled beyond a Stéphane crown, though her head was veiled from behind. She held her scepter firmly and passed her torch and a sheaf of grain that she had brought as a gift to the household to a maid.

The messenger Hermes arrived on his curved flying sandals, sparkling as he wore a short chiton just below his knees, a chlamys, and a petasos on his head. In his hand, he carried his kerukeion—the caduceus.

Apollo asked the maids to take Andrew away. He was gently but watchfully led to a door on the opposite side of the hall, then guided toward the guest quarters. There, he could bathe in fragrant waters and eat mortal food before being allowed into the council of gods.

When the time arrived, he was led into halls of enormous size and towering heights. Once inside the chamber where gods performed their divine duties, he was struck by its elegance: walls covered in gold shimmered, and massive silver doors stood proudly. The thrones all around made him feel small. In the center stood the largest throne made of black marble, decorated with goldwork, with seven steps and a golden eagle clutching a thunderbolt. This was the seat of ultimate power, the eternal seat of justice, reserved for the god of all gods sitting in a purple fleece. Yet Zeus, the father god, was nowhere to be seen.

Hera occupied an ivory throne with three steps, its back decorated with golden cuckoos and willow leaves, beneath a full moon. She sat on a white cowhide. Her long silver robe was cinched with a golden belt, and golden sandals adorned her feet, as if she had stepped straight from the east pediment frieze of the Parthenon's three goddesses. She stood there, lost in deep thought, mostly planning to confound the father god. Her perfume of myrrh filled the chamber, stirring even Zeus. Her pearl necklace matched her glittering diadem, an elegant mask, but couldn't conceal the penetrating eyes of artful duplicity in a lady at the height of bloom and beauty.

On the other side, Poseidon sat perched on a grey-green marble throne. His seat was draped in seal skin and bore the emblem of a horse. Restless, he gripped his trident tightly. Once, Athena, seated nearby, smiled and whispered something he failed to understand, which only increased his fidgetiness. Desperately, he sought Aphrodite's attention. But she remained utterly devoted to the rascal Ares, her companion, despite recent events. He was shameless to bring her here on his chariot. He glanced sideways at the cuckolded husband sitting beside him.

Hephaestus busied himself turning and tinkering with a new golden hammer, seated on a rolling throne adorned with his emblem—a quail.

Nearby, Ares, marked by his emblem of a boar and spear, looked so uneasy that even the slightest argument could trigger a violent fight. He sat beside the man who had so offensively humiliated him, maintaining a grumpy, irritable expression.

Apollo sat on a golden throne decorated with a lyre resting on the back and draped over a python skin. Above him, the twenty-one spokes of the sun hung. His one hand lightly rested on a white mouse.

Hermes appeared stern on a rock covered with goatskin, with a swastika at the back, flanked by a crane emblem and a staff decorated with ribbons.

Athena sat majestically on a silver throne decorated with Gorgon heads, with an owl emblem displayed nearby. Beside her, Aphrodite rested charmingly on a silver throne, featuring her dove emblem.

Artemis took her place on a wolf skin atop a silver throne, her symbol, the she-bear, by her side.

Hestia rested on a plain, undecorated wooden seat.

Moments later, Dionysus also joined them.

In a quiet corner, the three Fates—Moirai—sat weaving the thread of life nonstop: Clotho spinning, Lachesis measuring the length and course of the thread, and Atropos, who snipped the thread.

The council rose to its feet when Zeus appeared at the golden door.

■■

"The god of all gods, the supreme, is here,

He was, he is, he will always be there.

Wind and thunder, water and waves, cloud and sky,

Just and strong, he sees it all, up and high.

We see your kindness; we know the joy.

You move the mountain, you shake the earth,

Make fire, anger, wrath, birth, infirmity, or death

Love, happiness, and fortune; wisdom, power, and health

Be the beginning and middle; may we see you at the end.

Rip the unjust, punish the liar, and let mortals fear what you send.

God of gods, supreme is here.

He was, he is, he'll always be there."

At this moment, all the gods and goddesses took their seats, while the Muses sang their eternal hymn—a song celebrating happiness, life, and all about the Olympians.

Hebe and Ganymede were seen rushing around, filling cups with nectar and ambrosia for the hungry gods. Zeus smiled approvingly as Ganymede approached him to pour, gently patting him. Meanwhile, Hebe skillfully avoided Poseidon, who, with a mischievous grin, boldly squeezed her rear as he seized the opportunity with his rough, unclean hands. Ares openly talked with Aphrodite, while Hephaestus raised his golden hammer above the table as a silent warning — but Ares remained completely oblivious. Athena whispered a divine secret to Hera, who bit her lower lip hard, as if angry at Zeus, who seemed to ignore her entirely, taking a sip of nectar which stained his lips red. He beckoned Ganymede again for more.

Apollo then began by introducing Andrew.

"Father Zeus, protector of all and lord of the immortal gods, I apologize for bringing this mortal here, but destiny has chosen him for this difficult presentation, and I am compelled to seek justice." He paused.

"Justice?" Hera interjected sharply.

All eyes turned toward the dispenser of justice, presently, since one could see the annoyance in Zeus.

"Justice is relative; it varies with the adjudicator and the appellant—who judges and who is judged," Hera said deliberately, with an apparent swipe at her husband.

Zeus, unusually calm, seemed a bit restive and intervened:

"Why? Justice should be the same, Teleia," he said to her as the goddess of marriage, pausing for effect.

"Why temper justice now? Don't we all hold a flame in our hearts—the flare of truth that dismisses lies? Why must I keep harmony among men, nature, and the deathless?"

When the father spoke, the entire assembly of divinities listened—except for the Leukolenos, the white-armed queen Hera, who smiled knowingly.

"Additionally, I caution that without justice, no other virtue can stand. If justice is undermined by even the smallest mistake, bias, or preference, it will stop functioning properly. It must be fair to everyone, ensuring equality for all."

Hera refocused her attention, noticing Zeus nervously fiddling with his thunderbolt too forcefully. Andrew, anxious and with a dry mouth, looked around desperately for a drink, but before he could speak, a maiden approached and handed him a gold cup filled with cold-scented water. Everyone turned their intense gazes toward him, and he bowed his head in fear. A light-hearted rumble spread through the room as Ares spoke again:

"O Son of Leto, you must suffer for this deviant act. Why disobey Divine Laws?"

At this point, Apollo began,

"The gods created mortals for different ages: the Golden Age, when they revered immortals and befriended other mortals; the Silver Age, marked by decline that enraged great Cronos; the Bronze Age, born from spear ashes and fought relentlessly to extinction; then the Age of Heroes, when Helen's actions brought havoc to both Trojans and Achaeans alike. Now, gods and goddesses, hear me. In this Iron Age, where the future is undeniably bleak, we have the divine responsibility not to worsen the fate of all," he paused.

The ponderous introduction caused the gods to reflect, wondering what could be so grave that the fast shooter would raise such a serious disquisition. They all waited for him to open his heart and get it over with, especially Hephaestus, who was eager to bring up his matter of marriage reconciliation.

Father Zeus created the woman, Pandora, and you all helped him: Athena with her skill, Aphrodite with her charm, Hermes with his cunning, Hephaestus with her body, but look what came of it? She brought misery, pain, and hardship. This man, Andrew, will suffer no less with his Pandora. Why then must we rush to his ruin?

Apollo turned to Ares:

I have a strange feeling, god of Wars. This mortal is not an ordinary man to ignore, just as Paris wasn't the person Troy should have underestimated. He ultimately caused the extinction of such a mighty kingdom.

Andrew listened to the sermon, initially confused by everything he was told, but gradually his heart started to tremble. He wondered what Apollo had seen in him to speak so forcefully and why he warned of gloom and doom.

Ares squirmed in his seat. Since no one spoke on this matter, he chose to deride,

"Apollo, don't fret over the past. Immortals should take some responsibility for the Age of Heroes. You tried, didn't you? You unleashed nine days of plague on the Achaeans and destroyed Achilles by deceit. But that was their fate."

"Ares, was it your fate, or was it when Diomedes thrust his spear into you and also hurt my splendid wife, who happens to be… so caring?" Hephaestus sneered, and a small teetering broke out, but he finished firmly.

"Or perhaps you blame Hera and Athena for plotting."

Thus, the gods in council showed only minimal interest in a mortal's concerns. Although Zeus passionately spoke of justice, the rest of his retinue reminisced instead about past misdeeds.

"Agamemnon foolishly seized my priest's daughter, Chryseis, but please, listen to me now—this is our fate. Consider carefully: if we keep this Helen..." Apollo glanced at Andrew.

Andrew babbled, "No, no—not Helen. It is Rhea."

Yes, Rhea. Don't you think the mortals from the mainland will come to rescue her? And what's our strategy? We want no ripples—our backs are already against the wall.

The sun god attempted to raise others' awareness of the impending danger, but his warnings were dismissed. After perceiving his divine role in this seemingly trifling matter, he tried to inspire others' conscience, knowing no justice can prevail without a collective conscience, even among the deathless. Yet Ares resumed his old grievances.

But Hera, smug from her tremendous victory in the Trojan War, felt vindicated. After all, she had destroyed Troy and punished Paris, the man who had favored Aphrodite over her. So, she said,

"Phoebus, that's enough. Why are you so petrified? What can they possibly do?"

Hera realized immediately how pathetically self-evident she had become to the rest of the council, undermining Apollo's insecurities while her own were well known. She wondered why jealousy crowned her thoughts. Could jealousy ever be justified? Why does an endless stream of emotions erupt within her like an ugly green monster? Does he really love someone else? Did he belong to another—Alcmene, Io, or Europa? Why should she care about what he gave to others if he did not withhold his love from her? Her gaze shifted to the father and his evil eagle, and for a moment, she questioned herself:

Do I love my Cloud-Gatherer the same? Or have I changed since he courted me?

All this fuss about what he does—it was ridiculous! I'm no longer wasting my time on him. Jealousy might be what people think drove Hera, but I want to change. He had incredible energy to create, to generate, and to fill the earth with seeds of Heroism, Justice, and Order. Of course, he's the father of the world—without him, what could they do? He brought order from the chaos of the women goddesses before him; he was the Self within them all.

I, Hera, shall raise my own Zeus within me; I, Hera, shall create and nourish the hurler of thunderbolts—my soul, my Zeus.

Apollo continued,

"Though you helped the Argives' victory at Troy, what makes you confident to save this tiny island now? How do you manipulate the generals and commanders of this modern army? Paris chose Aphrodite as the fairest and gave her the golden apple, and yet you destroyed his kingdom. Now, Hera, this is a complicated war—air strikes by unmanned vehicles, laser weaponry, nuclear explosions, poison gas... what else?" He stopped triumphantly. Silence fell.

"What say you, Athena?" Zeus asked.

"Well, it certainly makes things difficult for me. This is no battlefield where I can mingle freely with mortals and offer them guidance. Yet during the Trojan War, I was with the Greeks, which enabled Odysseus to inspire his fleeing people to return to the fight. In truth, we all were together with the Greeks—including Poseidon. Though Poseidon was angry with the Laomedonians for not paying him after he had worked for an entire year building the walls around Troy."

 "I think it was all Heracles' fault," Hermes suggested.

"How so?"

"See, first, he killed Laomedon and conquered Troy. Then he took Priam's sister, Hesione, off to gift Telamon. When Priam demanded her return, Paris intervened—and the rest is well known."

It made them feel a lot better, but Artemis spoke out,

"Where is this mortal woman? Let us search for her."

"Indeed, we all should restore her to her lawful owner," Hera said cunningly.

Apollo beckoned Andrew forward. Trembling, Andrew began,

"Glorious people, gods, and goddesses of Olympus! I can't put into words how I feel. Am I dreaming? Or is this some divine joke? Everything I knew of you feels alive here before me. I can't tell you how I feel," he broke down.

His emotional appeal touched the present gathering, capturing the attention he desired and finding that he continued,

"So, honorable ones, please understand that I am here by accident—and on this island, I have lost my beloved girlfriend, to whom I had just proposed."

The council smiled sympathetically, all but mighty Zeus, who remained solemn.

Andrew concluded, "I do not know how to find Rhea, whether she is alive or hurt. I beseech your help."

The council began whispering, each god quietly speaking to the next—except for Zeus, who stayed solemnly silent. Over time, a deep divide appeared among the council; no one could agree on helping Andrew, for reasons only the gods knew.

Andrew added, "Greeks have always paid rich tribute and libations to all of you. Let me promise riches for all of you: the finest shining clothes, wild beasts, sweet vintage wine, and striking gold, platinum, and silver jewelry, and on top of it all, your name reaching as far as you travel on earth. I promise to be your disciple and to help the resurgence of your religion and its glory."

"Hold it! Why is a mere mortal assuring us of our lost glory? Why do we accept such a token tribute? Don't you all know the strength of my thunder surpasses all their arsenals combined? They are just creatures of mercy: destructible, perishable, and achievable—whenever and wherever we want." Zeus said.

Andrew trembled in fear, hope giving way to despair. This main is hard to appease.

"But, mighty Zeus, I have done no harm to this divine world, nor will I ever bring it any hurt. That is a promise. Furthermore, my father deals with modern ships in case you need any in the future."

Poseidon took offense,

"Well, I don't think we must work for his mate's recovery. His father has been actively building vessels, defying my role and domain. Hell with you, young man—you haven't seen my fury," he roared.

"Let us not succumb to emotion," Hestia said.

The council listened. Then the kind goddess rose and walked deliberately to the hearth, seeking strength for her statement. She rekindled the fire's glowing embers and spoke softly,

"Brother Zeus! You are the strongest among us, and we thank you for your help. But now we need to be wise enough to see that our power has diminished, and so has yours. Mortals have achieved incredible results with whatever Prometheus has given them," she paused.

"Foolish Heracles! He released Prometheus from his chains on the Caucasus Mountains."

"They are way ahead, and science attempts to clone people," Andrew informed.

"Never!" they all roared together.

"Silence!" Zeus commanded.

Athena remained untamed, but the others were shaken profoundly. Apollo opened his mouth again:

"Oh, Thunderer! Please don't lose your sense of justice. You uphold justice—now, show the same to this weak creature."

"Justice?" Hera interrupted mockingly. "Justice... it demands moderation and impartial wisdom. Can you assure us, god of gods, that you will remain dispassionate and fair?" She erupted into a symphonic, artful laughter that swelled and pierced the ears and minds of gods alike, with an uncanny trepidation.

Chapter Five-Poseidon.

Poseidon felt somewhat slighted in that council for a moment. In recent years, he had found it increasingly difficult to pass his domain over salt and fresh water to mortals. Though they undoubtedly built countless vessels, flaunting his territory without his help and reaching their destinations unaided, he had come to accept their arrogance—if they did what he initially set in motion: move and migrate, keeping the world in constant motion. Nothing is definite; nothing should solidify into lasting order, the very order that the big brother Zeus so passionately advocates. Yes, he struggled with his brother; though younger by birth to Cronos and Rhea, this brother had risen to a stature and glory that far surpassed what Poseidon could achieve.

Poseidon reflected. Furthermore, I don't even mind his status as the supreme god, he thought, telling others where they belong and what must be done to protect justice, honor, and continuity, so long as he pays me due respect and understands that the three of us brothers divided the world into three parts. We chose the heavens for him, the underworld for Hades, and the ocean for me. We left out Olympus and the Earth, for all of us, and we must not renege on these fundamental tenets of our existence.

For years, I have guided others to migrate all around. Who tamed the horses? It was I who urged the Aryans invading Greece to subdue this noble animal, which they then spread across the earth. Who thought of coupling in the form of a stallion with Mother Earth? To this day, they celebrate the Isthmia in my honor—every other year, horse races thunder near the Isthmus of Corinth.

Who is called *Poteidan* because *Da* was Demeter before the Olympians gave her any other name, and I am the husband of *Da*. I courted Mother Earth; thus, I am *Gaiaochos*.

I am not the destroyer they portray, nor the god of calamity they claim I am. I lead people to exotic and awe-inspiring lands, places they would never reach without my help. Think about what I did for Odysseus. Why should I help the Achaeans, then be so ruthless to one of their greatest soldiers—the one who made the Trojan War favor the Greeks, the one Athena favored the most among other Achaeans?

Poseidon thought, I have no shame in admitting my anger at the Trojans. The arrogant Laomedon, whom I served faithfully for a whole year as my penance for defying Zeus by building the wall around Troy, never kept his word to pay me and Apollo. There was more to it, but that made me furious.

Poseidon considered his role in destroying Troy. For a moment, he wondered what if he had helped the Trojans instead. Against the other gods' wishes, he once saved Aeneas's life. What if I'd drowned all the Achaeans' warships before they even landed near Troy? He could have changed history, stopped the slaughter, and prevented the Achaeans from desecrating Athena's temple.

Poseidon became critical of his actions and shook his head; the other Olympians would have prevented him from siding with the Trojans. No single god can change the whole world.

Achilles roared with rage. He had his spear in his hand, aimed at Aeneas. No one could stop that favored mortal from his wrath, except that I intervened at that critical moment. Aeneas was destined to carry the seeds of Dardanos across the sea to establish a new nation, and here Achilles was ready to lay him to ground for Hades. So, when I asked the gods at Olympus for help, Hera offered no resistance to such a plan.

I, the Earth-Shaker, moved quickly while rising a mist over the battlefield, obscuring Peleus's son's sight and lifting the son of Aphrodite above the noise and chaos of the fighting men, the determined horses, and the dying soldiers. I carried him far away, to a distant place untouched by death, so he wouldn't dare face the mighty Achilles again.

Now, he realizes what he had done after falling in love with Pelops and bringing him to Olympus, even before Zeus dared to bring Ganymede. His passion for Demeter and his courtship as a stallion, when she deceived him by turning into a mare, resulted in their union and the birth of Arion. With Medusa, he was so passionate that their union took place in Athena's temple, which led to her transformation into a monster. When she was slain by Perseus, the winged stallion Pegasus and a giant wielding a sword, Chrysaor, were born from Medusa and Poseidon.

As the god of the seas reflected on his past, he grew tired. His arms draped over the couch like a receding wave from the shoreline. Amphitrite, daughter of Nereus, watched him with eyes full of love. She remembered all the good years she had spent as his wife. She was no longer the carefree Nereid, dancing and frolicking freely, strutting atop the crests of massive waves, flirting with mortals and gods alike, yet never to be claimed—much like the goddess Athena. Then, one day, everything changed forever as Poseidon turned his gaze upon her youthful, tender self. She was so unrestrained, joyful, and oblivious to the harshness of male dominance: the strength, the brutality, and the sudden, ruthless ways they take control. So, the gentler, more delicate goddess found herself running away after he was done. Did she truly want nothing to do with it, or was that not the case? Wasn't there any joy, any reassurance, the mysterious desire deep in her heart that waited, lingered, afraid to be exposed— let someone come and take me?

Amphitrite didn't linger long, moving from east to west; the goddess of the sea wandered through her pain, shame, and agony to the other end of the ocean, where no one would see her, no one would ask her, "What happened, princess? Why are you so withered? Isn't there enough joy in your youth?" She had hidden in a distant palace, speaking only to the dolphins, easing her pain.

Poseidon is a fierce lover, a violent god who will reign at any cost, and he did find her. She was taken. The gods and goddesses watched the procession of dolphins, Nereids, nymphs, and sea creatures; all rejoiced as Poseidon became her rightful husband.

Amphitrite gently rested his hands on the couch to let him relax. He was pretty old; his ways were different from other gods, and she often felt the need for another companion—someone not so intimidating and threatening but with a sense of freshness and joy who could settle down instead of tearing everything apart. When Triton was born, a very unusual son, half-human and half-fish, it was hard for his mother to love or hold him. He inherited all the traits of his father, including a strong sexual desire, which made him ravish everyone he saw, regardless of gender. He didn't even spare the goddess Hekate.

Their daughter Rhodos married Helios, the sun god, and lived honorably. She had eight Heliades as her children.

Presently, Poseidon opened his eyes as if his daydreaming had been interrupted and asked,

"What does the gnomon say, dear Amphitrite?"

It's late; Helios is almost finished with his journey across the sky. How was the council meeting today? Was the father of all gods in good humor? How's Hera? And how are all the children?

"So many questions! Zeus seemed slightly lost; something was brewing in his mind. No matter how well I know him, it's often difficult to predict his next move."

The master of the sea paused, wiping his face before turning to his wife. Her ageless face, deep eyes, and affection brought him quite a happiness. His mind wandered, and he thought of many people—his other women and children.

He thought of Alcyone, daughter of Atlas, and their children— daughter Atheusa, son Hyperenor, and Hyrieus. Orion was born to Hyrieus, the great giant, so strong and beloved by Artemis. He

wondered why Artemis had killed him—was it in defense so as not to be ravished or out of jealousy over Eos' love for him?

Poseidon looked through the darkness outside, searching for his grandson's constellation.

"You'd better sleep early," Nereus's daughter said. "The sea gods are all coming to meet you at dawn."

"I know," he nodded absently, still lost in thought of his progeny.

People say many things about Scylla and Charybdis. Scylla was once in love with him, and Amphitrite grew fiercely jealous. One day, she poisoned the well where pretty Scylla bathed, transforming her into the six-headed monster who now haunts the Strait of Messina.

Charybdis was born from him and Gaia. Zeus couldn't tolerate her ferocious appetite, and after she stole Heracles' cattle, she was also transformed into a monstrous woman who drank the ocean in enormous swigs.

At the next dawn, while mortals on the island still slept, the water gods gathered and approached the palace of the god of the ocean. The waves crashed loudly on the shore in large proportions as the gods descended and made their way toward the mountain. From there, they took a winding path through the valley caves to reach the secret areas of the immortals, unknown to the residents.

They were all ushered in by the maid at Poseidon's door.

"Is Father awake?" Triton asked, curling and flicking his fish tail gently to avoid contact with the splendid furnishings of the grand palace.

"The master did not sleep well last night. Something is bothering him."

Ocean wiped the dripping water from his face with a towel and took a seat. Being a Titan, he keeps his distance from the younger gods.

His wife, Tethys, was more cheerful; she quickly proceeded to the interior of the house, saying,

"I will see Amphitrite and bring some ambrosia."

Leucothea and her son Palaemon sat quietly in the farthest corner, as if afraid of the actual gods. They struggled to adjust to their newly acquired godly status after being mortals for so long.

Proteus scrutinized the doors and windows as if looking for possible vandalism by the mortals. His paranoia persisted even though he could foresee the future.

Pontus remained deep in thought, emerging from the deepest parts of the waters.

Nereus tried to smile like an amicable father-in-law, but struggled wearily and kept brushing his overgrown beard with his long fingers. His fifty daughters, including Thetis and Amphitrite, were all grown, yet why would they constantly bother him for his advice?

Finally, Poseidon arrived. His sturdy, commanding silhouette, draped in a flowing silk robe, and his serious expression, with no hint of a smile, suggested grave matters to be discussed among the water gods.

They all bowed to him, as the gods in Olympus bow to Zeus.

"Let us gather in the council room," he ordained.

Once they were all seated and ambrosia served, the meeting resumed.

"May we know why the Earth-Shaker has summoned such a gathering of gods, as it entails great risk when all the waters of the world remain unattended by us?" Nereus spoke.

Poseidon raised his head gently, cast a swift glance over the curious faces, and said,

"My mind is restless, and my heart is distracted by an unknown threat…"

"Will the father ever think clearly before raising a tumult?" Palaemon sneered.

"Cease! Do not call me 'father,' Palaemon. You have shamed me," Poseidon roared. He could not forgive his sons for sleeping with their mother.

A profound silence fell. Then, Palaemon spoke with visible anguish,

"For the last time, let me clarify it was Aphrodite who cursed us to sleep with our mother after we denied her landing on our island," he hissed.

Amphitrite smiled as the ambrosia was served.

We need to stay alert. There's a suspicious mortal on our island. His mate is missing, and our all-seeing eyes can't find her. She's either dead or concealed. If dead, where is her body?

"Perhaps eaten by some fierce animal?" Tethys offered.

With no skeleton found anywhere. Was she dragged into the beast's lair? I am restless. Something is wrong—an omen has been sent. Did you sense any hint of it?

No one moved. The commotion grew into an atmosphere of distrust toward the Lord of the Oceans.

I know you all seem quite annoyed by this simple event in a mortal's life, but don't forget what led to the fall of Priam's kingdom. It was also unexpected that Helen's abduction could spell the end for that noble race, except for a few.

"That was a matter of justice. Zeus could stand for nothing less, as Paris had done by taking away Helen: it was unjust for a guest, impious for a king, and they had incurred the wrath of Hera, Athena, and you," Leucothea described.

"That is how mortals are shown the way," Amphitrite added, "so the gods set the paths of just and unjust, honor and dishonor, truth and falsehood."

Poseidon remained unsatisfied. He shook his head and declared,

I command all the gods and goddesses of distant and nearby waters to be watchful and cautious. Keep an eye out for upcoming signs of trouble. Something sinister is brewing somewhere, and we should ask Phoebus Apollo to consider this and reveal it to all of us, since he is the knower of the past, present, and future.

At this moment, all the Masters of Waters—those of the seas, rivers, and streams—rose from their seats and bowed deeply.

Within minutes, the ocean roared into massive waves; rivers overflowed their banks; streams surged with renewed power, as if they all had a single goal: to find a mortal, a remnant of a mortal, or even a group of mortals.

The next day, the island's citizens gathered in and around the small harbor. A rumor spread among the men working on ships, fishermen in their boats, and a few of their maidens. They had seen a small piece of land that had recently emerged southwest of the island, only a few miles away, and some claimed to have landed there. This had been going on for some time, but now skirmishes had arisen between the old settlers and the newcomers. The sheriff heard all the complaints and planned to resolve all the disputes that day. However, he was unsure who should control the smaller island or how to introduce the people to the controlling god. Heracles called an emergency meeting with Zeus to inform him of the situation.

The other gods had no problems except for Poseidon, who believed the virgin ground was formed from the ocean—his domain of endless waters—and that it had placed an offering to its master. Therefore, he claimed the new land belonged to him, vowed to build a temple there, and appointed a priest to perform the rites.

Athena took great offense at this claim and immediately staked her own claim on the tiny island. She believed she could build a civilized society by offering her advice and strategy, which she would use to guide her reasoning over emotion. She would teach mortals handicrafts and arts, including weaving, and protect the core values of the community, such as law and justice, which Poseidon would most likely lack.

All other gods were already weary of this quarreling duo, especially after Aris brought up the past dispute over control of Athens for discussion. They seemed least concerned with who had initially founded the town.

Therefore, Zeus asked Heracles to visit the island to settle disputes between mortals and these two immortals, and to make a decision based on whatever evidence they presented. By nature, Heracles was very daring and didn't care who his enemies were, but this time, he was worried about outsiders, especially the government soldiers. He knew that sooner or later, the map would reveal the new emerging island, and radar would detect it, prompting the Greek army to arrive and evaluate the land.

Heracles approached Poseidon, seeking cooperation in exchange for rights. Power is a strong motivator even for gods. It is the ability to impose one's will on others despite resistance. But how do these gods wield power? Heracles mainly uses brute force. He is strong enough to subdue any mortal and even an immortal. Others prefer persuasion, a familiar approach of Athena; she educates and convinces her audience through extensive knowledge and reasoning—the power of knowledge. Aphrodite, like Hera, offers earthly gains and wields power through wealth. Wealth, force, and knowledge are the three sources of power.

Why did Athena want to acquire Athens in the past? Why would Poseidon do the same? Were they driven by a desire to claim more land, or was it a hunger for power, to gather more followers for the future? What motivates the gods to pursue their goals with such relentless determination? How does this differ from mortals?

Mortals are naturally inclined to possess various attributes and possessions that support biological reproduction, mating, and procreation, such as land, shelter, food, money, and so on.

If gods couldn't restrain their desire to be in race, how would a mortal be expected to contemplate and appreciate what they already possess?

Did Athena need more land to demonstrate her power through material gains, such as shelter, agriculture, food, commodities for trade, social standing, or wealth, to find a mate? All of these seem unsuitable for a goddess, especially one who is a virgin.

Back on the mainland, as dawn began to shed its golden light, the farm cows moved restlessly with full udders. The enslaved people rubbed their sleepy eyes nervously, checking if their master was still asleep, and that's when Andrew would soon start his work. He would fetch one bag of grain at a time and carefully place it inside the shop. He had developed a routine; now he finishes his work quickly and has time to roam when the shop is closed.

Stepping outside into the morning chill, he stretched his arms and back, smelling the morning scent of the wildflowers growing in the surrounding bushes—smiling yellow crocuses, steady blue hyacinths, and fragrant white cliff roses. A sharp pain struck his healing wound. The cold breeze caused the chestnut and oak trees to sway, tilting their branches sideways. Andrew decided to walk toward the harbor. The harbor was small and sheltered a few dozen boats belonging to local fishermen. They have been in the same business for generations; their vessels bear the scars and marks of age. They wear oversized tunics and old hats; many have long beards and unkempt hair, and they always carry a scent of fish.

When Andrew arrived at the quay of the small town, he felt as if the harbor had remained unchanged for hundreds of years, with just a few shops and almost no breakwaters. Neither gods nor men had tried to build walls here, preserving the beauty and natural charm of the harbor. Several small fishing boats gently bobbed in the green waters, while buyers and sellers haggled over the left corner of the pier in a lively fish market.

A small group of men gathered at the pier, talking and appearing eager to board a few larger boats. Many of them could undoubtedly qualify as what the Greeks called monoxylons—boats carved from a single tree. The boats and canoes here were built further south, near the island's southern tip, where docks were used to make boats as large as ships and to repair them in dry dock. Fishermen still preferred large tree trunks, cutting or partially burning them to form hulls. Outriggers were commonly used.

A large fishing boat was sailing back to its assigned slip when the stern man harshly spoke a few Greek expletives in heavy accents to a young guide on the pontoon. The port side crashed against the pier, causing a loud commotion. The rowers stood up just before some were thrown overboard to the starboard side, landing in the shallow water and yelping for help.

Amused, Andrew chuckled. At the same time, one of the men swam back and spat at Andrew in disgust. He started helping the crew by bringing them onto the dry pontoon. The boat wasn't severely damaged, and calm returned. Andrew soon made friends with some of the crew.

Later, the crowd grew larger, and tension increased on the harbor side as rumors quickly spread that some land would be distributed on the newly discovered island later that afternoon. Many boats were prepared to set sail for the Aegean Sea, eager to find this new place.

Andrew sailed with one of the boats later that afternoon, as he had nothing else to do.

When they reached the new island, men scattered to different spots, riding sturdy donkeys to examine the land that had just appeared. After a few hours, the sound of bugles and drums drew people to the island's tip, where most boats were moored. Initially, there was some confusion and a lot of curiosity, but soon, a nobleman appeared on higher ground so everyone could see him.

Suddenly, someone announced loudly, as if introducing the current dignitaries. The names sounded like river gods familiar to everyone.

I am Achelous and live in the Achelous River. You all know me for my defeat in wrestling with Heracles and losing my sweet Deianira.

With me stands Alpheus, from his river, whom you know for his pursuit of nymph Arethusa to Syracuse before she was transformed into a spring by Artemis.

On his side stands our venerable Asopus, father of naiads including Aegina and Sinope.

After him, Inachus, the master of the river Argos, who gave his territory to Hera instead of our lord Poseidon.

Scamander is busy talking with his friends Cephissus, of river Attica, and Peneus of river Thessaly, who is well known for his daughter Daphne, loved by Apollo. Scamander fought against Achilles in the Trojan War, and when Achilles polluted his river with dead bodies, it overflowed its banks, nearly drowning Achilles.

Now, by the name of the Thunderer and the god who is fair to all, I name this land Poseidon's. He does not claim it for himself but for the people who have gathered here or who will soon arrive when the news of its emergence spreads, carried by the north wind. In return, he offers the ability and skill to control the waters, so they serve humankind's needs and churn the sea's treasures for the fortune of its residents. He will bring prosperity and power by saving the pious on stormy, struggling vessels and drowning the marauders, the pirates, and the deceitful diabolical.

The crowd cheered loudly, expressing their joy. Poseidon shook his head in response.

The din of applause, whispering farmers, and the rustling of a few handsome young men, oblivious to the proceedings, gathered more for *faut de mieux,* and it all combined to overwhelm Andrew. He slipped back toward a corner beneath the shade of a tall poplar.

Before he could settle into his reverie, a gentle yet firm hand tapped his shoulder. He turned to meet those fiercely green eyes he had only recently seen. Athena beckoned with a smile, and when he stepped closer, she whispered,

"Andrew, you must protest his claims."

"Why? Why should I get his wrath?"

She quickly murmured, "Poseidon cannot rule this land. He would destroy it. I alone must teach the people everything—agriculture, shipbuilding, weaving, pottery—and how to defend this country against invaders. Go, challenge him."

Andrew moved to the front and headed toward the center, where Heracles was discussing the agenda with his team of lawmakers. Frightened, he turned to leave, but a steady white arm, the goddess's arm, grasped his hair and whispered in his ear,

Go and speak. Fear not, mortal; fear not, you cannot be harmed. Hold onto this scarf.

She handed him a red scarf. Andrew started sweating as the absurdity of challenging the god of the ocean overwhelmed him. He was aware of Odysseus's fate. By now, he had long suspected these actors and actresses of being gods and goddesses.

His conscience wouldn't let him move, and his feet felt glued to the sandy ground as he approached the speaker.

For a moment, he couldn't speak. His voice wavered badly. Then, locking eyes with the goddess, he started:

"Why should we trust you? The Moirai only know our fate, while we toil each day for mere sacks of barley. You have all the comforts and desires we utterly lack: warm halls, fresh cheese, refreshing wine, and tender, pretty women. Here, we survive in poverty and abject deprivation, facing a bleak future." He paused, sensing the crowd's intense attention, and

he continued with reckless courage, "May the god of justice hear our prayers. May the gods and goddesses of Olympus be kind? Déjà vu—the familiar Athenian story of dominion and dominance by the King of the Ocean, the Lord of the Seas. Let us invoke the goddess Athena on this auspicious afternoon and pour a libation of the finest wine in her honor, as well as in honor of all the gods and goddesses."

The crowd eagerly accepted his request. From the boats, some Oinochoes appeared, and people started pouring wine for the goddess Athena. Despite his obvious discomfort with the mortal's suggestion, Poseidon kept a slight grin. One of his river gods whispered with contempt and scorn,

"Impiety. Disrespect! Foolish mortal!" he muttered beneath his beard. "Cousin of Odysseus. Imbecile. Let his scatterbrain drift to the ocean; let his vessel sail smoothly over peaceful waters—then let him ask for Athena."

The crowd gradually became restless, eager to hear the final word about the new town they would inhabit and claim. The susurration grew louder as Heracles stood to give his verdict,

In the name of Father Zeus, wielder of thunder, let us gather a council of citizens to carry on the management of this small island. People step closer, all volunteers for the same, and say loudly which god they intend to propitiate today.

They performed an excellent trick. About ten wise elder men stepped forward and started an informal discussion.

"Kalispera," the leader said to everyone. "Watch for the signs, listen to the trees, and seek divine guidance to decide who will lead us."

The people agreed, and they all looked around for divine auspices: a pair of doves flew past gracefully; a south wind rustled the tall oak trees; and a boat's crew sang an old love song.

Suddenly, the wind picked up with fierce speed. The tree moved violently; its rustling leaves became chaotic. Birds fluttered and flew in fear as people scattered in horror.

Andrew stood perplexed.

"Bad omen!"

"Let us run!"

"The gods are angry!"

Poseidon was nowhere to be seen. He had walked to the shoreline where his feet were submerged. Then, suddenly turning back to the crowd, he hurled his trident with great force. It struck the ground directly beneath him. Pure water gushed out, washing the faces of those nearby, and this happened again and again as more springs emerged across the tiny island. Everyone was drenched as a new fountain appeared out of nowhere near their feet, and people responded joyfully. Nothing was wrong, as the familiar signs of Poseidon were received with reverence and wonder.

"We pray to the god of the ocean, the mighty lord who wields the trident. Let us make him our patron," The older man declared.

People cheered wildly. From the large oak, the rest of the birds took flight in a circle. A tearing sound started to deafen everyone as they looked toward the tree with terror, for it was leaning dangerously and was being forcefully pushed by the wind before crashing onto the island. Few underneath ran for their lives as a loud thud echoed across the land—it was over. When the thick leaves and busy branches lay helplessly down, the sky revealed a new view of the island. People saw the orchard just beyond where the tree had once stood tall, hiding rows of gnarled-trunk trees with silver-green lance-shaped leaves that shimmered in the sunlight, along with small white flowers, which probably would produce green fruits.

Andrew ran toward the olive orchard and shouted, "Athena's gift! Let us honor her. She will bring us food; she will bring us prosperity!"

The people were so confused that they dared not speak, fearing the wrath of the other god. Before they could decide what to do, numerous wells or springs erupted all around them. Here was a spring, there a spout, here a stream, and there another spray. Soon, the sandy beach appeared submerged in water, and the men struggled, unable to keep their footing; they had to swim and wade through the rising flood. The force of the water increased rapidly, flooding the island in an instant. People were swept away as panic took over; realizing the danger of drowning, they frantically swam toward the boats, which were swaying so violently that it seemed they might not hold much longer. Andrew, along with several other men, swam to the nearest vessel and quickly grabbed the oars.

Soon, the remaining boats sailed away, and the people looked back at the island, now gone without a trace. For miles and miles, only the ocean roared and crashed, churning white foam that seemed filled with vengeance and divine wrath.

Great Poseidon wouldn't be defeated this time.

The fishermen on one of the boats opened a bottle of wine and a loaf of bread. They had barely poured the wine and broken the bread when everything shook violently from a massive wave that nearly tipped the vessel on its port side. The mast made a sharp noise, and the fishermen jumped for the rigging, some struggling to pull the halyards, others checking the sheets. Andrew couldn't hold onto anything and slipped quickly; as the boat tipped to starboard, he was thrown into the water, hitting his head against the rigging. Then the sail tore, the mast cracked, and the boat capsized.

Andrew tried to float but was tossed and turned by the towering waves. He saw great walls of water erupt from nowhere, swelling up before crashing down on him. Water surrounded him; there was nothing to grasp except more water. Eventually, he became sluggish and exerted more effort to survive. Around him, men bobbed helplessly with the current, feeble and forlorn. Feeling that the end was near, he gave up his struggle for life. He experienced profound peace, life gyrating with undulating sheets of happiness, moments of ecstasy from his childhood: his first baseball bat, his little Labrador puppy. He also saw his mother's eyes before she left his father: deep blue, heavy with guilt, yet void of tears. In that quiet farewell, he called out sincerely to Rhea, wishing she were there to know he was dying.

Later, when the sun set over the horizon, only a few boats reached the island; most never came back. Andrew was seen floating near the shore, wrapped in a divine scarf, until a large wave crashed again, tossing him over the dunes and pulling the scarf back into the ocean.

Athena was seen on the shore, with furrowed brows, drooping eyelids, and the corners of her mouth turned down, her pretty jaws tense as if about to burst.

She stood there in utter silence, a vanquished goddess.

Chapter Six – Athena

Athena sensed that Hephaestus was scheming against her father. He had seen the vehicle that had fallen to Earth and had even met the mortal. But he knew more than he admitted—much more. He was not perfect, far from it. Yet she owed him for his role in her birth: how he split Father Zeus's head with his mighty axe, allowing her to emerge; a warrior goddess born not from a mother's womb but fully grown, splendid, and armored. Métis was wronged, and Athena understood her pain, distrust, and betrayal when Father swallowed her to prevent the rise of a stronger god. But he could not bear the headache that followed, so she had to appear, clad in battle gear and shouting a fierce battle cry that made it clear to both gods and mortals who would be second in the pantheon.

She felt empowered by her own strength within the family of gods, along with many responsibilities, and often looked up to Zeus for guidance. Hera was more like a cousin than a stepmother. She never stopped whining and grumbling about their father's other relationships. How could she advise Hera about marriage when she had never been married herself? Once, Hephaestus asked Father Zeus for her hand as a reward for delivering her from his head, and Zeus had unwillingly agreed. Then the ugly god took her to his bed.

She was utterly shocked by his advances. She couldn't tolerate his touching, the proximity, and his warmth. She had repeated many times that she was not the bride he wanted, but all her protests went unheard. Driven by intense passion, he chased her unrelentingly. When he approached, his love seemed to ignite his grotesque body; she leapt to her feet and ran away without looking back. His passion raging, his masculinity had coated her alabaster thighs, and she wiped them as a virgin would. The seeds fell onto Mother Earth, Gaia, who had to carry her son Erichthonius.

Athena bore her son with great anguish. How could she hide him? What could she do to make sure the gods never find out she had a son? She entrusted him to Kekrops's daughters: Aglauros, Herse, and Pandrosos, trusting them with her little secret.

"Please, do not open the basket," she had whispered.

But alas! Aglauros, the same girl who once asked for gold from Hermes to meet her sister Herse, had pried through her secret. The sisters eventually had to end their lives by committing suicide, unable to bear the heavy burden of guilt from their deception.

Athena represents all wisdom, and she alone, aside from her father, can throw the thunderbolt. She oversees law, order, and justice just as she protects the city.

Unlike what happened recently when a new island emerged, long ago, when Kekrops became the first king of Attica, and they were deciding which god would preside over the land, Poseidon suddenly appeared and claimed the city. He was so furious that he struck his trident into the ground, and behold! A freshwater spring burst forth, providing water, the most essential element of life. But Athena was undaunted, and she cleverly called Kekrops to be her witness, having planted the first olive tree on the Acropolis. The gods favored her because of her witness, and Poseidon was outraged over the entire situation. He called the waters of the world to flood Attica. He is her uncle, yet he remains reckless, resentful, and capricious. She often had to keep him in check.

"Mother Hera would like you to meet her," the maid announced.

Hera called. I wonder if Zeus is planning some new splurge," she said softly.

The maid smiled.

Whenever there was trouble in their marriage, the goddess Hera would have a premonition and call all her trusted family members to gather information. Zeus might have been seeing someone new; he could love outside his marriage, which would challenge the rules of the relationship that Hera tried so hard to uphold. Hera never strayed from the rules of cohabitation. Once, she was outraged, but she still didn't sleep with anyone else; she had just borne a son by herself, Typhaon. Her other children were two sons, Hephaestus and Ares, and two daughters, Hebe and Eileithyia, who were well known in the kingdom of the gods.

Now Hera was troubled, and she called Athena.

It was worrisome. Athena hoped Hera was not planning anything unwise.

She walked outside, and the cold breeze gently stroked her face. Pallas Athena began to realize that something serious was in the air. They were talking about Andrew, a handsome man who had tried to make his case in the council. Andrew, whom she had recently chosen to help her, and whom Poseidon had called the cousin of Odysseus. Can you believe it? Odysseus—the king of Ithaca, a father, and a husband who would do anything to return to his beloved wife, Penelope, despite the tumultuous wrath of Uncle Poseidon against him. Athena looked deep inside her soul. Did she miss Odysseus? She is the goddess; she has no emotions and is barely a conduit of wisdom, which flows through her, unmoved by her feminine stream of desires. She shook her head, took a deep breath, and felt a void within her.

Then she pondered: why should things always go the way they had for all those years that passed without her, without her realizing her own dreams, the sweet dreams, the softer desires, the ripple she felt when she saw someone—someone strong, someone who would not buckle under mortal pressures, someone she could trust and still be the goddess she was; someone who would take her close to his chest and utter a few words that would bring a mild blush to her pretty cheeks; one from whom she didn't have to run, who wouldn't scatter his manhood on her, but would give it only when she was ready— and ready to merge with him in the most beautiful union that Athena had avoided, in a way that she wouldn't be ashamed of carrying the child, but proud to say: yes, this is my baby, another offspring of the god family, another bearer of wisdom, justice, and crafts.

Athena decided to look for Andrew's mate, Rhea. Justice required wisdom.

Is Odysseus back?

Athena took the narrow path leading to the colony of mortals.

The afternoons in Greece were warm and languid. The people slowed their pace; the agora lay quiet and heavy with stillness, while dogs curled lazily in shady nooks, quite content. Athena walked past the houses of the poor, where she saw the same girl in a shabby tunic pause again from her busy schedule of tending to the house, the pets, and her sick parents. What was lying in her fate? Would she ever escape this misery? Athena froze near the little house, cast her green eyes on the girl for a trice. Then, with a smirk, she walked briskly past the little girl.

The fruit seller tried to fend off the hovering flies with a piece of dirty cloth.

The tavern looked forlorn from the outside. Here, they all gathered for a drink, to forget their day's toil, to vent all their frustrations and abuses, and to share their dreams of being freed.

Athena looked around and, in a bold move, stepped inside. She turned her himation inside out to look like a commoner.

The dim light inside, from the candles, the soggy smell of the shoddy wine, and the putrid air of warm sweat, all of it turned her gut, but she stood valiantly. The wife of the owner spotted her and greeted her with a surprising shimmer.

"Is the lady lost?"

Athena thought quickly,

"No, I am truly thirsty," she replied.

"Please, come in. I'll serve you some wine," she offered.

Athena sat quietly in a corner booth. A man nearby nearly fell out of his chair, rubbing his eyes in disbelief; a fair woman was rare here unless she was a companion. So, he decided to move closer,

"Is the lady willing to share a pleasant moment?" he asked.

Athena nodded. He leaned in close, almost touching her side, then extended his palm, revealing a gold coin that gleamed, smeared with his sweat and embossed with Artemis' head. Athena smiled and accepted the coin. The woman brought wine and poured it into two goblets, all the while watching Athena with simmering curiosity. The man took a sip and coughed. Athena reached for the goblet but hesitated. The woman left.

"What should I call you? Your eyes are greener than the island's grass. You seem… different. Unlike our women," he said, intrigued.

"I'm here looking for someone… A man named Andrew. He's new to this island."

The man shook his head, then resumed as if ignoring her.

"I have more gold coins at home."

Athena poured her wine into his empty goblet. He drank with a mix of amusement, served by the lady, and wiped his greedy lips with the edge of his tunic.

"I take you where strangers dwell at this time."

 Athena took time.

"To the north side, where shops are better and food is fresher, where xenos wander the streets."

"Well then," she mumbled.

"Want me to do the dirty work? Come with me, and no one will bother you. Pantremeni?" he asked lustfully.

(Pantremini-married)

"I am not married. My family lives on the other side of the island, but they wouldn't mind."

Athena waited outside as the man paid for the wine.

They walked briskly toward the north side. He opened further, saying he heard someone crash here from outside.

"I know we are not supposed to entertain any strangers, but how long will our island survive with no contact?" he mumbled.

"We've survived so far, haven't we?"

He shook his head gravely. He wondered if this man was a harbinger of people with new faith soon to infringe on this island.

"Not if we stay united and protect our land. Zeus won't let us down," she assured.

"If he ever gets the time… with all he has to do."

"Like what?" she pressed.

"You know... I shouldn't, but it's all divine." He demurred, then, encouraged by Athena's steady gaze. "Finding another goddess or mortal to ravish, like many in the past—like Europa, Io, and many more," he sneered.

"There is a reason behind everything our gods do, whether it's creating Europe or preserving justice in this world through their lineage. Hey, the gods are just like us — imperfect. Would you believe in a god who is flawless?"

"Hum… The world outside tends to believe in flawless gods and a source of all good?"

"Why do we have to fabricate when we've had our gods for ages?"

He did not argue, but he hinted at what made the new gods more popular.

Athena tried explaining that their gods were omnipotent and omniscient, asking if he knew what that meant. She was surprised when the man asked,

"Not omnibenevolent?"

She wanted to say: well, the philosophers have created some models of human behavior—the ultimate human being, their god—and there could only be one. Because if there were more than one, both would be similar, since their qualities would have to be the same—the shining example. And don't you think it would be absurd to have more than one character with similar habits? But she didn't say it.

"Lady, who are you trying to give me all this heavy stuff?" he asked in surprise.

Athena turned her gaze to him unblinking, and he, for a flash, froze.

"I learned from my father,"

"He must be wise…"

Athena straightened her posture and smiled kindly. They saw a row of shops selling books and shoes, with jewelry, perfumes, and clothes in the distance. Here, people moved slowly and relaxed.

"See that lame guy, he was seen with the Xenos," he pointed.

Athena gently pulled Hephaestus aside, asking where Andrew was. Hephaestus was in no rush to answer and went back to looking at the silver cups being sold.

The man waited there for Athena to come. When she returned, they continued walking from shop to shop.

"He is not here," she predicted, closing her eyes briefly before freezing in her place, completely silent with her eyes closed as if in a trance.

The man looked at her with horror.

"Are you sick?" he asked.

Athena opened her eyes and said,

"Never been better. Let's head toward the theatre."

Andrew sat on a bench, watching people buy tickets. His face looked different, with some stubble grown. Every day was a surprise for him, and every meal felt like a gift. But he hadn't gone without food or drink so far, thanks to these people and their generous gods.

He heard his name and was captivated when he saw the source. Was he dreaming, he wondered? She was back again. He looked at her shoulders, arms, and breasts. He gazed firmly, unlike the Greeks, who don't prefer to stare directly. His mouth dropped open in awe, and his whole body felt a rush. He shook his head in guilt.

"Come with me," the goddess said, reminiscent of the moment years ago when she had pulled Achilles' hair on the battlefield to stop him from striking Agamemnon, and Achilles had obeyed her with reverence.

Andrew rose, and his tall figure stood beside her. His unshaven face showed a childish fear, for he had felt her strength by now, as if he knew who she was, and his face changed to one of pleading. The goddess sensed him as well and then trembled softly, so her feelings wouldn't give her away, and her womanhood remained hidden.

She quickened her pace, making it difficult for Andrew to catch up. Meanwhile, the older man who had spent the gold coin for Athena grew impatient and breathless.

"I can't walk so fast, I'd better go. My gold coin?"

Athena opened her palm, and the coin shone again. Then she took out several more coins from inside her chiton.

"You would be better off with your spouse," she said softly.

At last, they reached the same dense forest where he had been before with Apollo.

Andrew noticed it was a small dwelling, unlike what he had seen recently.

"I don't live here. Are you hungry or thirsty?" as if she could read his mind.

Andrew nodded. The goddess clapped her hands, beckoning a maid.

"Some fruits, bread, and wine," she requested.

After he had had his meal, she asked him,

"Now tell me about her. Who is she? What does she look like?"

Andrew wiped his face and began,

"By the way, you almost got me killed the other day. But now I understand why you offered me the scarf, and I'm very grateful. Now, as for Rhea, she is my life. After losing her, I realized how much I loved her. I've never felt this way before. She is helpless, alone, and I'm lost here, cut off from modern civilization. No one here understands me, and I have no way to connect with my people. How am I going to find out where she is?"

"Do not seek help from outsiders," she said grimly.

Andrew looked at her sternly.

Athena's cheeks flushed red at the mortal's arrogance, and her eyes locked onto his, unblinking.

Andrew was afraid of those eyes; they were so deep and beautiful, yet, for now, so menacing, and he trembled. Athena didn't answer, which made him feel even more helpless.

"I remember you're one of them from the council. Playing goddess like the rest, but don't you see where I come from? Besides, your powers seem questionable; otherwise, you wouldn't be hiding here in fear and isolation." He appeared reckless and impolite.

To this, the goddess spoke in the same voice that could silence a thousand guns, but now much softer,

"What is fear? It's believing something is dangerous because it's likely to cause pain. We feel no pain… we just think about pain, mortal.

We live for mortals. One day, we'll bring all the glory and piety back as it was in the past," she started.

It began to drizzle. Andrew watched the time seem to recede as if it were churning, while it rained. Each raindrop rose back up after splattering into pieces, returning as a shining, beautiful droplet, and the dust motes flew backward.

The fall of Rome meant that everything disappeared, gone. The people turned to Christianity instead, and the same altars that once celebrated her in the Parthenon now worshipped a new religion.

The more he spoke, the calmer she got, as if she were a proud mother handling a stubborn child.

"That is what history tells you. We couldn't stop humans from glorifying certain philosophies, certain attributes," she almost cried.

"See, Andrew, we couldn't stop the violence they committed in the name of their religion, and, unfortunately, their god remained silent during all their brutality. But then, look at what has happened to those same people now. Rome wouldn't shine ever again."

She paused, and Andrew gradually emerged from her frightful presence.

"Do you harbor faint hopes that Greece will embrace the Olympians again?"

Athena was looking beyond him, or rather, through him, and she uttered, as if from a distance.

"Gods don't die. We shall not perish. We watch the misery of mortals from our places as they choose new gods.

We observe the endless cycle of destruction and conflict, where one seeks to eliminate the other for not sharing their beliefs."

Andrew regarded her prophecy but shook his head.

Athena found it amusing that the child was challenging the mother, while the baby looked quizzically at his creator's authenticity.

Andrew looked at her with many possibilities, trying to relate her to his understanding of apotheosis.

In different parts of the world, natural forces seemed beyond human reach, magnificent, and animism followed with a spirit in each part of nature: sky, earth, ocean, air, and tall mountains.

But then, as agriculture, rivers, rain, heat, cold, storms, and floods became unpredictable, the sun and moon were revered and needed to be appeased. Personification then began: Zeus controlled the weather, including thunderstorms and rain; Poseidon ruled the seas, causing storms and earthquakes; Gaia kept the earth stable.

When other mortals were born later and performed heroic deeds, they all came to resemble gods by apotheosis.

People who believed in them after their deaths felt compelled to spread their messages through storytelling and myths.

Then they preached to kings and queens, who, in turn, converted their subjects and captives to these beliefs, leading to the emergence of new religions. The new priests took on the role of controlling people by depicting images of gods that could never be proven or seen.

"Describe your friend again. How does she look?" Athena changed the subject.

Andrew described Rhea as best he could.

"Medium height, sun-kissed skin, hair just brushing her shoulders. Pretty blue eyes, thin lips that open to a smile worth dying for... and soft-spoken," he continued.

"Tell me something only she and you know."

Andrew couldn't think of anything off the top of his head. So many things—her moles, her emotions, her actions—yet then, suddenly, he announced,

"She's carrying…She told me before the crash."

Athena felt his smugness, a triumphant male, proud like a pheasant strutting across Mother Earth, and an unexpected helplessness rose within her, awakening the goddess with a surge of maidenly emotions and virginal suffering.

She asked no more. Andrew slept peacefully that night. The next morning, he was taken to the town's central area, where ordinary people gathered.

Chapter Seven- Dionysus.

The winter had been relatively mild, but the relentless sea winds and saltwater had left the town looking weathered. Winter starts in December and lasts through February. On this tiny island, people eagerly welcome spring in March, when the average temperature rises to 21 degrees Celsius, with little rain and no snow. The landscape blooms with vibrant colors, lush slopes, flower-filled meadows, and the ocean's waves become calmer. Overall, witnessing spring's arrival is refreshing and invigorating.

The festivals on this remote island follow a calendar similar to the one in Athens. They have lunar months that start with the new and full moon and then proceed to the old moon.

During Anthesterion, Demeter Chloe is honored for the sprouting of grains. However, on the second day of Anthesterion, a festival for Dionysus takes place with grandeur. This five-day celebration features drinking wine, dancing, and singing in praise of their vine god—Bacchus. Even women shed their secrets and dance through the streets, around the agora, and some flee to the mountains at dusk in wild frenzy.

Naturally, Dionysus was delighted. As spring brought fresh air and new life to farmers, the wine had to be sampled. The festival would start with Pithogia, the jar opening, followed by Choes, the Wine Jugs ceremony, and end with Chytroi, or Pots.

The island decorated itself with its finest ornaments for the ghosts and strangers. Mortals busy themselves painting their doors with black tar. Slaves and laborers carry wine in clay or wooden barrels. Fruits are brought to the sanctuary as the first offerings. Priests dart around in their ceremonial togas, and among all this, the little children jump about most joyfully, hoping to have wine in their small juglets.

Dionysus frequently visited the town and watched mortals undertake significant tasks. Yet he wondered: Why? Why do these people continue to honor him, a member of the gods' family who couldn't protect them from the invasion of foreign gods, their supporters, and the spread of their cultural values? Look at Athens: nothing reflects its glorious past—neither the language nor the religion they practice, and indeed not any festival it once hosted for the world. It now follows the calendar from January to December; it celebrates Christmas more than the Panathenaia; and all the sacred sites have been abandoned and left to decay. How can Greece restore its honor?

The shop owner initially asked Andrew to haul heavy wine barrels just outside, but then changed his mind and told him to take them to the contest area instead. Poor Andrew couldn't even move his arms and legs after so many trips to the shop.

"These are heavy," he protested.

They aren't that heavy. Besides, why do I need you? Move them, and you'll get the money and shelter.

"I cannot do it," he gave up.

The owner hinted he might need to report him to the authorities as a stranger to the island.

Andrew knew the sheriff—Heracles. He remembered the small cell he was taken to after arriving, where skeletons still lay shackled. Oh no!

He headed to the contest area with his share of barrels, loaded onto his horse-drawn wagon. The horse showed its disapproval and stubbornly stood its ground as Andrew yelled and pulled the reins hard.

The little boy who had helped him with directions sat beside him, grinning.

"Why are you so happy?" Andrew asked.

"I drink wine tomorrow."

"What! Do you drink alcohol? You are not even ten!"

"Over three, you can drink."

"What a country! What will happen today?"

"We go to the sanctuary and wait until evening. The priest pours the new wine for the gods after the Jar Opening."

"What happens after that?"

"Tomorrow is the real drinking. My dad drinks a lot. He might even win this year."

"Win what?"

"You don't know? The Wine Contest. You know Orestes—the one who killed his mother? He was offered a drink as a guest when he arrived here."

"Watch it, watch it!" someone yelled.

Andrew looked back just in time to see one of his barrels almost sliding out, tilting on the street, and ready to roll away. He jerked the reins to stop the horse, hurriedly got down, and tried to push the barrel back up, but his hands gave out, tired from the day's work.

"Move a bit," a man in a beautiful synthesis said softly.

Andrew scooted for him, and together they pushed the barrel up and tied the rope tightly around it.

Andrew thanked him while gazing at his details.

The handsome man smiled softly. He seemed to be of noble origin.

"Who are you? Who is your master? You don't look exactly like a slave."

"I'm not a slave. Just passing through tough times. I must make a living here."

"We all must make our living, don't we? If we don't… we perish."
And with that, Dionysus walked away in his own style: his
expensive robe, gentle manner, and effeminate personality left
behind a friendly aura.

"Wow! Such a gentleman," Andrew chuckled.

"He called you a slave," the boy quipped.

By the time they reached the contest area, the sun was softer. The
little boy went inside to call the owner, while Andrew hauled the
barrels inside one at a time.

He was surprised by the seating arrangements, tiny tables each with
just one rickety chair, as if everyone drank alone.

At the end of the day, Andrew earned a few coins as his pay.

"You can live in the room behind," the owner said. "There's a small
toilet, but you'll have to use the public baths."

Evening arrived with a festive mood. People walked to the
sanctuaries, men and women dressed in chitons, children in tunics.
Andrew felt out of place in his old tunic, which had become
smudged, torn, and wrinkled over the past few days. He bathed at
one of the public places and had a bite of porridge; meat was
expensive here.

He stood outside the sanctuary with a small crowd, watching with
curiosity the events that led up to the real drinking, like a longtime
resident of the island.

The next day, Andrew woke up late. He washed his face and opened
the shop since the owner would not be working that day. It was the
twelfth day of Anthesteria.

His day was mostly uneventful, with little work and just a few
customers. In the evening, he decided to go out to meet people and
make some friends; he needed trusted friends in this close-knit
society. Although everyone was kind, there was always a limit to

what they would openly share. No one seemed to know much about the outside world, only a few hundred miles away, the entire scope of modern civilization. It seemed like they had chosen this life, almost like the Amish, but how they managed to block out any modern influence was a complete mystery. There were no churches, no post offices, no courthouses. Was this place even on the federal government's radar in Athens? If not, why? Was it because it was hidden beneath those two mountain peaks? What happened to people like Andrew, who accidentally stumbled upon this place? He couldn't have been the first. Or was he?

His radio on the plane was still dead. He planned to return to try to fix that junk.

Andrew remembered Athena's displeasure when his last attempt to contact Athens by radio—calling the outside world for help—failed. This land was their last stronghold, and they wouldn't want to lose it. Then that's fine, my god! Andrew muttered. If these people aren't faking it (which he believes they are, a bunch of clowns frozen in time), they shouldn't be afraid of anything. This could be one of Greece's most popular tourist spots. He couldn't accept it as real; the thought was terrifying. He wasn't very pious, given that he had met gods. Have any of the Christian saints or even Pope Paul ever met these people?

I don't care. Let me find Rhea, and I'm going to scramble out of here. He mumbled.

At the large contest area, men gathered to join the drinking contest. The wine was ready after the gods had been appeased, and the whole town was excited for the event. The strangers and the ghosts seemed alike.

An older man began speaking to the crowd, who delighted in hearing about their past, their heroic figures, myths, and deeds.

"When Agamemnon returned victorious from the Trojan War, he seemed the luckiest and bravest man alive. He was blessed; his fleet of ships arrived back with no problems. The whole town was all up there to greet him at his palace. But Clytemnestra had taken a lover, and everyone knew."

"Clytemnestra? Beautiful Helen's sister?" an older man asked.

"Yes. Her husband Menelaus was Agamemnon's brother, the son of Atreus. The gods had cursed their house after their grandfather feasted on the flesh of his own child. Death was destined to follow them for generations. When Agamemnon sacrificed his daughter to appease Artemis, he invited his own death."

"How?"

"Clytemnestra could never forgive the murder of her daughter, Iphigenia. She'd welcomed him with sweet words, while he presented his booty, the beautiful daughter of Priam, Cassandra, his prize from the war, to his wife. He pleaded gently, Take care of this maiden from Troy, my award for the grand victory.

As the couple stepped inside, Cassandra screamed in terror-This is a house of death. Two people are going to die tonight, and one of them is me."

A silence prevailed as the narrator went on,

Cassandra was killed immediately, but then another horrible shriek shattered the palace, that of the dying king himself. The queen emerged with her lover, radiant, bloody, and unrepentant, boasting under her breath- I haven't sinned. I brought death to a murderer, the killer of my daughter.

Where was her son Orestes?

He was sent away as a child. As he grew, his mind tormented him to avenge his father's death. But how could one undo one wrong with another by killing one's own mother? Apollo, at Delphi, guided him: "Go, kill the murderer, and then atone."

He returned to his town and met Electra. The rest is known: he drove the sharp knife deep into the breast that once fed him, onto

Clytemenestra, and left the town as the Furies pursued him. He reached Athens, where he found shelter, food, and drink. There, Athena convened the jury, and he was acquitted of matricide. The Furies had turned here into the Eumenides, the protectors of suppliants.

The crowd listened with reverence, and they all praised Apollo and Athena for their roles in preserving justice.

"Take your seats, gentlemen. Everyone will receive equal amounts of wine. If anyone who speaks after the drinking begins will be disposed of. Take the largest swig you can. The jar will be refilled. The winner shall emerge at the end." The announcement came swiftly, and people rushed to claim tables; those who failed to acquire one stood near the walls.

Andrew found a table near the back, shoved and jostled by the strong Greek men. He only wanted a free drink, but the magnitude of the event and the people's enthusiasm to participate left him awed. The whole arena was filled with hundreds of contenders who sat eagerly, while a multitude of waitresses—like swarming butterflies—scurried around filling jugs. The burgundy wine looked different in each jug, carried by those colorful Greek women draped in various shades: from deep crimson to rosette, dahlia, magenta, maroon, yet all shades sanguine like blood. The thick scent perfumed the air, the blood of Agamemnon and the beautiful Clytemnestra.

Andrew glanced around to find a familiar face. He spotted his master at one of the tables and smiled, but the owner did not smile back, looking tense because of the competition. His eyes landed on Apollo in a corner, smiling and chatting with several mortals. Did they know who he was? He wondered if revealing his godliness would even matter—most likely, they would laugh and call him crazy. People here lived in a surreal world - they knew the gods yet behaved as if they didn't. Was he the only one who knew their secret? Not possible. They came too easily to him, and they made no effort to conceal it. Impossible!

Then Athena appeared, weaving confidently and elegantly through all the mortals. She was coming towards him, and Andrew was happy.

She leaned close and whispered,

"Do not drink. Be vigilant. Look for clues, help me."

"I am here to participate."

"Andrew, listen. Don't drink. Get up and follow me."

The man at the following table overheard and chuckled loudly,

"Go on, go! She's sweeter than wine. She wants you—ha! Ha! Ha!"

Andrew dug himself deeper into the tiny chair—he wasn't going anywhere. He looked around and noticed other men watching him as well.

"Hey, beautiful, take me instead," someone leered.

"You shall repent," Athena hissed and stepped away to the side.

The drums began, beating a slow rhythm to stoke excitement further, then escalating to a wild cadence. The men, now agitated, poured their jugs over their faces like some ding-a-lings' winos.

The wine went down his throat with no effect, and Andrew knew he could take a lot more. He was used to late-night drinking of pure whisky, rum, vodka—name any spirit. This was syrup to him. The servers ran around refilling the jars. This time, Andrew was able to laugh and smile at people. Presently, he found the girls attractive and wondered if they would mind. The men laughed and flirted, while the girls spoke in an equally coquettish way, touching each other fondly.

There was a sense of celebration, and Andrew felt the sensuality creeping in as the evening progressed. Many tables were occupied by women, who were not behind in drinking compared to the men.

The jars were emptying relatively fast. Andrew wouldn't give up. He gulped his portion and turned his face around for the next.

As night deepened, the seats emptied. Contenders either stumbled away or were dragged out for inactivity. No one was permitted to slumber or rest. The patience of the organizers and crowd was astounding. Andrew threw back another round in haste and coughed. He glanced at Apollo, still smiling, but Athena was gone. She must have left in disgust, he thought. Who cares? No one would help him anyway. Why don't I have a good time? He felt the candlelight growing dim and dared to touch one of the serving girls as she came near him. He touched her ass; she moved her hip closer, and he sensed the passion. When she returned to serve him again, he felt her again, and she stuck to him. Her bosom near his face, he caught the scent of her sweat—an exotic, rural scent.

Only five men remained. Outside, the night was thick and black. The sound and the screaming of people who had left earlier broke through—singing for Dionysus, god of the vine. He wanted to sing, too. Two other men collapsed onto chairs—quickly pulled out by the identical girls, dragged toward the door, left for their loved ones to carry them later.

"After the drinking is over, please do not throw away your jugs. Carry them, with your garlands tied around the jugs, to the sanctuary, where the queen will be married," they announced.

When Andrew looked around for more wine, he realized his chair was now surrounded by a crowd: men, women, organizers, and waitresses, all smiling at him. He had survived.

They spoke reverently of Dionysus the great and lifted him onto their shoulders for the walk to the sanctuary. They were dancing and yelling in celebration, and some were still drinking. The men made wild advances toward the women, who turned like maenads in their frenzy, but were gently rebuffed.

Andrew felt happy, exalted, almost like a king. He thought of all the stories he had heard about this festival. Why don't we have something like this back home? He mused. They drank outside the sanctuary as if to atone, as if reliving the sin of matricide, just like Orestes had done.

Andrew again felt exalted like a king; his head was heavy and fuzzy.

King Ikarios, whom Dionysus had first taught to plant the vine and press wine, must have felt the same way. Ikarios had invited his friends to drink, but once drunk, they believed he had poisoned them. So, they killed him. His daughter, Erigone, found his body and hanged herself in despair.

Andrew grew a little nervous as the crowd passed through dense vegetation in the dark. Was he safe? Was he about to become a human sacrifice?

Well, the Greeks didn't like the human sacrifice. And he hadn't shown any disrespect to Dionysus, unlike King Pentheus.

The cymbals and the flutes, the dancing and drinking, intensified near the sanctuary.

King Pentheus had failed to recognize Dionysus as a new god and had ordered his guards to seize him.

Dionysus had come with no resistance.

"Arrest him," he had said.

"The gods will free me from your prison," God had said.

They had tried to throw him into the prison—yet Dionysus emerged effortlessly through the doors, which swung wide open for him. Then he asked the king again to acknowledge who he was, but the king humiliated him again.

So, the story goes, the king's mother and sister became maenads and fled to the mountain after drinking wine. When the king followed them to see what was happening, the women leapt on him, tearing him limb from limb.

Andrew shuddered. He pinched his skin, checked his hands, and looked at his own feet to assure himself he was still safe.

"God! I respect all the gods. Please, just let me find her, and I'll be out of your face forever."

They dropped him down in the center, and the dancing resumed.

Then he saw the same man who had helped him earlier that day when his horse buggy got stuck and the wine barrels were slipping.

"Hey, see you again!"

"See you, son. Having a good time?"

"It is cool. Maybe when I return, there will be a festival like this one in my hometown."

"No. They won't allow a festival for Dionysus."

"We cherish freedom of religion," he asserted.

"Really? Just celebrate with us while you're here. Let destiny decide what the future holds."

"How about a future here? I don't see any. Rhea is lost forever."

Then Andrew pleaded with him, describing her as a woman with blonde hair, tanned skin, and a thin figure, knowing very well how vague his description was.

He said he hasn't seen her yet, but he would look among the maenads.

Maenad? What! Who is he?

Time will reveal. For now, watch the Venerable take their oath in the temple.

The queen led the prayers, and fourteen women received the oath. They were called the Venerable, chosen to serve the queen. Then came the moment everyone had been waiting for: the queen's marriage to the god.

Ostentatiously dressed, the queen's jewelry glinted above all else. She seemed hesitant as her maids escorted her toward the god.

"Wow," Andrew whispered, watching the majestic queen and her aura.

Then he turned toward the man with golden locks, the purple robe, and wreaths of vine. Andrew was left alone with joy bordering on ecstasy, but as he searched more for him, it turned to mild terror.

Chapter Eight – Ares.

The thirteenth day of Anthesteria, marked by pots and cereal, was over. Life, in general, had grown tedious again. Andrew brought the wine-filled barrels from the countryside and stacked them one on top of the other. His work was both challenging and tedious, and he disliked mornings. Afternoons were slow, except when customers arrived, at which point he would haul wine to their horse-drawn buggies. He had seen no trace of Rhea so far.

Andrew planned to reach his plane after dark and see if he could fix the radio. He was afraid people might discover he was trying to contact the outside world and destroy his plane. He preferred to take his time and be cautious.

When he arrived, it was already dark. He lit his candle and forced the door open. Once inside, he felt safe and shut the plane's door behind him.

Suddenly, he felt a deep sense of loneliness and desolation. His past seemed to swirl around him.

After fiddling with the radio for some time, he managed to turn it on. He had some signals.

Speaking softly, his head bowed low, he whispered,

"I need some help. I can't give—"

"Hello... Hello... We cannot hear you clearly."

"I can't speak any louder, I need to reach my family... My dad..."

"Who are you, and where are you?"

I'm Andrew Burke. My dad is Charlie Burke—Burke and Burke Shipbuilders."

The Athens control tower answered his call and tried to gather information from him. He was told that his father was running ads in newspapers and on television. An award was announced for anyone who provided information about him. At that moment, he heard some noise and had to stop talking.

"Someone is nearby. I'll call again tomorrow."

He shut off the radio and stepped outside. There was a faint noise—he thought it was a deer. But soon, he realized otherwise. A couple was very close by. He paused, intending to give them privacy, but they heard his footsteps. The man sprang up and threw him to the ground.

"Who are you? What business do you have here at this hour?" he roared.

Andrew remained silent.

The lady emerged, and Andrew gazed at her in awe. She wore a chiton that sparkled even in the dark, a chain around her silky neck with a pendant in her suggestive groove. She stepped forward, serene, unabashed, and spoke.

"Aren't you the same mortal everyone's talking about?"

He nodded, bowing his head respectfully.

"Ares, let him be free," Aphrodite commanded.

Andrew, Ares, and Aphrodite walked silently. They reached a sanctuary, and he opened the door. Andrew was surprised to see the enormous frescoes.

How beautiful, what are these paintings? he thought

The gods exchanged glances as if they read his mind, and she spoke,

"Thracian Ares comes from the northeast, born of Hera and Zeus. Here are the Aloadai giants, Ephialtes and Otos, who trapped him in a jar for thirteen months before Hermes rescued him, half-dead."

Andrew's mind flashed Trojan war!

"Yes." She read his mind and continued to describe the frescoes.

Athena took his weapon away when he was furious and ready to fight for the death of his son, Ascalaphos, at the hands of the Achaeans. Here, Diomedes is thrusting his spear at him, and he runs to Olympus. Here again, Athena hit him, and he fell flat.

Ares uttered in a vexed tone, asking why his heroic deeds weren't displayed. But she carried on in her lilting inflection.

Here you are, pleading to us after killing Poseidon's son, Harlirrhothius, for his attempted rape of your daughter, Alcippe. You were acquitted for once, since no one other than Alcippe came forward as a witness. She finished.

Ares's face turned grave as he spoke,

"We are worried about your presence here."

The silence fell on the halls heavier than Ares's spears as he paced with long strides, his jaws set tight.

"Because the mainland is venturing for my help?".

"No, because there would be unnecessary death and destruction

The twin peaks of our mountains are deceptive."

"It's hard to believe there has been no outside interference. Because the mortals here believe they live on a special island, protected and blessed, and they would never go hungry. They are born here, and they die here in peace." He continued.

"So why are you…?" Andrew asked.

"We don't know how you survived this ordeal," Aphrodite interjected. "Perhaps Zeus or Mother Hera knows more. That is why Athena is working for you."

Ares hesitated, then added, "We can't find any trace of your friend either."

Andrew became restless.

"She must be alive; we just don't know where…" he added.

"True, but where is she? And if she is hiding or planning something, we must know."

Andrew felt a flicker of relief—they hadn't heard him on the radio.

"This is our abode in Greece…"

And he trailed off, as if he wanted to say, "If we run into any more trouble, we will have to leave this island forever."

"I would promise to cooperate fully to keep this haven safe," Andrew said.

Aphrodite asked. "Would you like to live here?"

They exchanged glances, finding no answer from the mortal.

I need to be safe here- Andrew was thinking fast, these people have the power to hold Heracles down.

Ares was thinking the same, as he knew what Andrew desired. Oh, Heracles has done me enough harm. *Oh, my sweet Pelopia, with whom I had my bloodthirsty bandit son Kyknos, who built a temple from the bones & skulls of travelers. Heracles shot him down in one strike, and Kyknos was transformed into a swan and was placed among the stars in his constellation.*

He declined further involvement to help Andrew. These gods would never act against each other in a serious way for a mortal. Zeus could banish Cronus to Tartarus but not kill him. Ares was wounded by Diomedes but returned safely. Was it Zeus' authority, fear of retaliation, which allowed petty squabbles but no real war?

Or maybe because they were immortal anyway.

Chapter Nine – Hera.

As a little girl, Hera saw her image reflected in the pupils of others' eyes—her own reflection, which, of course, changed depending on who she was looking at. Though she wasn't aware of the difference, all the images were part of who she was or who she would become. She was not troubled by this, as she didn't have the leisure of visiting her inner faculties; the difference in many images blended all together.

And if it did add up to her image any time, she would sketch it so other divinities would know from her what Hera was all about. This little princess knew who was significant and who wasn't, who would appreciate a little charm and who wouldn't. She turned herself like a sunflower turning toward the sun. Sometimes, she would effortlessly lie, or at least subtly distort the truth, and over time, she had learned to twist the truth to the extent that she could no longer recognize herself, whether she was in the company of truth or total falsity.

She is the only goddess with whom Zeus consistently shares his bed, and she is also afraid to upset him. Her largest temples in Greece stand at Samos, Tiryns, and elsewhere. She brings the institution of marriage to a sacred level. The cow, peacock, and cuckoo are sacred to her. She is worshipped under various epithets: *Pais* (the girl), *Zygia* (the uniter), *Teleia* (the fulfilled), and *Chera* (the separated). Her children with Zeus do not play any significant role in Olympus like Ares, the most hated one, Eileithyia, goddess of childbirth, and Hebe, the cupbearer.

In Latin, *Herus* means master, the masculine of *Hero*, and in Greek, it means Earth. Then was she the sky goddess before she became a symbol of marriage? Some say the name was derived from the Sanskrit word *Svar*, meaning sky. She was worshipped long before Zeus. Hera was born of Cronus—the second sky god—and Rhea. She was born before Zeus, most likely on the island of Samos, near modern Turkey, and raised by Oceanus and Tethys. The river god Asterius had three daughters who attended to her.

One must listen to the story of Grandma Gaea and Mother Rhea to understand the goddess Hera. Only then is Hera revealed in her proper form, which has evolved and strengthened the female presence in the pantheon of gods. Her mother, the lovely-haired Rhea, was a Titaness born of Grandpa Ouranous, showering his affectionate rain on Grandma Gaea, producing the rivers and streams that run all over the world.

But alas! Instead of festivity in the house of Gaea, years of despair followed as the great sky god kept pushing his own children back into their mother's womb. They lay there in total darkness until Gaea made Cronus revolt and slice off his father's genitals in the middle of the night. Mother Earth received the spurting blood and gave birth to more children—the three Furies, or Erinyes: Alecto, Tisiphone, and Megara, who punish mortals for crimes against their own family, the race of giants, and the ash tree nymphs. Father Ouranous called these children the 'Overreachers.'

Cronus, the least violent among the Titans, was afraid of losing the kingdom to one of his offspring, as his mother Gaea had told him. So, like his own father, starry Ouranous, he hid his children—rather, he swallowed all in his belly.

Mother Rhea fled to Crete while pregnant with the youngest, Zeus. She had spoken with her grandparents. In a place called Lyktos, she gave birth to the future king of the gods and quietly passed the baby to her mother, Gaea, who hid him. Zeus never saw the dark side of life as Hera and his other siblings had, after being swallowed one after another by the powerful Cronus. They waited in a hollow cave within the divine gut, bereft of any hope for their glittering future. They wept together, without plans or clues. Then, after Zeus's birth, a massive stone appeared in the hollow cave instead of him. They were all surprised. This was different—something was planned by fate that the sky god Cronus was unaware of and had missed. The divine club of little children waited eagerly for what was to come.

This time, the gut shook fiercely as if it would tear apart, and the stone shifted inside. Father Cronus was given an emetic by his brother Zeus, in conspiracy with Grandma Gaea and Mother Rhea. The mammoth stone was forcefully expelled, and they all could see the bright light shining outside, where the muses sang, the fates spun, and the gods reigned. Then the impossible happened—they began churning inside. Father retched, and as if trying to atone for his sin, he vomited each child one at a time into the lap of their mother, Rhea. Realizing he had been tricked, Cronus called them the Titans—the Overreachers.

When she was sent away to be raised by foster parents, she did cry—that was when she first felt real emotions connected to her inner self, the little girl losing her mother. She did not touch any ambrosia for a long time. Her pain reflected in her tears that gathered on her rosy cheeks whenever she saw the Oceanids running to their mother and Tethys lovingly gathering her daughters. She knew she could not have her mother's embrace and settled for less. Then she developed ways to draw attention, which earned praise from the adults for being such an understanding child, such a beautiful goddess. Though she continued to feel the lack of warmth, she compensated for her sadness with a radiant smile whenever one of the gods would pick her up and shower her with admiration.

Oceanus, the god of all the waters, took her around the world. The little princess would hold onto him, awed by the speed at which he swam—his upper body strong like a human and lower trunk scaly like a fish. Thus, she learned the strength of the land from Cronus and the waters from Oceanus. She dreamed of a place where she would be the one asking questions, and one day she promised herself it would happen. Oceanus felt uneasy around this tiny but inherently decisive goddess, and instead of being filial, he raised her almost subserviently. Though she always made an extra effort to show him the esteem she believed he deserved, he knew she had somehow chosen him for her own sake.

But the three thousand daughters of Tethys teased her brutally as the "fake goddess." Fake, fake, fake, Pais. Hera would fill her cow-like eyes with transparent, pure droplets but would not shed them so easily. In fact, the Oceanids failed to see her broken. She remained the perfect *Pais*—the girl whom heroes would worship, offering votives and sacrificing lambs whose spurting blood mirrored the deeply seated pain she nurtured.

Hera never understood why those girls were so jealous of her. When they played outside in the meadows, collected flowers, and chased butterflies, she tried her best to mingle. Though she could not run fast and would be exhausted, she never betrayed any weakness. At the end of play, when they were utterly exhausted, Hera would call them to play even more, so that they knew she had won. That was how she ensured her place remained intact, and she wanted it no other way than by letting others lose.

She continued to win long after her childhood.

So, Hera was very grateful to Oceanus and Tethys, her uncle and aunt, for rearing her. The nymph cousins were all around her, but still felt very different. From a few years old, she sensed a lack of emotional connection from her parents. As she began her curious search as a child, often turning her gaze back to her mother for affirmation, she found either no one or someone who mirrored her, but for the wrong reasons as to why she was loved. Hera was the perfect child, who tried to be what her parents, her siblings, and her foster parents wanted from her. She developed a strong awareness of others' expectations. She could change so rapidly—almost by reading silent faces—that she was often surprised and confused herself about which version was her true self and which was merely a performance. She began to learn that it did not matter what she desired or wished in her heart, but what others needed to see in her. They all conveyed this to her, and she molded herself so efficiently and quickly that she became the ideal child—and later, one of the perfect goddesses who remained unspoiled.

"I hate the nymphs," she would whisper, but when they were around, she smiled at them as if eager to play. Yet she always remembered who she was—the goddess born of Rhea and Cronus. She knew how special she was, how powerful she needed to be, and she worked tirelessly to maintain that image. The emptiness inside—the voice that told her she was of no value without being someone with power expanded as she grew up. That she was undoubtedly superior to others was just her outside veneer covering a hollow inside that cried, *"You are worthless."* As the years passed and generations of mortals were born and died, the goddess Hera developed a hard shell that reflected what she believed in her mind: that she was charming, the most desirable, the strongest woman, and so many other qualities that other goddesses could not claim.

Hera was a goddess in her own right long before she became the consort of Zeus—an earth goddess for the Minoan people, with temples in Samos and Argos. Hera Parthenos (the virgin) was no less a force than Hera Teleia (the fulfilled, married). The virgin embodied strength devoid of petty emotions such as jealousy, vengeance, and the zeal to shun other goddesses or mortal women; she was the goddess of heroes. Fallen heroes were consecrated to this earth goddess.

Yet, all this led to her becoming one of the most jealous and vengeful women the gods had ever seen. Zeus caught her lying so much that she had become almost shameless. She had to prove herself right, even when she was unholy, unjust, and unkind.

She never realized how her narcissism had hurt all her children later in life, the same way that she was when she was reared. Unwittingly, she became the greatest narcissist. She believed she was special— and, of course, the most beautiful. She felt that power was not granted simply by being a born goddess but had to be earned above all other gods. Relationships were merely tools where one had to assess the status of the other constantly and either draw inspiration or distance themselves if unworthy, and ultimately, one had to possess power as evidence of superiority. In her assumed strength, she made decisions unilaterally, judged and condemned indiscriminately, and violated others' boundaries.

Her tendency to adorn herself for every little thing, every turn in her life, and to look better than the others, only grew stronger with time.

But she acquired the beauty that she was not aware of till she was fully grown. And who but her own younger brother, Zeus, would remind her of her womanhood?

One would find Hera *Teleia* an extraordinary beauty, clad entirely in royal pelops, her head crowned with a jeweled diadem befitting a princess and later, a queen. She carried her cuckoo, adored the peacock unwittingly, perhaps as she wandered away from her inner quarters. She enchanted the world with her colorful tail, yet deceived herself into believing what she knew was not true at all.

Hera couldn't be blamed for consorting with her own younger brother. An earth goddess had to unite with the strongest sky god— a befitting union for the cosmos. Anyone less than that might have brought about the end of this great beginning in the history of gods and mankind.

In the divine realm, relationships must be formed with such care that one is left with no broad choices but their own family. However, she avoided him for many years, mortals say three hundred in total, before she was tricked by a drenched cuckoo perched on her window on a rainy, stormy day atop Mount Thornax.

The cuckoo wasted no time claiming her, transforming into the mighty Zeus.

She married him. But Hera would not simply marry; she was the first goddess to be married legally and with elegance. Not even Grandmother Gaea or Rhea could claim this milestone in their relationships. Thus, in preparation for their marriage, Zeus and Hera subsequently left Crete and landed in the Garden of the Hesperides. Before marriage in a ceremony, she was offered the hair cuttings of nubile girls before their wedding at the altar—a ritual also honoring Artemis. The gods and goddesses joined in the sacred marriage, heiros gamos, unbeknownst to their parents. Aphrodite was happy and visited the garden, so did a lot of others, like Hermes, Peitho, and the Charites. Gaea gifted Hera the Tree of Life bearing golden apples, which Hera later planted in her own garden. This sacred marriage stands out as one of the grand celebrations of the Olympians, a festival which mortals shall emulate, and which Hera would protect fiercely.

She had her most wonderful, unblemished, and uninterrupted conjugal pleasures for the first three hundred years, during which she bore three children to the King of gods.

Although Zeus could get her to agree after a deceit in the form of a cuckoo, he remained flirtatious with numerous mates in his extramarital relationships. She had no choice but to chase her bad husband or curse the women, like she did to Io, turning her into a cow, or coerce Semele, Dionysus's mother, to ask Zeus to reveal his true form, which he did unwillingly, arriving with a blaze of lightning and thunder, enough to immolate her, along with many others.

Hera fought with Zeus almost daily. Their conflicts sometimes turned violent; he had shown his anger when she tried to raise a revolt in Olympus against him. The gods conspired to tie him down on his couch while he slept. Thetis arrived with the hundred-handed Briareus, and Zeus was freed. In response, he hung Hera shamelessly in the air, with an anvil attached to her ankles and bracelets to her wrists. Hera had to promise never to oppose him again, enduring her worst humiliation. Her accomplices, Apollo and Poseidon, were sent to work in Troy for Laomedon.

But Zeus changed time and again, loving and engendering with women after women, while she cried in agony. Each time, she rose to her feet stronger than before, to carry on her life as the queen goddess and the sole exemplar of the institution of marriage.

She behaved much like any other mortal woman and took revenge on her enemies—those who sought to take Zeus away or disrespected the sanctity of her marriage.

She drove Leto from island to island while she was pregnant with Apollo and Artemis before she settled on Delos.

She counseled Semele to ask Zeus to show his real form as a god, and when he did, she was singed to death.

She drove Alcmene's son, Heracles, mad after her plan for his labors was foiled. As a result, Heracles killed his wife and children.

But now that she has seen it all and aged, her anguish and inner hatred have abated. She remembers how Zeus swallowed his first wife, Metis (while she was pregnant with Athena), after hearing that her son would usurp him as the next ruler. He loved and married many, producing children to provide the world with order: the Fates and Law from Themis; the Graces (Charities) from Eurynome; Apollo and Artemis from Leto; the Muses from Mnemosyne, goddess of memory; Hermes from Maia; and Dionysus from Semele.

Hera understood the need for the father god to make baby-gods from different sources. She connived at many plans to punish him, but they all backfired. For example, when Hephaestus helped her by ensnaring Zeus on his throne, Thetis rescued Zeus and, in response, he hung her from her ankles with an anvil. She tried to divert his attention during the Trojan War so the Greeks could win. Wearing Aphrodite's girdle of desire, she reached Mount Ida to beguile Zeus. He immediately fell for her and wanted to sleep. He raised a golden cloud, and she smiled as he felt exhausted and snoozed, while the battle raged down on earth among Achaeans and Trojans.

Mortals say she renews her virginity each year, but she laughs at such ridiculous tales. Why would a woman humiliate herself in that way? The spring of Kanathos brings her new zeal, a new determination to live her life the way she wants.

It is not merely a reestablishment of her *Parthenos* status—it is a time to live as *Hera Chera* (the unfulfilled).

Her anguish over not having a child she could be proud of, watch them grow, and take the lead in the family has not helped in her struggle for the rights of women. Her own trio, comprising Hebe, Hephaestus, and Ares, lacked any true leadership qualities. Heracles killed the strong Typhoeus. She had brought Typhoeus with so much zest, so much anger at Zeus, but all in vain. An animal! What a shame on her motherhood, nothing like the other gods, Athena, and very far from Apollo or Artemis. If her marriage to Zeus is so sacred, why does it not produce the strongest, bravest, and kindest child-god? Why doesn't it confer on two of them, as Earth goddess and sky god, a gift of unequaled potency?

Is there something lacking in this divine union? Is it Zeus, with his indiscretions, or is it the fates that determine the origins of gods from diverse sources? Or is it Hera herself who does not want to be duplicated by another Hera? Never again. Since she has shown the light, the independence, and she has claimed respect for all women, when she said to Zeus, "You have to marry me, " a sacred union, *hieros gamos*. She keeps this institution separate from her own feelings and has never jeopardized this bond. She has never encouraged amorous looks from anyone other than her husband.

That is how the goddess of marriage lived her life.

Hera often wondered about her own joy in this relationship. Has she truly lived her womanhood with Zeus? Has she ever felt the urgent passion he exhibited, the consummation he craved, and the unrestricted satisfaction he demonstrated afterward? She was not so sure. Wifely duties and motherhood overpowered her sensuality until she awakened from a jolt of his surreptitious indulgence. Then she became engrossed in negative thoughts, severe depression, and dark clouds hovering around her, and she escaped. She embarked on a journey to the ends of the earth to visit her foster parents, Tethys and Oceanos. Just as during the Trojan War, once in the past she yearned to see Tethys, for the couple was not doing well.

For some time, Oceanos and Tethys had separate sleeping quarters due to profound misunderstandings. Hera wanted to counsel them and restore their joy in marriage. Meanwhile, Zeus had become so engrossed in the war that he perched on Mount Ida, watching the Achaeans. He had commanded the council of gods: "Listen to me, all gods and goddesses... If I find any of you succor either the Trojans or the Danaans, they will be struck by my thunderbolt, and I will throw you into the pits of Tartarus."

Some blood-curdling words from the father god!

They all left the council shaken.

He was softer toward his daughter Athena when she spoke up, and he tried to reassure her,

"My dear Tritogeneia, I didn't really mean it…"

If Hera were to analyze the war and decide which of her acts were wrong or inappropriate, she would have to think about the whole decade. The beginning was almost a little game played by three of them, Aphrodite, Athena, and herself. She could hardly believe how they all behaved. Why would a queen mother compete against her own girls just to be validated for her pulchritude? She sought out Paris to utter the words she thought were right to claim that she was indeed the fairest of all. But the wretched shepherd was unimpressed by her promises and did not accept the offer from owl-eyed Athena either. He chose Helen, the most beautiful woman on earth. She was furious and did everything she could to avenge this insult, or at least, that is what everyone believed. But Hera knew that this game wasn't for her beauty or to avenge Paris.

In any case, she was bound by her honor to support the Greeks.

Phoibus, the silver-bowed Apollo, was shooting the Greeks indiscriminately when his priest sought justice. Agamemnon refused

to return his daughter and drove him out of the tent. After nine days of continuous death among the Achaeans, Hera intervened, speaking to the far-shooter to stop, as the Greeks realized their blunder and agreed to return the priest's daughter. Earlier still, she had saved Agamemnon's life when Achilles drew his sword on him. She had asked Athena to pull Achilles away. She tried to sway Zeus's mind from helping the Trojans, especially on behalf of Achilles, as requested by his mother, the fair-ankled Thetis. But her efforts were in vain. So, she had to stage the drama as the father god watched the war from a distance. He couldn't resist, so what if she wore the love-girdle borrowed from Aphrodite? And he fell for her, just as other sky gods had before him, with earth goddesses.

When Artemis lined up in the war with Ares for the Trojans, she used her fierce, motherly force, boxing her ear to chase her away.

She rejoiced at the destruction of Troy. She rejoiced not because the Temples were defiled and mortals were bleeding; she was delighted that, in the greater game plan, the Trojans would now achieve what no other human race could: establish the greatest civilization in the world, far away in Rome.

The son of Anchises traveled in despair to the shores prepared for him by the gods. Aeneas had taken the gods from his temple with him.

Hera knew how Homer and other poets painted her for ages as a jealous, crafty wife, constantly scheming deceit and retribution. She laughed at them for knowing so little about her. Yet our great queen, the pale-armed lady who sat on the golden throne beside her brother, the cloud-gatherer Zeus, continued to show the light to all self-respecting women and stood proud as the goddess who wed only once.

Yet Hera still dwelled on her deeds as years passed by and centuries broke into a new millennium, while mortals remained unchanged. Why did she trouble Heracles? He obeyed all the labors, cleansing the earth of giants, beasts, and dark forces, and whatever he was asked. Why did she drive him to madness, causing him to kill his own three beautiful sons? Why did he not spare Megara, the wife he loved so dearly? Was Hera so bitter against Heracles simply because Zeus shared a bed with Alcmene, or was her anger rooted in Zeus desecrating two marriages—his own and Amphitryon's? As the goddess of marriage, she was determined that no one, not even the immortals, would humiliate her domain—the lawful union of two sexes. She reproached the thunderer for his deeds and sought to ruin or, at least, tried to spoil the lives engendered from such.

One might be aghast or consider Hera's actions toward Heracles unjustified when she sent the goddess of Madness to his palace in Thebes, where Heracles ruled with impunity and his old, cuckolded father, Amphitryon, lived. When madness shrouded his mind, Heracles slaughtered each of his precious offspring like he did in his other labors against the wild beasts, and the cries of the imploring boys did not even register as if they were children of enemies. Then, when Megara fled to a closed room in the palace with a baby, he tore down the door with an axe and, in a final, cruel act, shot a sharp arrow tipped with dragon's blood, crowning his misery with two more murders.

Hera sighed and looked around. Why had she been so cruel? Was Heracles supposed to have been born from her womb—a worthy heir to the most fabulous pair of gods, a god who could rule after the thunderer? But Zeus knew this well; he would bring a god of similar caliber, but only as a mortal, unable to challenge his dominion. Hence, he shared his plans with Alcmenae.

But now Zeus should realize his days are limited. The Greeks have stopped praying for years; the temples lie in ruin, and the family is running out of resources. Hera has attempted many times to reason with the other Olympians, "Let us all dismantle. Let us all perish into the vast universe. Let us cease to be gods and goddesses. Let us release the three worlds and their inhabitants from our bondage." But no one heeds her. She is just the mother goddess.

Now, a new trouble involving a mortal is going to affect the family. Many gods have begun to suspect one another of some game or trick. No one knows how this iron-bird could be intact and its travelers not dead, something that has never happened.

Someone in the family has allowed the safe landing. Someone knows where the other mortal was killed. Something in destiny went wrong. The Moirai—the goddesses of fate must reveal what happened. The three Moirai—Clotho, Lachesis, and Atropos—spin the days in the lives of mortals, and even Zeus dares not interfere with their work.

But a lot was at stake at this point. Hera was tired of her marriage, the family feuds, and the ridicule from mortals since the fall of Rome, and it all reflected in her behavior. Nevertheless, she went for her bath to renew her virginity in the spring of Kanathos near Argos—her favorite city, very regularly.

Troy was destroyed, but she had to work hard for it. She hated Paris for siding with Aphrodite. Yet now she is uncertain if that alone was reason enough for Troy's fall. Were they not too grudging, not too pretentious with their egos? Perhaps she would act differently now. Let no more Paris steal Menelaus' wife—but if something like that happens again, she will have to ask Zeus to be very fair. The gods must embody all the positive attributes—the qualities mortals seek in a god, what they cannot be themselves, what they envision as good—the ultimate bringer of happiness. But is there such a thing? Why aren't they happy with something in flesh and blood like the Olympians, with their faults and follies, their greatness and strength, emotions and stoicism—a natural god?

Hera was always pleased during the month of the wedding Gamelion.

They have festivals all over Greece.

In Olympia, the Hera festival is celebrated every fourth year, featuring sixteen women from different communities. The athletic part includes races, singing, and the distribution of cow meat, among other activities.

 In Beotia, the Great Daedala festival occurs every sixtieth year, with wooden figures as brides on ox-carts, bridal processions, animal sacrifices, and the burning of everything at the end.

On this island, many activities are performed, mostly by women but in the presence of men.

Today, the festival will begin around her temple. She watches them as a silent spectator from a distance, ensuring she remains among the masses. She has asked Hephaestus to come; in case there is trouble. He looks so ordinary; no one suspects him of being an immortal.

The little boys in their short new cloaks, with their curly locks and their enthusiasm to carry the shields, followed by a procession of adults, make for a spectacular sight at the New Year festival. The priest follows with all the women on the island, and then multiple horses and buggies carry wooden figures of women as brides. Musicians with cymbals and flutes, along with the women's shrill voices, make the scene lively.

They all reach the sanctuary, where frankincense granules are scattered over burning flames. The priestess pours a wine libation, and prayers are said. This is followed by the sacrifice of a bull and a cow; the meat is given to the fire. Finally, all the wooden figures, the altar, and all the gifts are burned in an enormous pyre, accompanied by the chanting of Hera's name.

This is followed by women in a procession collecting gifts from all the houses in the name of the goddess. Women who desire a stable married life give whatever they can.

Andrew found the entire town in a frenzy over this festival. He saw hundreds of women he had never seen before. In the procession, he remained at the tail end, lest someone notice the presence of a strange man in an all-women festival. When they turned into the darker side of the island and deeper into the mountain, he thought of withdrawing, but Athena caught hold of his wrist.

"Let us go around,"

He obeyed. After darkness enveloped the entire valley, the women became slothful and spoke of returning to the sanctuary. They were exhausted, and no more houses were in sight. Suddenly, one of the ladies pointed toward a woman in ragged clothes, waving. Andrew wasn't even watching as the procession advanced toward the desolate corner.

"Wait, people, tell me what this place is? Where are you all coming from? What is going on here?"

Athena saw Andrew strolling, fatigued and disinterested. She pushed him.

"Look at her," she urged.

Andrew looked and almost ran toward the lady. He started sprinting through the crowd, pushing and shoving, not caring if he fell or died—his eyes fixated on this woman.

"Rhea, Rh-e-a, R---h---e---a," he gasped, speeding rapidly.

She saw him, and her face turned pale. She was afraid and turned around, then vanished to her right, in a way Andrew couldn't make out.

When Andrew reached her spot, she was gone. There was no sign of her. The mountain and the caves stood silent and dark. The dense forest seemed dead.

Andrew became hysterical and entered one of the pathways into the jungle. He ran, he jumped, he screamed in vain. The lady was nowhere to be found.

Athena stood there, perplexed. She pulled Andrew by his cloak and said, "Leave her alone, for now."

Andrew became angry, then frustrated, and finally started crying.

"Where did she go? Come on, Rhea, it's me, it's me, honey, come on. Come on!"

He screamed, and it echoed through the mountains. The procession began to move, and the women in the group pulled Andrew along.

"What is this place? Does anyone know? She is my Rhea. Where is this fucking place taking you? Is there any hidden path here? Come on, people, and help me. Ma'am, see, she ran away. Why did she run away? She is scared, I don't know why. Someone has done something to her. She really loves me. She is Rhea."

The women chanted,

"Herai—Herai—of Cronus and Rhea, you sleep in the arms of Zeus." "Herai—Herai—of Cronus and Rhea, you sleep in the arms of Zeus."

"Herai—Herai—of Cronus and Rhea, you sleep in the arms of Zeus."

Chapter Ten – Zeus

Chaos prevailed before any order was established in this world. Gaea emerged from her and gave birth to Ouranus, the vast sky. He showered all the rain on her, and together they created the grass, the trees, and the flowers. They then bore three giants with a hundred hands, three one-eyed Cyclopes, and twelve Titans. Ouranus threw the giants and the Cyclopes into the dark depths of Tartarus. The children of Gaea and Ouranus were Oceanus, Crius, Coeus, Hyperion, Iapetus, and Cronos. The daughters included Rhea, Theia, Themis, Mnemosyne, Phoebe, and Tethys.

Other Titans included Prometheus, Epimetheus, and Atlas among the males, and Leto and Metis among the females.

Among the Titans, the youngest, Cronos, dared to help Mother Earth (Gaea) and to attack the tyrant father, ultimately castrating him. The drops of blood fell on Mother Earth, and she bore three Erinyes (the Furies against patricide), as well as three Ash-nymphs.

Cronos became the ruler, no different from his father. The Greeks thought he was the time itself—a sacred crow, and he took Rhea as his wife. The Titaness Theia took Hyperion and bore Helios, the sun; Selene, the moon; and Eos, the dawn. Phoebe married Koios and had Leto, Artemis, and Hekate.

Rhea gave birth to Hestia, Demeter, and Hera, followed by Hades, Poseidon, and the youngest, Zeus. Fearing that one of his children would overpower him, Cronos swallowed them at birth. Rhea took Zeus to Crete and let her mother, Gaea, take care of Zeus. He grew up and returned to give his father a potion of emetics, and he regurgitated all the offspring.

Zeus and the Olympians fought for ten years to defeat the Titans.

Thus, Zeus survived the battle and became the ruler of the gods. He has since engendered countless children-gods and goddesses to ensure the continuation of the cycle of life.

He represents the intellect, the justice, and the order among both mortals and gods.

His first marriage was to the Titaness Metis, the goddess of wisdom. She had helped him give the potion to Cronos. Gaea had told Zeus that his daughter would certainly be like him in strength, but a son of Metis would surpass all and become god of gods. Zeus lured his wife near him with honeyed words, transformed her into a bee, and swallowed her, thus keeping wisdom to himself.

Zeus engendered Lacedaemon with Taygete; Pandia, daughter of the moon goddess Selene; the nymphs: Dryads, Hamadryads, and Oreads from Mother Gaea, the nine Muses from Mnemosyne; the three Graces from Eurynome; the Horae from Themis; and Tityus from Elara.

Zeus had Apollo and Artemis with Leto.

He ravished Io, who turned her into a cow when Hera showed up suddenly.

Zeus came to Danae, the mother of Perseus, as a shower of gold through the skylight.

Heracles was born of Alcmena, daughter of Electryon.

Artemis killed her companion Callisto upon discovering her affair with Zeus.

Zeus fell in love with Semele, a mortal, and they made love. Hera tricked Semele into asking Zeus to reveal his true divine form. Zeus appeared with his thunderbolt, and Semele was incinerated. Their son Dionysus was stitched by God into his own thigh, later giving birth to the god of wine.

He had Aphrodite with Dione and Ares with Hera.

So, Father Zeus made his efforts to seed the entire nation. No one had ever questioned his actions before, and the Greeks were very comfortable with his affairs. They laughed at Hera's jealousy and mocked at marital transgressions, but all in delight. Christianity came with bitter criticism of these gods and ruthless postmortem of their actions. The allegory, the respect for the broader aspects of godly behavior, was scrutinized by the human standards of the day, and past learning, feelings, and philosophy were discarded like an old garment.

Yet, on this island, Father Zeus has made his home. He continues to manage his business alongside his children and mortals, much like in the old days. The mortals here have remained faithful.

However, Father is now worried. This new mortal is seeking trouble. He can foresee a large-scale war approaching, like the Trojan War. But this time, he cannot simply watch it from Olympus, as he will be at the center. He wants to avoid a struggle with the mortals, unwilling to witness such terrible misery again. He has seen the bloodshed that these can cause in the name of new religions. He has silently watched Christians killing Muslims in the First Crusade and Muslims retaliating in the Third Crusade. He has seen how Muslims plundered in Southeast Asia and India and massacred peace-loving Hindus mercilessly for a thousand years.

Father Zeus often wondered when these mortals would allow others to follow their own paths, the way the land has grown, the natural way of religion. If all those people called missionaries stopped traveling to distant lands in the name of God and ceased proselytizing, then the original belief, the pure old natural religion, could survive without violence.

The new religions, which had destroyed his realm and other countries' spheres of influence of their land-born deities, made him wonder if they brought any authentic spirituality. All the wars, the crusades, the riots, aren't they all the fruit of such new religions?

And the hatred they spread, like the one in the *City of God* by St. Augustine.

But despite all that, Father Zeus feels sympathy for the mortals. He knows the time will come when they discover the real God, not one of them born in a foreign country and extolled by a group of disciples who spread that name for their own reasons. People from different lands will find God in their own backyards, in their own lands, and realize that the forceful conversions of their ancestors were wrong.

Father Zeus pondered the roles of his children in the Trojan War.

Zeus believes the war was necessary for the mortals. Since they were becoming so unruly, unjust, and demanding on earth, Grandma Gaea. She could no longer bear them on her broad chest. Yet now, that he reflects upon it, it could have been done differently. He tried to help the Greeks eventually win the war, since their cause was just against the Trojans, who had violated all laws of hospitality. Paris should never have taken Helen with him. But was Zeus lenient toward his own daughter, Helen? She survived all the rough weather in both camps.

Apollo, however, was very angry with Laomedon for being dismissed without his wages for rearing cattle. He initially helped Hector and later killed Achilles when he was out of control and began the genocide among the Trojans in his rage.

Now, Hera and Aphrodite were like any other women, angry for not being chosen by Paris as the fairest. Hera's anger knew no bounds, and she was bent upon destroying Troy.

At least Aphrodite had her son Aeneas saved for Italy.

Poseidon's wrath against Laomedon was excessive. Ares behaved like a lover.

Anyway, the past is the past. Now Zeus is worried. What will happen if things go wrong on this island? They are tired of moving and waiting for the Greeks to return and redeem their glorious past.

One fateful day, he had heard a lady extolling Olympians as she traveled in the sky. It was a large iron bird over this island, approaching fast and falling vertically as if it wanted to die. He was pleased and curious to meet this creature and needed to bring her down to the ground.

He had walked briskly to the shore and watched with horror as a great bird plummeted to the ground. As he came near, the smoke and the heat almost blinded his old eyes. The man lay unconscious. The woman pleaded for help.

"Who are you people? Where do you come from?"

"I am Rhea, and he is Andrew. Please help us…"

"You have landed on my island—that is a transgression. No mortals from outside are allowed to enter this land. This land is reserved only for people living here for ages," Zeus explained.

"What are you saying? Who is mortal and who is immortal?" she asked.

The god of gods pondered whether to reveal his identity - I am Zeus, god of gods, the cloud-gatherer and thunder-maker. However, before he could speak, she opened her eyes with distrust, as if she had anticipated his disclosure, and then collapsed in an apparent awe.

Zeus had no time to waste, as the mortals in the city were awakening. He pulled the door and took her in his lap—a beautiful creature, and she rested in his arms. He thought of Semele and gently kissed her. Then he hurried to a hidden cave where no one could find her.

Hebe responded as soon as she saw the beckoning rainbow in the sky. She realized Iris was looking for her to deliver a message from either Hera or Zeus, and she hurried to reach the cave before

Ganymede. She took the mortal and laid her down on a freshly made divine bed, crafted by Hephaestus with silver and adamantine, adorned with images of Zeus in various incarnations he chose, covered by soft white silk sheets that magically lulled Rhea to slumber. When she opened her eyes, Ganymede offered her a sweet mortal drink that would turn her thoughts of grief and loss to a serene awakening that does not seek reason or consequences. This way, Rhea slept and woke up and slept again for a few days before she knew where and what was going on with her, even remotely.

One dawn, as the sunlight fell on her window bright, she walked outside the cave, but soon she became mortified as two men and two women watched menacingly. Rhea thought she was confined forcibly at an unknown place by local people. She felt initially helpless and later outraged, and her agitation grew when she asked why she was confined, and they remained silent. Rhea considered escaping and walking fast, when the two guards came after her, so she ran out of fear desperately.

One of the sentries, named Bia, grabbed her and pushed, twisting her arms forcefully behind her back, and Rhea fell face-first on the grass, screaming in pain.

- You need not be afraid of us, she said. I never use my force on you unless… she waited to see Rhea's reaction.

-Get off me… you.

The second lady guard stood over her mumbling, "I am Nike."

Then they released her gently, but she kicked the first guard ferociously and scratched Nike's face in a frenzy so fast that the male guards came running.

The man named Kratos looked ominous and fiercely powerful.

The other guard, Zelos, said, "Hope you never need me, but if you do, I offer the same or more zeal you showed and a bit of rivalry."

She was subdued easily and escorted back inside the cave by those four guards of Zeus.

Rhea had recovered, but her behavior has been strange. She learned that those attending to her were not to keep her but to heal her from her trauma. She began to eat well and get some exercise. She had met the old man and complained vigorously. He listened to her like no one ever had in the past. He would always leave her with some fruits and flowers. She would arrange the flowers later and wonder why she felt this way. She never asked him why she was kept in a cave, what the old man expected from her, or why he was so benevolent.

Gradually, she began to feel a sense of security, as if everything would turn out well for her and her baby if she remained here under such care, isolated from crowds, serene and guarded from outsiders. So, when the old man asked if she should be transported safely across the ocean back to the mainland, she had a fit.

She refused to return until her baby was born. She thought that the baby would not survive in the real world as in the past. She had learned to trust the man who said his name was Zeus. She shared her belief in the Greek gods, mentioning that she liked his name, which was from the pantheon. She learned that Andrew was safe and trying to find her. She decided she would only reveal herself when the baby was born. Her fear was unjustified. Andrew was not Father Cronos, who swallowed all her unborn children. Yet she believed her fate was akin to that of her namesake, Mother Rhea.

Zeus stood near the cave, gazing all around, and turned left, hearing a quick thud on his right. The door opened.

"Rhea!" he exclaimed. She was sitting on a couch, her hands covering her face as if she were about to cry.

"Are you all right?" he asked gently.

She raised her head and gently wiped the tears from her face.

"I am so lonely. I miss him; this is enough. I want to go home now," she confessed.

Zeus felt her emptiness and her longing for her mate.

 He walked toward the mortal and sat beside her. Then, the god of gods took her face in his hands and gazed into her eyes.

Rhea remained still, her heart and mind gradually calming as the cloud-gatherer showered her with affection.

Rhea spread her arms and embraced him gently, like a small rose swaying in a soft breeze.

"I must be dreaming. Who are you?" she mumbled.

"Let it be a dream, oh mortal! Just a dream!" he declared.

Rhea closed her eyes as if sleeping, then opened them as if awakening. Seeing the apparition before her once more, she smiled and drew herself closer to him on the couch. She touched his cheek with a slender finger and swiped it to his lips.

Zeus shuddered, and she smiled playfully.

She felt a surge of emotion that she could not define in her mind.

Zeus turned his face toward the door, as though someone might enter.

"Oh, do not inflame my passion; you carry the seed of a mortal."

And he scampered out of the cave.

Zeus walked to the site where he had picked Rhea. The plane stood there like a giant bird, its roof and windows partially covered by leaves and dust. Zeus wondered if it could be repaired and flown back. How could he send her back? This island was isolated from civilization, and any attempt might end in disaster. Planes and boats attempting to approach the island usually meet a severe fate: they drown, crash, or burn, leaving no survivors. This couple was different; the woman was calling upon the gods. Was this a grave mistake? Now he couldn't imagine how one day Rhea could just leave, leaving her cave empty, infested with bats- damp and bare scarred rocks, and his visits would cease as if there was no purpose in her arrival.

Then he heard the footsteps.

Andrew walked near the plane. This mortal is a troublemaker. Zeus stepped away into the woods. Andrew entered the plane.

Andrew had been coming frequently whenever he had a little time. His master made him work hard for his stay on a meager salary. He turned on the radio and spoke softly; the control received him right away.

"I'm calling from this desolate island. No, no, I have no clue. We really need help. This is unbelievable—no, nothing like that, no animals. My fiancée was lost, but now I've found her. I really need assistance. No, it must be handled very gently. This is something you'll be amazed by—you'll have to go back in time. Not just a few years, how about a few millennia, or even more?"

Andrew spoke with the control for a long time. They asked him directions and other details, but he could give no idea. They will have to figure it out.

"Stay on the line, keep talking to us, and we'll figure out by your signal." At that point, the signal disappeared, and Andrew hung up.

Zeus quickly transformed his face. He turned his cloak inside out and smiled at Andrew as they came out of the plane.

"What? Who are you?" Andrew asked, perplexed.

"Nothing. Can you fly this bird again?"

"No. The engines are gone. But why?"

"So, you can go back where you came from."

"Who are you? I've seen you somewhere before, but I can't remember."

Zeus kept silent.

"I am Andrew, the unfortunate passenger of this wretched plane."

They spoke for a while, and Andrew revealed his frustrations.

He spoke without fear to the old man.

-I would appreciate it if someone could talk to me clearly and provide more information. However, this place is peculiar; time seems to stand still here. God knows when we'll get out of this mess.

-My son is a craftsman.

-No, that's all right. This is beyond any repair. Just don't tell anyone you saw me.

-Why?

-You never know. Anyway, I must get back to work.

They began walking back toward the town.

-Do you know what's going on around? I've sold a lot of food to women lately.

-Thesmophoria.

-What foria?

-Thesmophoria is a festival here. The women pray for Demeter and Persephone in their sanctuary.

Andrew had an idea.

-Do all the women participate?

-Not the virgins.

He told him it would last for three days and celebrated in a few sanctuaries, but the one outside town was most active. A large crowd gathers there each year. They say the statue of Athena comes to life at night, and sometimes even Demeter visits the women along with Persephone.

Andrew's gaze seemed inward; the sanctuary, people, women, and location, everything swirled rapidly in him, and he shook his head.

But why would she come? She might have no clue about Thesmophoria.

Zeus began to think as well. He must mention this conversation to her.

Andrew learned that men are not allowed in the temple.

- Bring someone with you who speaks Greek and understands the customs.

Then a mortal walked alongside a divinity on a desolate, uneven dirt path in stillness, only broken by the whistle and the whisper of the wind.

The old man walked effortlessly, as if his feet were kissing the ground beneath him, his mind flashing back hundreds of years and into the future, occasionally pausing to clear a fallen tree without help from the mortal. But Andrew felt the cold breeze on his face as he carefully stepped away from the ditches, wincing in pain while watching the old man, who otherwise seemed so serene, askance. He believed there was power in stillness and in how a person moved on the ground.

They walked together until they reached the shop.

Chapter Eleven – Thesmophoria

Thesmophoria is celebrated on this island from the eleventh to the thirteenth of Pyanopsion. The women have been waiting all year for the chance to leave their homes and spend a few days and nights with their friends. Men and children were not invited, except for the infants.

The deep red reflection of Helios on the water, the gentle rays caressing the land, and a cool morning zephyr heralded the dawn on the island. The grass was still moist with dew; the birds were chirping around; and the din of the slaves before their masters could open their eyes made the land feel so predictable despite the presence of gods.

The gods didn't change anything here. They just lived alongside the citizens, neither boastful, harsh, nor interfering in anyone's life. How wonderful or how impossible? Aren't gods supposed to discipline sinners? To be above humans? To regulate, manipulate, and influence their agents, always spreading their names? Not on this island. They lived like anyone else, falling for the same temptations as humans, including falling for pretty mortals, squabbling among themselves, and complaining to their father, Zeus. The residents here still believed they were godly; if they happened to meet one of their gods, they simply spoke openly with them, without guilt, not a bit, because they were not told—"you're a sinner from birth." They didn't constantly strive for redemption. Everyone lived their life to the best of their ability, unpretentiously.

So, when the master woke up and saw Andrew still snoring in his small room, he was furious and dumped a bucket of cold water over his head.

"What the hell?" Andrew screamed.

That's right. I'll show you the gate to Hades' world, you tembelis," he meant lazy.

"Get lost, you fu..." Andrew paused, thinking about his job.

"Go ahead, swear as much as you can, American!" the master said.

Andrew awoke, rubbing his eyes, and dashed to the bathroom.

When he returned, Protagoras was already hauling sacks of grain outside the shop.

"Today we sell the most," he said.

"Why?"

"The women buy their food and grain for three days of their celebration. They love to get away for their own—you know what I mean?" His eyes twinkled with some ribald pleasure.

"Really? They do that?" he asked.

"All kinds of stuff, you name it. They eat cookies like your—you know what-and cookies like their-you know what..." he teetered on his words.

"Hey, that must be fun. Maybe we can join them."

"Join them?" he was shocked.

They kept working. Protagoras remained silent after his outrageous statement.

"I mean, what is the big deal about men not going there?"

"You have no idea. They do all kinds of things—no one knows—not even the gods."

"So let us find out."

"Listen, you fool. If you want to waste your feckless life—go ahead, but I know it better."

"Come on, Protagoras, this will be fun. Watching those pretty women—doing kinky stuff. Let us take a chance."

Protagoras took a piece of cloth and cleaned his seat. Andrew made another gesture.

"See, this may be my only chance of meeting her..."

"You don't understand, do you? It's not only forbidden but very unbecoming of men. In fact, treacherous."

"I'll give you my watch," Andrew waved his wrist.

Protagoras seemed tempted.

"Hum... I can take you there. But you go inside alone."

The deal was made, and they started whispering thereafter—the conspiracy began.

"Have you heard of Aristophanes?" Protagoras asked.

"Comedy writer?"

"You know what happened to Mnesilochos in *Thesmophorazusae*?"

They discussed Euripides and Mnesilochos. Then Protagoras hurried home, and Andrew waited outside. He confided in his wife. At first, she refused to cooperate, but with much persuasion and the promise of an ornament, she agreed to help him.

The process of depilation for two hairy men was not only arduous and prolonged but also very uncomfortable for a lady. Yet she performed the task. Her eyes nearly shut, her face crimson, and the men in pain—as she clipped, cropped, trimmed, and lopped. When they "ouched," she shrugged and smashed their faces with the sides of her elbow. Then, with pity, she used some of her liniments to smooth their turtle skins.

Two sisters followed Protagoras's wife to the yearly festival at the temple of Demeter.

The sisters had to be introduced to the other women since all new members needed initiation.

Women from all over the island surrounded the temple as they arrived; three chaste girls of considerable strength guarded the only door. The termagants screened the supplicants with hawkish eyes.

The two sisters paused, whispered, and then shuddered as they saw their herald approaching the door audaciously.

"Halt!" the vixen commanded.

The sisters almost froze with fear.

 "Virgins?"

Their big sister saw the trouble. She screamed,

"Virgins, like your mother! They are my neighbors. Let them come."

The sisters walked past the guards, holding their breath.

Inside, the lamps were too dim to banish the darkness and the dampness. Some women struggled to hold back their piglets, which caused a terrible stench in the room. The sisters found a cozy corner and unloaded their belongings. A tall but thin lady stood near the altar and scanned the crowd. Then she began the announcement:

"We will begin soon, ladies. Please listen."

There followed a general commotion. But soon the women gathered around and were ready to listen to the person at the altar.

"In the name of the sacred Olympians, we have gathered to celebrate our Thesmophoria..."

A baby cried.

"Lady, feed the baby," someone suggested.

"In the name of the goddess of grains, our lady Demeter, and her daughter, consort to the king of the underworld, let us begin our prayers," the priestess started again.

A commotion erupted near the entrance.

"They must have caught a virgin," someone whispered.

"Let us sing and dance for Apollo, the great singer.

Let us sing and dance for his sister Artemis, the great huntress.

Let us sing and dance for Hera, the keeper of marriages."

The women began to sway and move in rhythm.

"We sing and dance for Apollo,

We praise the huntress Artemis,

We seek the blessing of Hera."

The sisters tried to imitate them in low voices.

One of the sisters glanced around, a bit skittish in her attempt to find someone.

"Do you see her yet?" Protagoras whispered.

"No. I can't even see their faces," Andrew replied.

The lady standing nearby gave them a reproachful look.

"Why don't you pray, lady?" Protagoras asked.

She turned her face away and resumed swinging her arms.

"Let us go around and look for her," Andrew suggested.

"You go. I'm out of here," Protagoras said.

"I'll give you my camera,"

"You'll ruin me," Protagoras moaned.

Moving with the dancing rhythm, they peered at the devout faces.

The priestess announced,

"Now, by the name of all the gods and goddesses,

Let us give the piglets to the earth,

Let us begin our days and nights of devotion."

The screaming piglets, crying infants, and worshiping women created a noise filled with commotion and strong emotion. The sisters hurriedly moved, unprepared and without offerings.

"Look at her, Andrew, she is not a resident," Protagoras found someone.

"I can't see her face," Andrew said helplessly.

"Do you need to see her face to know her?"

Andrew stepped close to the woman and stood beside her as if with no intention. As she moved and sang, he watched intently from the corner of his eye but seemed disappointed.

The place grew darker as night fell outside. Temple keepers lit more lamps along the walls. Women gathered into groups, babbling, chuckling, and gesturing. Protagoras searched for his wife; she was supposed to stay nearby, just in case.

He became nervous.

"Need any help, lady?" one of the keepers asked.

"No, just looking for my neighbor."

Then he noticed someone in the corner. He moved fast,

"Rhea!" he exclaimed.

"Do I know you?" she said apathetically.

"Rhea, look at me."

She turned her face toward him and trembled with a surge of disbelief and joy. A faint, sweet smile broke across her face, and she looked around with that intense relief, but it soon faded into trepidation. Then she tried to walk away quickly.

"Don't run," Andrew whispered.

She kept moving, and Andrew nudged her sideways to avoid drawing attention. They were close to the enormous chasm where piglets were thrown.

"Let me go, or I'll jump in the pit," She warned.

Andrew grasped her hand firmly; she trembled.

"Don't make a sound. They'll kill me," he implored.

"Leave me, or I'll cry. It hurts," She commanded.

Andrew relaxed his grip, and she darted toward the other side.

Protagoras found his wife, and they came near him.

"She is here," Andrew informed them.

As night fell, the women became unruly. They ate, drank, chattered, and laughed. The temple had turned into a clubhouse.

"Hi, hi, hi. My husband has no clue," one of the ladies revealed her secrets.

Andrew paused, scanning her.

"He knows when to come. Then he asks the maid whether the master left any instructions—hi, hi, hi—to see if he's gone to work."

"Where do you...?" her friend asked.

"In the barn, hi, hi, hi, on the hay bed."

Andrew spotted her again.

He ran toward her; she didn't see him coming.

Rhea, for God's sake, listen to me. I'm going crazy here. Why are you hiding from me? I'm your only friend here. Has someone turned your mind against me or what?

"Don't come close, Andrew. I have a baby in my womb."

"I know. You told me."

"Stay away. Let me have the baby," she implored.

"What? You think I don't want the baby?"

"No, Andrew. I have lost twice, both times you…" She paused.

"I didn't know, and you didn't tell me."

"It is our destiny. My first baby will be born away from you," she announced.

"Is it your imagination, or a divine forecast?"

"Whatever you think," she said earnestly, eyes wide, breasts heaving, nostrils flaring, so distant from Andrew.

"Oh, Father Zeus has got hold of you?" he derided.

"Don't speak of him. Please, it may hurt you," she warned.

"But Rhea. What am I going to do without you anyway?"

"Andrew, please, just for the sake of our baby…"

"Exactly. That's why we should leave this wretched place and go home."

The women guards came.

Will you two shut up and join us for the prayer?

"Rhea, let us get the hell out of here."

She hesitated but nodded reluctantly. Suddenly, there was a noise, and someone screamed,

"There's a man! A man among us!"

Andrew trembled. He was close to the door and could run, but for the sentry standing firm.

They dragged Protagoras toward the altar. His wife reached out, pleading,

"Let him go. Let him go. He is my husband."

"He has seen everything. He has witnessed our sacred rites." Someone in authority said.

"He should be punished for his crime!" the women screamed.

"Hang him! Torture him!"

"Whip him!"

"Throw him with the pigs down there!"

Andrew didn't know what to do. He wanted to save his master, but it was risky. Rhea moved toward the exit, unaware of the disaster. Andrew, torn by his conscience to save Protagoras, followed behind her.

Protagoras screamed:

"Andrew, don't leave me! Do something!"

Andrew turned around. Rhea pleaded urgently,

"Don't go back. These women are vicious. Come with me."

"Rhea, stay here. I must do something, just a minute," and he proceeded toward the altar. Once there, he forcibly pulled Protagoras free from the hands of the two guards. Then they darted toward the door. The women screamed, and a full brawl broke out. One of the girls slapped Andrew, and another kicked Protagoras in the crotch, causing him to fall to the floor. Andrew grabbed his hand, trying to lift him and run, but suddenly someone pushed Andrew hard, and he fell as well. The women laughed at this and closed in on their victims.

A shameless, pudgy woman sat on Protagoras, and he couldn't breathe.

"Get off, you big fat lady!" Rhea said, coming closer now.

The woman didn't move and sat there like a big boulder, swearing fiercely:

"We will teach you. You'll see that women aren't weak!"

"You're not weak. You're heavy, move your fat ass!" Rhea said.

Suddenly, another woman charged at her, knocking Rhea down. As she fell, the larger woman kicked her in the abdomen, screaming:

"Who are you? We'll teach you how to stand up for your sisters! These men aren't worth your pity anyway!" Rhea doubled over in pain. Andrew acted fast and rose to his feet. He pulled Rhea and Protagoras aside and then pleaded,

"Ladies, please! Stop the violence!" He screamed.

Protagoras stood up, but Rhea couldn't.

The group of Valkyries surrounding her looked on with curiosity. They were no longer angry. They all saw what Andrew and Protagoras had missed and could not notice. One approached gently,

"Sister, is it hurting badly?"

Rhea nodded. This lady then asked the men to stay away as she and others tried to hide a puddle of bright red blood collecting near Rhea.

"We need a physician."

"We should take her to her husband."

They all suggested various remedies. Protagoras spoke sharply,

"Ladies, look what you've done—hurt your own kind. See why men don't trust you? Now move and let us take her out."

They all scattered back. Andrew carefully picked up Rhea and carried her out. Rhea groaned in pain, and he tried to soothe her.

"Trust me, I know who can heal you. Apollo, yes, and I'm serious. I know him, Rhea."

Protagoras looked at them, befuddled.

"Andrew, take me to my cave," She whispered.

"No, I'm taking you somewhere safe." He hurried his steps. Protagoras followed.

"Andrew, please... just take me home. I want to sleep,"

Rhea was bleeding heavily. Andrew felt the warm blood soaking through his clothes. Rhea was weakening, her eyes shutting in exhaustion. Andrew thought she was slowing down and increased his pace.

He broke into a run.

"Don't give up, Rhea. Don't. We need this baby. Soon, we'll be home."

He mumbled, sprinting, and cursing those vixens responsible. This is how the loving couple celebrated the festival of fertility and feminine empowerment with secret rites as one bled life onto the other, turning him crimson, a sign of deep passion. Andrew was now seen running and confabulating.

Chapter Twelve – Andrew.

Andrew spent the whole day in the shop. He carefully stacked the grain sacks, counted them, and then listed the inventory. The master has been unusually kind since their unfortunate experience at Thesmophoria.

Protagoras seemed to have changed. One day, he expressed his gratitude—'You saved my life, or they would have thrown me with the pigs into the death pit. I would do anything for you if you ever needed me.' Little did Protagoras know if Andrew would need someone ready to die for him in exchange for a divine plan. Just like Alcestis offered her life for King Admetus—the ultimate gift—or whether Andrew would be willing to offer himself for someone else. One day again, for the same Protagoras.

But days passed, and the nights only brought more desolation. Rhea refused to see him. She made friends among the locals. Andrew saw her a few times in the market, always with her own companions. She did smile at him, but that was all he could expect. She didn't ask him any questions, nor did she respond to any of his. Andrew was at a significant loss with her. Someone so lovely and so kind… how could she change?

The other day, Andrew found her in the market and approached her with a smile.

"I haven't seen you for so long," he said.

"I was sick," she whispered.

"What happened to you?"

"I don't know. I had a fever and was very weak, no pep at all."

"You should see a doctor."

"I'm fine now."

"Rhea, let us go back."

"How?"

"My radio is working again. I fixed it."

"Did you contact anyone?"

"Not yet. I wanted to talk to you first."

"Let us wait."

"Why? Wait for what?"

"Just wait," she commanded.

"Rhea, be honest. We have no life, everything's a mess, and you seem so detached."

"Really? You have to say that? You... who ruined everything."

"How?"

"Everything. You flew the plane; you flew into the storm..."

Andrew just listened to her. She was no longer looking at him.

"Just because I wanted to take you somewhere nice…" he mumbled.

"Andrew, why did you barge into the temple? Why?"

Andrew searched for an answer in his mind as she continued.

"Why did you have to do such a stupid thing? And because of you…"

"Because of me? You came running back to save me?"

"Exactly. If they hadn't pushed me, if I hadn't fallen, if things hadn't been so violent, if…"

"You wouldn't have lost the…"

Exactly. Why does it have to be you? You. There's something in us, in me or in you, something unfortunate, I mean unfruitful, unproductive, and sterile about our relationship. And after three times, I believe we will never have a family.

"That's not true. You base your judgment on unscientific reasons, like people here do with these old gods," Andrew suggested.

"Don't, Andrew. You'll bring their wrath upon us. These are the real people. Don't you understand? We are so lucky, so destined to be with them. See, you don't even care. Fine, I do—and if you don't care, why don't you take your bloody plane and leave?"

"Come on, Rhea. Be real. This is all a dream, a surreal experience. You think these gods are real? They're impostors to control the villagers."

"Would you please stop!" she cried, covering her ears with her palms.

"Someone might be listening, Hun?"

"Maybe. And I think you should leave…"

"If that's what you want."

Rhea walked away. Andrew watched her receding figure in the crowd. He felt sorry for how their misunderstanding had grown deeper. There were so many things he wanted to say. I miss you; I want to spend time with you, and I'm curious about where and how you spend your days and nights. Why can't we be together? If this is the place you like, fine, let us live here as long as you want. No, she wouldn't listen. And he couldn't bring those words to his lips. His life, his love, everything was slipping away, withering slowly like the autumn leaves turning rusty and sailing every direction aimlessly with any draft.

God, give me strength. Let me regain control. Women don't know anything, especially Rhea; she's such a nice girl. She's fixated on the idea of having a family and a baby. That's all. Just because she had a few miscarriages doesn't mean anything. I'll have her checked by the best obstetrician in the world. I don't believe what she said about not being able to have babies anymore. Who the hell told her that?

Protagoras entered the shop. Andrew stood and feigned busyness.

"Andrew, there's an order."

"I'll do it. Give me the list and the address."

"Are you sure?"

"What's your problem?"

"It's the cave address—you know where?"

Andrew hesitated. Should he? Wouldn't she react again?

But love finds reasons for assignation, no matter how perilous, and Andrew was no different. He collected the sacks of grain, picked the fresh bread, and chose the bottles of wine he had enjoyed before. Then he pulled the horse cart and carefully loaded his goods.

He was on his way, whistling a tune that exuded love.

When he reached the cave, the sunlight diminished—red and yellow flickering near the entrance, with a vermillion patch illuminating the side wall. A gentle breeze tousled his blonde hair; his head was bathed in a yellow-orange glow.

He knocked gently.

No one responded.

He waited.

The light receded from the doorstep, and he stood in the shade. He knocked again, this time giving it a gentle push, and the door swung open. Andrew stepped inside the cave. Dim candlelight revealed a fairly spacious area, but no one was there. He saw a door with a silk curtain leading further into an inner chamber.

Cautiously, he moved the screen aside and protruded his head inside.

He saw a man's shadow leap over a woman, their faces inches apart. His fists clenched, jaw tight with rage. He turned away quickly.

Behind him, a pair of pretty eyes opened, surprised, embarrassed, and panicked.

She had seen him leaving.

Frustrated, he dumped the merchandise outside and whipped the poor horse in rage.

Jealousy grew in his heart day and night. He felt betrayed, humiliated, and, of course, furious. Now he understood why she wouldn't leave the island. His love was no longer enough for her. His caring, his sharing their lives—none of it mattered now. She had other reasons to live, hidden from him. His love for Rhea has been unconditional so far, even though he did not say it out loud. He wasn't the perfect lover before, but he was always there for her.

Why would she choose someone here? Who's this person? How long has she been with him?

Jealousy shifted to suspicion. His reasoning became cloudy, and he started to imagine a scheme. His mind began filling with plans as his heart burned with hatred. He decided to take revenge on this person. Rhea had only seen one side—his love; now she would see the other—his dark side. He was determined to make sure she learned a lesson; hurting others should not go unpunished.

Every part of his body burned with anger and vengeance.

Yes, he will kill that bastard. No one knows him here anyway. There is no real justice on this island. Then he will escape.

A few days later, he reached the wreckage of his plane. The radio was working.

Hello? Hello? My name is Andrew... He described the island in greater detail this time.

The other side asked him questions, many of which he was now able to answer.

 The east of the island has... the west is covered with... and the ocean looks like...

There are two peaks—no, two separate mountains. There is a large meadow, with a wide gap in the middle where people live. You might not see it from the air. When you come here, make sure it's dark. I don't know anything about their defenses, but don't shoot or do anything. No, I don't want any guns. Tell my dad to stay out. I don't want an army here.

These are very kind people. Too kind for us. They still live in the past; they have no electricity, no radio or TV. But they are not uncivilized. They are god-fearing, as if gods live among them.

"Really, have you seen any?" they mocked.

Maybe I did. Any of you? Andrew retorted.

They laughed on the other side.

Have I seen a god? These villagers are amazing, almost divine. You won't find people like them in Athens. Anyway, I need a ride back, a boat—no planes, no fights, no media around. Tell my dad to ensure this island keeps its special status like before, with no one within twenty miles. It should stay protected as it was.

Am I alone? Yes. What happened to my girlfriend? She left me. No, I don't want to find her. She's lost, lost forever.

Commandos can find her. Look, I just said—no military, or I won't cooperate. You come here; you won't find me either.

I'll call you tomorrow.

Andrew didn't care about anything; he just wanted to escape. But he ensured the island remained as it was, isolated, pristine, unspoiled by civilization. Let these gods live their lives as they wish and not our bloody way. What has a thousand years of development brought us? Mammoth concrete buildings, rushing citizens with incurable social problems, their lives riddled with distrust and dishonesty.

Suddenly, Andrew realized he enjoyed living here. He repented of his earlier decision.

He turned toward his shop.

A lady stood in his way. She wore a long chiton of sky blue, her neck adorned with a choker bearing a solitary diamond at its center. Her eyes shone bright green, her lips a pink smile.

"Why are you so happy?" Andrew asked.

"Talk about your happiness. I'm always glad to see mortals with courage," she said.

"I am fake. My life has halted here."

"You remind me of Odysseus."

"You must be kidding. Did he lose Penelope here?"

"Have you?" she asked.

He didn't know how to explain himself. Will she understand? She seemed calm and collected—why wasn't she wearing her battle gear? Andrew couldn't think as her eyes held him in place.

"Why don't you find her?"

Andrew wanted to say he did not prefer finding her anymore; instead,

"It's hard for me," he said.

"Men have wandered from homes for ages; have traveled to exotic places seeking riches, bringing back gains. You are no different," she paused.

"My gains…?" He trailed off.

"You see the losses only. Cowards brew on losses. Are you giving up in tough times for fear of facing pain?"

"Maybe. But Rhea is lost because she wants to be. I don't mean much to her anymore. We're done. It's over."

Athena listened carefully; she had stopped smiling.

"Do you love her?" she asked abruptly.

He fumbled for words. His hesitation created the silence. He tried to break it and assert himself, but he couldn't; he had definitely paused.

"Let no man and gods infer anything from your silence," she said.

Andrew lowered his head, saying,

"You think I'm complaining?"

Her radiant smile returned, eyes shimmering with a glow.

"Go claim what's yours. Be strong not only to face your love, but also those who snatched it. You have a formidable task."

"Are you inciting me?"

"I'm showing you how to do the just, even though I foresee peril and strife for our family that you will bring. Do not doubt my integrity—no one has in ages."

"What can I do?"

"Get ready. This won't be easy. You will face many tough choices, but remember, peace can come from this struggle, not bloodshed."

She walked away. Andrew followed her but couldn't keep pace. She disappeared into the woods.

The next day, Andrew gave exact directions to the advancing boat from the mainland.

He waited at sundown in the bushes near the shore. The boat had only one crew member as requested and advanced stealthily in the darkness toward the uninhabited corner.

Andrew saw a flash of light, and his heart leaped with joy at the prospect of freedom. Finally, he would go home.

Now he could see the boat clearly. He stepped near the shore. The captain signaled twice. Andrew hesitated; should he jump into the water?

The captain waved and brought the boat very close, and Andrew saw the outline of his face, a bearded man. Andrew stepped out from the bushes and shrubs; he wanted to be seen. But he couldn't dare, as a fireball shot from nearby struck the boat. Andrew saw the scourge with shock as the fireball hit the deck, igniting it in a flash. The captain couldn't be seen due to the intense glow, but there followed a loud human cry. The boat was engulfed in flames. Andrew scanned for the culprits, but smoke and heat blinded him. He retreated to the bushes and watched the conflagration. He wanted to reach the boat and save the captain, but he was frightened.

At that moment, a few men emerged into the open, speaking in Greek, and approached the boat. Andrew couldn't see their faces in the dark. After a while, they pulled a body ashore. Someone whistled for the horses. Three horses trotted up to their riders. The men loaded the body onto one horse, and two rode alongside to cover it. Andrew couldn't tell if the captain was still alive. He sat still behind a small mound of earth; his eyes fixed on the remaining men. They looked around and, at one point, gazed in his direction. Then they headed toward the trees, shielding Andrew. He took a quiet breath, ready for anything that might happen.

Andrew tried to hold his breath as the Greeks towered over him.

"Who are you?"

Andrew thought about running away, but someone hit him. In the next moment, the same man crouched on his back as he lay face down on the ground, writhing in pain.

"You called the outsider to this island. Traitor!" someone hissed.

"I can't breathe," Andrew squeaked.

"Take him to Heracles."

"Oh no. Please, let me go."

The Greeks helped him onto a horse and rode for half an hour through the dense forest. Andrew moaned in pain; his side ached, and his face burned.

Finally, they reached their destination, a façade with no windows.

"You will stay here," the leader said.

"Where are we?"

"This is where traitors live… or die, whatever."

They shoved him in and shut the gate.

Andrew was scared. He looked around for any way out. He was very startled when he heard the clanking of the iron door shutting. He walked over to the door and pressed his ear against it. The ocean breeze swept past, smelling of salt. He stood there as if someone might walk by, and he could call for help. But no one did, and the night grew darker.

Andrew fell asleep right near the door.

The sun rose over the island as usual. It peeped through the mountains, tall oaks and pines; it shone on the houses and fields, then finally bathed Andrew's face in warmth. He squirmed and felt the sharp pain where he was hit last night.

Then he sat up in horror, surrounded by men and women, all confused. The men looked mostly unkempt and unshaven, with grim expressions. The women appeared scared, with pale faces and hair that was tangled and matted. They all wore the same clothes—togas—many with ram's horn nails.

"Signomi, ti ora ine?" Andrew asked the time.

They gazed at each other hesitantly and embarrassingly. Then someone said,

"Den eho ora."

Andrew smiled, wondering how they could possibly know the time.

"Ti ora servirete to prono?" he asked, feeling hungry.

"Around nine," a man in his thirties came forward.

"You speak English?"

"I'm from Florida."

"Andrew."

"Charlie."

They shook hands. Others gradually dispersed.

Charlie arrived a year ago. He and his friends were lost at sea but managed to bring the boat to this island. What happened afterward was a sad story.

"Did some people fire at you suddenly?" Andrew asked.

"How do you know?"

"It happened to me last night. I called for help; the boat was almost there when people started firing from nowhere. I don't know what happened to my rescuer," Andrew said ruefully.

"They killed all my friends. I survived by jumping out of the boat, but they caught me anyway," Charlie said.

At that point, the large door opened with a clatter, and inmates rushed. Two tall, hulking men shoved them back with fists. Then another person brought the food: bread and dark coffee.

Though hungry, Andrew showed no eagerness. After all were served, the Greek soldiers looked at him.

"Pos sas lene?"

"Me lene Andrew."

"Sou aresi o kafes?"

Andrew hesitated. Charlie elbowed him.

"M' aresi para poli," he said he would like the coffee.

The soldier nodded approvingly and poured. Andrew took bread as well.

The soldiers left.

"Don't ever refuse the food," Charlie whispered.

"Why?"

"Against Greek hospitality. I was roughed up a few times before."

They ate silently. The day grew warm; people scattered lazily in their spaces, slothfully.

Andrew grew despondent. How could he escape this hell? What will happen to him?

"Do you ever think about…?"

"Sh…sh…sh, someone might be listening," Charlie cautioned, scooting near him. Then, looking around, he whispered,

"I have tried once."

"Really?"

"Yeah, but I was alone. No one helped me."

"What happened?" Andrew asked.

They spoke softly. Andrew realized it would be nearly impossible to escape from here. They always came prepared; if someone tried, two guards waited outside to capture and torture the escapee until satisfaction.

After sundown, Charlie lit the brazier near his wall. The coal burned, emitting smoke. Andrew liked the heat and the smell.

Then he took a deep breath and planned as he spotted the black heap in the corner.

The prisoners keep the brazier burning at night by adding coal to keep it aflame. By day, it slows down to keep the fire buried under ashes. All they need to do in the evening is to blow out the ashes and refill with new coal.

Andrew took some coal in his hand, pieces of various shapes and sizes. He lit one brazier piece and blew hard. The flame rushed upward, and sparks flew.

Charlie looked at him.

Then they whispered again.

"First, see how it goes tonight," Charlie suggested.

Andrew shook his head approvingly.

"You shouldn't rush. If you fail, they'll kill you."

The gate opened again. Only one soldier brought dinner, which was some souvlaki.

The soldier seemed not so indifferent. He smiled at a woman.

Andrew and Charlie took the food without exchanging a word. The guard barely paid attention, his gaze fixed shamelessly fixed on the same woman. She noticed and smiled back.

After dinner was distributed, the soldier stood in a corner watching the inmates eat. The woman approached him and whispered.

"He is flirting," Charlie noted.

"Who is she?"

"Anna."

Outside, the moon never revealed itself; the countryside remained silent in complete darkness. The prisoners got ready for their nap. The female inmates moved to the other side and shut the door behind them. The men settled down to sleep in the main hall.

"I want to speak," Andrew whispered.

"Wait till morning," Charlie advised.

"No, it'll be too late. Let's go to her now."

"You'll enrage the others."

Andrew insisted. They walked to the door.

Charlie knocked gently.

"Ti thelete?" someone asked.

Charlie asked for Anna. She heard and emerged. They sat near the door and began to whisper. An older woman finally closed the door behind them.

Anna had arrived just a few days earlier, having been thrown here for a crime she disputed but had lost. She insisted she never seduced the man they accused her of. She received two years. Anna looked thin and tall for a woman, with a sharp chin. Her eyes were not submissive for a prisoner. When she smiled, Andrew thought her lips never gaped much.

She turned her neck, revealing a blue vein beneath her fair skin on her collarbone, a fragile tenderness. She barged forward, aware that the guards watched her with lustful eyes.

"No, no breakout. They will catch us, and I'll spend more years here," she refused.

"What if I take you off the island? To Athens," Andrew suggested.

Her eyes brightened, a moment's hesitation.

"You're not safe here anyway," Charlie said.

Anna pouted, then shrugged. Andrew felt he could still reach her. He looked at her earnestly, and she inhaled deeply. He wondered how such a fragrance could survive in this hell.

"I can handle these pigs. They already tried last night."

Anna was listening quietly now. Andrew spoke slowly, glancing around and whispering close to her ear as her scent overwhelmed his senses. He took a few extra minutes to elaborate on the plan. The other two nodded. Suddenly, she stood up and left for her cell.

Andrew awoke to a scream. Inmates lined up again for breakfast as a beam of bright sunlight struck the door. One of the soldiers stared as he opened his eyes.

He shot upright and joined the line.

Milk and bread were given out.

"What's your problem?" the soldier asked in Greek.

"Insomnia... couldn't sleep here. This is not a luxury place."

He paused, watching the soldier's indignant face.

"You want luxury? Heracles runs a few of those. Wait till you meet him today." He made a scornful face.

"Heracles? No, I'm fine here. No trouble. Did I complain?"

"Heracles oversees all our security. He likes to meet new jailbirds..."

Andrew felt humiliated but suppressed it. His plan won't be safe if foiled. He felt dejected. The guard noticed.

"No one likes Heracles. He's tough but is a very good man. He wouldn't hurt anyone unless they threaten the island."

"What is he? A god or something?" Andrew chuckled.

His jaunty words drew consternation among the soldiers. Even the inmates gawked rather uneasily.

"Sorry, shouldn't have touched religious sentiments," he apologized.

"You must be Christian?" the soldier suggested.

"Well, yes and no. I was baptized but have never gone to church."

After the soldiers left, inmates quickly dispersed back to their routines. Andrew thought hurriedly; he needed to speed up the plans.

Anna, Charlie, and Andrew drew closer for another meeting. They spoke so softly that they couldn't hear each other clearly.

"I will not like anyone killed," Charlie said.

"But with our plan, some people are going to get hurt. They won't back off unless they are injured," Anna explained.

"We'll cross that bridge when it comes," Andrew said.

The afternoon passed uneventfully. Anna spoke with a few, while Charlie gained the confidence of others. Everyone seemed very nervous about flying the coop. Andrew spoke only broken Greek and stayed out of the main arguments.

"Why do we risk ourselves? The chances are we will be caught on such a small island, and then what? It will be worse."

Andrew couldn't promise a getaway to the mainland for each. He wasn't sure what vessel he'd acquire and how.

Evening twilight broke beneath the massive door. Birds scurried back to their nests. People busy with their lives returned to their homes after a day's toil. Some laborers shared comments about the women they saw on their way.

Heracles hurriedly made his way to this remote place. He had been told that one of the troublemakers was kept here after the beach incident. Occasionally, he dealt with outsiders trying to reach or escape the island. He realized that keeping them alive was a burden. They never stopped trying to escape, and if one managed to succeed, the island's safety was at risk. The outside world was hostile; they wanted to change everything—culture, traditions, and impose their own gods. Who needs a new religion? Aren't we happy here? The Greeks and Romans always appreciated their gods until outsiders forced change, crushing dissent with swords and guns. They have silenced the rest of the world, except for this tiny refuge where old traditions still survive.

Heracles would ensure that nothing vanishes. He was helping Zeus and the others keep a tiny flame smoldering for a long time, so that when people needed it again, it would be there to resume, to live, and to take a shape and form of our old religion, which was so beautiful, with no hatred and no wrath against other faiths.

They argued that the gods were absent when the Christians advanced, to protect the worshippers of the pantheon. But that was not true. The gods don't protect the weak just because they are followers. What happened to the gods of Judaism when they were in trouble? The gods watched and let them fight their own wars. They are there to inspire, instill values, and guide, not to pick up weapons for you. Yes, during the Trojan War, a few took swords, but then it was against the rulings of the god of gods.

Heracles reached the prison after sunset. He opened the gate with his keys and stepped inside.

Suddenly, all hell broke loose.

One of the female inmates screamed for help, crying and yelling. Behind her came two men.

"She is evil, she is evil. She corrupts men here,"

Heracles turned toward her and tried to speak with her.

He wanted to have some idea, and he asked her to stop crying,

No one can hurt you. Just compose yourself. I am Heracles.

And then everything seemed to turn upside down. Hot, burning coals flew everywhere, some striking him right on the face as he shut his eyes to shield himself. The ash turned the hallway into a dingy, dark place, filled with gray clouds. The skirmish that followed was totally unexpected and chaotic. The same lady screamed even louder,

"I told you. I warned you. They will kill me! They are bad..."

"Shut up, let me think,"

"Think fast, Sheriff... think fast,"

"I will, if you stop bothering me! I can barely see—my eyes are burning!"

"Wait, I'll get you water," she said.

At that moment, someone approached and struck Heracles on his head. Memories of his past labors flashed before him—the Nemean lion, the Hydra, Artemis' stag, the Boar of Mount Erymanthus, the filthy stables of Augeas, the Stymphalian birds, Poseidon's bull, the mares of Diomedes, the girdle of Hippolyta, the cattle of Geryon, the golden apples of the Hesperides, and Cerberus from Hades. Those were far more difficult tasks compared to what he is doing now. He felt dizzy.

Then, great Heracles howled a cracking noise —groaning in intense pain and rage, followed by a snapping sound as if he had broken his arm, and finally a loud thud as he touched the ground like a large, felled oak in a forest.

The mortals nearby, passing by his side, couldn't help but watch him with awe – did Heracles, a mortal turned god, fall from grace, felled by similar mortals? They would have moved it out of the way if it were a tree, but a felled god was not easily understood.

Andrew hurried out of the prison, not daring to look back until he needed to stop and catch his breath. His chest heaved, and his heart pounded with exhaustion. Several of the other prisoners were still running beside him. In their eyes, he had become a hero.

He looked around in the darkness of the night. They were not far from the main town; he could see a few streetlamps in the distance.

"Where do we go from here?" he asked.

They looked at his face for an answer. For once in his life, he felt exalted as if he were leading others like him or wiser than him, and he wondered if he was beginning to be favored by the gods, if he would be stronger, less indecisive, and able to see through where he had failed in the past. Were there levels of apotheosis for mortals?

His feelings soured quickly to helplessness. He stood there, utterly confused, with no idea which way to go to find safety. The darkness was so thick he couldn't see the details of the path he was walking.

Then he felt her hands pulling him along. He saw a disappointed look in Charlie's eyes, as if he had been abandoned, prompting him to take a different path into the night's thick shadows as Andrew turned toward her.

She was walking briskly, and not once did she look back at him.

They reached a small dwelling with dim lights glowing on the porch and an entrance that looked inviting. Exhausted, he sought a place to rest for the night before continuing on.

His mind slowed down; his body slumped, and he fell asleep.

He woke up once, drawn by the subtle scent of jasmine; oh, how he loved it. He pulled her closer. His heart told him it wasn't right, but his body yearned to ignore that. He commanded his mind to stay still.

Andrew had a beautiful dream as he turned away from the jasmine-scented, warm silhouette, and she withdrew. In the vision, Syrian King Theias and his daughter Myrrha slept in incest because of Aphrodite's curse, for Myrrha claimed she was more beautiful than the goddess. The guilt-ridden King Theias chased his daughter to kill her, but Myrrha transformed into a myrrh tree, and soon the trunk split open, giving birth to an extraordinary prince—Adonis.

Andrew, in his dream, felt as if the jasmine-scented silhouette woke up and took baby Adonis far away to the underworld, a place darker than the incest where Persephone stood in her flowing robe, smiling. Would you care for the baby? Yes.

Now, Adonis seemed to have grown up into a very handsome man. Oh, the jasmine-scented is playing with him as Persephone stood irate, jealous, and rushed to snatch him away. There is an old man with a beard separating the two women, giving a verdict: Adonis shall spend four months with each of you and four months by himself.

Andrew began shouting, moaning in terror in his sleep as a wild boar ripped apart Adonis. The jasmine-scented woman stood there wailing desperately to stir up Ares, whom she knew was the deadly killer. She turned Adonis' blood on the ground into so many vibrant, colored flowers- red, purple, pink with dark centers. Andrew babbled, Anemone! Anemone!

But jasmine-scented Anna was wide awake. Watching Andrew babble, she smiled, but not with the same mortal intent. Her eyes flashed fiercely at his mortal body as if to immolate him for some abhorrent sin. Now he was the object of the same relentless gaze she once bore, when Hephaestus had allowed him to witness what no mortal had ever dared.

"You will pay for this… I will make sure… Ares will hear the gossip and act mercilessly. No anemones will ever bloom from your blood. You will perish like Adonis, but I shall never weep."

Andrew changed to the other side of the bed in his deep sleep.

"Unless, of course, someone else offers their life for you. But you are not King Admetus, and you would never have anyone here. For Admetus, Queen Alcestis offered her life. Ha! Ha! Your only mate has also abandoned you, just as it is."

Anna vowed to herself.

Aphrodite could appear among any Anna, but most Andrews of this mortal world would never notice her presence. Jasmine will blind them on most occasions. Will Aphrodite, in the end, have the last laugh?

The next day, Andrew arrived at his shop and opened the back door. He was still in a trance, yet aware that a jasmine-scented spirit had visited him, wrapping him tenderly. However, he did not realize there were many others: Nyx cast darkness into the wilderness, and he lost his way. Her son, Hypnos, poured lead into his eyes as he slid into deep sleep. Twin brother of Hypnos, the psychopomp, Thanatos, excused himself to help someone dying in the corner of the village. Those spirits were in conversation with three Moirai. Clotho said she was done when Andrew was born, Lachesis pretended to be busy spinning a few more yards of life for him, but Atropos had a smirk and kept all of them guessing when, how, or whether she would snip…snip…snip.

Andrew lived unaware that a single mistake from the day before could ultimately determine not only how and when his fortune would grow or collapse, but also if he would survive the snip.

Chapter Thirteen – Apollo

Apollo liked Andrew. His freshness, zest for life, and unapologetic ways made him a good mortal. His fearlessness and unbelieving eyes made him a formidable enemy, if that ever came to it. He ought to find his mate, or Apollo believed something terrible might ensue.

The war for Helen could not be so easily forgotten. Who truly won, and who lost in that war? Apollo still could not decide. Was it right for him to be angry with Laomedon, the king who never paid him for tending the cattle and helping Poseidon build the fortifying walls around Troy?

Could he justify the pestilence he sent upon the Aegean army to castigate Agamemnon for his ravishing Chryseis, the daughter of his priest? And later, was he justified in making Orestes kill his own father, and later, also to save him during his trial?

But he will not regret killing Achilles, who had surpassed all human limits and showed total disregard for other living beings. He felt no remorse for ignoring Poseidon's challenge to fight directly when all other gods had established boundaries outside Troy.

Was he glad that Laomedon's city was washed away after total annihilation for such a trivial fault as not paying him?

Do gods tend to follow their egos rather than being just and virtuous?

Do we need to change?

But the mortals never understand why gods do what they do; they always find simpler explanations for all our divine deeds.

Apollo struggled to remember all his childhood days. He had heard from Leto how, after his birth, she had walked into the temple at Delphi with a baby in her arms. It all seems very impossible now, but it did happen. The baby saw the dragon, cozy in its place and always protected by its mother, Gaia. Apollo drew his bow so intently that he nearly tipped his mother, Leto. The scream that erupted from Python shook the earth, but to no avail. Thus ended a matriarchy and began the oracle Pythia's reign to sing for Apollo—a new beginning for patriarchy.

Currently, Apollo walked briskly toward the southernmost secured place reserved for aliens, since he was told that the mortal was incarcerated there.

He stood near the gate and immediately sensed a mishap.

The gate was wide open and bereft of any residents.

He turned around and, as he proceeded to return, he heard the groans of an injured lion in pain.

He entered and found Heracles unconscious. Searching quickly, Apollo gently splashed water on him. Heracles stirred, pushed him briefly, and then opened his eyes.

"What happened?" Heracles asked.

 "You tell me. Who hurt you?"

Heracles took a sharp breath,

"I was taken aback by the inmates. A woman bolted like the wind seeking succor, and I stood there comforting her. Then a violent gang erupted, hurling hot coals at me. I was blinded, then someone struck me on the head..." he said.

Apollo did not know whether the mortal was involved in the revolt and prison breakout.

"Did you see a man with..." he asked, describing Andrew's features.

Heracles uttered, pondering over,

"My memory must be failing, but I had seen this person somewhere else..."

They spoke for some time. Apollo took Heracles back to his palace for treatment.

"I have a serious concern…" Apollo broached.

"Serious indeed. We never had the whole prison empty like this,"

"Exactly. Something is brewing… an ill wind that brings no good."

Heracles struggled to recognize the danger, but his thoughts were muddled. He was shaken by the breakout. Suddenly, he let out a sharp shriek, clutching his head and venting his anger.

"You need anger management, Heracles… you can't afford the same mistakes. Times have changed."

Heracles looked at him with displeasure.

"What else does my dear cousin have to say? Is he bothered again with the world being unreasonable?"

"I'm worried about our world now. There is something you should know. You know how you sacked Troy and took Priam's sister…?"

Heracles scratched his head and nodded.

"What followed many years later? When Priam wanted his sister back, he sent Paris?"

"Paris was smitten by the beautiful Helen."

"And he ignored the laws of hospitality…"

"So, is someone now repeating the story?"

Apollo paused, then walked again, saying,

"There is a woman missing… and her lover is stricken with grief over her disappearance. He is no ordinary mortal… destined to cause turmoil in our lives. We need to act now."

"Is that a prophecy?"

Apollo did not respond.

"Maybe we should ask Athena to take charge?"

"No… she is not the right person."

"Why?"

"Heracles, do you ever think? You haven't heard this from me either, she has a fascination for strong, wily mortals—like Odysseus."

"True. But what can he do?"

"He already tried to call for help from the mainland. The boat for his succor was destroyed, and you know better than I all about the security information."

"So that boat was called by the same man? That makes sense. I'll tear him apart."

"No. You would be wise not to act on your rage this time."

"Why?"

"Why? Don't you see how the entire world has lost confidence in the true gods? They'll rather believe in some mortal as a god—someone no one has seen but who appears strong and divine. They'll make up stories and pass them down through generations until they seem all true and divine. And if anyone resists, swords, tanks, or even United Nations resolutions will do the rest."

"What, United Nations?"

"Hermes will tell you all about it."

"Come on, Apollo, I am not stupid."

"It's an organization supposedly meant to protect the world, but it only acts according to the whims of a few Caucasian countries."

"It doesn't represent the world population?"

"If they make it representative, it will have Africans and Asians."

"Why don't we correct it?"

"No, Heracles. "

Then they discussed a few more worldly happenings.

There was a lot of news about child abuse by the church and its priests, and the head priest knew all about it.

They would have punished their priests if something like that happened among Olympians. They were open and didn't hide their feelings, even though they had anger issues.

They talked about St Augustine, who had said, " The church is the mother of us all." They wondered if he was concerned to see what was happening in Churches.

"Why was he so critical of the Greek gods?" Heracles asked.

"He was born in Africa in 354 and converted and baptized at the age of 33. For no reason, he started writing extremely derogatory statements about the religion and the Greek language as well."

"Like what?"

"Mostly baseless allegations, like we didn't rescue Regulus when he was tortured to death by his enemies, or we didn't give moral teachings or the right way of living to the worshippers. He also criticized the theaters and shows about gods and goddesses done with humor."

"Did he recognize the humor?"

"No. He merely grasped at his last straws from wherever he could. He forgot that we gave the Greeks a society of order, peace, democracy, art, and philosophy. Our pantheon evolved to offer so much that the Western world continues to follow and enjoy those achievements. Can one person create such a vast world and a magnificent heaven? It is preposterous to think so. It is natural to believe a god behaves close to a human being."

"Exactly. Now they see that throwing other people's religion away with the sword will not do them any good."

They seemed pleased with their discussion.

"So does the great Phoibus believe we will be back to reclaim our place among the commoners?"

"I believe people will emerge from organized religions and think independently of gods and goddesses without form or attributes, so they remain enigmatic and inexplicable."

"That seems very hard to imagine…"

"So, they will create shapes and forms inspired by their local customs—heroes dressed like them, speaking their language, and relishing their food. And as their minds evolve, they will abandon those figures and pray to the unknown, the supreme, the true divine god."

Heracles nodded approvingly at the god of light. They both seemed satisfied with their exchange. Apollo stood under a tree to rest. He pulled out a lyre and began to play gently. The tune fascinated even the uncouth Heracles, who closed his eyes, pitying St. Augustine for missing such a magnificent creation as Phoibus—an embodiment of truth, the great healer, lord of the silver bow, and the unceasing source of melody. In Delos, people learned to speak only the truth and nothing less to their oracle, for brilliant Phoibus taught how to cleanse and expiate from sin, because men commit sin only after they grow up in this world.

Men are not born sinners, and children do not sin by crying lustily for milk.

Chapter Fourteen – Zeus

When Zeus mates with mortal women, a hero is born; but when he mates with a goddess, another god is created. Heracles was mortal and was later made a god. Dionysus is a real exception, born of Semele, a mortal.

Zeus sat on his throne today, very lonely. Hera has been busy with many things. He had breakfast with her. She seemed perturbed again. Her pretty face displayed no mirth while serving him the nectar. She remained restless, as if about to ask a question, but held back until he spoke.

"Is my fair queen contemplating some unrest with our son Hephaestus?"

That was enough to infuriate our queen mother, and she turned her eyes back to him without betraying any anger.

"I suppose a wife has no choice but to endure humiliation. But doesn't the thunder maker realize his days are numbered? Mortals have chosen gods who consistently show none of their traits—none. They do not have any temptation. But, oh, king of my heart, can you be truthful to me, for all the love and care I give to you and our children? Is it too much for a wife to ask where her husband has been passing his precious time? Is it another divine responsibility or a desire to mate with someone else?"

At this, Father God smiled gently.

"Mother of Hebe and Hestia, what nonsense are you speaking? Do you truly believe in your heart that gods could be created as mortals imagine and fantasize?"

"Athena's father knows my answer well. But it has been almost two thousand years since we lost our grounds, and the mortals have been fooled into believing in gods that follow all moral codes..." She paused.

"Well, go on... the same code of conduct we break—the temptations humans easily fall for, and we get caught by just as easily, if not for carnal reasons?"

"Exactly. All those temptations, all that fascination with mysterious power that leads you to engender unions of strength with fertility, reasoning with sentiment..."

"The raw masculinity blending with melting femininity, the ruthless shearing of the sword paired with the undying love of a recent widow..."

"Oh god, please. Dear Zeus, either stop loving me or cease your ubiquitous presence among all that is charming, all that blooms toward the future..."

"Mother of Ares, neither shall I ever cease to love you, nor pretend not to exist. Since I will never be destroyed and you will stay my wife for eternity, while myriads of mortals will be named gods, and their priests suffer humility at the peak of their glory and puissance," Zeus declared.

"So, is it true that a mere mortal is bothering you?" she broached carefully.

"He has not bothered me. He has broken our laws, and Heracles shall find him."

"Do you care why he is so desperate?"

"Hera, everything is predestined. Don't weaken me, as you did during the Trojan War, with all your charm to disarm me, just as Poseidon incited the Greeks. We ended up with carnage, slaughter, and defilement of our own temples—an unnatural denouement."

"If so, why not change the course of events, so death is avoided, destruction stalled, and we remain in the hearts of our followers as saviors, as deliverers?"

"My sweet seductress! A contrived world? The way mortals want to believe a god should be is to protect and to redeem when they recall us. So, they have created their own religions—unnatural, one god possessing all positive attributes who performs miracles and saves sinners, even though they cannot find examples to impress others; whereas it takes many to complete any task: to build a house, a bridge, a school, or a hospital."

"Even the rainmaker cannot change the course of events. Save poor lives ready to be slaughtered by enemy forces?"

"The wars must be fought by mortals. Who loses and who wins, who dies and who survives, depends on so many things that divine intervention should not even be called for. No. I know some will try to take advantage of these situations, arguing that if we did not save pagans, we do not exist; but eventually their own sins will catch up, rotting the system of false praises for some supernatural force."

"What will happen to us?"

"Let the daughters of Themis—our sweet Moirai—dish out the fates. Let Clotho, Lachesis, and Atropos spin the threads of life..."

"And you?" Hera asked.

"In disputes, I'll weigh with my golden balance who shall live and who shall not."

The father of fates and seasons smiled, keeping the queen enthralled for ages.

But Zeus did not remain complacent with Hera. Disguised, he walked out to evaluate the situation himself. He reached the cave where Rhea lived. She showed delight, knowing instantly who he was.

"Am I unable to hide from you?"

"Father of gods has a countenance..."

"Of senility? I am not competing with Apollo or Ares here, am I?"

"Neither. You are quite handsome for an old man. Anyway, I have not met all your children. When will you take me to the palace? Will I ever meet your spouse?"

"Don't even think about it."

"Why? What's wrong with me?"

"Not with you. Do you want to turn into an animal? Say, like a cow chased by gadflies as with Io, or a bear, only to be killed by Artemis as with Callisto?"

"I'll speak with her, and she'll understand."

"Instead, you should talk to your mortal mate," Zeus suggested.

"Now what is he doing?"

"He called for help from the mainland, which was foiled—and then he escaped our jail."

"Oh god!"

"Yes."

"No, not you. It was just an exclamation," she explained.

"Tell him to cool it. Tell him not to seek succor from distant people. Our island is threatened by this world. We need a place not in heaven but within our subjects. We must endure the sacrilege until it all ends."

"So, you believe paganism will return?"

"Not paganism, but the true religion of the land. The original gods all live in different parts of this planet, just dormant."

"You mean hibernating?"

"Don't use that word; it smells like a frog."

Rhea had another issue to talk about, and she hesitated.

"Something bothering you?" Zeus asked.

"No, nothing…"

It was hard for her to talk about her own problems. This man was supposedly the strongest and capable of granting her wish. So, why wouldn't she ask? She had failed so many times that now she could neither hope nor dream of anything new. Life was short for mortals, and she would die without experiencing the joy of motherhood. She didn't want to have children before marriage, but who knew when Andrew would propose again? She was getting there, and in a few years, her risk of birth defects would increase. So, this was her chance, with some divine help.

"You have to help me…"

"Help?"

Rhea couldn't be more explicit and turned her face away. Her eyes filled with tears; her voice faded. How could she ask for what she genuinely believed would help? Zeus has been kind to her, showing his affection in more than one way—and she found it very acceptable. Zeus was just a good man. Yeah, she thought. He may be the god by name, but he was so normal, so humane, that it is hard to see him as a god. Her upbringing doesn't allow her to accept any god so close to her own kind. Yet here is one so sensitive, who listens to every word she has to say, who visits her regularly, who laughs with her, and touches her only when appropriate. Her eyes welled up, and she felt the tears streaming down both cheeks unbridled.

Zeus sat quietly, lost in thought about this world. He had many more problems than just comforting Rhea. He wanted to speak with the Moirai—the Fate sisters. Zeus bore the responsibility not only for the continuation of humans but also for the immortals. Just because he liked his creation, this group of mortals, he found it hard to annihilate them as he had in the past. But he is the one monitoring the limits of sin and the one who will bring a new race.

He remembered what Ares said during their last argument with Aphrodite. Ares asked Aphrodite if she had slept with a mortal. She didn't answer, which only made him more upset. The Fate sisters must have already decided the mortal's destiny by now.

Zeus felt deep pity, not for the loss of the mortal but for how poor Rhea would react if or when she ever learned what Andrew had done and what he was fated for.

He saw her face and could think no more. He rose and pulled her close to his bosom.

"Would you despair for your mortal mate if some unforeseen misfortune befell him?"

Rhea heard him and felt something break inside her, shattering into a million pieces under the weight of the unknown. She felt helplessness creeping under her skin as she fought against the old man.

And as the most powerful man on earth or heaven pulled her closer… she relaxed slightly, deciding she would ask him later about Andrew's fate.

Wouldn't it be difficult for Rhea to stay still and stiff? Wouldn't it be easier for her just to give up? Give up in her bewildered mind, in her dry heart, and in every tired, hankering cell of her body?

She buckled gently like a tiny wave lapping the shore. The one who created everything smiled and played with a limpid teardrop at the tip of his finger.

She allowed him, but only to wipe her tears.

The town square bustled as usual. No one bothered to foresee the future. Zeus pulled his shawl up to cover his lower face. He stood in a corner watching the crowd. How innocent, how vulnerable this human race appeared. They seem so engrossed in their mundane lives: buying grain, tending business, cleaning, and sweeping the streets. They have no inkling of what is stored soon.

Where was he? He should be back at his shop. Zeus wouldn't stir up any problem at this point. He was weighing something. Then Zeus thought of a little trick and walked close to the shop.

Andrew carefully balanced the weights and sugar until the balance seemed perfectly level. He needed to add some sugar. Then he tried again, and this time had to remove some. The customer grew impatient as Andrew struggled. The scale seemed faulty. He moved to the larger scale usually meant for heavier weights. Again, he needed to add sugar.

The owner stood beside him as Andrew kept adding more sugar. The customer smiled in delight; he would get extra for nothing. The owner decided to take control and moved Andrew aside. He took some new weights and replaced the ones used earlier. The balance tilted heavily toward the sugar side, and he smiled gleefully as he scooped the extra sugar away. He had to remove a large amount before the balance would even respond. Now there was only a modicum of the commodity left. The buyer became restless and protested. By this time, a small crowd had gathered, discussing how citizens are cheated every day by merchants. Andrew stepped back, sensing their hostility. He would not get involved in any trouble at this point.

The crowd grew impatient, and one of them stepped forward to weigh.

The balance behaved perfectly, and the amount now seemed correct. The crowd cheered victoriously and sneered at the owner with contempt. Someone grabbed the owner's collar and lifted him up, accusing him of deceit. A middle-aged lady approached and spat in his face. The people enjoyed the reproach and suggested various punishments for the dishonest merchant.

Andrew noticed an old man in the corner watching the episode. Where has he seen him before? Who is he? Is he dreaming again?

Zeus stood smiling. The god of gods knew this mortal was certainly no ordinary man, and he noticed some portending signs that made him uncomfortable. He was walking toward him. Zeus knew he had to do something, but felt some strange, unsettling premonition in his heart. No, the Fates were against his plan. This mortal would not perish so easily. It would take a lot to impair him.

Andrew came closer. Zeus looked at him with those bright eyes that made people stop.

Andrew couldn't come any nearer; he stared in awe, rooted to the ground. His face turned pale. His courage vanished, and words wouldn't come. Beads of sweat appeared on his forehead.

Andrew felt weak as the old man gazed at him with knife-sharp intensity that rattled his knees.

He could say nothing.

His head dropped as if in deep obeisance.

Zeus turned around and walked away briskly.

People on this island waited eagerly for a day of fun and frolic. They call it Karneia, a festival honoring Apollo Karneios. Protagoras was selected by his group, along with four other rich merchants, to raise the funds for the festival's expenses.

His excitement for the joyous occasion faded as he thought about his share of the costs. Usually, they assigned this task to unmarried men, but it seemed they couldn't find five bachelors willing to agree.

Still, like all Greeks, he was not a killjoy and was eagerly getting ready for the day.

The stadium was closed to the public for foot races and other events. Tents were erected on a clear area where the men would stay, sit, and eat together as comrades. The pillars, gates, and streets were adorned with laurel leaves and twigs. Little boys and girls ran everywhere, helping their fathers. The Stade-track for the foot race was cleared and marked.

Andrew visited the area a few times. No one had bothered him since. He grew his hair and stopped shaving. Even Rhea would have a hard time recognizing him.

"The old king and his family are expected," Protagoras announced.

"The Karneia seems like a major festival here," Andrew observed.

"The king decides how to reward the runners…"

Andrew saw a glimmer of hope. What if he won? Would the king reward him? He could ask for his help to find Rhea and set them free. That was it. Once Rhea left this place, she would change. Everything could be turned back to where they started, the two people in love, the way it was -Andrew and Rhea, meant for each other. If the gods wouldn't help, perhaps the king might.

"I want to be a karneatai," he declared.

"Are you sure? What if someone…" Protagoras questioned.

"I don't care. The worst is getting arrested again."

Protagoras was surprised. These Americans were wretched and would do anything to achieve their goal. His heart told him to remove Andrew from all danger. He could hurt himself. No, he was not helping him.

"I'm sorry, but I don't think you qualify as a grape runner…"

Then he noticed his face change color. He was disappointed. This was an opportunity to eliminate this trouble forever. He didn't even have to fire him. Let him become dejected and flee this place, which was so ominous for such a nice gentleman.

But Andrew looked at him again, and this time artlessly demanded to be included.

"Fine, let's go. But don't get me into trouble. I don't know you… all right?"

Andrew nodded.

Protagoras brought two masks from inside.

Two bears or Arktoi commenced for the festival grounds.

They dismounted and tied their horses in a safe, shaded place. The sun shone brightly, and the air grew warm. A little boy came running to feed the horses. Protagoras initially howled at him, then threw a few coins.

The stadium could seat at least ten thousand people. The king and his family sat in the royal box—the pulvinar—and behind them, the senators, priests, and vestal virgins in rows behind. The common people sat at a distance.

"They will have a foot race in the stadium?" Andrew asked.

"No. Behind the stadium is a clear area. We will cross through, it's a shortcut."

They came to the ground where Andrew saw nine tents, each tended by men from different communities.

"See those five people together?"

"Yeah?"

"They are the Karneatai—chosen to pay for the event. They are all bachelors."

"Should we talk to them?"

"Let us try."

Protagoras introduced himself. They started laughing when they realized they wanted to participate as well.

"We're looking for a victim, you know? Someone who will run against us."

"What does the victim get?" Andrew asked.

They didn't answer. Someone chuckled darkly.

"Death!" one of them shouted.

Protagoras pulled Andrew away.

They walked off. Andrew was surprised.

"Well, actually, no one is sacrificed anymore. Our king is against all violence."

Suddenly, the place started bustling with a growing crowd. The tents were packed, and groups of people rejoiced. Small shops sold ornaments, clothes, and toys. A few horses ran free. Andrew saw togas everywhere. His eyes searched for Rhea.

The procession of gods entered the ground. People carried statues of Zeus, Apollo, and Artemis. The chanting of praise for the gods submerged all other noise.

"Zeus, the king of gods! The Thunderer and Maker of Rain, oh Zeus, father of worthy Athena. Oh, Zeus—who rules the world!"

"Oh Father, keep this land safe. Vanish all the invaders like you vanished, Typhoeus.

Send your powerful thunder against any ship approaching us!"

"We are the last children of the gods. We belong to you."

Andrew was moved, overwhelmed as he saw people crying, women in tears. These people were loyal to their gods.

Next came the procession of the king and his family, accompanied by knights. When everyone took their seats, Andrew could see three men near the royal seats. They all stood tall and were ready to deliver their tasks.

The first was the hierus – a priest dressed in a long-sleeved purple chiton, floor-length, with a himation covering his upper body. His waist was tied with a deep violet sash.

A mageiros who would be slicing meat stood defiant in white short chiton.

A kreonomos, looking like a commoner, waited to distribute the meat.

The hiereus at the altar raised his hands and read aloud the prayer, propitiating the pantheon.

The fire was lit on the altar, and a goat was brought in for sacrifice. The priest sprinkled the holy water, and it bleated helplessly.

A maiden with a crown of flower wreath approached with a knife in a basket.

The knife shone in the bright sun. The head of the animal was held down tight by a man, and the heiros raised his weapon high and brought it down in one swift blow to stun the goat and slice its throat.

Women cried out ololyge—ulu-lu-lu-lu. Ulu-lu-lu-lu.

The gushing blood was collected in a bowl and poured onto the altar.

The mageiros began his swift cutting, and after tending to the animal, he threw the meat into the fire.

The kreonomos took the meat and distributed to people close to the altar.

The king raised his hand signaling the sport to begin, and five naked men started running fast. They were chasing after the fat man covered with wool, who struggled to reach the end.

People cheered. One of the runners closed in on the victim. The crowd seemed to get a kick from one of the clowns who tried to come in between as if saving the victim.

But instead, the clown pushed the victim, nearly causing him to fall.

"Get him! Kill him!"

"Don't let him go any further!"

The purposely appointed victim could have been Andrew. He showed no anger and continued to walk briskly, rather than running, weighed down by his heavy clothing. They caught him.

The crowd erupted in uproar. The race was over.

Andrew and Protagoras left the ground before chaos broke out.

"What will they do to him?"

"In the past, they killed…"

Andrew did not ask more.

"Karnos was a seer killed by the Heracleidae before the invasion of the Peloponnese. This festival is their atonement, a ritual for relief against plague in the army by Apollo," Protagoras explained.

Andrew walked in despair. Nothing had changed. How would he ever get Rhea back from these crazy people?

"The chariot race is our best sport. She may come there…" Protagoras whispered, as if he read his mind.

Chapter Fifteen – Athena

She likes many of the epithets that the Greeks have used for her in the past, except when they called her "the terrible eye." She prefers green-eyed Athena Polias (protector of cities), Athena Parthenos (temple of the virgin), and Athena Pronaos (since she stands before Apollo in Delphi). She is ambivalent about Pallas Athenae and the stories connected to that name—did she kill the giant Pallas and use his skin for her aegis, or was Pallas her playmate who died accidentally in her hands? Similarly, she feels conflicted about Athena Persepolis—the destroyer of cities. She helped bring down the fall of Troy, where her own Palladian stood tall for generations. Yet, when the Achaeans entered, she stood silent as they desecrated her altar with the murder of Priam and the unnecessary spilling of the blood of men, women, and children. Hector's baby was thrown from the walls of Troy, and the Greek generals carried his mother and wife as war prizes. Athena did not move to save those helpless people.

But Athena works in her own way. She could not save the Trojans because of what they had done in the past—inviting the Greeks to their own destruction by keeping Helen, even after knowing what Paris had done by abducting a married woman from the friendly palace of Menelaus. Her wrath at Paris for declaring Aphrodite the fairest may have had a small effect, but mostly, it was the deterioration within the Trojans themselves and the need to move forward in creating a new nation that would bring light to the rest of the world, in Rome, that led to the total downfall.

Pallas Athenae never gets restless. Among her siblings, she has the most excellent understanding, but she is somewhat disturbed by recent events. This mortal is not good news. Andrew is becoming a nuisance for this island, and if she is right, he will bring deep trouble. The people here are so vulnerable and so loyal that Athena feels it is her responsibility to ensure their safety and victory if a struggle occurs. However, Andrew has the right to find his mate and leave without causing carnage. It sounds like a simple task, like when Helen was abducted, but it has already become a bone of contention among various gods. Hera is furious, suspecting that Father Zeus has something to do with this mortal woman, and she has already spoken with Hephaestus. This is causing such division within the family that all old rivalries and grievances are once again resurfacing.

Ares told Hermes to locate her as soon as possible. Apollo seems to agree with finding her and sending her away with Andrew to the mainland. This time, all the gods want to be on the right side—so justice is served, irrespective of their own feelings. Poseidon is keeping his forces on alert after a boat was sunk from the mainland.

This is the last place the gods' family would like to see destroyed. A few thousand islanders know Zeus as their king and Hera as the queen. They also believe their royal family never ages and never dies. For whatever reason, this small population has remained safe and free from significant natural disasters for over two thousand years. They believe the gods are kind to the royal family and will not bring other religions here. In the past, Christian missionaries who landed on the island disappeared mysteriously, with no one knowing what happened, and no one lamented their fate.

Milk and cheese are abundant here. Olive orchards bring all the oil they need and more. Wine is made locally. Bread, eggs, meat, and vegetables cost almost nothing.

So why would anyone want the mainland's culture, religion, or prosperity?

Athena was waiting for Andrew to come out of his shop. She wanted to know his game plan. She would like to help him.

Andrew saw her and paused. The glaukopis goddess, with her blue-green shimmering eyes, gazed deeply into the mortal. He mumbled,

"Athena Polias!"

"Andrew!"

He remained frozen at a safe distance, his eyes hesitant on her. Her body was adorned with a silk robe, her neck covered with a glittering necklace, and her feet in bright sandals. Why doesn't she wear her terrible aegis, and where was the shield with Gorgon's head? She could be mistaken for any mortal with such a beautiful figure and features—maybe a princess. But mortals do not possess such strength or an intense power that inspires awe, as Andrew felt now. Andrew was facing a force —a natural phenomenon that could turn against him in an instant and wipe him out completely. He knew she could not be made unhappy; her enemies did not live long.

"You made a fool of yourself the other day…"

"I wanted to win the contest."

"And what would you have gained?"

"Favor from the royal family."

Athena remained silent. Andrew's supplication softened her. She wanted to help him even more now. Not letting her emotions betray her, she thought, "Never have I felt such sympathy for a mortal except for Odysseus and, maybe, Orestes. I make the earth groan and the ocean foam as I walk, and now I…"

Andrew took courage and looked at her innocently. She walked closer, and an unknown fragrance suffused the air. Andrew felt lighter, as if he floated into the sky and was taken with her—much like she had done with Achilles, pulling his hair just as he was about to strike Agamemnon with his sword.

"Pandrosos!" he called her, the maiden who gave us the olive.

"Don't, no. Andrew, please. Even gods, I mean, that is not what…"

Andrew took a chance. What could a mere mortal think other than his own benefit, his selfish gain? Even a goddess could be used if he could impress her, a virgin goddess.

"Is it true what people say about the daughters of Kekrops? You trusted them with your son, and they opened the chest out of curiosity to find your son, Erichthonios. Why did they jump from the Acropolis to their deaths?"

The goddess looked distraught at this story. Why did she have to justify herself to a mortal for anything?

"Aglauros, Pandrosos, and Herse broke their promise. No one knew my secret, and I did not give birth to Erichthonios—so why should they know and reveal something that goes against my beliefs? Anyway, it was their guilt that drove them to their deaths."

"Mortals are laden with guilt and remorse?"

"And us…" she said, her face flushing auburn with embarrassment.

Athena wanted to talk about the present, but Andrew lingered on the past. He thought of her origin—was she really born from Zeus's skull, or was that a metaphor? A mountain peak where she was found? Was she fully grown and armored as she appeared? Her lack of aegis and shield bothered him. Is she vulnerable like any other woman, or is he just daydreaming? Is she here to warn him or to caution him? Andrew, after all, was struggling against all of them. He smiled, deducing that she was trying to get information from him. He decided to exhaust her.

"Athena Persopolis! Why would you trouble your own disciples? Why did you not let Odysseus return safely to his nostos?"

"Andrew, since you called me Persepolis, yes, I was. But there was a fair reason, and what the Greeks had done after the fall of Troy was hardly heroic. Crafty Odysseus was to blame for many of the post-victory ills, and his ten years of peregrination were a suitable reproach for the best of the Achaeans."

"Then why spare his life? And kill Agamemnon?"

"Odysseus was essential to save Ithaca from those worthless suitors of Penelope. I had to protect the country. And Andrew, call me Athena Polias instead. Will you?"

At this, her terribly green eyes brightened. The slim neck of the goddess stiffened, and her immortal shoulders—bearing those supple arms that had once helped Atlas hold the earth with ease—strengthened.

"I need your help," he whispered.

She looked perplexed at his supplication. What if she refused? What if he calls the ships from the mainland? This island cannot withstand any sophisticated naval force. Where would that leave us again?

"I inspire men's passion to fight, and I admire the war hoop. However, here, it feels so destructive and unnecessary that I will do everything to avoid conflict. Still, if I help you, you must promise me something…"

"Yes?"

"No harm should come to this land from your conspiracy. You will not be the agent of misery among the mortals here."

"I have no grievance against the simple folks living here. It is only Rhea and whoever she is…"

Athena smiled at his helplessness. Did Paris realize how Helen truly felt for him? Do most men even try to think before falling in love? Poor Andrew. Did Penelope wait ten years for Odysseus out of love, or...? Athena grew restless. Why was she so crafted to feel for both sexes at the same time? Why couldn't she be simply a woman—the one who loved weaving, tamed horses for the chariot, hid the baby Erichthonios in a basket, and used Peitho- persuasion, to transform the Furies into the Eumenides—the kindly ones?

Chapter Sixteen - Artemis

When the other gods were busy managing affairs in the Trojan War, did Artemis care? The Potnia Theron (Mistress of Animals), as she was called, wandered freely through the woods, meadows, and dark crevices of forests, as well as the clefts and peaks of mountains, chasing wild beasts in her own ecstatic delight. Known as the virgin goddess—the loveliest one, or Kallisto—the terrible one, or Semnotata—her mother Leto rejoiced in her girlish, untamed beauty and even helped her when she was scoffed at by her stepmother Hera. Artemis stood fearlessly against Hera and supported the Trojans. Still, at times she endured great humiliation, especially when Hera pushed her, boxed her ears, and ridiculed her so severely that this terrible goddess had to run back to Olympus and whine to her father. Leto, ever calm and gentle, would gather her scattered arrows and neatly return them to her quiver with a tender smile and quiet demeanor.

Presently, Artemis sat by a brook, wondering what had gone wrong and why she could not understand Athena's behavior. Pallas was supposed to join her at a small festival where the town girls were being initiated into Artemisian ways. They all were so excited after traveling from different parts of the island, aged between nine and fifteen, supposedly all virgins. They wore small chitons and sported short hair, just like their goddess. They danced in circles with small plants or phalluses on their heads, like the village of Karyai, for their Karyatis. The beating of drums and the shrieking crowd enlivened the temple outskirts, much like the old times near Athens. The giggling nymphs, their lustrous eyes, and wild cries echoed alongside the piercing sounds of sacrificed animals. The Arktoi, or she-bears as these girls were called, sang and invoked the goddess with cries of "Potnia! Potnia! Semnotata!" Artemis does require sacrifice—but only of animals. The Greek tales of human sacrifice do not please our Semnotata.

Iphigenia was a different matter. Agamemnon did kill a stag in her sacred temple at Auli, but that was not the reason she asked for Iphigenia's sacrifice. Her father, blinded by pride, had gathered thousands of warriors to wage war against Troy. He was ready to kill all the Trojans for his glory and to save his sister-in-law from the hands of her lover, Paris. So, the virgin huntress forced him to face the cruel dilemma of sacrificing his own daughter before the winds would cease and his ships could sail. Agamemnon had called Clytemenestra and Iphigenia back with the pretense of marrying her to Achilles. The poor maiden came rushing with her mother, only to face her father's knife for the sake of the Greeks. She implored him, clutching his knees, for mercy—pleading to live, to grow old, to marry, and bear grandchildren—but to no avail. Agamemnon turned to stone, deafened by the battle cries. He drowned his wife's and daughter's tears and pleas in his cruel misdeed—a crime to any other father, a heinous act of detestable quality for any parent to spill the blood of his own offspring to please a goddess. But Artemis had flown poor Iphigenia away from that altar to a distant land, where she had placed her safely in her own temple for many years, until Orestes recovered her from the region of Cherronese. So, Artemis was not the bloodthirsty goddess people thought her to be.

Men do sacrifice stags and goats before hunting for her. They also perform Kordax dance for their Kordaka. She accepts their prayers as she does those of her Arktoi.

Artemis was a virgin, but she was not devoid of all the feelings any young maiden carried in her bosom at that time, like her mortal disciples. Yet, she was bound by her own rules and limits as the goddess of childbirth, wilderness, and weddings. She knew Aktaion, son of Autonoe and Aristaios, uncle of Dionysus (cousin to Semele). He had wandered off while hunting and must have fumbled just as she was getting undressed to bathe. And in that fateful hour, as she stood near the brook with nothing on her, his eyes beheld the most sacred, the purest of the gods—unconcealed—and he was awestruck by those splendid prospects that even gods had never seen unrestricted. For once, she thought he would leave, and she waited, holding her immortal breath and biting her slender lips tightly with her marble-white teeth to the point that her ichor would seep. Still, his desire had peaked, and with valiant, gentle steps, he ventured slowly toward that very sacred, that very unattainable presence.

The unclothed virgin girls, ready to bathe with the goddess, frozen on the grounds in shock, suddenly exposed to a mere mortal. But the prince was oblivious to all.

"What am I seeing with my eyes? Is this an apparition? Why do I feel this way—as if I've waited all my life for this, as if the gods designed this maiden in the wild for me?" he whispered.

She trembled as his princely hands began to explore her, and she closed her timid eyes. His warm, fragrant breath fell upon her face as she tried to cover herself with her fair hands, but he was so impassioned. She had nothing on her mind, absolutely nothing. She wished her fate to be controlled by the Moirai. Gradually, she found herself giving in and slid into his arms, strong yet gentle. They slumped on the soft grass. The South Wind rustled, and inside her was a unique calm yet overpowering desire: to know, to feel, and to be close to someone so innocent, so refreshing, and so different from the gods.

But why was he so eager? Why wouldn't he understand she was a goddess? When she awoke from her short ecstasy, her eyes met the hateful gaze of her disciples, almost asking, imploring her to stop. She felt the emergence of a strong current within her, which was what she was meant to be and what mortals and immortals expected of her.

Suddenly, she pushed him aside and stood up, her chest heaving from passion and desire. Then she threw a stag's pelt over him as he weakly, almost unwillingly, recoiled. She glanced at her virgins and stepped aside to let the prince walk away. He had stood there for a moment as if waiting for a last word from her, but she could not say what she felt. Her lips pouted, and the marble-white breasts shone defiantly.

He walked away in disgrace, head bowed and eyes downcast in shame.

Later, when the sacred grounds shook violently, and shrieks echoed through the dense woods, a flock of birds took flight in fright. Artemis shivered in pain.

The prince Aktaion was ripped apart by his own hounds, muscle by muscle, after being disguised by the stag pelt the goddess had thrown over him as a gift. He chose not to oppose the beasts. How could a mortal remove the gift of the goddess from his mortal body? It was a gift of death.

And mortals still believe that male sexuality, in its attempt to tame feminine purity and the untrodden meadows of the maiden's mind, finds its most significant challenge in Artemis, the protector of maidens. She dwells in the wild side of mortal life, tames the animals, and castigates any attempt to violate female chastity.

But Artemis wished to live an everyday life. She was so different from her sister Athena. Undoubtedly very strong, she was also deeply feminine—unquestionably ruthless only when challenged by the beast. She was sweet, kind, and inspired to live, to frolic, and to survive the coming marauders, invaders, and destroyers of the wild.

But currently, our virgin goddess was concerned about Athena. What had kept her away from the festival? Why was she so preoccupied? What was the matter with the old lady Hera again?

Why was she traveling all over to search for someone? The family of gods had been peaceful for a long time until something very unusual happened: the landing of this iron bird. This was a bad omen. Something very sinister was brewing, and no one seemed to discuss it in detail. Why would the gods care about a mere mortal? But then this was how things were two thousand years ago—so much reverence, such a good cult, such glory, and what a splendid following for all of us. It all vanished like a dream. The people, the rulers, the priests all turned around and ceased to worship, suddenly stopped all the rites and rituals, and turned the temples into history. So, Artemis felt something was changing again. It couldn't get any worse, since there was very little left anyway, or could it?"

Athena might be busy with serious business. Was it a family feud? The beginning of another war? If it were a war, Artemis decided she would show it to all this time. Hera wouldn't be able to box her ears and chase her away. She would certainly protest or, better yet, she would actively fight her stepmother.

The virgin goddess made a promise to herself; she would help the mortal against her own mother, Hera.

The islanders flock to the stadium for the chariot race. It all starts a week before the real race when people begin to prepare. They have teams, each colored just like the old Roman custom: The red, orange, yellow, and green teams. Training starts after the chariots are made and players are selected. It is a professional sport that can bring considerable prestige, financial rewards, and lucrative sponsors. Since it is such a small place, the rich and poor, common and powerful, men and gods, all are involved. Traditionally, if a team realizes it has the support of a powerful family or the royal family, it feels much more secure, knowing abundant resources will be available to prepare. But the outcome is not dependent on the sponsors; rather, it depends on the players themselves and their horses.

Protagoras has a cousin who participated in the race for ten years before he had an accident, and he now advises the green team only.

"What experience do you have as a charioteer before?" he asked.

The friends looked at one another but offered no answer. The old man got impatient and closed his eyes.

"How can I ask this of you? My conscience prevents me from hurting you, first my team, then you. It's certainly very exciting when people roar and horses fly, but in a flash, you can hit the side or another vehicle and break into pieces, torn flesh and broken bones."

The silence that followed this harsh remark made Protagoras hesitant, and Andrew weak. His resolve flattened, and he thought better of it.

"Only if you are totally fearless, unconditionally dedicated—maybe Hades will spare you, and you can give your best, even if your best may not be enough…"

"That will give me a reason to live. They say the winner becomes the king's favorite, isn't it?"

The cousin smiled at his childish suggestion.

"And losers bite the dust."

Finally, he agreed to have a training session before presenting Andrew to the other sponsors and advisors of the green team. The team had not been so fortunate in recent years. The last time they won was seven years ago. They had a hard time finding sponsors. It is expensive to train the horses, buy all the latest equipment, and feed the animals and the charioteer. People of noble descent usually spend the money for the prestige it brings in society. The winner is adorned with the sacred wreath made from olive. Every year, the king offers prizes to compensate the winner for his expenses, such as jars of olive oil, gold kettles, and amphorae painted with pictures of gods and goddesses, among other items.

"I will bring you honor," Andrew said confidently.

The old man stared at him, then slowly nodded.

As they walked back, Protagoras remained silent, skeptical, and fearful for Andrew's safety.

"You don't know the consequences..." Protagoras mumbled.

"No, I don't. I have never done this sport," Andrew answered.

"You should ponder and decide."

"Look, I'm a fine rider, so it can't be that dangerous. If I feel during training, it's not for me; I'll quit."

Protagoras knew Andrew wouldn't change his mind. He prayed with his hands raised in obeisance to Nike, hoping either to be helped or at least protected.

For four weeks straight, Andrew was drilled alongside four other Greeks for the event. The team would field two chariots, each with a backup rider. Training began before sunrise, involving feeding and cleaning the horses. Protagoras hired temporary help for his shop and occasionally visited the camp.

The training chariot had two wheels and a central pole. Two horses were yoked to the pole. The basket rested on the axle between the wheels, with sides and front guards to protect the rider; the open back allowed easy mounting and dismounting. The basket was made of light wood and reinforced with bronze in certain places. The wheels had about four to eight spokes and were fitted with iron tires.

The pole ended in front into two yokes. The horses had saddles, bridles, and leather reins tied securely around the charioteer for safety.

"Learn to let go of the left or right rein depending on your turn. Slacken them as you face the deadly pillars, so the steed understands how to turn."

The trainer Theomnestus preached.

"Don't race recklessly. Negotiate the curves and other chariots."

"How do I win the race?"

"You do not win…let others go down. Just watch and keep your horses away from the fast ones," Theomnestus added.

Andrew fell off the chariot many times at first, bruising all over. He returned to his small room, determined not to show up the next day. But somehow, all the pain and anguish seemed small in the hollow of the night, and he walked to the ground carrying his despair and bodily pain. By the end of the week, he was riding comfortably, falling only when he attempted to speed up. His horses would lick him when he lay flat on the ground in despair, as if sensing he might not make it. The trainer was tough and kicked his ass a thousand times.

"Racetrack has no mercy," Theomnestus said.

Andrew began to believe in his cause. He started to race with zest, and his partners were pleasantly surprised as he gradually showed his mettle.

One day, he was told to go home very early. The next day, the festival would begin.

All the gods met in the palace the same evening while Andrew slept soundly, exhausted from weeks of training. Zeus and Athena spoke about the upcoming event, while Ares and Aphrodite flirted unabashedly. Ares continued to bother Aphrodite, asking about her recent dealings with some mortal men. She laughed and assured him he could do whatever he desired if he knew about some ungodly happenings. She did not care.

Hera and Hephaestus concurred on some issues as Hermes coaxed Apollo to agree not to disrupt the event with his mood. Hebe served nectar, and Heracles stood guard outside. Artemis sat silently near Demeter, who cautioned Persephone on her next trip to the Underworld. Dionysus seemed tired but smiled for no reason at everyone.

"The tradition dictates that we select a winner for the most important event," Hera stated loudly.

"Hera, this is not an issue for the Olympians," Zeus requested.

"The winner is blessed by us and naturally protected from all evils," Hera replied.

"Does Mother want any special favors?" Ares asked.

Hera scowled at her son. Ares returned her gaze but was not truly present in this exchange with the queen. He was planning to punish a mortal. He wished Aphrodite would not repeat her liberties with unknown people. But he had no control over her affairs, so he planned to end the mortal's life and set an example for the future. He will find out the whereabouts of the man she holds dear. He hoped his siblings would not side with the mortal.

He stood up defiantly, then sat down again as if to apologize. Athena wondered why this simple mortal event so perturbed Hera.

"Whoever wins fairly shall become our hero as well, and we should bless him forever," Apollo suggested.

Zeus, the knower of all and father of the gods, became restless.

"Justice will be served to a holy person. No deception, no perfidy."

Athena did not like this simple yet profound verdict.

"The winner becomes holy. His present act is what we reward—victory or loss."

The prayers to Zeus started the day, followed by sacrifices. They offered lamb and healthy oxen at the altar. The priests burned lamps, incense, and meat, along with barley and olive oil, to the gods. The king indicated his happiness, and all the trumpets blew in unison, shaking the ground and inciting the crowd as they thundered with loud noise, supporting their teams. Before the race began, Andrew noticed Rhea walking close by. She watched him in his full gear; the horse remained calm, as if it knew its master needed nurturing just before the race. She stood there firmly, her face uplifted in her festive gown, hands clasped behind her back.

"Why? Why, Andrew?"

He was so pleased that his hands began to shake, his heart raced, and he knew she loved him. He did not utter a word.

"What happened with Aphrodite? Why did you anger her?"

Andrew looked around. The gates will open at any moment. He couldn't fathom the connection with Aphrodite; when, where, or what might have happened, he could think no more.

He wanted to leave the race ground and take Rhea with him. He wanted to say, 'This is all for you.' Now that you are here, let us go somewhere else. I need to hear you talk to me, get angry at me, and I shall not argue. Can we please leave?

The gates at the start line opened with a thunder, and the steeds emerged gracefully before leaping forward as the charioteers pulled the reins and cracked their whips sharply across the gleaming hides. The clamor of the gates and the wheels rolling stirred everyone alike. The last to appear was our Andrew.

He remembered every word the trainer had uttered: there is no race, no winning—only staying on the basket as long as possible. The sawing and swerving, the sharp turns and pillars, all made him nervous, waiting for disaster. But nothing happened as he trailed behind the other chariots.

They raced fast and collided. The drivers who fell were either trampled or died instantly. The horses kept running in different directions without their masters. Andrew moved slowly on every lap. Only two other charioteers remained besides him, and he felt better as he scanned the track. Then, he lashed his horses and crossed one of the vehicles effortlessly. Pride swelled within him as the crowd cheered for the green team. Andrew pressed the reins harder and struck the horses mercilessly. They listened and galloped swiftly. His chariot sailed around to complete the seventh lap. As his chariot neared the opponent, a rival suddenly stopped. Andrew swerved to the side to avoid a collision, and then saw a dangerous pillar close ahead. He struck it head-on. The axle broke into pieces. Andrew was still tied and tangled in his reins. The excited steeds would not stop as they ran toward the end.

Andrew bled profusely. His body had hit every pillar hard; his bones cracked, and his skin sloughed away, exposing rippling muscles torn and bloody. The enslaved people caught the horses, finally, and he was cut loose to be left on the ground as if he were dead.

As the winners were announced and prayers begun, Andrew saw an apparition. The sky filled with chariots, not one or two, but twelve, gliding past him with gods and goddesses smiling and whispering in his ears.

The four wind gods drove Zeus, who saw it all and smiled. White-armed Hera came close to Andrew as she gripped the reins of her Hippoi, whispering, "Stay on your course, mortal, and you shall find what you seek."

Then Aphrodite flew past on her chariot of doves, accompanied by a pair of winged Erotes. She seemed distant, but felt a wave of sorrow sweep through her chest when she saw Andrew, knowing what Ares was planning—hope, not today.

Swans drove Apollo slowly above him, and hinds carried Artemis without any clamor. Winged dragons pulled Demeter's chariot, and panthers drove Dionysus. Fish-tailed horses worked for Poseidon, and lions roared as they took Rhea, the Titan mother of all.

Andrew watched the divine procession in awe, though his pain remained unbearable. Fresh wounds spurted blood onto the sand. He tried to rise but failed, slumping back down.

The ground was empty as soon as the spectators and organizers had left for the feast, except for the unfortunate charioteers who had fallen and had no one to care for them, the dying horses that neighed from time to time in pain, and a few men who had breathed their last instantaneously during the crash. Then, broken chariots, straggling wheels, and the detached limbs of humans and horses made a mockery of the noble sport.

Andrew gave up. He buckled in pain, cried, and searched for his legs. His eyes were covered with blood and sand, but he could still make out someone approaching him.

As the wind blew more sand and twilight danced on his pupils, and as he slipped into a deep slumber, someone laid a staff beside him. Andrew opened his eyes with all the strength left in his body.

"Psychopompos!" Andrew mumbled, as if welcoming a stranger.

Hermes, Psychopomps or Argeiphontes, known for slaying the many-eyed giant Argos, who guarded Io. He had taken Euridice back to the underworld from Orpheus and brought Persephone back to this world.

He bent over and examined his wounds. He wore a long, heavy cloak, and his face was obscured by a beard that had grown over the ages. He seemed well-built and kind in his mien.

"Touch me with your caduceus again," Andrew implored.

"Why?"

"So, you can take me down to Hades. Just like Euridice… when she was almost out with her Orpheus… don't spare me…"

The transgressor of different worlds, the messenger of the gods, did not get upset with his taunting. Andrew needed help desperately, both for his wounds and his troubled mind.

"Why did you lie about the race? You are not Greek?"

Andrew laughed. "Look who's talking."

Hermes, son of Maia (daughter of Atlas) and Zeus, was born on the fourth day of the month, in a dark cave on Mount Cyllene in southern Greece. As a newborn, he had already shown extreme cunning and ingenuity. He emerged from the cave, ripped open a tortoise, strung seven strings of sheep gut across its shell, and sang beautiful songs to the gods. He then proceeded to steal fifty of Apollo's cows, for which he was dragged before Olympus. Zeus laughed at his wily ways but insisted that he make peace with his brother.

He gave Apollo the lyre and returned the cows. Apollo returned the favor by giving him his staff and the status of god of the herdsman and shepherds. Zeus made him the escort of the dead and messenger of the gods.

Andrew laughed again at the clever accusation. Lie! He had convinced the team that he was Greek; otherwise, he could not participate.

"How does it matter now? I have lost anyway," Andrew said.

"Exactly. Goddess Nike wouldn't let you win."

Andrew groaned. His eyes could not focus, and his lids felt heavy. He wondered if any god would let him die unnecessarily, whether gods cared about his fate. Back home, ambulances, paramedics, and doctors would have at least tried to save him. But here he was, perishing.

"Andrew! Andrew! My god!" Protagoras finally located him and ran toward his fallen form. Andrew tried to raise his hand, but could not move much.

"Protagoras, you were right."

"Oh, my god, you're bleeding badly! Help me, help!" he yelled.

Hermes sprang to his sandaled feet, caught two stray horses, and yoked them to an unbroken chariot. Protagoras tried to lift his friend, but he was unsuccessful. Hermes stepped forward to help. Andrew moaned in pain as the messenger of the gods carried him to safety. Protagoras rode beside him on another horse and wondered about Hermes.

"Listen to me, foolish mortal. I could take you to the dark Tartarus in a moment if you do not cease your mean acts against us: no more assaults, no invasions of this island. You are fortunate I carry your mortal body to a place here on earth and not to the dwelling of Hades. So, try not to hurt these people, or you shall..."

"So, the gods are against me now?" Andrew asked.

"Not everyone. We follow our own precepts, so this world remains. Fortune and destiny unfold, and cycles of creation and destruction should alternate."

"I don't believe it. The strong prevail, and the weak perish…"

"For a short while. Even the strongest crumble when fate decrees."

"Pardon me, I'm not disrespectful. You have become extinct, for most of the world."

"Everything inexplicable and unobtainable finds a place in history. But you are still alive, talking to me. We are immortals; you will find out."

"If so, why are you afraid of me—a mere mortal?"

"Because of the consequences, the mayhem that will ensue."

"Then just help me find Rhea. I shall leave the island peacefully."

The messenger god smiled. Protagoras looked for help as they reached his house to get his friend inside. Hermes smiled again and walked away. Andrew shut his eyes in exhaustion, bleeding from his wounds. Protagoras and his wife were kind to him. They took him inside, cleansed his wounds with water, and applied herbal remedies all over. Then they asked him to open his mouth and poured a thick green potion from the medicine man. Andrew soon lost consciousness.

After many days, when Andrew finally opened his eyes not to close them again, the couple stared at him. As he tried to speak, they broke into joyous smiles.

"Andrew!"

"Hey!" Andrew whispered.

"Andrew!"

"Protagoras!"

The couple brought a bowl of goat's milk, and Andrew tried to sit up. He drank slowly, in several, and milk spilled a bit at the corner of his mouth. He was weak.

"You have a visitor," the lady said.

Andrew tried to sit up on his bed. Rhea walked in, looking at him with a hint of a smile. She wore a pastel blue skirt with forget-me-not flower petal prints; her bare legs gleamed in the sunlight. Small rings adorned her ears, glittering faintly. She is never without these pretty earrings. Her arms looked slimmer than before. Though she seemed peaceful on the surface, Andrew felt her unease, as if she needed explanations.

"I'm glad you came."

She came closer and hesitantly sat down on the edge of the bed, though a small chair was nearby. She lowered her face and asked,

"Is it hurting?"

They remained silent for a while. Then Protagoras came with hot tea and bread.

When alone, she put her palm on his forehead, as if checking for a fever. Andrew felt as if she had come back for good. After a while, they were found smiling and laughing gently with each other. She asked again about Aphrodite. Andrew did not remember anything.

"Did you?"

"What?"

She waited.

Then, like a bolt of thunder, he realized she hated him. He remembered the night when he had escaped from jail. He did not see Anna when he woke up the next morning. He had stepped outside, knowing exactly where to go, to his own place.

He remembered the jasmine flower. Where was that flower?

"You know, Andrew, once upon a time, there was a princess called Myrrha. Her queen mother thought she was more beautiful than the goddesses."

"Like you," he said laughingly.

"Maybe, I don't know how you feel now, Andrew. Anyway, goddess Aphrodite was not happy and made Myrrha lust for her own father, the king. For nine days, he kept her locked away in darkness, but one day, he could see who she really was. He was angry at his own incest; he chased her with a sword. She ran, then froze and turned into a tree—the myrrh tree."

"Oh, stop." He didn't want her to continue.

"Yes, you need to know about her- the goddess of beauty."

"Stop!"

"Not yet. Myrrha was already pregnant, and a son named Adonis was born. He was very handsome. Aphrodite and Persephone both fell in love with him. Zeus let Aphrodite and Persephone share him, but Adonis chose to stay mostly with Aphrodite."

She paused and sighed.

Andrew knew what had happened to Adonis; his mortal body was found covered in blood by Aphrodite.

"Was it Ares?"

"No one knows, Andrew. But Ares is bloodthirsty." She suddenly turned silent, averting her gaze.

Andrew was initially filled with fear and then experienced a feeling of self-loathing for his actions. He knew no one anywhere loved him anymore. The contempt grew gradually, and he developed deep despair for his own life.

He became careless, no longer afraid of death. Even if the gods had ordained that he die for being with one of them, he would accept their verdict.

The days that followed were filled with happiness in the household.

Two weeks later, Andrew was able to return to work. He sat at the register, adding all the gold and silver coins. Protagoras toiled around with heavy sacks of grain and blamed Andrew for his misery.

"Never again, you should know. This is it, the last time I help you," Protagoras riled.

Andrew smiled and agreed. But his mind kept working, missing Rhea again. "What is going on with me?" he wondered most of the time. "Why can't I find her and just get the hell out of this damned island?"

Andrew was often seen limping through the woods toward the wreckage. He tried the radio again.

"Hello, hello..." he whispered after gazing all around.

"Hello, this is Athens."

"Yes! This is Andrew. I'm still stuck on this island."

"Wait a minute. Hold on..."

"No, please. Look, I'm in danger. This is an emergency. I need to be airlifted."

"Sir, hold on." The operator made some quick noise, and Andrew heard a lot of voices buzzing on the other end. "Yes, Andrew. This is the ground supervisor. Tell us your exact location."

"I don't know. That's the problem. The boat arrived here but was fired on."

"Tell us what happened."

"They sank the boat after firing at it. I think one of them was captured."

"There were ten people on that boat, and none have returned so far."

"Oh man! I saw only one body. Please send help."

"We will. This must be a Navy and Air Force joint operation."

"No! Don't involve them. This is not a war. Just send a helicopter or a boat and let me know the time and place. No firing. No signals."

"Can you go around the island and note down the thick forests, plain areas for landing, rugged mountains, accessibility, and call us?

The next couple of days, Andrew was busy noting the rakiness of the island. He understood where the land was flat and where it was fortified. The densely forested areas were not accessible to any transport, nor was the rugged terrain.

Here he was confronted by Herakles.

"What are you doing, mortal? I need to take you in," he roared.

Andrew was frightened. As he began a conversation with Heracles about his miserable existence, he seemed to soften and ask him questions that showed compassion.

"Do you know your mate is staying not so far from here in a cave attended by the guards of Zeus? I have met her and found her to be a very kind and likable lady. We can walk to her place, and if she allows you a few days before you surrender, I will not mind. I trust her."

Rhea was happy to see him. The guards seemed carefree and remained outside.

Ganymede brought water in a gold Hydria with three handles, and a silver kylix cup with a stemmed foot and two handles.

"Heracles, would you leave us alone, please?" She commanded.

After he walked through the door, she came close to him and embraced him for some time. Her eyes filled up, and she sobbed uncontrollably. Her body shook against him like a soft tendril, and when he reached her lips, she became pliable initially, but she held him with such strength that it filled Andrew with unexpectedly intense love, a feeling he had been craving since she was lost. They kissed for a long time.

"Andrew, Heracles told me a story of his friend Admetus, king of Pherae."

"Rhea, he is cruel. Heracles wants me to surrender."

But Rhea continued to narrate the story. When Admetus knew he had to die unless someone would die for him, he asked his parents and everyone he loved. No one volunteered except his dearest wife, Alcestis.

"I know the story, please stop."

But Rhea wouldn't stop.

When Heracles heard she had died for him, he went to her tomb and fought with Thanatos, bringing Alcestis back to his friend.

Heracles entered as if he could hear his name being called. He agreed to let Andrew be free for a period before he should return either to the mainland or surrender.

Chapter Seventeen – Zeus

The women he loved varied, and he begot some of his children who later were part of his Olympian team: Maia, mother of Hermes; Semele, mother of Dionysus; and Metis, mother of Athena.

But the whole mortal world knew Zeus; the god of all gods was a sentimental, amorous ladies' man. He fell in love with so many mortals and goddesses that sometimes even his own family was confused about their status.

Today, Zeus decided not to bother his mind over any silly trifles from Hera or any other woman. He has been in deep thought for months about the future of this island. Something would change things around here, and he is sure it would begin with a mortal. One would think it easy to tackle a mere mortal and solve any problem, but that is just an underestimation of what the Moirai have stored. The Fates decide who will live and who will die; that is written in stone. No one, not even the Knower of All, may alter such a fate. The Trojan War was a completely different story, where most of the gods played a role on each side, and Father Zeus ensured everything was justified. From his throne atop Mount Ida near Troy, he observed the carnage's minute details. And Troy had fallen despite Apollo, Aphrodite, and Ares' efforts to support the Trojans.

But now this island is at stake. Somehow, this man called Andrew is very bothersome. It would have been simple if his fiancée, Rhea, had agreed to return and leave happily. But she is unwilling to go for her home. She said she wouldn't leave 'til she had a baby. Can you believe this preposterous demand? These mortal women remain fixated on motherhood as the only testimony to being a woman. And who can say if she truly loves Andrew? There is nothing in her statement that could be used to decide either way. He is no object in her life now, no matter what he did to convince her.

Now, if Andrew is seeking help from outside, more rescue missions would follow; that is what is so worrisome. Zeus did not want any more bloodshed of innocent mortals. But Poseidon had been alerted and assured him that no sea vessel would successfully reach the shores.

Yet Zeus is uncertain of such claims. Modern technology has produced massive ships with tremendous capacity to hit any object they choose with precision. These ships even carried iron birds on them like swarms of flies on heaps of filth. How could the gods tackle such aerial assaults?

Zeus thought it should never escalate to such levels. And so, the god of gods decided to trudge to the peak of one of the hidden mountains, and as he reached there, his breath almost froze. He looked with surprise and knew this was a bad omen.

He saw rows of modern boats and Greek soldiers lined up on the decks. The ocean was dotted with approaching ships. Zeus took a deep breath and thought again; why should everything happen just the way he had seen in his mind? He remembered the Achaeans under Agamemnon outside Troy many years ago.

But they were there on the gods' command, and these are here, and the gods do not even know.

Zeus hurried to the council.

Once inside, he summoned Poseidon, Apollo, and Athena first.

"Father, why would you bother your daughter at such an odd hour when most women are in bed or near their loved ones?" Athena asked.

Zeus nodded and heralded for her to be silent and sit beside him.

"Brother, have you seen anything unusual that made you call us so urgently? And if you have, why couldn't you settle it with all your strength?"

"Poseidon, I cannot and will not oppose any action arising from necessity and just cause. But I am helpless against those we disfavor but who are righteous and morally correct."

Hera walked inside the chamber and seemed surprised. She sat near Zeus and spread her fair, right arm to hold his left hand in a gesture of support.

"Poseidon, my brother, what is going on? Have you been sleeping in your palace?"

"Why say such words, Zeus? Just because you reign over much more than me?"

"No." Zeus shook his head.

Then the grave, deep voice of his tore through

"What I have seen exceeds everything you have ever subdued. Mammoth sea vessels are arrayed around our sacred shores," he paused ponderously.

They all grew concerned. Ares came. The hall remained uneasy, as if the air was thick and heavy. Aphrodite whispered cautions to him about the latest developments.

"The boats, the mortal beasts," he began, "have not carried enough weight, and even though they look gigantic, so unlike their makers, but alas, so akin in their vulnerabilities."

"You shall not attack unless it is crystal clear they intend harm," Zeus spoke.

They sat silently. Athena nudged Poseidon.

"God of seas! How have mortals come so far? Have you ceased to reign across the bluest waters? How have your keen senses allowed such an invasion?"

Poseidon stared at her, neither helpless nor angry, but with acceptance, as if she knew him well. Suddenly, he woke up, touched his beard, and uttered,

"Yes, need to hold them away, far from our shores. No one, no one should sneak on our land. Yes..."

Zeus looked at him,

"Figure out means to restrict their movements until we know their purpose. Do not let any step upon the land."

Poseidon nodded, and the gods left the council chamber.

That night, Andrew was unable to sleep. When he found all the lamps dark and the island sluggish, he set out briskly toward his destination. Halfway through the forest, he became lost. He could not tell if he was moving toward the shore or away. After an hour's wandering in vain, he sat down, hands on his head, deep in despair.

Then he saw the tiny lights far away, and they blinked in a special arrangement. Yes, he knew they were here. His heart leaped, and he rose. He was indeed very near the beach, and out on the sand, he could see the boats. He was cautious and stepped back into the thick bushes. How can he reach them? It was perilous to swim. He had seen the firing before. Unless this time no one was watching, but he wouldn't take any chances. No, no more prison. This is the last time he would reach the boat, no matter what, and he wouldn't hurry.

It has already been a year since he arrived. Now, there is no rush. No hurry.

Suddenly, he felt a tender hand pulling him deeper into the thicket. Andrew panicked, but the soft hands urged him onward.

"Don't move. They are waiting for you."

Andrew smelled the lady's fragrance and remembered the heavy legs pressing on his chest when he was spying on Apollo.

"Artemis! The virgin goddess!" he whispered.

"What do you know about these vessels?"

"I know nothing. I was wondering myself…"

Artemis tried to look at his face, but it was so dark that even a goddess had a hard time ascertaining whether he was telling the truth. Andrew remained firm.

"Since you have arrived, we have noticed activity on our shores."

Andrew said nothing. She was so close, and the darkness of the night seemed to draw them nearer.

Artemis wanted to find out a bit more from him, but instead started walking. Andrew was frozen to the ground with fear. She came back and pulled him along again.

"The night at the ocean is full of danger. There are guards all over. Come with me, and you shall be safe."

Andrew felt reassured by her words. Did she figure out why he was there? Andrew did not know. Was she casting a net?

He walked silently for a while. She gave him her hand as they crossed a brook. This was a different path.

"May I ask you something?" he said hesitantly.

"You may."

"Why are you so much against me? I mean, us… the men in general?"

She did not respond immediately. Suddenly, Andrew hit his foot against something hard, felt pain from stubbing his toes, and then stumbled over, almost falling. She supported him, and he fell into her arms. He found her chest as comforting and fragrant as any woman he had ever known. She stood there with a mortal face resting on her bosom, feeling her ichor thicken, divine veins throbbing. A goddess could not help but pause all her plans for that moment. Why was this happening to her, the goddess who had begged her father to keep her a virgin forever? Was this mortal any different? Should she punish him for his indecent proximity?

And while such thoughts crossed her mind, Andrew steadied himself, holding her waist with his hands. Such curves, such softness, and yet such strength, he thought.

"No, I certainly am not. That is false. But I stand firmly for all women, for their choices, and anyone trying to violate that shall not be my friend," she whispered.

"Um… why so ruthless?" Andrew asked.

The huntress suddenly turned, and she pushed him away forcefully. The tip of his nose scraped the sharp border of her peplos, along the grooves. His left palm slid against her pale, soft, damp armpit. He wondered whether it was he who was sweating or the goddess.

"Andrew, it is you whom we should be talking about," she cautioned.

He got the hint and resumed walking behind her. They spoke till the forest cleared and a dirt road became obvious.

"I must go now. Be careful."

He couldn't figure out whether it was a veiled threat or friendly advice. He nodded, and with a gentle swish, she crossed to the dark far side of the hill.

Andrew did not head toward his home. Instead, he wanted to reach Rhea's cave before it was too late. He walked for almost another hour until he saw a dim light flickering where the road curved sharply at the cave's mouth.

He knocked.

He looked around. No one was there at this late hour. Even the insects had tired of trilling. The door didn't open at first, but then a sweet voice erupted,

"Who is it?"

"Open the door, Rhea."

The door opened, and she appeared, clad in a long chiton that covered almost her entire body.

"Why are you here? Andrew, oh my god!"

Andrew went inside quickly and stood in the center, watching her.

"Rhea, listen to me. The boats are here to take us back. We have to leave; this is our last chance."

"What are you talking about? Please, please sit down."

Andrew sensed her reluctance and grew restless. His body trembled slightly.

"Rhea, what is wrong with you? Do you want to die here or get me killed? Come on, babe; let's get the hell out of here. This place is spooky."

"Spooky? No, not correct. You can say holy… place, Andrew. Feel it. The gods live here. We are so fortunate, so lucky that we serendipitously or by destiny reached here on a day when we thought we were going to perish, it was so dark, so frightening, and we had no hope."

Andrew could say nothing against her words. He knew she was right, but he also knew they had to leave. This was not their home. He couldn't live there forever, no matter what she said or how many gods and goddesses he met. It was a languid apparition, as if he were hammered high, and the effect never waned or waxed but stayed the same. Nothing he saw was truly atrocious or unreal. Even Rhea made sense to him because she had experienced the same things he had. It was all so surreal! He wished he could argue, persuade her, and leave, but found no suitable words to express or deny.

He felt exhausted after all the planning, all the secret walks, and the exciting opportunity that he had recognized with the arrival of the ships—a definite escape. But now all that seemed less significant, and what mattered most was what Rhea had just uttered: she was staying, and he could not summon the strength to say, "Fine, I have to leave." No, he could not. All he hoped for was to sit on the backless dipthroi covered with ornamental stones. There was also another throne trimmed with gold and ivory, the one he had seen Zeus rest on in the past. Then he collapsed onto the couch as if resigning.

She sat somewhat apart from him on a klismos, a chair with a curved backrest and legs. He lowered his head in despair, noticing the tiny space between them, just a few steps, but he could not call her closer. He sat there, wishing she would rise and come to him as she had in the past, to take his head in her lap after a hard day of work, gently comb his blond hair, and often lower her face to his, as if to infuse a little life into his lips. No. She did none of that. She just sat there, leaning back slightly, as if she had no memory of the past, as if she was waiting for him to rise and announce, "Well, you seem tired. I'll see you later," or something similar.

"I'm so hungry," he said suddenly.

She got up and brought him some food and fruit. Andrew began eating slowly, taking his time, as if she were asking him to leave once he was done.

"You look awesome!"

Rhea smiled. It seemed she had gained a little more flesh around her bonny, slender limbs. Of course, she was happy. And Andrew was losing. He wondered why two different outcomes followed from calamity on two seemingly similar people. Do women change so quickly? Or do they adjust? Or is it he who couldn't? Rhea was never opportunistic; in fact, he was the one always taking advantage of her, yet she had always remained faithful. He had seen many others, but she was always present whenever he returned. What happened to this unpretentious but forthright person?

"You look bedraggled. Awful!" she whispered.

"It is killing me."

Rhea said nothing. She took the plate and poured a drink from a kantharos.

"Hey, so listen, what's going on? I mean, I see a change in you."

A long pause followed, as if she were gone, before her face began to move, yet she did not answer.

"You know them? Who are these people? Have you joined a cult? I mean, you think you are one of them now...?"

"Never..." she mumbled.

As she said "never," she wondered about her position on this remote island she had never been to before. She has changed so much that she wouldn't even respond to someone from her past. She wouldn't know what she would say if her parents showed up one day. What if her family asked her to return to the US in this condition?

But she cared for Andrew deeply. She had been extremely worried about his fate—about how he would end up here. Will he be able to fight the wrath of the gods? One day, she spoke to Apollo about her concerns.

"Is he safe here?" she asked Apollo when the god mentioned him.

Apollo did not answer. He didn't know what had passed between Ares and Aphrodite after their conversation.

Then Apollo told her about the past, when he was banished from Olympus for an entire year.

"I served King Admetus dutifully. When he wished to marry Alcestis, he came to me for help. The father of Alcestis, King Peleus, required the groom to perform a heroic feat, yoking a lion and a boar to a chariot and driving it around the racecourse. So, I helped him with Heracles, and he won his bride, Alcestis. But he forgot to pray to Artemis before the wedding, and guess what, she was offended. He came to the wedding chamber and found coiled snakes instead of his naked bride. I spoke with Artemis, and she agreed to relent, only if someone else would offer to die in his place. His parents refused, but the brave bride offered herself, and Admetus was saved, for now."

Then Apollo asked if Andrew had someone like Alcestis for Admetus. Rhea did not know what to say. She had no answer, and inside, she felt as if she could not breathe. Apollo smiled ruefully and walked away.

They continued to talk for a while. The darkness of the night could not erase the distance between them, and all their whispering centered on everything except their own lives.

Finally, Andrew rose and walked out.

He promised he would come again.

In the meantime, Poseidon had left for the shores. He stood there in the light of dawn, watching the boats. One of them was large and already had a few crew members up on the deck. Why were they here? Was this a friendly vessel? But then, there had been no message beforehand. They resembled Greek government ships, except they had no flags flying high atop the mast. He did not want to act in haste, lest some mortal life be put in peril.

Why not approach and find out? He thought.

The next thing the islanders knew was that Poseidon had been taken aboard the ship, captured for trespassing.

On the ship, the crew was certainly fascinated by a bearded Greek who demanded information from them and threatened that they must leave the shore immediately, otherwise they would face unpleasant consequences. He did not elaborate on how unpleasant it could become, as he remained rather humorless but solemn.

"Who are you, sir? Who sent you here?"

He remained uncooperative.

"What is your name? I need to record it. Do you have family, children? We can inform."

He looked up, annoyed, and answered,

"Yes, my wife is Amphitrite. My sons—Triton, who may be lurking nearby; my daughter Rhode—I'm not sure where she is; and you know my other son Polymphemus, whose vision is poor with one eye."

The sailor wrote down his report without distortion and with no understanding of the strange names, as if facing an old man from his own town.

"I came here on my own. Listen, boy; you must leave before sunrise."

They were not so serious about the old man. But the captain was informed, and he was taken inside. Poseidon was told about their mission and the loss of crew in the previous rescue mission.

"We want Andrew and his girlfriend Rhea," the skipper said.

"Who are they? How will you locate them?"

"At sunrise, one of the units will land on the shores and investigate."

"No, do not send troops. Our people dislike mainland armies. We are a protected island, autonomous for hundreds of years. No government has ever interfered in our administration."

The captain was surprised. He could hardly believe his eyes and ears: a small island that doesn't even appear on the state map, yet enjoys autonomous administration.

"Sir, wait here."

Then he contacted his superiors in the naval offices. They were also surprised. There followed a lot of activity in the naval headquarters, and the ministers of defense and home affairs were informed by their respective secretaries.

Then he received a call,

"Yes, do not do anything till legal matters are discussed. There were a few islands left autonomous when the Greek constitution was written, and all of them had diverse populations that had undergone no change over thousands of years of Greek history. Some of them were never formally visited by any government heads."

"But then what are we supposed to do? What about Andrew and Rhea?"

"Wait for further instructions."

Poseidon was taken to the dining hall and offered breakfast. He did not touch anything, which annoyed the captain.

"Have some coffee, my friend. Have a little bread," he asked.

Poseidon cringed at such a request. They asked numerous questions, but he avoided direct answers.

"Sir, we will have to keep you on board," a soldier informed when he tried to leave.

"What! What an insolent order. You will confine this old man here? Do you think you have the power to hold me?" He laughed at the soldier.

"We will, we have to, until we know more,"

Poseidon shook his head, and with that, the vessel began to shake. There followed a loud thud, and the soldier seemed to tilt over. As he tried to stand up, everything in the cabin started to move: the chairs, the table, and the dish full of uneaten food scattered all around. Poseidon got up and stood in the corner, still shaking his head. Then came further noise, emanating from all over the ship: the lower and upper decks, the crew cabins, and even the engine room. The vessel trembled heavily, and waves of water splashed against the windows as if trying to break them open. The soldier looked at Poseidon and fled, screaming,

"The old man—he is evil! He started it… the old man, the old man!"

The captain and his crew came rushing. They caught him and shook him.

"What happened? Why are you screaming?"

"Stop the old man! Stop him! He is shaking his head. His eyes—they are not normal. He's angry. He's making the water so turbulent!"

When he was speaking, the captain noticed warm air rising from the water's surface.

"A typhoon!" he announced.

Suddenly, a gust of rain rushed in. A vast wave splashed over the deck, and they were all swept toward the ocean's edge. They lay flat near the edge, holding the railing. The captain stood up and ran inside. The ship was flooding and about to capsize as trained sailors all over were busy trying to lower the lifeboats and rafts in utmost panic.

Within minutes, it was all over.

Poseidon stood on the shores, sad, wet, and repentant. When would these mortals learn to respect others? He wondered.

No vessels were floating anywhere close by.

The wind blew, and the waves were drawing anything drowned near the shore to the deep inside the ocean, where almost fifty crew members and their boats would find their new home for eternity. No one would ever rescue them alive.

The angry god took a deep breath and searched his soul for answers: why? Why, and how long? When would the times change? When would mortals realize and cease making their new gods on their own, whoever, wherever, whatever?

In the council, the gods were stunned upon hearing the details of Poseidon's report. For some time, a great silence fell over Olympus, as if an irreversible grief had settled upon them all. Hera sat rather indifferent, whispering to Athena. Ares looked tired and closed his eyes, feeling no urgency to decide. Apollo, Hermes, and Artemis listened very intently and, in this unusual pause, chose to stay quiet.

Zeus broke the silence.

"Poseidon! Do not repent now. You should have thought it over before you chose to hurt those poor mortals. But anyway…" he paused.

Hera was keenly listening to his suggestion, but turned her gaze away as Zeus looked directly at her. Hephaestus saw them and became restive. Some sinister clouds seemed to spread over their realms. He looked at Aphrodite, who shamelessly stared back at Ares and then gently elbowed the god of war to rouse him. Startled, Ares looked around in embarrassment.

"Why don't we find the mortals responsible for this intrusion and send them back?" Hera spoke.

All the gods and goddesses felt the strong sentiment in their queen's words and looked at Father Zeus. They saw his face turn red, anger sweeping across it. There was more going on than what was spoken at the council, Athena thought.

"Why should we live under constant threat? We have lived here in peace for so long; why take this nuisance? Let us get rid of the problem." Hera pressed her rhetoric.

At this, Zeus raised his head, looked at her angrily, and said,

"I do not know where you get such vengeance, but it should not cloud our reasoning. We have a moral responsibility to shelter those who seek it and to protect them from outsiders. So, save your contentious words for our domestic issues."

Hephaestus seemed uncomfortable and heralded Ganymede to serve another round of nectar. Athena spoke up.

"Father of all gods, may I suggest we all work together on this serious issue? Despite all our strength, we are vulnerable. Think, if we faced a large army of mortals, would we be ready to use force against them, knowing we are indestructible, and they are not? We are not like the Achaeans to achieve our goals with carnage and endless annihilation. Are we?"

Ares was quick to protest. He said whenever mortals race against the divinity, it is in their best interest to be punished. Apollo sat thinking and brooding over the past, but made no real speeches. Aphrodite said,

"Why don't I ask Rhea to speak to Andrew and put a stop to his rescue operations?"

The sudden mention of these two names made the gods and goddesses rather tense and discomfited. They thought of her again with mixed feelings and silently hoped she would say no more.

"That may not work. Poseidon, Apollo, and Athena will review our existing security measures, meet with Heracles, and decide our response. In the meantime, let Hermes go to the mainland and seek a meeting with the Prime Minister to explain the treaty signed when the constitution was written."

With that, Zeus rose and left the council.

But the gods sat there long after he was gone. Hera sat with her head bowed, thinking, why was he so rude to me? Why do all such meetings end with an insult directed at her? He had most likely realized by now that she was aware of his mysterious handling of the mortal woman. He left with a strong animus toward her, his eyes full of vengeance, just like when she had chastised him in the past for his numerous other amorous relationships, his lack of respect for their marriage, and his urge to create varied creatures all over the planet, which he thinks necessary for the greater purpose of life's continuity. But life for mortals, which he always overlooks, is so brittle anyway, and moreover, they no longer care for us. Why should he spend his time on their good, or even for the sum-mum bonum? Hoping for the day when the very same people would turn around and pray again at his shrine. They would visit the Parthenon, walk the streets of Athens, and worship Athena and Apollo.

Most likely, the temple of Zeus at Dodona would bustle with kings and queens. Also, the temple of Apollo at Delphi would be rebuilt, and new priestesses would be assigned to serve as oracles. Huh! What wishful thinking. Preposterous. Never, never would these Greeks abandon their new philosophy of monotheism to return to the original, pure, and ubiquitous gods and goddesses that had helped them become the greatest race on earth. But Hera would never say that to him or any of her children, because hope is all they have—the very same hope Zeus decided to keep for mortals when Pandora opened the box that Epimetheus had forbidden her to open. Well, now history repeats itself, and they hope that glory shall return, and the gates of all sanctuaries will come alive as people return with their sacrifices.

Of course, Hera would rejoice and willingly share her part to help them again, in marriages, in childbirth, and in whatever else is assigned to her. No doubt that, if this happens, Zeus had better think right and cease all his previous practices. All of us should change, because human beings cannot comprehend a god who is like them. Hence, we would become what they want to see, hear, and pray to, only good, without weaknesses, no wishy-washy stuff, and only the best possible show.

 But for now, where is the damn mortal woman? Hera spoke with Hermes.

"Why don't we all speak to her and return her to the man?"

They all had different ideas.

"We must never go against Zeus's will. He can be vengeful," warned Hestia.

"You stay out of this! I need a few of you to help me. Who can I trust?"

She looked at Hephaestus, Athena, and Apollo.

They were all silent; she knew the times were changing.

"I see that you all strongly believe in what Zeus has just said, and that is fine. But think, and think hard, what is the future? That reminds me of Apollo; why don't you see it and tell us what the future holds? Whether this is just a small calamity, or does it portend some greater evil that can engulf us all, like what happened to the Trojans?"

Apollo was listening but uttered no word. He closed his eyes and walked toward the window, a gentle breeze touching him. Then came the soft words from the oracle's mouth,

"I see large-scale war. I see death looming large. I see the god of gods shrinking, yes, physically shrinking, and I do not know what it means. Is it that time will turn back and great Titans take over, just as when Zeus was born to Cronos in power?"

They all listened with fear. Apollo's words were penetrating, reminiscent of the destruction these gods had suffered in the past. They had left Olympus and deserted their sanctuaries all over Greece and Turkey to avoid the bloodshed and devastation that evil human forces brought to their fellow mortals to impose each other's faith.

And now, it was back again. The sinister, ruinous, all-devouring feeling had returned. The gods and goddesses knew the mortals would not cease fighting, and they could once again become the cause.

But Father Zeus, who can always see and reason, seemed harried as he made his way toward the town center. His mind was occupied and weary from everything that had happened over the last few months. He knew this was a rather trifle compared with the serious events he had handled in the past, and how he had been able to keep mortals flourishing, regardless of whom they chose to pray. The sun god and the moon goddess still rose and fell; the south and north winds blew and soothed in just the right proportion; the nymphs in the water and trees nurtured gently; and all the planets and constellations revolved in their proper orbits so that life could be sustained here on earth.

Now, after seventeen hundred years, he is worrying again. It seems like a minor trouble, a man and a woman lost on this island, with the man frantically searching for her, except she does not want to be found. What is the role of divinity? Should they not protect her and stand for her freedom and honor? Or, as Hera said, should they hand her over and rid the island of the threat? But that is such an unjust and cowardly act. Even if all the Olympians agree to Hera's suggestion, Father Zeus will vigorously oppose it in the council, and hopefully, they will see his point. See, this is where polytheism works so well; otherwise, one supreme god can decide the fate of all without debate, discarding noblesse oblige.

The only thing that bothers him at this point is Andrew's position, not because of what he wants, but because he feels as if Andrew was not given enough time to present his case. Perhaps he has his arete, a virtue that only a lover can explain. In that case, it may be worth knowing his mind.

Zeus stood near the shop. He wore a long chiton, a himation draped over him, and leather sandals. His head and the lower part of his face were covered by the end of the himation.

He entered the shop.

"Yes?" Andrew asked from a corner while cleaning the shelves.

"Yes!" the god proclaimed.

"What? What do you need?"

"I have no need." The god answered.

"No need? Fine!" Andrew seemed perplexed by the old man. He scratched his head. Where, where had he seen him before? He couldn't figure it out. An old man, but powerfully built, must be a laborer with those sinewy arms, or a farmer. But those eyes! Piercing!

Is he one of those moles Heracles keeps? Possible. He'd better be careful. What happened to the boats? Man! They vanished from the sea in minutes. These guys are something else, and they have no technology. He might have come to interrogate me. My lips are sealed.

"Andrew?" he asked.

Andrew nodded.

"Why?"

Andrew didn't quite know what to say. Why, what? Why is he here, or why has his fate brought him here? Why did Rhea come with him? Or maybe, why is he so unfortunate to be stuck here? Or even, why did he choose to lead a different life than the one his father had designed for him? Like, he could have been running the shipbuilding business and living in mainland five-star hotel suites, never having to worry about these small, unknown-to-civilization tiny islands.

 "Why are you so keen to?" he paused again.

So keen? Man, keen about what? Here he is wretched. He has nothing left, and he couldn't even be enthusiastic about anything.

"Why is it imperative that she leave with you?"

Suddenly, Andrew knew who this gentleman was and where he had seen him. Oh yes! That's him. He was leaning over her...on that half-lit evening in her cave.

He smiled wryly. She chose a good one. He could be her father, even her grandfather. Rhea, you have lost it, baby; you're really sick! And he dares to ask as if he is claiming her from him. Maybe he should know it better. He needs a lesson in relationships, specifically age-appropriate ones. That's right!

"Why do you care? Who are you anyway?"

The old man smiled at this childish query from a mortal.

"Embarrassed? Aren't you? You may have a daughter or a granddaughter her age. And here you are asking me why?"

The old man maintained his grin effortlessly. His mind was perfectly still; his heart had no animus. He felt pity for the mortal before him. He had already assumed a certain link between his lover and this stranger. How strong was his trust in her? How deeply did he love her if such demeaning thoughts could even arise? Even if it were true, he should never have mentioned it so openly, in such a blatant way, to taint his own relationship in a rush. Does it have anything to do with the new religion, the one that teaches them morality far more exacting than ever before? Are these mortals truly any better than their ancestors? Why are they decaying so quickly?

"Embarrassed? No. Relationships are invisible; you can color them however your heart decides."

Andrew listened carefully. Invisible! Yes, it is certainly invisible—impossible to be found. Where did the bond, the tie, the caring, and all the mutual feelings vanish? As if there were none, as if they had never lived close, watch each other in tender moments, never felt their own weaknesses, or supported one another's inconsistencies. And now, Andrew must carry on as if a new life is usurping the old one, in which there would be no place for Rhea. Is this what he came here for? Was this his fate, as the locals say, the fate the goddesses had in stock? Andrew felt weak and couldn't think clearly.

"Invisible, not imperceptible," he muttered.

It is certainly imperative that I take her back. Where she belongs— where I brought her from, he thought. She is so naïve.

Zeus could see his desire to hold on to what he believed a man ought to do. He saw the desperate eyes trying to conceal the soul within, as if the world would know and then reveal him to her. As if he must continue to love her no matter what, until she recognizes and rewards his earnestness. Or at least stay with him even if her feelings differed—because that is what his religion had taught him: the everlasting bond, monogamy, and all that is so farcical, so unaccepting of human frailty, and an un-affirming negation of the reality of life itself. Behave! Behave, my children. Do not increase the burden of your sin. What nonsense!

"What if she wishes to stay here? Will you compel her?"

Andrew did not expect such a blunt assessment from an old, decrepit farmer. How does he make such a naked assumption? Old fool! She would want to stay here, not if she knew who they were. All these cults and their antiquated habits! Why would he force her? And Rhea isn't listening anyway. She couldn't be persuaded now, not on this island. Something distinct had changed in her. These people have done their job well. But then why would such a hoary fellow stick by her side? No, it couldn't be just what he thought earlier. He doesn't look that way. There is something sinister, something more, and it is not what his soul waited for. As a man, he felt the farmer was frank. Andrew couldn't fully justify his outrage against the old man, though he couldn't shake it off thoroughly. I will get him if he continues to stand in my way, he resolved.

Yes, if push comes to shove, I wouldn't hesitate to use all my strength, he promised himself.

Then he noticed a rising steam in the old man's eyes, as if he had heard what he had resolved as something impious, very improper, and he almost froze in the corner—his eyes wide open, jaws clenched, and his right hand raised as if to draw strength from heaven. Andrew was sure he had offended him with his thoughts alone and wanted to hide. But then darkness fell outside, and a thunderous noise broke through their agonizing silence. The small shed adjacent to the store, where Protagoras stored all his grain, was in flames, lighting the backyard with bright golden tongues of the glow.

"Lightning!" Andrew muttered.

Andrew rushed to get a bucket of water. Neighbors came running to help.

The fire had caught the stored sacks of grain, splattering the corn all over. The flames leaped up and down in the air, advancing towards other sheds.

The old man seemed distressed, coming out of his burst of anger, but then walked away as if the fire did not concern him.

When the fire was under control, one neighbor asked,

"What happened?"

Andrew had no answer. He searched for the clouds, the thunderstorm, any sign of impending rain.

But all he could think of was the old man and that moment when he drew his right arm. The gods were there to help the old man. Should Andrew be more discreet? Was it truly possible?

Andrew trembled. How could he handle a man like this?

Is he what he seems, or is there more of him? Why was he here, and what did he want?

Did Rhea have anything to do with it...?

Chapter Eighteen – Olympus

The sun rose in the east as usual, and the wind god turned around, just as he did every day. The islanders emerged from their homes, their shops, and wherever they had been. Yet, the sky and parts of the island were burning, not with sunlight, but with fierce missiles hitting certain areas. Leaping flames, loud explosions, and the cries of victims stunned the island.

People had no idea why this calamity suddenly struck their island, and they did not even try to hide. Heracles was busy rushing around with his team, urging people to get inside and take shelter—preferably in underground areas or basements where the approaching explosives from the attacking planes might not reach.

Zeus stood, watching the carnage. He couldn't believe what he saw: the same mortals he had saved from disasters for ages, the ones that he decreed to live, were now killing each other ruthlessly. Why? Who is behind such a massive assault on this island? The government had requested help from different nations, which might indicate a foreign power. They wouldn't care for this tiny island. He was not only shocked but utterly disgusted. He looked around and found the same cruelty, the same destruction that had been ongoing on this planet for years.

But he is the protector. He should stop this ferocious attack. Yet why and how could he succeed? They wouldn't talk or listen. They sneak through the air, dropping explosives with pinpoint accuracy.

He walked into the midst of the field.

Hera came closer.

Then came all the other gods and goddesses.

They all looked at the carnage, the rising fires from the dwelling on the island, burning fields and crops, the scurrying women and children, and they were filled with anger.

They asked questions, expressed grief and frustration, and resolved to stop the attackers from destroying their home. They decided on a strategy, left the palace altogether, and gathered in the center of the island so the people could see them and stand with them when they needed them most.

So, when the gods and goddesses were seen among the people, when there was a large crowd in the town, Apollo began the warfare with his dangerous arrows. However, he soon discovered their ineffectiveness against such a formidable machine, designed by mortals.

Then Hephaestus raised a flame that shot up to the sky and caught the planes. Unfortunately, the fire spread rapidly across the island, consuming people and their homes as well. Hephaestus had to stop.

Zeus stood helpless as miles of pristine land burned.

Suddenly, Hermes appeared from nowhere. He had brought the mortal woman with him. Rhea stood amongst all the gods. She looked scared. She did not know the reason Hermes had pulled her from her bed. She saw the destruction upon arriving in the town, and she cried.

Zeus knew what to do. He raised the arm that had comforted Hera, protected mortals, and destroyed the perpetrators for thousands of years.

Dark clouds filled the sky, swallowing the iron birds, which vanished from sight, then he struck with his weapon. The fierce thunder, the brightest lightning, and the divine energy had just begun to take shape and scatter. The gods and goddesses stood terrified as a low-flying iron bird came very close, releasing a massive missile toward Zeus. They shut their eyes and clung to one another, fearless in their unity.

Zeus was seen to place his hand over the mortal woman and speak words of benediction. She stood frozen in fear as Zeus walked away from her toward the other gods and goddesses. He wrapped his arm around them, stretching it to encircle all of them—Hera, Aphrodite, Ares, Apollo, Hephaestus, Hermes, Artemis, Athena, Hestia, and Heracles.

The clouds descended, hiding the Olympians.

When the clouds dispersed, the town was strangely silent.

The survivors were seen searching for their family members and crying.

Andrew was frantic. He staggered through piles of fallen walls and houses, stopping repeatedly to help the injured.

He reached the town center just before sunset.

The last rays of the sun had fallen on several people on the ground. As he walked closer in search of Rhea, he fumbled and nearly fell over an older woman. Then he heard a cry and turned his head toward the corner.

Unable to make out what was happening, he walked near the source. A newborn!

Oh, oh! Andrew leapt forward, gently wrapping the baby with his own shirt. The cord looked dark red.

Andrew sat beside the mother and took her wrist in his hand. Her face was bloodied and turned away; her slender neck was smeared, and her tangled hair fell over her forehead.

Yet she still wore her familiar tiny earrings on both sides. Andrew didn't know if she was alive when people arrived with stretchers and took the baby from him and the mother as well.

People say Andrew never left the island. He refused to go with the paramedic Greek soldiers who were seen surrounding the area, resuscitating the woman who had no pulse and labored breathing.

He named the baby of Eumelus, son of Alcestis, who led eleven ships in the Trojan War.

Andrew never knew whether she had offered herself as a sacrifice for his sin, and how the gods had accepted another Alcestis to perish instead. So Admetus would live on…

Did Aphrodite have the last laugh?

Where was Heracles? Andrew was seen frantically calling him so he could return Alcestis from the clutches of Thanatos.

The End.

NOTES

1. Zeus and his consorts

Maia — mother of Hermes, born on Mount Cyllene, the beautiful mountain nymph, the mother, the midwife, and the mysteriously dark-eyed goddess who seemed never ready to hang out with others. One fateful evening, Zeus came to her and thus Hermes.

Electra — mother of Dardanus and Iasion, another daughter of Atlas, named after the color of amber, the dark-faced, bright sister of Maia. After union with Zeus, she went to Palladium but was thrown out to the earth by Athena, as she was no longer a maiden. After the city of Troy lost, she faded from the constellation of Pleiades.

Taygete — mother of Lacedaemon, from southern Greece, Laconia, another sister Pleiades had refused Zeus, so Hermes changed her into a cow for Zeus.

Semele — mother of Dionysus, the only mortal we know that Zeus turned into a goddess, Thyone. She is the one who asked Zeus to appear in his divine form; as he did, she burst into flames as all mortals do. Zeus sutured her baby Dionysus in his thighs.

Alcmene — mother of Heracles, Danae — mother of Perseus, Leda — mother of Helen and Plydeuces.

Metis-- She was so bright; she even helped him plan his revolt against Cronos. People say that when she was pregnant with Athena, he swallowed her. Hard to believe. Maybe it was a symbolic act? To completely overtake another person to the point she did not exist for the world, not for love but something else unknown, not well understood by mortals. But then we know Athena was born, and Metis remained deep inside Zeus to guide him forever, without the threat of a coup d'état by her unborn son.

Themis – She was his favorite aunt, and they had fates and seasons.

Demeter produced Persephone.

Leto had-- Apollo and Artemis.

Zeus came to Danae, the mother of Perseus, as a shower of gold through the skylight

2. The Horae (Seasons)

were Eunomia (Law and Order),

Dike (Justice),

Eirene (Peace).

3. Moirai (Fates)

were Clotho, Lachesis, and Atropos who decided the mortal's lifespan. Moera is for a share, representing three phases of the moon: maiden, nymph, and crone.

Clotho spins on her spindle,

Lachesis measures with her rod, and

Atropos cuts it off.

4. Graces

Eurynome produced the Graces:

Aglaia- Beauty

Euphrosyne- Grace

Thalia--charm.

5. Muses

Mnemosyne bore nine Muses after nine nights of mating:

Clio — history,

Euterpe — music and poetry,

Thalia — comedy,

Melpomene — tragedy,

Terpsichore — dance,

Erato — love poetry and marriage songs,

Polyhymnia — sacred song and oratory,

Urania — astronomy,

Calliope — epic and heroic poetry.

The Muses—still sing on this tiny island for the gods.

6. Rivers in the underworld

In the underworld ruled by Hades, there are five rivers:

Styx — hate,

Lethe — forgetfulness,

Phlegethon — fire,

Cocytus — grief,

Acheron — pain.

7. Mother Earth Gaia

Mother Earth was very prominent before the Indo-Europeans invaded northern Greece and turned the matriarchal society into a patriarchy ruled by Zeus. After the birth of the three Hecatoncheires—the hundred-handed giants—and the three one-eyed Cyclopes, she bore twelve more children, including

Theia, goddess of light, who married Hyperion, god of the sun, and bore Helios, the sun god; Selene, the moon goddess; and Eos, the dawn goddess.

Rhea, earth goddess who loved the oak and fell for clever Cronus—the youngest and bravest—produced the Olympians: Hestia, Demeter, Hera, Hades, Poseidon, and Zeus.

Themis maintained law and order and was the Delphic oracle. She is represented by the zodiac sign Libra.

Mnemosyne was the memory goddess and mother to the nine Muses.
Tethys, goddess of the sea, favored Oceanus, the firstborn, and the primordial rivers.

Crius—father of Astraeus.

Coeus married Phoebe—who became the Delphic oracle after Themis—and bore Leto, the kindest goddess, and Asteria.

Iapetus—the father of Prometheus, Epimetheus, and Atlas

8. Festivals with seasons

The New Year begins with Hekatombaion, dedicated to Apollo, occurring in July and August, followed by Metageitnion, with the Metageitnia festival in August–September; Boedromion in September-October (for Apollo); Pyanopsion in October–November; Maimakterion in November–December; Poseideion in December–January; Gamelion in January–February, dedicated to marriage; Anthesterion in February–March; Elaphebolion, dedicated to Artemis the Huntress, in March-April; Munichion, also for Artemis, in April–May; Thargelion, for the grain harvest, in May–June; and finally, Skirophorion in June–July, marking the end of the year.